I renamed this book ***'He's behin***

info by a (US) author on the Inte

my few followers so I have republished it with its original title.

'Below the Belt' is back.

The title is fitting because what happens to Hunter and his family is a kick in the teeth, a punch below the Belt in boxing terms.

JB. Woods

This novel is a work of fiction. Names and Characters are a product of the author's imagination and any resemblance to actual persons, living or dead, is entirely coincidental.

The author also willingly admits to having stretched local geography to suit his own ends.

JB Woods
18/02/24

Acknowledgements

George Carr a friend who painstakingly critiqued my first unedited version.
Colin Fearn and Ken & Kay Theaker close friends who I have co-opted as characters into the book and who also read it and gave their opinion.

Cover design: Brian Platt
Lounging Model: Iain Powson

CHARACTERS

GB Hunter (Orion) (Venator) aka H. **(Book 1)**
Jacquie Hunter nee Riccardi (Artemis) aka Jay**(Book 1)**
DI Colin Fearn - Police
DS Carrie Priya Long (British/Malay-Indian ethnicity) - Police
Senior Agent Gus Thomas SIS
Agent Simon Bell (Doyle) SIS (Pt 2: Blue) (Tall & short blonde hair)
Agent Penny Farthing SIS
Demyan Orlov aka Dimitrov aka Marcus (Professional hitman)
Patrick O'Hearne - Pro-IRA Local Commander Belfast
Aiden Cronin - Pro-IRA Sniper & wife Naomi **(Book 1)**
Sean O'Reilly & wife Karen Pro-IRA sympathisers **(Book 1)**
'C'
Andy Roberts - Neighbour retired DI
Jamie McDuggan
The Voice - NI MP and Pro-IRA Organiser (Martin McGovern)
Kath – Hunter's sister. **(Book 1)**
Iain Hunter age 11. H's Son in his last term at Primary School.
Lesley Hunter age 8½ H's Daughter
Tim ex-Parachute Regt and Afghanistan veteran and Springer Spaniel Sasha his Sniffer dog also an Afghanistan veteran.
Bill - Landlord of 'The Swan Inn' public house & daughter Sharon
Kay & Ken
Agent Duncan Williams (Ernesto) (**Book 1**)
Dr Kerr SOCO
Dr Mrs Isobel Wearne - Trauma surgeon
DS Newlove (Effie)
DC Jordan (temp)
Charlotte - Jacquie's PA
Martin Parr (Doyle) – Simon's brother (Pt 2: Red)
Sir Henry Jackson-Milburn – Deputy Chief of GCHQ – (Pt 2: Gold)

CHAPTER 1

Saturday evening

Peering through the telescopic sights in the fading light of a late spring evening he was able to pick out the individual 1930's era houses and bungalows stretching along the lane on the opposite side of the Recreation ground. One by one lights were going on as the shadows lengthened and he was surprised by the number of houses that didn't close their curtains but gave every passing observer licence to look in.

He panned left until he came to a large modified bungalow with a conservatory stretching across the rear and was pleased to see that they were helping him in his cause. The lights were on and the three occupants in the conservatory clearly visible and his target highlighted in a white shirt with narrow blue stripes.

He eased the bolt back and forward on the rifle and slid a polished round up the spout and placed the cross hairs squarely in the target's chest before he took a deep breath in, exhaled, held it and began squeezing the trigger and then quietly cursed as he released the pressure.

'Keep still, you bastard.'

He was short of training but with the target a little under three-hundred metres away he figured he'd have no problems and there was little or no wind to cause him any undue pressure on the shot. Once more he lined up the target who had turned side-on. He allowed a little lay-off for the double glazing and aimed breast-high just behind the left arm. He took up the first pressure, exhaled, held it for a couple of seconds and squeezed the trigger. As the weapon recoiled the view of the target blanked out.

'What the...?'

A dog began barking furiously directly to his front and his reaction was swift. With practised ease, he dismantled the rifle, packed it into its holder and sliding back through the long grass which had sheltered him he reached the rough ancient right of way down the side of the field. He raised himself on one knee and then became aware of another person just thirty metres down the path.

He froze and watched while reaching for the handgun strapped to his thigh. The other figure carrying only binoculars climbed off the ground and in a crouching position moved with athletic ease downhill along the path between the allotments and the hedge separating it from the gardens at the rear of some more early 20th Century bungalows.

He waited while anxiously looking across the field to where the dog was barking and then dodging brambles and overgrown shrubs in the dark he also beat a hasty retreat down the path towards the narrow historic lane some two hundred metres away.

He reached the footbridge over the Old Mill stream at the bottom of the valley where the ancient track joined the main footpath and congratulated himself for vandalising the single light on the bridge during a recce run two nights earlier. He hung back in the shadows of a large bush as a white 4 x 4 completed a three-point turn on the wide grass verge and drove hastily away. The driver was taking no chances and drove without lights.

On the opposite side of the valley was a 1960's Public Housing estate and after he had crossed the bridge he glanced left and right before he ran over the grassy verge and climbed the steep bank leading to the road along the front of the houses and with a wary eye and his gun bag held vertically pulled tight into his body he made his way to his car parked behind a playground.

He paused momentarily in the shadow of the hedge surrounding the playground but nobody stirred and keeping low he ran to his car and placed the rifle and his handgun in the boot before stripping off his camouflage jacket and throwing that in.

Satisfied no one had seen him he slid into his car and drove slowly keeping the engine noise to a minimum. Only one thing disturbed his thoughts. 'Who the hell was the peeping tom spying on the Rec who drove a BMW X5 which is not the sort of vehicle you left unattended in the middle of nowhere.'

~~~~~
~~~~~

CHAPTER 2

It wasn't Jacquie's reaction when she threw herself back from the conservatory door but the crash of the outside pane of glass of the double glazed conservatory window as it disintegrated into a thousand shards and the inside pane changed into a diamond-encrusted backdrop to the bullet hole which appeared.

It was an instinctive reaction bred over years of service to Her Majesty's Government. His age made his response slower and he winced at the impact of a missile in his upper arm and the barking of a dog out on the recreation ground went unnoticed as he recovered.

Hunter, clean-shaven and his dark hair belying his sixty-eight years pulled himself up using the back of a cane chair. He brushed bits off his shirt and the knees of his cavalry twill trousers and cursed, 'What he Bloody Hell's going on?' as he stooped to help Jacquie as she scrambled to pick up pieces of the coffee set scattered over the floor either side of the door separating the bedroom and the conservatory.

'I don't know, H,' she answered, 'but it's cost a bomb in new china. There's blood on your shoulder, are you okay?'

He picked up a broken cup and looked at the name on the bottom and withheld a groan before he said, 'That's your grandma's old set?'

'Yes. How's Ken and Kay?'

'Oh, shit,' he said, 'I'd forgotten them.'

He glanced across to see how their guests were doing and breathed a sigh of relief to see they were shaken but unharmed. Both Ken and Kay seated on the cane sofa were shading their eyes and looking out across the Rec through the deepening gloom trying to spot what was causing the manic barking of the dog.

Hunter stood up and went over to them and breaking into their thoughts, said, 'I'm sorry about that, it's not our usual way to welcome guests.'

Ken looked up at him. 'We're okay, George, but I wonder what your neighbours are up to. That sounded like a shot and that window says it all, and what's the matter with your shoulder and that dog?'

That's when Hunter first became aware of the dog.

'Jeezuz,' he muttered.

He went to the damaged window and winced as he moved a chair out of the way and instinctively grabbed at his shoulder. As he surveyed the mess he felt something through his shirt embedded in his flesh and exploring further realised it was the remains of a spent bullet.

'Bloody hell, it's for real. What's the matter with that damn dog?'

Peering out across the Rec he could see nothing because of the crazed reflection in the glass and his mind was made up.

'Jacquie, I'm going to see what hells the matter with that dog. Dial 112 and report this to the Police.'

'Hunter, you're not going anywhere until I've looked at that shoulder.'

'It's a bullet.'

He fiddled with the object under his shirt and winced as he twisted it and pulled it out.

Dropping the bullet on the table he was about to open the sliding doors when something made him fetch his mobile phone and a torch. Muttering to himself, 'There's something weird going on here,' he went out into the garden and down the path to the back gate leading to the Rec.

Against the backdrop of the dark bluish evening sky and the first twinkling stars, he could see the silhouettes of the houses on the other side of the Rec and the hedge separating the allotments from the playing fields but the barking was coming from the centre. As he walked aided by his torch he could feel every stud mark and missing divot made by the weekend football players.

The dog sensed help was coming and the barking intensified as he came closer and when he raised his torch he saw a Labrador sniffing and barking around a hunched up body.

As he approached he spoke calmly. 'Easy, boy. What's the matter?' The animal calmed at his presence and Hunter continued talking to it. 'Easy now, let's see what's up.'

He could see it was a woman by the clothes and he bent over the body and reached to check for a pulse in her neck and then hesitated when he saw the blood soaking her collar, her scarf and the surrounding grass. Suddenly she shivered and exhaled with a big sigh. Hunter knew the signs. She had bled out and passed her last breath as he watched powerless to help.

The dog went quiet and began whimpering and nuzzled up to Hunter as he carried out his checks but he knew it was hopeless and his worst fears were realised when he could feel nothing.

'Oh, shit, what happened here?'

Pushing her scarf down he saw the bullet hole and without moving the body he felt underneath and was able to feel the exit wound on the other side of her neck.

'A through and through.'

He stood up and fumbled for his phone and dialled Jacquie.

'What is it, H?'

'Update that call to the police, Jacquie, we have a body. Get an ambulance also, although it's too late, the lady's dead. She's been shot.'

'Okay,' Jacquie replied, 'they're on their way already. Are you okay?'

'Yeah, I'm fine.'

'You'd better be.'

As she rang off he could hear the klaxons and two minutes later one car pulled into the gateway by the Village Community Hall and onto the Rec and bouncing over the muddy grass surface it stopped thirty metres away with headlights and spot-lights lighting up the scene. A second car went down the lane to the front of the bungalow. Hunter flashed his torch as a policeman and woman climbed out of the vehicle.

'Lower that torch and walk towards us slowly, mister,' shouted the policeman who had been driving, 'and keep your hands in sight.'

Hunter muttered something under his breath but did as he was told.

'Call your dog, don't want him spoiling the scene do we?'

'It's not my dog. It belongs to her. You might want to throw a ring around that scene.'

'Smart arse, aye. Stand by the car and don't move.' He spoke to his colleague. 'Helen, check out that body while I get his details.'

Helen went to the boot of the car to fetch the regulation blue and white cordon tape and before she approached the body she laid out a twenty-metre ring around it. Keeping in line with the car and using her torch to search the ground in front of her she lay a strip of tape on the ground behind her and proceeded cautiously towards the victim.

Meanwhile, Bob, her companion pulled out his notebook and spoke to Hunter. 'Name and I.D. and where do you live, mister.'

'Hunter, George Hunter,' he pointed across the field, 'and I live there where all the lights are blazing and your oppos are looking at the damage. My ID's in my back pocket, is it okay?'

'Aye, Get it, but slowly.'

As Hunter reached for his wallet the policeman's radio crackled and unintelligible words came from his radio to which he responded by flicking a switch and pressing the earpiece firmly into his ear. '1212, go ahead.'

He listened intently for a few moments and when the distant voice went quiet he said, 'I'll pass it on. We need SOCO and the brains department. 1212, over.'

He returned his attention to Hunter who was holding his driving licence at arm's length. 'Mr Hunter, it seems you were one of us, what do you reckon?'

'I'm retired,' said Hunter wearily as he put the licence back in his wallet, 'but it looks like some idiot was playing with illegal toys and either took a pot shot at her or she just got in the way. The bullet by the way was a through and through and went on to smash our window. That's why I'm here and your mates are checking my house out.'

An approaching Ambulance could be heard as Helen rejoined them leading the dog by a length of cordon tape threaded through its collar. She gestured towards the body with her free hand. 'She's been shot, Bob.'

'Aye, Mr Hunter here was saying as much,' and with a nod of his head in Hunter's direction, 'and he's on our security list.'

'How do you do, Mr Hunter. What did you do and is that blood on your shirt?'

He ignored the first part of the question and replied, 'The blood is from the same bullet that hit her. Is it okay for me to go back home now? My wife will be worrying.'

Sure,' said Bob, 'I'll take it from here but we'll need to interview you later. Would you mind looking after the dog?'

Hunter shook his head. 'Sorry, but I'll get the RSPCA out for you.'

'That's okay, I'll call the station and they can do it.'

It was dark now and as Hunter prepared to walk back across the Rec to the bungalow he thought to himself, 'A late-night tonight, time for a stiff'n.'

—

When Hunter entered the conservatory the Police Sergeant who was interviewing Ken and Kay lowered his notebook. 'Are you okay, Mr Hunter, your wife said you were injured.'

'Aye, it's only a scratch.' He pointed over his shoulder across the field, 'but it didn't do her any good. She took some of the pace out of it and the window did the rest.'

'Take a seat, I'll be with you in a minute. Your wife's filled me in on the details but I'll need your version.'

Hunter nodded and dropped into the nearest armchair just as Jacquie arrived with a tray loaded with mugs of tea. 'Oh, you're there, would you like some, H?'

'No, I'll have a beer. Sergeant, can I nip to the fridge?'

The Sergeant looked up. 'Yes.'

'Would you like one?'

'Not on duty, thanks.'

Hunter stood, stretched and rubbed his right hip and thigh before making his way through the bungalow to the kitchen where he got not one beer but two and balancing a glass under his arm joined the others in the conservatory. Returning to his seat he opened a can and filled his glass. He'd just taken his first mouthful when the Sergeant came across dropped his notebook on the table, pulled out a seat and sat down. 'Tell me your side of things, Mr Hunter.'

Pointing across the conservatory he said, 'I was stood by that door that leads into the house to take the coffee tray off Jacquie and just as she was about to hand it to me the window exploded. I felt this thump on my shoulder as I ducked down at the same time as she dived for cover and when we looked up, as I said, the window was in its current state. I went over to the window to check the damage and as I did so I felt a twinge and fiddling around found the bullet lodged in the fleshy part of my shoulder and at the same time heard this dog going bananas out there so I went to investigate and found the woman's body. She'd been shot through the neck.'

They both looked up when they heard voices coming through the house and moments later a grey-haired man of indeterminate age wearing a tweed jacket over brown cords and suede boots came into the conservatory followed by an attractive young woman of British / Malay Indian ethnicity with close-cropped hair in the Audrey Hepburn style and dark eyes made more attractive against her golden skin dressed in a modest but well-fitting trouser suit.

He nodded, 'Evening, I'm Detective Inspector Fearn, and this is Detective Sergeant Long.' He gestured to the uniform Sergeant. 'Fill me in, Jim.'

'Mr Hunter here and his wife and guests were just settling down for an after-dinner coffee,' he pointed across the conservatory to the mish-mash of splintered glass, 'when that window imploded.' He took a plastic bag from his pocket and in it was the bullet. 'Mr Hunter was wounded and when he investigated he found this embedded in his shoulder and clothing.' He gave the bag to Fearn who immediately tossed it across to Sergeant Long. 'Unfortunately, it was distorted by the impact and probably of little use as evidence. We also have the body of a woman in the field over there which Mr Hunter found.'

'Thanks, Sergeant. Do you need any medical attention, Mr Hunter?'

Hunter shrugged. 'I'm fine, but it's made a mess of my shirt.'

Fearn marvelled at the stoic old-world attitude and couldn't help thinking that with all the modern health and safety crap if it had been one of his officers there would have been para-medics in attendance, six months off work and a full enquiry later.

He acknowledged Hunter's reply with a nod of his head, 'That's alright then.' Turning to DS Long, Fearn said, 'Stay here, Carrie and get a catch up from the Sergeant. SOCO will be here shortly. Mr Hunter, can you show me where the body is?'

Hunter led the way out to the field where a circle of lights and a blue tent were being erected. Closing the garden gate behind him, Fearn spoke. 'You're on our high security list, Mr Hunter, what's all that about?'

As they walked Hunter gave Fearn a brief background history, ' ...and I've been retired ever since so I don't think there's much to worry about.'

'And, Mrs Hunter?'

'She's on the list also.'

'Is that how you met?'

'You could say that.'

They stopped at the blue and white tape cordon and a SOCO operative in white disposable overalls came over to them. Fearn greeted him with a nod. 'Evening, Dr Kerr, anything yet?'

'Not much to report, Inspector. The lady appears to have been shot while out walking her dog. She was shot through the neck and bled out there. From the position of that shattered window...' He swivelled around and pointed to where torches were moving around in the gloom on the far side of the field. '...the shot was fired from over there. Ann Judge is there with uniforms checking the area but it will be morning before we can properly evaluate it. To add anything more would be conjecture at this point.'

'Do we know who she is?'

'Not yet, but the RSPCA will be checking the dog to see if it's chipped and the uniform boys can follow that up.'

'Thanks, Doc. Seal the field off and I'll leave you to it. See you in the morning.' The Doctor left them and Fearn said, 'There's not much we can do here, let's go back.'

—

When they arrived back at the bungalow everyone was assembled in the lounge and Jacquie offered them a mug of tea which Fearn accepted but George declined and ignoring Jacquie's disapproving glare opened another tin of beer.

Fearn chuckled to himself and approached Ken and Kay. 'Mr and Mrs Theaker, you come from Preston?'

Ken nodded, 'That's right.'

'When are you going home?'

'We're staying with George tonight and intend to drive home tomorrow.'

Fearn rubbed his chin thoughtfully before replying, 'Can you stay a bit longer. I don't envisage it will be too long but just in case?'

Ken looked over to Jacquie. 'Will that be okay, Jacquie? We can go to a hotel tomorrow if you want.'

'No you won't,' she said, 'what sort of hostess would I be if I let you do that? I'll ring H's sister and arrange for the children to stay on another night or two and I'll pop round tomorrow with some extra clothes for them as they have school on Monday.'

'That's settled then,' said Fearn with a hint of relief, ' I don't think there's anything more to be done here tonight so I'll leave you good people in peace. Good night, come on, Sergeant, let's go.'

Hunter showed Fearn to the door but as he was about to leave Hunter stopped him. 'Is it alright to sweep up that glass and seal the window?'

Fearn turned to the SOCO operative behind him 'Have you done?'

The SOCO nodded. 'Cover the window as we may need to use the hole as a guide for the shot, but you can sweep up.'

The section of the Cheshire Police Department left and when peace had returned Hunter said, 'Anyone for a nightcap. I've got a good single malt.'

~~~~~
~~~~~

CHAPTER 3

One month earlier

Demyan Orlov, aged forty-six, five foot eleven and bronzed, with a six-pack which sent women wild, shut down his smartphone with a sigh and pondered his position as he watched his wife Elena playing with their two children in the surf. The sun was hovering above the horizon of the Gulf of Mexico casting a red aura across the western sky and he was at peace with the world but that last call troubled him. It sounded like a routine job but all jobs in his line of business came with a certain amount of danger but his bank balance was healthy so did he need it?

He sat down and ran his fingers through his trimmed blonde hair which was tinged pink in the evening light before he rested his head on his hands between his knees trying to shut out the happiness wafting towards him up the beach. He looked up when he heard Elena calling and she waved to him to come and join them. His heart skipped a beat. This was what he had worked for all his life after the torrid time spent in the Moscow ghettos.

The youngest sniper ever employed by the Spetznaz he did a two-year tour in Afghanistan where his skill had been recognised with promotion and medals which boosted his claims to a State provided module in a better suburb of the capital where he housed his ageing mother, but he always longed for more.

His dream was America with its freedom and choices, not a life of scrabbling for black market food wherever it was available or looking for work in a corrupt society.

It was the collapse of the USSR in December 1991 which opened the door but first, the State required him to show his worth in Chechnya both in the First Chechnyan War and the Second where the death of school children and other civilian atrocities sickened him. In the year 2000, he absconded and made his way via Georgia, Turkey and Greece to the West.

Several visits to the US Consul in Athens persuaded them that he was a genuine refugee and they gave him free passage to the States where the underworld of New York beckoned. His early interviews were daunting as at first the authorities didn't consider him but the more information he gave them about Spetznaz operations the more they believed his intentions to the good life and they passed him through the system. He obtained his green card but the work he had in mind involved functioning underground using his Spetznaz skills but not content with working for the Russian Mafia in 2004 he became a freelance hitman. His prowess earned him many recommendations and jobs provided by the Agency as it was known took him all over the world in many guises.

In 2008 he met and married Elena and in 2009 he was given legitimacy with the arrival of his US Citizenship and Passport. Given the nature of his employment, his income was considerable and he invested well in a Scuba Diving and Surf Board school on the shores of the Mexican Gulf in Florida at the same time honing his golfing skills at the Innisbrook Copperhead Club.

With a handicap of three, this made him a favourite in club matches and the many PGA Professionals who visited the course were keen to play him as he gave them a run for their money. This was his dream, a wife, children, the beach life and Golf.

He thought many of the people he assassinated were personal grudges that were unnecessary and he became more selective as he tried to back away from paid murder and so the call he received in 2014 came as a surprise.

Should he or shouldn't he? The offer of one million dollars at the same time as a demand from the IRS was tempting. He shut it from his mind and with a heavy heart ran down the beach to play with his family.

—

'Demy, what's the matter?' Elena snuggled up to him and traced her fingers around his muscular chest. 'You're very quiet tonight.'

'I've had a call from the Agency. They want me to go to Paris and talk to some holiday company from Oman. It means I'll be away for about three weeks.'

'I thought you'd finished with them?'

'I have, but they asked if I could do one more job.'

'Are you?'

'I said, yes. It's paid offshore and with that demand from the IRS, it couldn't have come at a better time. You'll be okay and I'll call every night. Just this last one.'

'Okay, if you must, but you know how the kids miss you. Send them messages on their pads and if you get a chance, Skype.'

'I'll make it a quick one and this comes with a good bonus if I get it right.'

'When do you leave?'

'There's an overnighter from Tampa to New York tomorrow and I'll fix the Paris bit from there. The sponsors are paying and it's all first-class so not so bad.'

'Good. Let's go to bed and you can placate me intensely up there.'

Unable to resist his beautiful blonde temptress he stood up and in one swift movement scooped her up and carried her towards the stairs.

~~~~~
~~~~~

CHAPTER 4

It wasn't the best day of the year to travel and Jamie wished he had paid more attention to the weather forecast and waited until Wednesday but his mother demanded that if he was going then he must do it while it was uppermost in their minds and nothing must distract him from his promise. Since leaving home from his rural retreat in South Armagh that morning it had done nothing but rain and comfy though the bus was it made his journey no more enjoyable. Most of this passed him by as his meeting with the local underground Pro-IRA heavies had unsettled him and the prospect of meeting someone higher up the chain was quite unnerving.

The Europa Bus Centre in Belfast did nothing to lift his spirits and after wasting fifteen minutes trying to find his next bus he gave up and decided to walk across the city to the Falls Road. On a whim, he stopped a bus driver who was clocking off.

'Hey, mister, can you tell me the way to the Falls Road?'

'Aye, lad, wander round yon corner and get the 215 bus.'

He endured five minutes of nature's battering which was blowing the rain parallel to the ground before the bus arrived. Ten minutes later he was in the Falls Road looking up and down and trying to judge which direction was the most likely way to his destination. He was no city lover and wished to be back home but a promise was a promise and slinging his backpack over his shoulder he pulled a scrap of paper from his coat pocket and made a quick check of the name of the Bar he was looking for before he lowered his head and trudged off to his left with the wind trying its hardest to persuade him the opposite direction was the right way to go.

Fortune favoured him and a few minutes later he arrived outside his destination. It had recently had a facelift and did not match the instructions he had been given. The paintwork was still green but no longer faded and peeling but the name was right and with an inner feeling of trepidation he entered the 'Shady Tree Bar.' Immediately he was aware of the silence as all eyes turned to see who the stranger was and the barmen was barely less than hostile when he ordered a pint of lager. This made Jamie uncomfortable and he wished he could go back home but he had promised and taking a piece of notepaper from his inside pocket he called the barman and slid it over the bar.

'Yeh! What is it?' was the less than friendly question not in a manner designed to encourage new customers.

Jamie bit his lip and nudged the piece of paper further across. 'Do you know where I can find this guy?'

The barmen picked it up and studied it. 'Who wants to know?'

With uncustomary bravado and holding his temper in check, Jamie thrust his head forward, stared at the barmen, and said, 'Me!'

The barman took a step back. 'He's not here,' and walked to the other end of the bar. Moments later Jamie saw him speaking to two hard-looking men and immediately felt the atmosphere change but he stuck it out and ordered another lager.

The older of the two men left the bar only to return fifteen minutes later and he said two curt words to Jamie as he walked past. 'Wait here.'

He rejoined his mate and they sat talking for around half an hour all the time watching Jamie. A mobile phone rang and the older one answered it and after a few muttered words he closed his phone. Giving his mate the nod they got up and made as if they were leaving the Bar when they suddenly turned on Jamie and stood on either side of him and took an arm each. The older one scooped up Jamie's backpack and together they propelled him to the door.

Outside was a dirty black Vauxhall with the rear door open and he was roughly thrown in. The younger one got in with him and from inside his jacket took out a pistol and held it to Jamie's head. 'Lie down and stay there.'

The older one climbed in the front and with a squeal of tyres, the car accelerated away. A few hundred metres along the road they made an amateur fierce left turn and the tyres screeched in protest. The same shoddy driving exercise was repeated several times before they did a final vicious right turn into a back entry. Jamie was no fool and realised it was all for show and guessed they were back at the bar albeit at the rear entrance.

They dragged him out and with the gun thrust into his ribs

they pushed him up a fire escape and into a sparsely furnished upper room. The smell of the kitchen downstairs pervaded the air and it reminded Jamie that he had not eaten since he left home. At one end of the room was a kitchen table left over from the wartime utility years and in the centre, a chair was set ready and Jamie was shoved onto it and his arms tied behind him just above his elbows in a manner that made him helpless and to further complicate his discomfort they blindfolded him.

Jamie heard his bag being tipped upside down spewing the contents across the table at the same time they searched his pockets and took his wallet but an additional noise entered his brain, another person had entered the room wearing proper shoes and was walking towards the table. He could hear them rifling through his belongings when a voice with only a mild trace of an accent, said, 'Well, well, what have we here? A bit off your territory aren't you young man?'

Jamie next heard a tearing sound and guessed it was the brown envelope his Gran had given to him and he heard an audible whistle when the bundle of fifty-pound notes tumbled out. The Voice addressed him again. 'Jamie McDuggan from South Armagh, what's this?'

Although his heart was pounding Jamie spoke firmly. 'Are you the guy I asked for because if you are there's more of that if you want it?'

'Oh, yeh, and how does that work? And don't waste my time otherwise you'll need a Zimmer frame for life.'

'Are you the guy I asked for?'

The Voice replied in a manner that needed no interpretation. 'I'll ask the questions. Now before I lose my patience what's your game?'

Jamie shivered inwardly and his short show of bravado disappeared. 'My Gran won the lottery and wants revenge on the English bastard who shot her man, that's me, Grandad. That's a down payment and she's willing to pay more but she needs you to organise it. If you're who I'm looking for we got your name from the local Commander who said you and some guy call O'Hearne could fix it.'

The Voice showed renewed interest. 'And when was this supposed shooting and where?'

'South Armagh in **1983**. That's what I'm told anyway. I wasn't born then.'

'Do you have this guy's name?'

'No, that's why we need you.'

'How much is here?'

'Five thousand pounds.'

'I want one-hundred thousand as a goodwill gesture and then more if we fix it. How much did your Gran win?'

'I don't know.'

'Right, son, you go back to your Gran and tell her I'll look into it but to be prepared to pay out a million and maybe more to close it as I need to pay off people.'

Jamie's heart skipped a beat when hands started searching his body and relief surged through him when they stopped immediately they located his Smartphone and took it from his pocket.

The Voice which Jamie thought was familiar but he couldn't put a name to it, said, 'Check that out, Pat. You, Jamie, will communicate through Pat, my Belfast Commander. He'll give you a phone number and when you let him know if the deals good I'll put the wheels in motion, but I warn you if this is a set-up or you renege on your payments both you and your Gran will need to book a funeral which will take place only after my chaps here have had their fun with you which could be long and drawn out. Is that clear?'

His heart in overdrive but trying not to show his fear Jamie nodded and then he heard a rustling noise like money being scooped and footsteps coming towards him. His phone and something else was stuffed into his top pocket. 'There's fifty quid, you'll need that to get home.'

The footsteps went towards the door but before he left The Voice said, 'Pat, a word.'

The two left the room and the young heavy removed the blindfold and untied Jamie. 'Get your stuff and you can go but mind on what he said, he doesn't like to be messed about. Take the back stairs and shut the door on your way out.'

Outside in the corridor, The Voice spoke to Patrick. 'I'll pass that mobile number onto Red in GCHQ so we can keep tabs on him. You follow him home and shop around to check his story, here's two hundred pounds to tide you over.' He took the money from the envelope, 'On your way before you lose him.'

'Thanks, Boss, where'll I get hold of you?'

'I have some business in my London office so call me only if it's genuine with the standard precautions and give Jamie the account number and we'll go from there. If it's not genuine look after them the usual way. Have we still got those books about the SAS from the seventies and eighties and that hardback from ninety-one? There were three of them all together with pictures in.'

'They're in my loft.'

'Dig them out.'

Patrick knuckled his head and hurried downstairs and paused only long enough to grab his coat and went out just in time to see Jamie a hundred metres away walking back to town.

Jamie didn't hurry and went into the first takeaway he came to and idly leant against the wall to devour his late lunch of sausage, curry and chips which annoyed Patrick who, try as he might, could not disguise his presence. It had stopped raining but the chill North-easterly wind was making life uncomfortable and Jamie stopped for coffee while watching Patrick through the window as he took time out to make a phone call. After five minutes with no attempt at evasion, he continued his walk to the Europa Bus Centre.

Two days later...

'Hullo, Boss. His Gran won four million and the deposit money's in the bank already. What do we do now?'

'Wait for my word, Pat. I'll get in touch with Gold and Red in GCHQ and Blue in SIS while you read up those books and see if they give a clue as to who or what was responsible for that mission, and I repeat, do nothing before I give the word.'

~~~~~
~~~~~

CHAPTER 5

Demyan settled in the white leather armchair and decided this five-star luxury life was something he could get used to but he wasn't impressed with the view from the penthouse window. For this money, he thought you should get a better view than a building fifty metres across the street.

His dream was disturbed when an elderly Arab gentleman dressed in the way of a Sheikh came through from the stateroom next door. He was escorted by another Arab who was wearing expensive western garb and carrying a briefcase. The fine stitching around the lapels of his silver-grey suit gave distinction to one of Saville Rows finest. Black patent leather shoes complimented the suit but the colourful tie he wore appeared somewhat incongruous.

Demyan stood up but the Sheikh ignored him and sat on a matching white leather sofa that stretched along one side of the room. The Suit spoke to him.

'The Master does not approve of your profession so names will not be used, but welcome, please be seated.'

He, himself sat down at a white leather veneered desk with a matching leather office chair opposite Demyan and between them was a matching white coffee table. Suit turned to face Demyan and took three books, one a hardback, some scribbled notes and a photograph from his briefcase and placed them on the table. Demyan noted the title of the top book was in English; *SAS – Operation Oman.*

The Suit pointed at the picture. 'This research which was given to us from another source is now extinct which includes those books. It leads us to believe that this man was responsible for the death of my Master's first son some forty years ago in Oman. It was during a skirmish in the Saudi Empty Quarter east of Deefa when soldiers of the British Army Training Teams (BATT's) employed by the Sultan were lured into an ambush. We, or rather, he wishes to avenge that death according to our *Jebali* traditions so that his sons and their sons can live with ease in their own society.

In the scriptures, it is called an eye for an eye...'

Demyan raised his hand, 'Hold it there. If his son lured this man into an ambush isn't he responsible for his own death? So why do you want this guy dead?'

The Suit spoke to the Sheikh in Arabic before answering Demyan's question rather sheepishly. 'It is the tradition amongst *Jebali* tribes to avenge the death of ones kin, be it in battle or man to man combat. It is called the *thaa'r* and until it is carried out or it is seen that attempts are being made to carry it out one loses respect amongst ones fellow-men which you must have if you have any desire to lead your tribe.'

To an ex-soldier, this seemed bazaar and Demyan shook his head in puzzlement before replying. 'Tell me what you want.'

The Suit pulled some papers from his briefcase and threw them on the table. 'There is your contract. You will be paid twenty-five per cent up front and the rest on proof of completion plus a bonus if you finish it quickly. You have a bank account?'

'I have an account in the Cayman Islands and I want thirty per cent up front as I have a Tax bill to pay plus two-hundred thousand dollars in hand for expenses. I'm might have to grease a few palms.'

The Suit had a quick interchange with his Master before he replied. 'That can be arranged but because of your demands, I must warn you that if you don't finish it we will come after you. We want our money's worth. Anything else?'

'Yes, why the hurry?'

'My Master is well advanced in age and he would like to see this gift to his sons completed.'

Demyan stood. 'Very well, I will take the contract and read it and if I agree, which I don't see any reason why not, I will drop it off tonight. Can I have the picture and the books?'

Suit nodded. 'Take it all but the information is quite old. When you return your expenses will be waiting for you in reception. We do not want to see you again. Good day!'

Demyan was frozen out as both The Suit and his Master walked past and retired to the Stateroom without so much as a glance in his direction. Feeling more like the persecuted rather than the executioner he made his way back to the cosy family hotel which he had used on previous occasions.

—

Demyan went shopping for a set of golf clubs to be delivered to his hotel. He browsed for half an hour before settling on a set of Ping S56 clubs with which he was familiar. He spent the rest of the day reading and did not break off for his lunch brought to him by the room service. His main interest was in the operations of the BATT's during the conflict in Oman in the nineteen-seventies which he likened to his service in Chechnya but a damn sight warmer but he still had difficulty with the idea of revenge for what was a combat death between two warring sides. It didn't make sense. War is War which means casualties on both sides which was regrettable, but fact.

Mulling his thoughts over dinner that evening he decided that if they were paying he would carry out his mission so without further ado he took the contract from his inside pocket, signed it and sat back to wait for dessert and looking forward to his evening entertainment which he had arranged earlier.

After dinner, he walked to the hotel where his prospective Arab employers were staying but delayed only long enough to leave his contract and collect the stuffed brown envelope left for him in Reception before walking back to his hotel were waiting for him was a lissom blonde chosen for him by Madame Brouchard with whom he had been a client for many years and whose shape encased in faux leather leggings and blingy T-shirt could only have come after many hours in the gym.

He knew his night was going to be exiting by her wandering hand in the elevator and she found that he was already a willing client.

—

The following morning when more favours for his prowess were given willingly, and a good Continental breakfast he made his way to Reception where a package courtesy of the Agency was waiting for him and from there it was a taxi to the Gare Du Nord train station and a trip on Eurostar.

He spent the time travelling under the English Channel

studying his latest alias. His new surname was Dimitrov domiciled in Frankfurt, Germany as a civilian IT worker for the US Army going on a golfing holiday and he had a room reserved in the five-star Chantry Wood Hotel just outside Chester, wherever that was, and he was booked to play at a links course in Hoylake close by.

He was met at St Pancras Station by an Agency chauffeur who took his cases and golf clubs and showed him to a limousine for the short journey to Euston Station. After Demyan had handed over the receipts for his new clubs, not a word was spoken during the five-minute ride to Euston Station and the chauffeur refused the offer of help with the bags and the heavier set of clubs which had been substituted for the ones Demyan had brought over from France but he was pleased when offerings of a gratuity were made. It was all for show and done with the correct amount of gravity between an employer and his hired help.

Safely settled in his first-class seat Demyan sat back with a newspaper to enjoy the delights of the English countryside on a journey to the North West with only one end.

~~~~~
~~~~~

CHAPTER 6

One month later

The Voice stood over the table looking at the photographs displayed in two of the three books from Patrick's loft. He pointed to a photo in the one entitled, *SAS – Operation Oman*.

'That's our guy, I think, Pat. Gold says it was an agent under the code name, Orion, who was assigned the mission and that fella there in the Oman picture is an SAS Sergeant by the name of Hunter who must have left the SAS and the Army just after that picture was taken as there's no trace of him and in the Parachute Regiment records he's shown as demobbed. We know the SAS keep no records and when you leave you to revert to your own Regiment. Putting two and two together, Orion is the mythological Hunter of Greco / Roman times and therefore a not so good cover name for our ex-Sergeant Hunter.'

Patrick walked around the table and peered closely at the pictures. 'Okay, I'll get some copies made of that but how do we locate him.'

'I'll try my contacts again to see if there's an old address he retired to while you get one of your whizz kids to search online and see if we can trace him through phone records and if not we'll try the Census records. This may take some time because in my experience when you type your name into Google there are thousands of you. Meanwhile, find someone to do the job.'

'I know just the person, Aiden Cronin. He has a grudge against the bloody English especially since they put him away for five years in ninety-two. That really got him going.

'What was that for?'

'He was with Tim O'Reilly's brother, Sean, when they spotted a woman who had been posing as one of us in the early eighties but she was an English undercover agent. A tall model who went under the name of Siobhan Milligan...' The Voice nodded, as his memory was stirred, but he remained silent. '...Aiden and Sean chased after her and her sidekick and took a couple of pot-shots at them in Liverpool of all places. It didn't take the cops long to pick him up. Come to think of it she was there when McDuggan's grandad was shot.'

His face remained inscrutable as The Voice said, 'I've heard of her. What happened then?'

'The bitch dropped off the radar until she was spotted in Cyprus by O'Reilly. Cronin, who lives in Liverpool with his wife went over to the States and did a snipers course at a school run by an ex-Navy Seal and ever since then it's taken a lot to stop him going alone on some harebrained scheme. O'Reilly lives close by which helps us as checks on the airport and the ferries won't suss them out.'

'Has this Cronin got access to weapons or does he expect us to supply him? We want no cock-ups.'

'Okay, Boss. I don't know about any weapons but as soon as we find our quarry I'll go over and see him.'

'Good, I'm off to a meeting in Stormont and then I'm nipping down to Dublin before I fly to London. You know how to get me.'

—

Patrick was lounging at the rear of the Bar in the 'Shady Tree' watching and listening to the local Irish Folk group when his attention was drawn to the barman who was waving him to come over. 'What the hell does he want now. Not another wandering vagrant looking out for his Gran.'

He heaved his fourteen stone up from his seat and went over. 'What is it, lad?'

'There's a call for you.' He gestured with his thumb. 'Take it through the back.'

Patrick sighed and decided it was time to retire his days as Commander would end after this mission. Nodding his thanks he went to the end of the bar and through a heavy door into the back of the premises. The phone was off the hook lying on a small table in the hallway waiting for him.

He picked it up and said in a bored tone. 'Hullo!'

'Patrick.' He didn't need an introduction The Voice was instantly recognisable. 'Have you got a pen?'

He took a pen from his inside pocket and pulled a small pad towards him. 'Yeh, Boss, go ahead.'

'Take down this address and then check it out against phone records. It may be our man assuming he hasn't moved house.'

Patrick scribbled as the instructions were read out over the phone. 'Right, Boss, we'll get onto that straight away and I'll pop over tomorrow, Cronin's anxious to prove himself.'

'Good, and warn him to be careful. I don't expect our secret agent has lost much of his wariness even though he's in his sixties. Good night.'

Patrick put the phone down with a sigh, an old age pensioner ex-agent wasn't high on his list of priorities at this moment. 'I'm too old for this,' he muttered as he meandered back into the bar and assumed his seat. Guinness was his priority that night.

—

Patrick cursed his overindulgence the night before and looking around his fellow passengers on the mid-morning flight out of Belfast he wondered why people departing always looked happier than those coming back.

His mood was further soured when he had to wait for more than an hour for Cronin and his tone when he called on his mobile was less than complimentary. After five rings he was about to press the cancel button when the phone was answered. He didn't give the other person time to speak before he bellowed, 'Cronin, where the fuckin' hell are you and why the fuck am I hanging around this bloody airport?'

He immediately wished for the ground to swallow him up when a mellow Irish female voice replied, 'There is no call for that sort of language and if you persist I'll hang up. What was is it you wanted?'

'Aah, err! Sorry! Is that no good peasant, Cronin, around?'

'Who wants him?'

'The name's O'Hearne. He's expecting me.'

'Are you sure? He was working nights last night and he's still in bed and he said nothing about someone coming to see him.'

'Never mind, wake him up and tell him I'll meet him in, err... What's his local pub?'

'Bunch of Grapes, Aigburth.'

'I'll meet him there in half an hour, got that?'

'Yes, Mr Manners, and while you're there wash your mouth out.'

She immediately hung up and left Patrick with an apology hanging on his lips. 'Bloody women.'

If he was going to get the afternoon flight back he had better get a move on and unceremoniously pushed through the exit doors and jumped in the first taxi disregarding the smartly dressed tanned young man wearing a faux Burberry coat who followed him and with a flash of his ID commandeered the next taxi.

Outside the Bunch of Grapes Patrick alighted and reached in to pay the driver ignoring the taxi that cruised past and stopped two hundred metres further on. He may have been concerned had he seen the young man watching him through the rear window of the cab and get out moments after he had entered the pub.

With an imperceptible glance around the young man entered and made his way to the bar where he ordered a pint of lager. Taking his pint he surveyed the room and chose a table. Being right-handed he picked one where he was covered by a left-hand wall in a position where he could observe Patrick and have the pick of the exits at the same time. Spreading out a copy of the Racing Post he pretended to be studying form. A few minutes later Aiden Cronin entered and after purchasing a pint of Guinness he joined Patrick.

The welcome was less than cordial and Patrick came to the point immediately. 'Cronin, if you're this lax now I'm wondering if you're up to it. I've half a mind to look for someone else.'

'Whoa, Pat, I'm sorry and it's my fault. I've just finished my last night shift and I forgot to tell the misses you were coming.'

'What do you mean, your last shift?'

'I've packed my job in. I can take a break after this in Spain or somewhere.'

'Bit previous aren't you? You haven't done the fuckin' job yet.'

'I was pissed off and I'm doing a bit of keep-fit to get ready.'

'Are you tooled up?'

'I've got a stash in a lock-up.'

From his inside pocket, Patrick took out some folded A4 papers and a photograph which he pushed over to Cronin. 'That's our man and here's his last known address and according to the BT website he's still there.' He slid a stuffed brown envelope under the table and pushed it over. 'Here's a grand for expenses. You'll get another thirty-thousand on completion and we want proof, okay.'

Cronin nodded and then looked across to Patrick's stalker who was shaking his mobile, banging it and waving it around as if trying to get a signal and unbeknown to Cronin taking a full-face photograph of him during the moment. Swigging the last of his pint he stood up, dropped the mobile into his pocket, angrily rolled up his newspaper and without a glance left or right walked out of the pub.

Turning his attention back to Patrick, Cronin said, 'Haven't seen him around here before.'

'An' you'll probably never see him again. He needs to pay his phone bill by the look of it. Going by the tan he probably overran his credit on holiday. Have you got all the details you need because I've got to hurry if I want that flight back this afternoon?'

'Yep, it looks good.'

'There's no rush but the sooner you do it the sooner both you and we get paid.'

'And how much did you lot get?'

'Never you mind, but the Boss had to give a lot out in backhanders in high places and the funds from over the States are a bit thin at the moment. If that's it, I'm off. Have you got your car?'

'Yep, I'll drive you to the airport and then I'll Google this lot and get the lay of the land before I make a move.'

—

Aiden pushed his computer away and fished his wallet from his back pocket, opened it and withdrew two fifty-pound notes and threw them on the coffee table before he spoke to his wife. 'Naomi, buy yourself something nice we're going house hunting this weekend.'

Naomi paused the film she was watching. 'Like what? and anyway, what for, I like it here.'

'I can't say much but it's to do with the job I'm doing for Pat. A bit of scouting.'

'Aiden, you're not starting that again. It's old hat, no one cares today.'

'It's only a one-off easy touch but I need to find out the lay of the land and the place we're looking at is in the same postcode as my intended target. The wonders of Rightmove.'

'I that case I'll need more than a ton.'

'Bloody women.' He pulled three more notes from his wallet and threw them down with the others. 'That's all you're getting. Saturday morning, okay?'

—

Andy Roberts, a tall balding man of eighty, slightly overweight but upright for his age, turned the latch on the front door and stood to one side to let his visitors out when Cronin who had stopped to look at some pictures spoke to him. 'Lovely place you've got here, Mr Roberts, what about the neighbours?'

'It's a community where everyone looks out for everyone else. I wouldn't leave but I'm moving nearer to my daughter now my wife's died.'

Cronin pulled a photo from his inside pocket and showed it to Andy. 'I used to know this lad when I was in the Army. He lived around this way somewhere. Do you know him?'

Andy hesitated, his Police brain was telling him to err on the side of caution. Something about the Liverpool Irish accent triggered a reaction he had not felt for thirty-five years. His time seconded to the Royal Ulster Constabulary where everyone was conscious of even the slightest question and the photo of Hunter in combat gear set alarm bells ringing.

'No, I can't say I have,' he said, as he glanced at his watch, 'you might try the pub. It's after eleven so they should be open.'

Cronin shoved his hand out. 'Thanks, Mr Roberts, we'll be in touch with the Estate Agent, goodbye.'

Andy held the door open for them and replied, 'And thank you Mr... Sorry, I didn't get your name.'

'Smith.'

Andy watched as they walked down the front path to the road and he closed the door thoughtfully. The woman hadn't spoken a word during the whole twenty minutes. He was also intrigued when he saw Cronin's white Vauxhall Astra car driving back up the lane a couple of minutes later and slow down almost to a crawl when passing the Hunter bungalow. Surely he should have slowed down when passing number thirty-five the one he was interested in buying.

Andy concluded that being a policeman for forty years had clouded his judgment but he made a mental note of the car registration although he wasn't sure he would remember it as his short term memory wasn't that good these days. He became more concerned when he saw Cronin make a hash of a gear change as he accelerated past Jacquie who was driving down the lane on her way home. She pulled her maroon Range Rover to one side to allow Cronin to pass and as he acknowledged with a wave he recognised Jacquie and fumbled with the gears and cursed at the same time.

Andy went into the kitchen and made a note on the pad which lay alongside his daily pill box while it was still fresh in his mind.

Outside in the lane Cronin rammed his car with a resounding crunch into the next gear and cursed, 'Fuckin' hell, that's the Milligan bitch who got me five years. Sean and Tim recognised her from the eighties. She was supposed to be working for us and all the time she was a snitch. What's she doing here?' He fished the picture of Hunter from his inside pocket and threw it across to Naomi, 'Living with him do you reckon? Forget the pub she's all the proof we need.'

—

Sat in the corner of the crowded bar of the 'Bunch of Grapes' Sean O'Reilly kept his voice low as he discussed the day's events with Cronin. 'Are you sure it's her? We don't want any clangers this time.'

'Sean, you can't mistake her even after thirty-odd years. Anyway, she's nowt, it's Hunter I'm getting paid to get. Maybe Pat will have something to say when it's blown over. Do you want another?'

Aiden's dismissal of Jacquie inflamed Sean's mood even more and he said feistily, 'Yep, with a whisky chaser.'

Aiden stood up and pushed his way to the bar while Sean stared moodily into his drink and muttered, 'She's nowt, aye, well she means something to me the bitch, never mind McDuggan, she did for Tim in Cyprus and stitched up Karen's brother Jimmy.'

Memories of his brother Tim who had been apprehended for Arms dealing in Cyprus after Jacquie had broken his shoulder and Karen's younger brother Jimmy who had been ambushed and shot dead following an anonymous tip-off during the 'Troubles' were still fresh in his mind and muttering under his breath, 'Your time's come, you fuckin' double-crossing bitch.'

He picked up his glass and swallowed the dregs as Aiden returned and plonked a whisky and a pint of Guinness in front of him. 'Here, Sean, get this down yer before the girls join us.' He looked up as the tavern door opened and Naomi his wife came in and threading herself between indiscriminately placed chairs and tables made her way across the room. 'Too late, mate,' he said to Sean, 'get your stuff we're going into the lounge.'

Naomi arrived at Aiden's side and Sean looked around for his wife. 'Where's Karen?'

'She's taken the dog for a walk. She'll be here in a few minutes and said to get her a Gin and tonic with a slice.'

Sean stood up, 'Hang on here while I get the drinks. What are you having, Naomi?'

'The same as Karen.'

He manoeuvred his way to the bar pulling his wallet from his back pocket in readiness but when he asked for his order he was still feeling the animosity for what he considered a personal grievance not a tit for tat scenario in a war that was not a war and he added a double whisky which he threw down his throat before getting down to the more mundane business of entertaining the women in their life. When he got back to the table Karen had joined them and they retreated into the lounge where the local Ceili band had already begun playing.

~~~~~
~~~~~

CHAPTER 7

Sunday

The habits of a lifetime were ingrained into Hunter's psyche and lie-ins were not to be. He awoke with the dawn a way of life he had tried to break since his retirement but nature was having none of it.

Making every effort not to disturb the slumbering Jacquie he gently swung out of bed always conscious of his right hip. Not that he considered it necessary as from the day of his operation he'd had no difficulty continuing a normal life.

Retrieving his glasses from the bedside table he crept from the room scooping up his dressing gown from a hook on the back of the door and quietly made his way down the Hall so as not to waken Ken and Kay in the guest bedroom. In the kitchen, he closed the door behind him and cursed the noisy kettle while making himself a mug of tea. Denying himself a date with his favourite weather lady he went instead through to the spare bedroom cum office, part of the extension which they had added when the children arrived, and quietly opening the sliding patio doors he went out into the conservatory.

Through the early morning haze, he could just make out the blue tent covering the crime scene and the red and white marker pole where forensics suggested the fatal shot had come from. He had been contemplating for a couple of minutes when a homely Yorkshire voice said in his customary manner which was always using proper first names, 'What do you reckon, George?'

Hunter spun around to face his inquisitor. 'Morning, Ken. I'm not sure. If I didn't know any different I'd say that someone was taking a pot shot at me. I was in a direct line. It could be my imagination or just coincidence.'

'With your background, George, I guess you could be right but what makes you think that?'

Hunter pointed towards the striped marker across the Rec with one hand and at the broken window with the other. 'Taking into consideration the deflection caused by the bullet hitting that woman and the height it hit that window I'm bloody certain, but don't say anything to Jacquie although I suspect she has thoughts along those lines anyway.'

'Are you sure, George?'

'Yeah! If it was some idiot out pinging cats with a .22 it wouldn't have reached us or not enough to smash the glass anyway. That was a high powered rifle.'

'Do you think the Police will suspect that?'

'When forensics get that bullet they'll soon know it wasn't a pea-shooter and then the place will be swarming.'

Hunter nodded towards the Rec where the Police were conversing in small groups. 'Shift changeover. I wonder who she was, Ken, that woman, I mean. I've never seen her around before and I know most of the dog walkers.'

'It's peculiar, George, although I imagine an open space like that is a magnet with all the building going on and not all of it in the best places. Where's Tess anyway?'

'She'd normally be keeping watch at the end of the bed 'til Jacquie gets up. She'd get in with us if we let her but there are some things a man won't share. His woman and his bed but today she's with the kids at my sisters playing guard dog which annoys the kids no end as she never lets them out of her sight and I mean, never.'

Hunter glanced at the clock at the end of the conservatory. 'Come on, let's make coffee and get the girls up before the fuzz arrives. Jacquie is no fun without a caffeine fix. At least I haven't got the school walk this morning.'

'You walk the kids to school? You must be the only person I know that does that.'

'I have my own opinions on that, Ken, I had to do it so they can and it keeps me fit.'

They made their way back to the kitchen but this time Hunter left the door open and filled and switched on the coffee maker. It wasn't long before it was burbling nicely delivering its caffeine juices and a sleepy voice said, 'Do I smell coffee?'

—

DI Fearn put his mug down on the coffee table and leaned back in his armchair. His fingers caressed the fine leather of the chair and he let his eyes wander around the room taking in the details for the first time. It was then he realised that this 1930's bungalow was not only tastefully furnished but was of a standard better than your average household and had been extended both into the roof space and lengthways. 'He's landed on his feet,' he mused before he opened the morning's discussion.

'Well, Mr Hunter, there's not a lot to tell at the moment. We're chasing up the RSPCA to check out that dog and we have SOCO out there in the Rec. We have no leads as yet but it appears that there were two people about thirty metres apart over there last night and the ballistics specialist fancied that the bullet you found implanted in your shoulder although pretty mucked up appears to be a Russian 7.62mm and used primarily in...' he flipped open his notebook... 'a gun called a Dragunov.'

Hunter screwed his face up in disbelief. 'A Dragunov! That's a Russian sniper rifle.'

Fearn nodded. 'Yup! That's why we've doubled our efforts. One of the theories was that you may have been the target and because of that, we've alerted Scotland Yard. Do you know of anyone bearing a grudge against you?'

'Why me?...' just then Jacquie joined them from the kitchen pulled her fleecy dressing gown tighter and flopped down in a deep leather armchair. '...Did you hear that, Jay? They're thinking I may have been the target.'

'I'm not surprised. Who've you upset now? It's not that girl from the supermarket is it?' Jacquie turned towards Fearn. 'You know what he did, Inspector, we were stood in a queue at the checkout and this girl in front of us instead of concentrating on paying was talking on her mobile holding up the queue. He grabbed the phone and threw it down the counter after her shopping.'

Fearn grinned. 'I can imagine,' he said, 'but this is something a little bit more than aggro. As of now, Mr Hunter, until we prove otherwise be on your guard. That is, close your blinds, keep away from windows etc... etc... You know the drill.'

Hunter pondered for a moment and rubbed his chin thoughtfully before coming to a decision. 'Jacquie, love, we'll leave the kids at Kath's. I'll explain things when I go around. Pack some extra clothes and I'll add some of their games and things.' He turned to Fearn. 'Apart from that we'll carry on as normal and if someone is trying it on we may lure him out.'

Fearn nodded his agreement, 'I'll arrange for extra patrols in the area.'

'Not too many, this is a cul-de-sac and patrol cars are not a feature.'

Fearn stood up. 'I understand but the village may see more than it's used to. On that note, I'll go.' Acknowledging Jacquie, he added. 'Keep him out of harm's way, Mrs Hunter.'

'Before you leave, Inspector,' said Jacquie, 'you'd better change the coffee machine in your office. Sergeant Long says ours is better.'

Fearn muttered, 'She did, did she?' as he went up the hall.

Hunter closed the door behind Fearn before he spoke. 'I'm for another cuppa, how's about you, Jay?'

'Hunter, sit down. We need to think this one over. After all, this time who would be after you?'

Instead of sitting Hunter stood with his back to the fireplace and looked at her snuggled up in the large chocolate brown leather armchair holding a mug of coffee. Feeling very pleased with himself, he answered, 'I don't know and besides we shouldn't be bothering Ken and Kay with this stuff.'

Ken spoke for the first time since they had come in from the conservatory earlier. 'Carry on, George, having read your memoirs it would be interesting to delve into your murky background. Which reminds me, when are you going to publish that book?'

'When I find an agent. Getting back to our problem. I retired after the Afghanistan epic so there is nothing recent. When was that, Jay? Two-thousand and two or thereabouts...'

'Two-thousand and one,' said Jacquie.

'That was a war situation so nothing there. No, everything I did before that was undercover and from a distance and before the SIS it was military-like when I was in Oman with the BATTS. No, I can't think of anyone who would be that way inclined. It's probably some idiot popping off at cats with something he doesn't know how to handle.'

'But a big toy, George,' said Kay who had been quiet up to this point. 'Who would buy something like that? Surely an air rifle would be more appropriate or a .22. I had one of those when I was a child.'

Hunter swivelled his head to look at Kay. 'Kay, I'm looking at you through different eyes. What did a nice girl like you want with a gun?'

'Ha...ha...' laughed Ken, 'she keeps it under the bed now to keep me in line like if I want the bathroom first.'

Kay punched him playfully on the shoulder. 'Take no notice, George, it's just that I was a bit of a tomboy when I was young. I had a train set for Christmas one year instead of girly stuff.'

'You never told me,' said Ken, 'what happened to it?'

'I got bored. It just went round and round but my Dad was pleased, he took it into the attic and as you know, Ken, it covered most of it.'

'She's right there, George, but I didn't know it was Kay's first. It would be worth a lot of money today because it was in damn good condition. He kept all the boxes etc...'

'Jacquie!' said Hunter, 'that's something I've always wanted, a train set...'

'No! Now go and get cleaned up while I sort some stuff out for the kids but before that pull the blinds down in the conservatory and move your car from Andy's drive?'

Hunter snapped to attention and saluted. 'Yes, ma'am.'

Ken held his hand up. 'Hang on, it's our fault your car's over there. Would you rather we went into a hotel?'

'You're okay, Ken, Andy likes that car there. He says it makes it look like someone young lives there. He'd love to have a go with it but he doesn't drive anymore.'

'Okay, but tell us if we're an inconvenience.'

Jacquie interrupted the exchange. 'Ken, how could you? You know how much pleasure we get from your company. Would you like more tea or coffee?'

—

Kathleen, Hunter's sister looked at him with the disdain that all older sisters reserve for their siblings. 'And how long is this likely to be for, George?'

'I dunno, Kath, how often do you get shot at?

'Knowing you—lots. I thought you'd finished with all that?'

'I'll have, you know it's more than ten years since I packed it in. Besides, I can't run away anymore.'

She laughed which Hunter thought unusual. 'You never had the sense to run away. That's why you're in trouble now. Who've you upset?'

'We were talking about that this morning before I left and I can't figure it out. I never did anything that was face to face or personal.'

'You did. What about those little jobs you did on the side to help your SAS pals?'

The vision of a Merseyside loan shark flashed before his eyes. 'By God! You're right. I'd better check, but that was a helluva long time ago.'

'People have long memories and whoever it is may have good connections assuming that's what it is.'

'Thanks, Kath, for reminding me. Where are the kids?'

'They've gone for a walk down Burton marshes with Auntie Helen.'

'Okay, I won't keep you. I'll ring 'em later. Thanks for the tea.'

He scooped his keys up from the kitchen work surface and disappeared out of the back door.

Kathleen watched her younger brother as he drove off. 'What hornet's nest has he disturbed this time?' she wondered.

~~~~~
~~~~~

CHAPTER 8

4 a.m. Monday

In the gloom of the witching hour at the bottom of the valley, a shadowy hooded figure dressed in black from head to toe eased itself out of a nondescript small car parked close to the bushes and went to the rear and opened the boot lid. Lifting out a small bag they lowered the lid until it rested on its catch and then closed it with a gentle push.

Glancing left and right the figure walked leisurely to the road and ignored the footbridge over the Old Mill brook instead walked a hundred metres to the bollards restricting traffic from crossing the 12th Century road bridge which had effectively split the Mill road into two opposing cul-de-sacs.

Sheltering under the trees on the banks of the stream the shadow looked up the road and although it was a moonless night you could still make out the entrances, walls and hedges dividing the driveways of the bungalows and houses on either side.

After waiting two minutes the figure ran to the first gateway, paused by the nearest post and listened before nipping smartly across to the opposite side. The manoeuvre was repeated six more times when headlights suddenly appeared at the top of the road. The ghostly shadow ducked into the nearest garden and lay down along the bottom of the wall under a low privet hedge while a Police patrol car drove slowly past. The car did a noisy three-point turn at the bollards and began its journey back up the road and stopped opposite the gate.

A muffled radio conversation could be heard as the crew called in their situation report before driving on. On elbows and knees, the figure edged along the hedge to the road and peered around the gatepost. When the Police car had disappeared the figure with the bag clutched tightly to its chest continued with a look, listen and dart progress up the road.

The road became steeper and the gardens on both sides were now stepped as the buildings were built on top of the banks but at each new gate, more time was taken checking the cars in the driveways. The figure stopped at the drive with the maroon Range Rover parked on it, listened and waited before darting in and sitting with its back to the vehicle. After a brief moment, a slim solid object was taken from the bag and the ghostly figure crawled on its stomach up to the driver's door where it examined the object closely before turning it around and then carefully peeled the backing off the industrial doubled sided tape stuck on one side.

With arms outstretched, the figure slid underneath the vehicle and firmly stuck the package to the floor panel above. A fine split pin was cautiously removed and making sure not to touch anything the interloper slid away from the vehicle, recovered the bag and ducking low made it back to the gate and ignoring all caution but keeping low ran recklessly down the road through the bollards and to the car.

As it drove away the first light of dawn was appearing over the horizon and it was just light enough to show the dull red outline of the vehicle.

~~~~~~
~~~~~~

CHAPTER 9

Monday

The pinkish tinge from the sunrise on the fluffy clouds whispering overhead on a light breeze was at odds with the tension in the village but the morning came without any further disturbances and although there was activity out on the Rec it was still off-limits much to the disgruntle of dog walkers and those wishing to take a shortcut to the local shops. There was no update from the Police which prompted Jacquie to get ready for work as usual.

Hunter admired her as she approached down the hall. Her long, soft, brunette hair surrounded her face which made her look ten years younger than her fifty years and because of the mild weather she had her Gucci leather jacket draped over her shoulders which topped her ultra secretary look of white blouse and a black leather pencil skirt and patent sandals.

'Hey, lass, you got a date or something?'

'No such luck, I've got that meeting with the proprietors of the 'Golden Bloom' Garden Centre. They're still holding out on the offer I made them but I'm in no mood for haggling. I'm hoping the outfit might distract their CEO but if they don't agree then I'm withdrawing my offer. Later I have a meeting to discuss the new coffee franchise and I'm hoping for the same effect so the finalities shouldn't take long. They have already agreed to keep my staff on and continue with our food line as well as their own.'

He grabbed her around the waist and pulled her towards him. 'Looking like that you can't lose. Have you got time?'

'Whoa! Steady boy, watch your blood pressure.'

They kissed gently and he reluctantly let her go.

He waited as she went through the front door before he went through into the lounge to watch her from the front window. He told Jacquie it was to check the rear car lights as she drove off but he knew it was a deeper feeling.

—

Jacquie locked the front door behind her and edged carefully past

Ken's now Classic SAAB down the sloping drive towards her Range Rover. Habitually she would click the remote as she approached the vehicle but this morning she was distracted by one of their neighbours who was out walking his dog.

'Hi, Jacquie, how's the old man?' he called, 'is he over that rumpus the other night?'

Jacquie answered cheerily, 'Morning, Tim, he's doing fine,' and nodding over her shoulder towards the front window where she knew Hunter would be watching, 'but I hope he can't read your lips or you're in trouble.'

She and Hunter liked Tim. He was an Afghan veteran who had been invalided out of the Army when he lost the lower part of his leg in an IED explosion. He had been a Search Dog Handler with the Parachute Regiment and they let him keep his dog, Sasha when he was discharged.

Before Tim could answer Sasha began straining on her lead with her tail up and nose pointing up the drive. Jacquie stopped by the Rover and raised her remote when Sasha began barking and pawing the ground. She pulled harder on her lead and broke away from Tim and with the lead trailing behind her she ran towards Jacquie. As she reached the driver's door she stopped and began pawing the ground as she sniffed below the door sill.

Instinctively, something from Tim's service past made him shout, not at the dog, but Jacquie. 'JACQUIE! STOP! DON'T TOUCH YOUR REMOTE! Come towards me slowly and hope to God nobody calls your mobile.'

He saw Hunter stood in the window and made a signal towards him like a telephone to his ear, he then shook his head and did a cut-throat movement before waving for him to come out. As he did this Jacquie was edging past the exited Sasha who was still sniffing under the car with her tail rigidly upright and pawing the ground.

Moving slowly down the driveway Jacquie joined Tim. 'What's up, Tim?'

'Jacquie, do as I say. Put your car remote on the ground and make sure you don't press it and then back off twenty metres. I may be wrong but Sasha hasn't forgotten her training and has sussed something. Silly question, you don't by any chance keep any explosives in the car? Not even a firework?'

Jacquie shook her head. 'No! Why?'

'Good. I'll explain later. Now move away.'

Hunter came out of the front door of the bungalow and was about to close it when Tim shouted. 'DON'T SLAM IT! Come to me slowly, George, and don't touch the Rover.'

Hunter eased the door closed and warily eased himself past the two cars and exited Sasha. 'What's up, Tim?'

'Sasha is acting like she's sensed explosive, George. Seriously, she only does that for the real thing. Go to a neighbour and call the Police and Bomb Squad on a landline and then alert all your other neighbours not to use their mobiles or car remotes, shut all windows and get to the back of the house.'

'We've got guests, Tim. I'll alert them first.'

'Okay. No! do the Police.'

Hunter turned to Jacquie who was now some twenty metres away. 'Jay, take my car and go and do your business before they lock this place down, Hurry! I'll call the Bomb Squad from Andy's and then alert Ken.'

Jacquie hurried to Hunter's side and they made their way to Andy Roberts house where Hunter gave her the keys to his car. 'Remember, Jay, the wiper lever works upside down to yours and use the key element, not the remote.'

As Hunter rang the doorbell she took the keys and kissed him on the cheek. 'Yes, Dad,' and nipped around the car before he could respond.

Tim, with a barely noticeable limp, approached Sasha.

'Good girl, Sasha. Now Stay!'

Sasha lay down with her nose pointing towards the car. Tim reached into the thigh pocket of his Military style trousers and took out a mauled yellow tennis ball. He waved it in Sasha's eye line. 'Here, gal, get your prize.'

Sasha reacted immediately and rolled towards Tim and wagging her tail madly she took the ball from him as he picked up her lead and eased her away down the drive. 'Good girl. Let's hope it's for real or we're for the high jump.' He reached down and stroked her behind the ear. 'But I know you, lass, you're never wrong.'

—

Andy shuffled down the hall and opened the door. 'Oh, hello, George, you don't need to tell me when you take the car.'

'Hi, Andy, it's not that. We have a bomb alert over at the house and it's a bit dodgy using the phone, you know, Wi-Fi and all that and I wondered if I could use your landline?'

'Of course but what do you mean... 'A bomb alert?'

'Let me call the Old Bill first and I'll tell you all about it.'

Andy stood to one side. 'Okay, it's there on the hall table.'

Hunter went in and shut the door behind him and breathed a sigh of relief to see that the phone was still the older dial-up version albeit with push buttons. Two minutes later he joined Andy in the kitchen where he gave him a quick run down of the situation and when he was finished he said, 'I've got to go now, Andy, I've got to tell the neighbours to stay indoors and not to use their mobiles although that's probably too late.'

'You go, lad, and do what you have to. There's something I wanted to tell you but I can't remember what it is. Don't get old, George.'

'Cheers, Andy, you don't think sixty-eight is old?'

'You know what I mean you nearly old git. Go and do your business.'

Hunter patted him on the shoulder. 'Will do, mate. I'll pop around later when it's all sorted. It's probably nothing but you can't take risks and that dog is a veteran.'

Hunter opened the door and gave Andy a nod as he closed it behind him and to the tune of the closing emergency vehicle sirens, he began to warn the neighbours.

—

The 'Swan Inn' hadn't seen so many customers since the previous pre-Christmas Day dinner rush of husbands and partners dismissed by overworked wives and mothers. The landlord was rubbing his hands at the unexpected windfall.

'How long do you think it will last, Hunter?

'I've no idea, Bill. You know what they're like with all this elf and safety crap. You'd think it was a nuclear bomb the way they act and right now we are waiting for the assessors to see if it's okay for assessors who are checking it's alright for a bomb disposal expert to assess the bloody problem. I reckon it'll be at least two days.'

'In that case, I'd better order some more stock. Do you reckon I would be alright getting stuff for a full English breakfast, besides booze that is?'

'Do they eat that stuff anymore, Bill, although looking at some of them fire crew guys they live on it.'

'You wanna see the cafe in the supermarket, Hunter. It's full of families stuffing themselves on it. Yeah, I'm gonna do it. If there's anything left over I'll put it on the menu as traditional 'English Fare.' How's that sound?'

'Don't tell, Jacquie, but I only eat double yokers, and my sausages have to be Cumberland.'

'Hey; don't push it, by the way, there was a stranger in here earlier mixing with the crowd. He was here a couple of weeks ago taking a big interest in your plaque.'

'Have you still got that bloody thing? Where is it?'

'It's a bit grotty but I put it on the end of the bar when we upgraded. He was stood by it when he ordered and just seemed interested in it, that's all.'

'Jesuz! I thought you'd got rid of the damn thing. What did he look like and is he still in here?'

'Nah! He only had a half and left. He was about your height, good build with blonde hair and he had a peculiar accent. He was well-spoken but it was a sort of American and something else. English but neutral if you know what I mean. He was dressed very smart like he had money in an American manner. You know, his trousers were too short, open neck shirt and a sun tan.'

'Right, Bill, get rid of the bloody plaque and if anyone else starts asking questions, call me. A bomb scare and a possible shooting are too much of a coincidence.'

'Are you serious, Hunter? You think someone's after you?'

'I hope not, Bill. I'll know more when this show's over. Until then keep stum, between old soldiers, okay!'

Bill gave a mock salute. 'Right on, Hunter.' He gestured down the bar. 'I'd better sort this lot out.'

Hunter emptied his glass and was about to leave when DI Fearn came in followed by DS Long and a distinguished grey-haired man wearing a Burberry raincoat. A face that Hunter knew from his past. He was accompanied by a tall man in his mid-thirties whose short dark hair was tastefully cut and he was casually dressed in the standard ex-service desert boots.

'Mr Hunter,' said Fearn, 'I'd like you to meet the experts. This is Senior Agent Thomas and Agent Bell from SIS.'

Thomas was in his late fifties, a stockily built man of about five foot nine with greying wavy hair wearing a tweed jacket and cavalry twill trousers and like his Nº2, military-style suede desert boots. Thomas shoved a hand out. 'How do you do, Hunter, long time no see. What the hell have you been up to now?'

Hunter shrugged. 'I'm okay, and you, Gus?'

Fearn glanced from one to the other, 'You two know each other?'

Thomas nodded. 'He was my mentor many years ago. How's the lovely, Mrs Hunter, and do you still play snooker?'

'I play golf now.'

'What's your handicap, Hunter?'

'It's fifteen and I play Wednesdays and Saturdays. Enough of that. Mrs H was well the last time I spoke to her. She's a bit miffed because she's driving my VW. It's a bit of a drop from a sporty 4 x 4. Would you lot like a pint?'

Thomas looked around. 'Is there anywhere we could talk?'

'I'll talk to the boss.'

Hunter attracted the attention of the barmaid, a fresh-faced buxom girl called Sharon with a nipped-in waist whose charms were almost overflowing her décolletage. She immediately stopped what she was doing and came over to him and spoke with some respect. 'Yes, Mr Hunter, what can I get you?'

She took their orders and as she was about to return to the bar she added, 'Is there anything else?'

'Yes, lass, can you ask your Dad if he can spare a moment?'

'I'll just set this order up, Mr Hunter, and I'll get right onto it.'

‘Thanks, lass.’

He returned to Thomas and Fearn. ‘Won’t be a minute and I’ll speak to the boss.’

Thomas nodded towards the bar. ‘You’ve got a good friend there, Hunter. You ain’t up to something are you?’

‘More than my life’s worth, besides, I couldn’t keep up.’

They laughed together as Bill came over to them. ‘What can I do for you?’

Bill,’ said, Hunter, ‘these people are from the police and they would like to talk with me. Have you got somewhere quiet we could go otherwise it’s the car and no drinks?’

‘Yeah, sure. You can use the snug. It’s closed right now as we’re decorating it but it’s okay for what you want. Give me a minute and I’ll nip round and open it up. Can I get you anything?’

—

Bill dragged a table up from the cellar while Bell and Long pulled the dust sheets off some stacked chairs and amongst the discarded paint tins left by the decorators with Bell and Long sitting a respectable distance behind their respective bosses they passed the time of day.

DI Fearn was the first to speak. ‘How about your guests, Mr Hunter, are they okay?’

‘Aye, they’ve volunteered to look after the oldies over in the Village Hall until the fuss is over.’

‘That’s good of them seeing as how they don’t come from here.’

‘They’re that type of people.’

Sharon, carrying a tray of drinks pushed the swing door open with an out-thrust hip and Fearn, who was the youngest of the trio, showed his obvious delight and interest.

‘Here we are, gentlemen,’ she said cheerfully, ‘sorry about the decor, it’s called shabby chic. It’s the latest thing.’

‘Sharon, love,’ said Hunter, ‘tell your Dad we like it and the removal of the cobwebs has taken away the atmosphere of gloom and doom that was prevalent in that old sixties box room that was here before and we will now grow older with the benevolence of his foresight.’

Sharon laughed, 'I'm not sure he will understand that Mr Hunter, but if it means you and your friends will call again I'm sure he'll welcome it.'

They settled themselves around a table and each took a welcome swig from their drinks before DI Fearn opened the conversation. 'Firstly, Mr Hunter, the woman on the Rec. She was a local and lived on the other side of the main road. It was very unfortunate but she had only stopped by the Rec to give the dog a last run before returning home after visiting friends. Wrong time, wrong place, unfortunately. We are treating her death as suspicious but things have now taken a new twist with the latest events. Over to Mr Thomas.'

Hunter raised his hand. 'One moment. Inspector! Can you give me the woman's details? I'd like to pay my respects and secondly, drop the polite shenanigans, call me Hunter...'

Thomas chipped in... 'Okay, Hunter, we got your message but right now let's concentrate on the problem at hand. I don't think you realise what sort of predicament you're in. Somebody takes a pop at you and now they try to blow you up. What message do you need?'

Hunter held up his hands in a gesture of surrender. 'Okay, maybe I've been trying to hide from the obvious. I was sort of hoping there was no connection and it was all a hoax or something. What you're saying, Gus, is that it's a genuine bomb? Not the dog having a fit or anything?'

'It's a bomb, H. It's a bit old tech, the sort of device that did for Airy Neave in '79. A ball bearing in a tube, which, when the car changes its incline the ball rolls down the tube and closes the contacts and, BOOM! She was a very lucky girl. It was all down to that dog not forgetting his training and sniffing the explosives. Not IED's this time, but your car. What we need to know is why. Any ideas?'

Hunter shook his head. 'None.'

'An historical vendetta or revenge?'

'It could be but I've been out of circulation for years and apart from when I was in the forces all my work was done at distance and the stuff behind the Iron Curtain was a Cold War thing long forgotten. Did you say that this bomb is old tech?'

Thomas took out his notebook and flicked over a couple of pages. 'Yes, and according to the Bomb Squad, it is the type used by the IRA in the seventies and eighties. They're a lot more sophisticated now. They don't use ball bearings anymore they use mobile phones etc... Do you think that's relative?'

Hunter sat thoughtfully for a few seconds rubbing his chin before nodding. 'What if the target wasn't me, but Jacquie?'

Thomas and Fearn immediately became attentive and Fearn wiped his mouth with the back of his hand before he spoke. 'What do you mean? Why would anyone want to harm Jacquie?'

Hunter glanced at Thomas. 'Will you tell him or should I?'

'I'll do it, H.'

Thomas shifted uncomfortably in his seat reluctant to disclose information considered sacrosanct amongst SIS operators. With a sigh, he continued. 'What you are about to hear stays in this room, okay?' and looking at Bell and Long, he added, 'and that goes for you two also.'

Fearn nodded his compliance and Thomas continued. 'During the 'Troubles' in Northern Ireland, Colin...'

The use of his first name had now introduced Fearn into a personal circle and he felt privileged to be with them as historically the Secret Services had never willingly shared anything with the Constabulary.

'...not only did we have troops over there but as in every conflict we had undercover operators as well. Jacquie was one of them. Working out of our Lisburn office she was operating in Belfast for several years until her position became untenable. She worked herself into a position of some influence amongst the upper echelons of the Provisional IRA. If she had been caught her end would have been slow and as she was an attractive woman it is not unlikely sexually-orientated and gruesome. Her cover to explain her absences was as a model going on assignments, which she did, and she appeared in catalogues and supplements quite frequently. She gave us a lot of stuff that helped us capture or remove many of the leading IRA operatives so much so they couldn't fart without we knew. That is all you need to know, but what is going on now is likely because of those undercover activities. Someone has recognised her and is seeking revenge.'

Fearn shook his head as he spoke as if he couldn't get his head around the facts. 'Are you telling me she was a spy?'

'Spy is a term only used by the media, Colin, although spooks seem to be the latest fad, we prefer to call them operatives or agents,' said Thomas, 'It is fair to say that she used her feminine charms to good effect.'

'If you don't mind me saying, Mr Hunter, she doesn't look like your typical spook. Hollywood depicts glamorous women in the James Bond movies but I never thought...'

Thomas held his hand up. 'Stop there, Colin. Let's concentrate on the problem at hand. Who is it they're after and what do we do about it?...'

Thomas's phone rang and he paused to answer it. 'Hallo!'

He listened attentively for a few seconds before closing it down and continuing. 'That was the Bomb Squad. They've made it safe and removed it. Everybody can go home now which brings us back to what I said before. Any ideas?'

Hunter remained quiet taking it all in at the same time his mind was whirring with possibilities about Thomas's query and his family's safety. At the forefront of his mind was the security of his children and the conversation between Thomas and Fearn went over his head.

Fearn leaned back in his chair. 'Let's assume it's Hunter. They take a pot shot at him and then go for the 4 x 4 thinking it's a man's car. This to me is the logical answer and I think SOCO can do their donkey work while I, meaning the Fuzz, can take the case and chase it up.'

'Not so fast, Colin, I know you want the glory, that stands to reason, but what if it's Jacquie they're after. A pot shot and then her car. The Irish line seems to be more likely.'

Hunter broke out from his thoughts and spoke. 'She wasn't in the conservatory when they took the shot so that blows your angle, Gus.'

'Was she in the doorway and inline when the shot came?'

'No, she was in the bedroom approaching the doorway which

would mean a snapshot and speaking from experience, although the distance was insignificant, whoever it was would have to take into consideration the refractive angle of the double glazing which makes it a no-no. He or she wouldn't take the risk. Snipers don't take snapshots especially through glass or in this case double glazing. They do it deliberately as you only get one chance. The best in the world would take three seconds with a bolt action job or two with an automatic to get an accurate second shot in but by this time, like us, we were down on the floor.'

Fearn raised his eyebrows and smirked. 'I think that puts me in the driving seat.'

This time it was Fearn's mobile which rang as the opening bars of Carl Orff's 'Carmen Burrana' filled the room. He let it play for several seconds before he turned away to answer it lowering his voice and shielding his face at the same time. 'Fearn here.'

Both Hunter and Thomas looked at each other and shrugged as Fearn's head bobbed up and down with the conversation for half a minute or so and when he rang off he faced them but not with any serious conviction. 'That was SOCO. From the metallurgic analysis of the bullet, they have determined it was a Dragonuv round and they also found DNA from one of two possible firing points. What they are saying is that there were two people on the other side of that field about thirty metres apart. That puts a new light on it. Were they working together or was it a coincidence that two possible assassins were there at the same time? They are doing more tests to determine positively which of the two positions the shot came from.'

Hunter stretched and yawned before butting in. 'Quite often when working in the field we used to work in pairs but that sounds a bit extreme for a tit for tat job.'

'Quite so,' said Thomas, 'and that also makes things more complicated. Are we dealing with one, two or three people and are they connected? Colin—it's time to drop inter-departmental differences. I suggest that you follow up on the evidence you've got and find the shooter while we go in a different direction and look for out of work snipers and bombers on an international basis. Use my phone as the link but don't use it for passing on information. When you call I'll give you a new number to ring.

Conscious that things had taken a new twist outside of his jurisdiction Fearn looked uncomfortable if not a little upset but kept his feelings to himself but couldn't help having a little dig. 'I'm quite aware of phone procedures.' He waggled a finger pointing to himself and Sergeant Long. 'Am I right to assume that the same respect will be given to us?'

Thomas acknowledged Fearn's disquiet and nodded. 'Sorry, Colin. Yes, of course. Now, Hunter, what are we going to do with you?

Fearn stood up. 'I think you can manage without us. We'll get back to my team and keep things moving. Keep me in the loop as they say.'

Thomas and Hunter stood up and shook hands with Fearn and acknowledged Sergeant Long and as they manoeuvred around the scattered paint tins Thomas called out. 'Sergeant Long! Have you got a licence to carry?

'Yes, sir,' she replied.

'Colin, I'd like to borrow Sergeant Long until we can get someone in from the 'Firm.' Would that be okay?

Fearn demurred for a moment before nodding his consent. 'Yes, but we're short-staffed and I would like her back a.s.a.p.' He turned to Long. 'Sergeant, come to the station and collect a firearm and then get back here soonest. See you lot later.'

As they left the room Thomas picked up his glass. 'Right, Hunter, do you fancy another?'

'I'd love one but I think I'd better get back. Jacquie is still unaware of all this and I want to get round to my sister's to see the kids.'

'Oh, shit! I'd forgotten about them.' Thomas rubbed his chin thoughtfully for a moment. 'Will they be okay at your sister's?'

'I think so. It's me they're after.'

'Or, Jacquie.' Thomas took his phone from his pocket. 'I'm going to arrange an escort for her. Bell can do it. Where is she?'

Hunter looked at his watch which Thomas admired. He knew Hunter wasn't known as an egotistical person but a Rolex Oyster? Back to the present. Hunter continued, 'She had two meetings today but I reckon she's back at her main office by now. She never stops. She's looking at expanding the business as if three wasn't enough. I'll give her a call and check.'

He slid his hand under his sweater and fumbled a mobile phone from his shirt pocket. Thomas smiled when he saw it was still old school. What a contrast between phone and watch.

Hunter pressed speed dial number two and waited. Four rings and Jacquie answered. 'I give in. You found me'

'Hi, Jay, be serious. Where are you?'

'Home base, why? What's up?'

'Things have taken a big turn, Jay. Stay there and a back-up and escort will join you.'

'Hunter! What's going on?'

'I'll explain later, lass.'

'Are you alright, Hunter?'

'Yep, I'm ay okay! I'm going round to see the kids shortly and I'll see you when you get home. Wait for your back-up.'

'I'll do that. You take care. Love you. Bye!'

Hunter put his phone down. 'She's five minutes down the road at her head office, Gus.' He took his wallet from his back pocket and extracted a business card and after scribbling a car registration on the back of it he threw it over the table. 'You'll find her there. She's driving my car, a white VW Golf GTI instead of that monstrous tank of a Range Rover.'

'You don't like Range Rovers, Hunter?'

'Have you ever tried parking one of those damn things?'

'As if I could afford one.'

Thomas turned to Bell. 'Simon, I'm sorry if you feel you've been left out but Hunter and I go back a long way. Feel free to butt in if you have any ideas. Right now though I want you to go...' He handed Bell the business card, '...and accompany Mrs Hunter wherever she goes until we can arrange something. Take a taxi.'

Bell rose from his chair. 'Okay, sir.' He looked at Hunter and flicked a Scouts salute off his forehead. 'Don't worry, Mr Hunter, I'll take good care of her. See you later.'

As Bell departed Thomas took a swig from the dregs in his glass before continuing. 'He's good and comes from a military background like us. Before we go, Hunter, you appear to be well off, tell me, do you think there's any jealousy involved? Has there been any blackmail attempts or such like?'

'Gus, let's get one thing straight. We have money or should I say, Jacquie has money. She inherited her father's Fletton Brick manufacturing business in Stewartby and immediately sold it. With the proceeds, she started her Garden Centre business up here and she has no siblings so I don't think anyone would go to this extreme just for that.'

'How much are we talking about, Hunter?'

'Gus, I don't discuss our finances with anyone but let's just say a lot of zeros are involved.'

'Oh, and you still live in your modest but extended bungalow?'

'Yep! It does us and we both like it and the neighbours who I must say take a lot less interest in our income than you are.'

'Sorry, Hunter, but I'm trying to build some kind of picture for what has gone on. Did she sack anyone recently?'

'Not that I know of. She likes to keep all problems in-house and generally keeps her staff loyal. She even lends them money.'

As he prepared to leave Thomas, said, 'It's looking more and more like historic revenge. Don't you or Jacquie go anywhere without Long or Bell from now on? We'll leave it there, let's get back.'

—

Bell eased himself from the polished black saloon and paid the driver before crossing the car park to the Garden Aspects №1 entrance. He took note of a newish VW GTI parked in the first bay by the door and checked the registration with the one on the business card. It was Hunter's. Inside he paused and looked around and liked the way the place was set out. Almost military but homely. It was bustling with customers and the staff he could see in their green-based uniform were all busy either helping or keeping the place stocked and tidy. There was a Customer Service desk a few metres in and he liked the welcoming smile from the attractive young receptionist as he walked over. Sat alongside her was an older lady in a wheelchair.

'Good afternoon, sir, can I help you?'

'I'm looking for, Mrs Hunter.'

'One minute.' She lowered herself down beside her wheelchair companion. 'Here we go, Lily, can you remember Mrs Hunter's line?'

Lily nodded. 'I think so, it's our busiest one.'

Lily picked up the handset and flicked a switch before pushing a button on the keyboard in front of her. After a few seconds, the call was answered and a muffled woman's voice could be heard.

'Mrs Hunter,' said Lily, 'we have a man here to see you.'

The muffled voice spoke again and Lily looked up. 'What's your name, sir?'

'It's Mr Bell of SIS.'

Lily's eyes widened in surprise and she looked across at her companion before passing the message on. Then she put the phone down and pointing down the Garden Centre she said, 'Follow this aisle to the Cafeteria and to the left of the serving counter you'll see a door. Just knock and go in, she's expecting you.'

'Thanks, miss.'

He turned away and with an unhurried stroll followed the direction given. When he came to the door it was marked 'OFFICE' with a sign underneath saying 'Staff Only.' He hesitated momentarily, shrugged and knocked. The door opened instantly and a young man greeted him. 'Mr Bell?'

'Yep.'

'Come through.'

The lad held the door long enough for Bell to enter a long modern office with three staff working with the latest computer equipment and then he took the lead and led him across to a door at the other end of the room. The lad knocked and a cheerful feminine voice answered, 'Come in.'

He held the door open and Bell stepped inside, stopped and did a mental whistle as Jacquie smiled at him. What confronted him was not his impression of a 'spook.'

Jacquie eased the situation. She stood up and held her hand out. 'Mr Bell! Come in and take a seat.' They shook hands and she sat down again behind a large Waring & Gillows Georgian style desk and ignoring the leather sofa along one side of the room Bell chose instead to sit on the leather office chair opposite. 'Can I get you something, Mr Bell? Coffee or tea?'

'Err, coffee, please.'

'What do you fancy?'

'Americano, please?'

Jacquie got up from behind her desk and went to the door conscious of the eyes that followed her. Poking her head around the door she called. 'Charlotte, can you get us two Americano's, please. Put it on my tab.'

She returned to her desk and the most comfortable office chair he had ever seen and immediately eased into a conversation. 'Now then, Mr Bell, as we are about to get more intimate, I mean that in a practical sense, what's going on?'

Bell wriggled uncomfortably smiling at his charge's dry humour. 'You probably know as much as me, ma'am...'

Jacquie laughed, '...now I do feel grand. Ma'am, aye. I've never been called that before but as I said earlier, as we are going to be in each other's company a while longer why don't you call me, Jacquie, and what do I call you? Mister is too formal and just plain Bell doesn't have a ring about it.'

He was liking this woman more and more. 'Ha! Okay, ma... Jacquie, call me Simon.'

'Right, Simon, now tell me why you're here?'

There was a knock on the door and an attractive woman in her mid-thirties with long chestnut hair came in, placed a tray with two coffees on the corner of the desk and quietly left the room.

Jacquie nodded after her. 'That, as you may have guessed is, Charlotte. She's my right hand who is worth her weight. Now, we were saying?'

'As I understand it, Jacquie, that bomb was real and following your ordeal on Saturday evening, it is now a security issue. The feeling is that this is a historical revenge assault. I am aware of your background and I can see where they're coming from.'

Jacquie cocked her head a little to one side and rubbed her chin thoughtfully. 'Are we talking me or Hunter here?'

'It's a conundrum. You weren't in the conservatory when the

shot was fired and then your car?'

What she said next startled Bell. 'Are you carrying, Simon?'

Caught off guard he hesitated before uttering, 'Err, yes.'

'Let me see it.'

'I don't think I should.'

'Simon, I was using before you were born, just.'

He reached under his jacket with his right hand and withdrew a handgun. She held her hand out and he passed it butt first over the desk and he sat back and admired the professional way she unclipped the magazine, cocked the weapon and noted that he didn't have one up the spout, unlike Hunter who never went without. She put the magazine back and returned it.

'Sig Saur. I like it but I'm a Glock girl.'

'Seventeen or nineteen.'

'I don't do target shooting, Simon, I use a seventeen.'

'You still carry?'

'I'll put that in the past tense. I did use a seventeen.'

Somehow, he had a feeling, she still could.

Jacquie stood up and smoothed her skirt down. 'Enough, Simon, let's go home.'

As she walked around the desk she scooped her jacket from the coat stand and opened the door and with a nod of her head she led Simon out into the Garden Centre. His eyes flicked from side to side taking in everything and everybody and as they walked through the Cafeteria section in his peripheral vision Simon saw the movement of a blonde-haired man rising from his seat at a corner table. An inkle stirred in Simon's brain. He thought nothing of it at the time and when the aisle became wider he moved up alongside Jacquie.

'Nice place you have here, Mrs Hunter. Smarter than the ones down my way.'

'And where's that, Simon?'

'Essex, just by the Dartford bridge although I'm not there all that often.'

'Are you married?'

'No, but I have a partner who's making the right noises if I could stop Thomas from roaming the country long enough.'

'I know the feeling although in my case it was Hunter. We'd no sooner met and he was shipped out to Afghanistan.'

'With the Army?'

'No, with the 'Firm' undercover. He didn't make a good native and I think they sussed him immediately but he got the job done thank goodness. He retired then.'

'Lucky him.'

'He wouldn't say so. He had too much time on his hands and it allowed his memories to flood back and disturb his mind. He's okay now.'

'I had a hard time after I left the service but I got roped in by the 'Firm' which helped a lot.'

They stopped by the car. 'You don't mind a woman driver?'

Simon laughed. 'Do I have a choice?'

'No.'

He swivelled and went to the passenger side and saw the blonde man sauntering across the car park and stop by a white BMW X5 and something registered in his memory banks as he fastened his seatbelt and, Jacquie, with practised ease pulled out into the traffic on the main road.

Speed limits were not her forte for when traffic allowed she regularly broke them. He lowered the sunblind and using the mirror embedded in the back he checked the road behind and noted the BMW four cars back. Not unusual but on a hunch, he said to Jacquie. 'Mrs Hunter, pull into the next bus stop and pretend to answer your phone.'

Two hundred metres further on she did just that and pretended to fiddle with the Bluetooth phone connection on the dash. Simon sat back and noted the number plate on the BMW. 'Okay, Mrs Hunter, wait ten seconds and we can go.'

She mentally counted to ten as Simon wrote the number down in his notebook and with a glance in her rear-view mirror they rejoined the traffic. A few minutes later sweeping off the main road at the by-pass exit they drove through the village and turned down the lane leading to the Hunter bungalow. There was still a police presence outside the house and she had to park the car in Andy's drive. As she clambered out she waved to Andy who was looking out of his front room bay window and side by side with Simon they walked back to the house where she was stopped by a young Constable.

'Excuse me, ma'am, have you got ID?'

Taken by surprise Jacquie hesitated and Simon came to the rescue. He flashed his ID and said, 'It's okay, son, she's with me. I'll see she gets up to no-nonsense.'

The constable saluted and stepped back. 'Sorry, ma'am.'

'It's okay, officer, I live here. Take no notice of him, he's one of the staff. Come on, Simon.'

As they stepped across the threshold, Jacquie said, 'Hang your coat there, Simon and then follow me into the kitchen. She walked down the hallway and called out, 'Hunter!' and as she approached the kitchen door Ken came in from the conservatory.

'Hi, Jacquie, he said, 'George has gone round to his sister's. He said he wouldn't be long. What's the latest?'

'Oh, hello, Ken. Has he left you on your own? Wait `til I see him.'

Kay joined them. 'It's okay, Jacquie, he hasn't been gone long and he has his minder with him. Can I make you a coffee or something and who's your friend?'

'Coffee, please, and this is Simon. He's my minder and Hunter better watch his step.'

'Hello, Simon, welcome to this madhouse. How do you like your coffee?'

'He's in the club, Kay. Black and no additives.'

They all laughed and Simon could feel a warm glow in his cheeks as they crowded into the kitchen and Kay busied herself making coffee.

They sent out mugs of tea to the Police guardians at the front and rear of the property and when they had all settled around the solid oak kitchen table, Ken addressed the subject which they had all steered around. 'Tell us what's going on, Jacquie.'

'I'm not sure, Ken. Simon probably knows more than me. This double attempt to cause us some harm has sort of triggered a major alert and has moved a step up from the local police because of our background. I don't want to say this, Ken, but if this is what they suspect then things could get nasty. I think for your safety you should consider going home out of harm's way.'

Kay nodded. 'We were just discussing that when you arrived, Jacquie, and after dinner tonight we are going home. We've already packed.'

'Oh, Kay, I'm sorry for the way things turned out.'

'Don't worry, love, 'said Ken, 'we understand and without us hanging around your neck and causing worries about our safety you will have more freedom and an easier mind and we feel it is the right thing. 'Nuff said, that's it.'

Jacquie knew Ken and there was no point trying to persuade him otherwise. She got up from the table and went around and gave Ken and Kay a big hug. 'When this is over we are going to celebrate and it's on us, okay?'

The door swung open and Hunter entered the room followed by Sergeant Long. 'What's on us, Jay?'

She explained about Ken and Kay and then said, 'And what about the kids, Hunter?'

'Huh, don't worry about them they think they're on holiday. Kath's okay too but says to keep her informed.'

'Good, so let's sort out sleeping arrangements. Simon, you're in the back office. Hunter, tidy your stuff up and put the Z bed down. Sergeant Long, what's your first name?'

'It's Carrie Priya but Carrie is good, Mrs Hunter.'

'Right, Carrie, you sleep in the guest room when Kay and Ken move their stuff out. Have you got any clothes or overnight stuff?'

'Only what I'm stood up in.'

'You look close to my size so it shouldn't be a problem. What about you, Simon?'

'I'm in the same boat.'

'Hunter, sort something out while I prepare dinner. We've got plenty of travel stuff like toothbrushes etc...'

~~~~~
~~~~~

CHAPTER 10

Pat O'Hearne put his glass down and wiped his mouth with the back of his hand. 'Right, Aiden, explain yourself. The boss is going apeshit. What happened? You fucked up, twice?'

'Once, and I didn't mess up. I had the bastard dead to rights and as I squeezed the trigger his bloody good fairy walked into the line of fire.'

'You didn't put the bomb under his car or is that media bullshit?'

'I don't know. I went back on Monday to check but the place was swarming with Police and Army. I did get into the pub for a half but they were using that as a refuge for the locals so I learned nothing. The rumour was that they were making a film. There is something else. While I was making my shot there was a peeping tom there at the same time and he did a runner ahead of me.'

'Don't give us the crap, Aiden. You messed up.'

'I didn't. Okay, I missed him but it wasn't my fault and this other shit who was there was some thirty metres away from me and nearer the road with what looked like binoculars. He had a posh 4 x 4 by the way. It was the woman who messed it up but what was this other guy doing.'

'It was a fella?'

'I don't know but he or she was pretty big.'

'And you didn't try again on Monday?'

'No, Pat, I've told you.'

Pat shook his head in dismay. 'The Boss isn't going to like this. Are you having another go?'

'I've got a contract but I can't get close at the moment. Can you lot keep tabs on him?'

'The Boss won't be happy. Get it sorted, Aiden, I want to retire. Get me another pint and then I'm off. Easy-jet calls.'

As Aiden stood up to go to the bar Sean O'Reilly came into the pub.

Pat grunted. 'Aiden, you're not using that dickhead are you?'
Aiden shook his head as he walked away.

—

Demyan heaved himself onto the side of the swimming pool and sat contemplating his weekend. Someone had mussed up his plans. His target was clear but who else was trying to kill him. It appeared that our Mr Hunter wasn't a popular figure. 'What have you done to deserve that?' he mused as a muscular mermaid thrashed the last few metres of the pool and held an arm out for assistance. Demyan obliged and let go a silent whistle of appreciation at what he saw and he wasn't too displeased when she sat alongside him. Discreetly he let his eyes wander and laughed gently at the drops of water that sprayed around him when she pulled her swimming cap off and shook her dark brown curls loose. He was also quick to notice that she wasn't out of breath following her speedy sprint down the pool. She glanced across at him and smiled and he was immediately smitten.

'Enjoying the workout, miss?'

A voice of caramel and honey twanged his innermost feeling and the pheromones surged as she said, 'Yes, I love the freedom. It clears the cobwebs from my brain. And you? I noticed you pounding up and down.'

'Likewise. I do this when I have business conundrums and suchlike and like you, it clears my head. Do you have a name, miss?'

She looked at him and spent a moment weighing him up before replying. 'Yes, it's Penny, and you?'

She offered her hand and captivated he let his guard down and shook her hand and at the tingle of her touch he felt urges rising within him. With a sharp intake of breath, he said, 'Demyan.'

'That's unusual.'

'I'm American,' and realising his slip he added hastily, 'my grandparents were Russian. I'm living in Germany at the moment.'

'Oh, that explains it. Welcome to the UK. Business is it?'

'No, purely pleasure which I'm hoping could get better; and you?'

She smiled at the covert hint and captivated him even more.

'Business but I make a point of getting away early when I have these facilities thrown in.'

'That's nice. How would you like to join me for some liquid refreshment?'

'Okay, Demyan. Give me fifteen minutes and I'll meet you in the pool bar.'

'Sure thing.'

They helped each other to their feet and she 'accidentally rubbed up close to him. She smiled up at him and as he watched her make her way languorously down the opposite side of the pool to the female changing rooms his thoughts were on anything but his mission.

—

SMS - Contact made. Name – Demyan? Russian / American? Based in Germany? On holiday—allegedly?'

Penny sent the message and slipped the smartphone into her bag before she patted her hair in the mirror and headed for the bar where Demyan rose to meet her and was more than pleased with what he saw.

'If I may be allowed to say so, Penny, you look stunning.'

As he came around and pulled the seat out for her Penny smiled and replied, 'You may say so, Demyan, although there are some poor souls in this country who would be offended. It's not PC.'

'It's the same in the States,' he said as he held the chair for her as she sat down before returning to his seat and when the waitress approached he asked, 'What can I get you, Penny?'

'A long G&T, please.'

He ordered her drink and a small lager for himself and leaning forward in his seat, he said, 'Tell me about yourself, Penny.'

'Not a lot to tell,' she said, 'I'm twenty-eight and a rep for a reputable drug company. And you?'

'I'm in I.T. and support the U.S. military in Germany. That's it. I get to go back to the States regularly but this time I chose to come and play my golf at Hoylake. That's some damn course that is.'

'You're not married?'

She noticed the involuntary covering of his left hand as he spoke. It wasn't obvious but there was a paler band around the third finger. 'No, I'm looking for Miss Right.'

'The ladies in your State must be slow. Where was it again?'

Caught off guard and unlike a serial philanderer he stuttered, 'Flo...' and realising his *faux pax* he feigned a cough and said, 'Sorry, Fort Worth, Texas, but I'm relocating to Florida where the golf's better.'

'You prefer it in the south.'

Demyan nodded. 'I heard stories from my Gran about Russian winters and chose the south but your English early summer isn't very warm and it's wet.'

'You get used to it. You're in Germany, do you get much golf there?'

'I play at the Frankfurt course but it's a bit out of town and full of boring old people who go slow.'

'Oh, I see, and Hoylake, you find that tough?'

'Yeah, it was windy the other day which made it hard but a good challenge, and you, are you married?'

Penny smiled coyly. 'No! I left my partner a few weeks ago. When I'm not working I like to keep fit. Swimming, cycling, that sort of thing but I'm not keen on running.'

'You live where?'

'Mostly from my suitcase.'

Penny's alacrity to tell of her home did not alert Demyan and he assumed she was protecting herself until they got to know each other better so he didn't pursue it, instead, he nodded towards the window, and said, 'It's a nice afternoon how about we take a walk in the grounds before dinner?'

Penny declined. 'Not today, Demyan, I've been up since six so I'm going to lie down for a while. It's been nice talking to you.'

As she stood to leave Demyan felt a surge of disappointment and what he had earlier hoped was going to be a day finishing on a high note appeared to destined to wither and he swiftly changed his plans from a further reconnaissance trip to a more what he hoped would be a passionate pursuit. 'Penny, we must meet again. The restaurant here is excellent, can I treat you to dinner tonight?'

She paused and pondered for a moment before smiling down at him. 'Why, yes, I'd love that. Eight o' clock then.'

With that, she spun away and he sat mesmerised as she swayed sensually from the room.

Penny's thoughts were less on the sensual but more on the practical as she said to herself, 'Got him.'

—

SMS: Check out Frankfurt Golf Club and location. End message.

Penny put her smartphone on the dressing table, dropped her clothes where she stood and with the air of someone comfortable with their body she walked naked across the room to the shower while shaking out and raking her hair with slender fingers.

—

The decor and the subdued lighting designed to give an oyster pink glow added an extra dimension to her flawless complexion and highlighted her hair. Demyan admired her lissom figure as she advanced across the room and he liked the way her hair curved sensually around her face. Her figure-hugging black metallic button-through dress and jewelled high heel sandals added to her allure which she hoped would have a soporific effect on his mind and make him drop his guard.

He greeted her warmly when she got to the table and he came around and held the chair for her. He took little notice of the clutch bag which was only zipped three-quarters of the way and which she placed on the table between them.

When he returned to his seat, with a degree of certainty, he said, 'I took the liberty of ordering champagne, do you like it?'

'Yes, I do.'

Before the Maitre-de could oblige Demyan lifted the bottle from the ice bucket and poured her a generous measure and raising his glass, he said, 'Here's to a fruitful friendship.'

They touched glasses and she replied with a more forthright, 'Cheers.'

They sipped their champagne and Demyan never took his eyes

off her until reality clicked in and he said, 'Penny, would you like me to order or do you have any preferences?'

'Demyan,' she said, 'this is your night, surprise me.'

He nodded and called the waiter over, who, with pen poised, said, 'Yes, sir?'

Demyan ran his finger down the menu, paused and replied, 'Are these scallops hand fresh?'

'Yes, sir.'

Good, we'll have the scallops with black truffle vinaigrette followed by the wild venison and could we have a bottle of good Californian Malbec, please?'

'Yes, sir. I'll inform the wine water. Would you like more Champagne while you wait?'

Demyan looked across at Penny who shook her head. 'No, thanks.'

He took a sip from his glass and reached across to touch Penny's hand. 'Now then, what shall we talk about. I know, they have music here later would you enjoy a little dancing.'

'I'd love to, Demyan, it will work off this wonderful dinner.'

He squeezed her hand and liked the response as the waiter arrived with their first course.

Dinner was a pleasant interlude of three courses complemented by excellent wines during which Demyan took every opportunity to touch her. While he held her hand his knee gently rubbed up against hers. Like a rabbit transfixed by a stoat his eyes never left her face the real reason for his being in the UK forgotten.

Midway through the meal, Penny said. 'Demyan, stop looking at me like a lovesick calf I think people may have noticed.

Demyan jerked upright in his seat searching for words. 'Oh, Ah, yes! I'm sorry, I was just thinking what a shame it is that we haven't met sooner.'

'I don't think anything would have come of it as I was in a relationship.'

'I know,' he said with a lilt of laughter in his voice, 'but a man can dream.'

'Let us finish our dinner, Demyan, and we can talk later.'

He nodded his consent and they continued the rest of the meal with benign chatter about the recent weather etc...

They pushed their plates away and faint music could be heard in the distance. Wiping his hands on his napkin with a flourish Demyan said, 'That was perfect. Good company and excellent food. Let us finish the evening with more wine and some good music. Will you join me in the lounge, Penny?'

She dabbed her mouth demurely before she smiled at him. 'I most certainly will. That meal was perfect. You must allow me to go Dutch.'

'Go Dutch. What is that?'

'I wish to pay half.'

'Penny, what sort of a man would I be to allow my guest to pay. I won't hear of it.'

'Oh, Demyan are you sure?'

'Have no fear, Penny, I shall charge it to expenses.'

With that, they made their way to the lounge. Demyan was annoyed that the table layout didn't allow him to walk by her side so he contented himself with the svelte outline that shimmied before him.

In the lounge, they chose a secluded low leather two-seater sofa from where they could watch the dance floor but maintain their privacy.

'Champagne, Penny?'

'Oh, Demyan, you shouldn't, but yes, I'd love to.'

He attracted the waiter and ordered a bottle of Moet Chandon Nectar Imperial and then carelessly flopped down beside her with his arm across the back of the settee. 'Have you had this brand before, Penny?'

'No, outside of weddings I don't bother with champagne but I think I could get a taste for it.'

'You'll love it.' He let his arm casually slip from the back and his hand rested on her thigh and her response was not immediate but then she lifted his hand away and instinctively pulled her skirt towards her knees.

The waiter brought the champagne and after their first drink, Demyan noticed the '*The Carl Blackwell Four*' who were the entertainment for the evening were playing a slow tune which he loved. They were not a young band, in fact definitely retired, but their version of Nat King Cole's '*Unforgettable*' was so rhythmical he loved it.

'Would you like to dance, Penny?'

Keeping Demyan preoccupied with things other than his true purpose was uppermost in her mind and she obliged immediately and they joined the other couples on the floor.

She liked the way he held her with the back of his hand pressing into her back and pulling her in a rather old fashioned technique but with enough pressure so as not to be uncomfortable but intimate in a romantic manner. With her high heels, there was little difference in their height but she deferred in a shy way when he tried to nestle his head into her neck.

Instead, she leaned back slightly, and said, 'You dance well, Demyan, do you and your wife dance often?'

His thoughts were on more down to earth activities and unthinking he murmured, 'No,' when reality clicked and he hesitated before adding, 'Err, that is we used to. I learned a lot from my Mother and I enjoy this style of music and the company of course.'

'Does that mean you would marry again, Demyan?'

'Err, yes and no.'

'I'll put that down as a maybe.'

'And you, Penny?'

'I had a bad time. I'll have to wait and see.'

He pulled her closer and she responded by thrusting her hips into him and she could feel his manly response.

'Apart from golf, Demyan, why Florida. Wouldn't Silicone Valley have better prospects for an I.T. specialist?'

'I work from home and I like surfing, the oceanic sort.'

She squirmed into him a little more and she felt his breathing quicken. 'You're on the East coast?'

'No, the Caribbean.'

Alarm bells rang in his head and with a gentle alacrity he eased her away just as the music stopped and with the other couples, they stood for a moment and clapped politely before returning to their seats. They sat a little apart and after topping up their glasses, he said with a hint of misgiving, 'You ask a lot of questions.'

'Demyan, darling, I had a hard time with my ex and I'm being cautious.'

He watched her thoughtfully as she took a drink and replaced her glass on the table. There was no knee jerk reaction. Her movements were natural and without any degree of uncertainty and he concluded that she was probably telling the truth although wildly out with her assumptions about Florida but before he could respond she moved closer to him and spoke in a manner that suggested she was unphased by his reaction to her questioning, and said, 'My ex was in I.T. He worked in the automotive industry mainly to do with F1. You know engines and things, way above my head. What do you specialise in?'

This was not going to plan and he rubbed his chin thoughtfully for a moment. 'Oh, mainly business computers and phones and things. These androids cause many problems in the military.'

'Oh, do they?'

She fiddled in her clutch bag and withdrew her phone and with a disarming smile, said, 'I've always wanted someone who could sus these things out. Mine's refusing to play ball. Could you look at it?'

'Women,' he mentally muttered as he took the phone from her. The screen was blank and didn't respond to a stroke across the face. He pressed the home key and still nothing. As a last resort, he pressed the power button and held it for a couple of seconds. He shook his head at what appeared before him before he handed the phone back to her. 'The battery's dead,' he said, 'your apps are probably updating continuously.'

Penny took the device from him. 'Oh, is that all.'

He nodded and topped up their glasses and looked across the room. 'Would you like another dance?'

'No, thank you, Demyan. I have an early start.'

With the prospect of a satisfactory end to his evening, he immediately became attentive. 'Of course, Penny, how insensitive of me.' He raised his glass. 'Thank you for a lovely evening. You are the most beautiful lady I have met this side of the pond.'

Penny winced. 'Why, thank you, Demyan.' She put her glass down and stood up. 'I really must go.'

Demyan arose also. 'Let me show you to your room.'

'Thank you, Demyan, that would be nice.'

He stood back and allowed Penny to go first but as they left the room he caught up with her and put his arm around her waist. Penny didn't resist but neither did she respond.

Upstairs they stopped outside Penny's room and paused long enough for her to unlock the door and leave it slightly ajar.

'Thank you for a lovely evening, Demyan.'

'The pleasure has been all mine,' he said, and leaning forward he rested one hand on the door jamb and lowered his head to kiss her.

She responded by giving him a quick peck on the cheek and whispered, 'It's too early, Demyan.'

She turned away quickly and with a swift movement slipped into her room and seconds later Demyan heard the lock click over. From the other side of the door, she heard him curse in Russian and bang his hand against the wall in frustration before he stormed down the corridor.

In his room, he arranged with the Concierge for more willing company.

—

In her room Penny took the smartphone from her clutch bag and before replacing the battery proceeded to peel off the thin plastic screen protector and placed it carefully in an evidence bag. That done she extracted the digital recording device from her purse and with the knowledge that there was not much information on it she put that in a similar protective bag and after taking time to undress and pouring herself a whisky & ginger from the mini-bar she sat on the edge of her bed and sent a text...

SMS—Russian with US citizenship. Check out the West Florida connection. Have prints and DNA? – End

—

'I'm awfully sorry, Mr Dimitrov, but the lady checked out early this morning and left no forwarding information.

'Did she have a surname?

'No, sir, the room was booked by her employers, GB Chemical Import & Exports.'

'Thanks.'

Demyan turned away and tossed the bunch of flowers he was carrying into a nearby waste bin and walked towards the exit but something was worrying him. Import & Export was a cover often used by the likes of the CIA or SIS.

He retraced his steps to the Concierge and left his car keys and called the car rental firm to collect the BMW and then he searched on his smartphone for a replacement vehicle and other hotels in the area.

~~~~~
~~~~~

CHAPTER 11

Tuesday

'You're up early, Hunter, you planning on going to work today?'

'Yes, Jay, I feel guilty. I left them short yesterday and I've no excuse. Want some coffee?'

'Yes, please, but what about, Carrie?'

He got up from his stool and as he walked across the kitchen he said, 'She can watch me through the cafe windows.'

Rubbing the sleep from her eyes and her hair all tousled the object of their conversation entered the kitchen wrapped in one of Jacquie's dressing gowns. 'Mornin,' she said.

'Mornin,' lass, coffee?'

'Yes, please.'

Carrie sat on the stool vacated by Hunter. 'I hate these security watches. Simon insisted on two hours on and two off and I'm knackered.'

'I can understand that lass, he thinks he's still on stag in the military. Four and four like the Navy is better when there's only two of you. I'm going to work and you can sit back in the cafe and relax while I whistle some trolleys around. I'll join you for a break. Have you got a good book?'

'No.'

'Jacquie's got loads. We'll find something and you can have breakfast on me. I leave in forty-five minutes.'

He gave Carrie her coffee and sat down opposite her as Simon strolled in looking fresh. 'Hi, everybody. If that's coffee I smell, count me in.'

Hunter pointed to the end of the work surface. 'Help yourself, mate, and if you want toast, it's at the other end.'

'No, thanks, I'll get something at the Garden Centre.'

'What about the officers outside?' said, Jacquie.

Simon stopped pouring coffee long enough to say, 'They went home at six. With Carrie and I here their Chief didn't reckon they were needed anymore.'

Carrie slid from her stool. 'I'll go and get ready. I won't be long, Mr Hunter.'

'Carrie,' said Simon, 'you had a rough night why don't you go with Mrs Hunter and you can chill out on the sofa there and I can troll around with Hunter. Is that okay, Hunter?'

Hunter nodded, 'It's okay by me.'

'That's it then,' said Carrie, 'I'll be as quick as I can, Mrs Hunter.'

As Carrie left the room Hunter scooped up his jacket. 'Come on, Simon, I've got work to go to.'

Simon took a swift gulp of his coffee and followed Hunter from the room.

—

'Come through, Carrie, make yourself comfy on the sofa. I'm going to be busy for a few hours.'

Carrie plonked her bag down on the office sofa when Jacquie said to her, 'You've had no breakfast? Go to the restaurant and get something.'

Jacquie went to the door and popped her head out. 'Charlotte, Carrie here is going to have something to eat. Make sure and put it on my tab.'

'Okay, Mrs Hunter, will do. Do you want coffee or anything?'

'Yes, please, the usual.'

Jacquie returned and sat behind her desk. 'Off you go, Carrie, and when you get back you can get your head down.'

'Thanks, Mrs Hunter.'

Carrie scooped up her bag when Jacquie stopped her. 'Leave your bag, Carrie, it'll be alright there.'

'I can't let it out of my sight, Mrs Hunter.'

'Oh, silly me,' laughed Jacquie, 'you're carrying?'

Carrie nodded and followed Charlotte out to the cafe area while Jacquie opened the first of a pile of letters.

—

An hour later Jacquie threw her pen down and leaned back in the chair with a sigh of relief. 'It's no good,' she thought, 'I'll have to get myself a P.A.'

She looked across at the slumbering Carrie just as the internal phone rang and she picked it up smartly. 'Yes, Charlotte?'

She listened for a few moments before saying, 'Okay, put him through.'

She clicked on the loud speaker before she said, 'Good morning, Mr Dodds, I understand you want a delivery.'

'Yes, please, Mrs Hunter, the same as my previous order and can I have it at the same price?'

'Hold the line.'

She pressed the mute button and then clicked a switch for the intercom. 'Charlotte, have you got the Dodd's file there?'

'Yes, Mrs Hunter.'

A few moments later there was a polite knock on the door and Charlotte entered and handed Jacquie a file. 'It's all there and he's paid up to date, Mrs Hunter.'

'Okay, Charlotte, thank you.'

She opened the file and perused the latest bill lying on the top before she pressed the mute button once more. 'Hello, Mr Dodds, sorry about that. Yes, of course, you can have your order. Can you call this afternoon?'

'Yep! About three-ish.'

'I'll have it ready.'

She put the phone down and glanced at Carrie who was still fast asleep. Pushing her chair back quietly she got up and on tip-toes left the office and as she closed the door quietly behind her she tittered quietly at the incongruity of her actions as moments before she had been talking loudly on the intercom.

When she entered the main part of the building she noticed a quick upsurge in activity amongst the Staff as she walked down the main aisle to the Reception desk where she found one of the gardeners talking to Lily. She didn't need the name tags she insisted her employees wear as she knew them off by heart.

'Chris, just the man. Are you busy?'

'Err, yes. I was just going over the main road. Some pillock has left one of our trolleys in the lay-by over there.'

'Leave that, I'll do it. Can you get an order ready for this afternoon? Charlotte has the details.'

'It's no bother, Mrs Hunter, I can do both.'

'Thank you, Chris, but I need the exercise.'

Chris had a quick word with Lily and with a nod to Jacquie made his way to the office.

Jacquie spoke to Lily. 'How is it going, Lily? You up to speed?'

'Yes, Mrs Hunter. I can manage on my own now.'

'Good. Let me know if there's anything you need for your wheelchair access. If anyone wants me I'm over the road and I'll be back in a few minutes.' She pointed to some jackets hanging on pegs at the back of the desk. 'Can you get that coat for me?'

Lily spun away from the desk and smartly scooted over to the coat hooks and grasping one of the works green quilted jackets in both hands pushed upwards and let it drop in her lap before spinning and returning to the front of the desk.

She held it up. 'Here you are, Mrs Hunter.'

'Thanks, Lily.'

Jacquie grabbed the jacket and put it on as she turned and walked to the Exit out to the car park. It was a dull overcast day with a chill north-westerly wind blowing and Jacquie pulled the jacket tightly around her and zipped it quickly as she walked across the car park to the gate leading onto the main road. She paused long enough for a gap in the traffic before dashing across to the lay-by on the other side where some itinerant shopper had abandoned one of the garden centre trolleys.

She muttered a few choice words about whoever had left it there and was just about to grab the handle when there was a loud revving of an engine and a screech of tyres. Looking round she saw a small red nondescript car surging out of the Garden Centre car-park straight towards her when it suddenly swerved to the left and as it did so an automatic pistol was thrust out of the rear window and began firing.

For a split second, she faltered in disbelief and then instinct kicked in and she threw herself to the right behind the trolley. A sharp painful impact in her thigh spun her over and a piece of shrapnel caused by a bullet striking the metal trolley embedded itself in her ribcage. She crashed to the floor and as she rolled her head impacted heavily on the kerb and knocked her unconscious.

With wheels spinning and screeching on the tarmac the car slid sideways into an approaching car before zigzagging away causing oncoming motorists to brake sharply and swerve. A lorry carrying pallets was unable to stop and shunted the cars in front of him like a loose domino pack and sprayed its load across both lanes of the highway.

At the far end of the lay-by Paramedic, Rick Peters taking a well-earned break in his Ambulance Service Rapid Response Vehicle watched the whole episode unravel before him and his actions were instantaneous. He dropped his water bottle into the foot well as he grabbed for his radio. 'Echo Papa five-one. Require immediate back-up at this location plus Police. Shots fired. Female gunshot wound and RTC.'

He automatically hit the 360º emergency dashboard light switches and reversed his car thirty metres to make a protective shield for his new patient. He ran around to the rear of the vehicle and lifting the tailgate grabbed his Essential Emergency Response bag and quickly covered the last few metres to Jacquie.

He noted the blood spatter and the wet patch growing quickly as the blood pumping from her ruptured femoral artery seeped through the material of her slacks. He grabbed for his radio. 'Echo Papa five-one. Breach of the femoral artery. What is your ETA? Over.'

His pulse was racing as he grabbed an oxygen bottle and mask from his kit.

'Calm down,' he muttered to himself.'

He took a deep breath and began again.

'Airway.'

He opened her mouth and did a sweep with his gloved finger to check for any obstruction. 'Clear.'

'Breathing...shallow.'

He fitted the mask and turned the oxygen on.

'Circulation.'

He didn't waste time counting her heart rate for thirty seconds instead he unzipped her jacket and manoeuvring his gloved hands under her blouse he attached defibrillator pads to her chest.

'Sixty-two. Let's hope you're fit.' He glanced at her thigh.

'You're bleeding out, lady.'

His primary intervention stopped. His priority now was to check the bleeding and he hoped those sirens he could hear were his colleagues coming to assist. He extracted a pair of surgical scissors and knowing she was unconscious he was able to apply his actions firmer and began cutting lengthways up the leg of her slacks until he had uncovered the wound. 'Oh, jeez,' he said shaking his head, 'this is a bad 'un.'

He elevated her leg onto his shoulder and grabbing a wad of bandages he tore them open and pressed it onto the open wound before looking around at the gathering audience.

'Any of you lot know first aid?' he shouted.'

A young girl pushed through and said, 'I'm a First Aider at work.'

'What's your name?'

'Amber.'

He took a pair of surgical gloves from his bag. 'Right, Amber, put these on and get down here, lift her ankle onto your shoulder like this and then press on this dressing as hard as you can while I apply a tourniquet and get some fluids into her.'

She quickly put on the gloves and knelt beside Rick and they changed places.

'Press a bit harder, girl, like you do CPR, she won't feel it. We need to slow that bleeding or she's had it.'

'Okay.' She put her body weight behind her arms. 'I've got it.'

'Good girl. This won't take long.'

He took a tourniquet from his bag and applied it to the upper part of Jacquie's thigh.

After a few seconds, he said, 'Right, Amber, ease off and let's see if this is working.'

Amber sat back while Rick examined the blood flow from the wound. Satisfied he patted Amber on the shoulder. 'Okay, lass, it looks good but keep the pressure on.'

He began to cannulise Jacquie s he speculated if it was wise to do so as the approaching sirens were not close enough in his book.

—

Charlotte shook Carrie hard. 'Wake up, miss! You've gotta come quick. It's Mrs Hunter.'

'Oh! Err! What's up? Shit! How long have I been asleep?'

'Quite a bit, miss, you better hurry, it looks pretty serious.'

'What happened?'

'I don't know, miss, but there was shooting and crashing and Mrs Hunter was in the middle of it.'

Carrie struggled up, straightened her clothes and taking a quick peek in a mirror she grabbed her bag and ran after Charlotte who was halfway down the aisle of the Garden Centre. At the Exit, she acknowledged a customer who held the door open and she raced across the Car Park to the main road. Traffic was in chaos but following Charlotte's lead, she weaved a way through the stationary vehicles to where a small crowd had gathered.

She waived her Warrant Card and shouted above the noise. 'POLICE! Stand back, let me through.'

The small crowd mumbled incoherently and shuffled about until a narrow gap opened down which Carrie pushed her way to the front. She stopped suddenly and took a sharp intake of breath and put a hand over her mouth when she saw the prostrate form of Jacquie with Amber holding a raised leg over her shoulder and Gus working feverishly to fix the drip.

'Oh! My God! Is she alright? What's happened?' she uttered.

Charlotte who was close behind clutched Carrie's shoulder in despair. 'Mrs Hunter!,' she screamed...

The steady voice of Rick intervened. 'You know the lady, miss?'

Carrie spoke for the both of them. 'Yes, it's Jacquie Hunter the proprietor of the Garden Centre.'

'And you are, miss?'

The sirens were close now as Carrie replied, 'DS Long, Cheshire Police.'

'Okay, Sarge, clear a space for an Ambulance. We need to move quickly.'

Carrie turned away and lifted her Warrant card. 'POLICE! MOVE BACK! Give us some room here, this is critical.'

There were more rumblings from the onlookers as Rick busied himself attaching the drip. When he'd done that he called Charlotte.

‘Can you hold this?’

As Charlotte took the drip from him, Jacquie moaned.

‘Thanks, lass, hold it about waist high. She may be coming round. I’ll give her a shot of morphine.’ He turned to Amber. ‘You okay?’

She nodded. ‘Yes, will she be alright?’

He cocked his head thoughtfully to one side for a moment. ‘I don’t know. There’s a lot of blood. Fingers crossed.’

An Ambulance arrived followed moments later by several Police cars and as the crews secured the area and moved the crowd further back two Paramedics moved in quickly to help Rick and his fragile patient.

~~~~~
~~~~~

CHAPTER 12

Hunter was pushing a line of shopping trolleys into the holding enclosure while Simon watched as shoppers surged around with complete disregard for the staff. Hunter had no sooner finished putting them into place when he was nudged to one side and the first trolley snatched from his grasp.

He was about to react when his mobile jangled followed an instant later by Simon's smartphone. Reluctant to use his phone during work time an inkling made Hunter pull it from his pocket. As he stepped out of the way of shoppers he noted the number calling and answered. 'Yes, Inspector, what is it?'

'Mr Hunter, Listen up. I've got bad news. Your wife has been involved in a drive-by shooting and she is now in The Countess Hospital in a critical state. Get yourself down there.'

'What the hell happened?'

'I'll fill you in later. Just go, and take Bell with you.'

Hunter cancelled the call and turned to Simon who was doing the same thing. 'You got the message about your missies, Mr Hunter?'

'Darn right.' He threw his car keys to Simon. 'Get the car while I see the boss. I'll meet you here.'

Simon ran around the store to his right while Hunter ducked inside and went to Customer Services. Ignoring the queue he called the girl to him with frantic hand signals. She apologised to the customer she was attending to and came over. 'What is it, Hunter, I'm busy.'

'Sorry, Josie, but something's happened to my wife and I'm dashing off to the hospital. Can you tell the boss? All the sheds are clear but I haven't done the baskets by the tills.'

'Okay, Hunter, you go. I hope she's okay.'

'Thanks, love, I owe you.'

He spun around and dashed from the shop as Simon pulled up.

He jumped in and told Simon to go like the clappers and they would worry about the consequences later.

—

Resisting the urge to run he hurried into the A & E Department of the Countess Hospital with Simon in tow. Inside he was stopped by a member of the Security Staff. 'Whoa, there, sir. You can't come in here. Go round to the drop-in door.'

'But, but...'

Simon flashed his badge. 'Agent Bell. You've just had a Mrs Hunter brought in with gunshot wounds?'

'Yes, sir.'

'It's his wife. Where is she?'

'Hold on, sir, I'll check.'

The Security man ducked his head into an office door and amongst the unintelligible chatter, Hunter heard the word 'theatre' which meant, he hoped, that she was still alive. In a few seconds, he came back. 'She's been taken down to theatre, sir, and then she'll be going upstairs to the High Dependency Unit. There's a police presence already.'

'Thanks,' said Simon, 'which way?'

In the corridor outside the HDU ward, they were met by DI. Fearn and Carrie who stood back with her head bowed.

'Mr Hunter,' said Fearn, 'your wife is still in theatre. It was touch and go when they got her here according to Sergeant Long.'

'I know she's bloody critical,' said Hunter, 'now tell me what happened?'

Fearn turned to Carrie. 'Sergeant, fetch some coffee and you're paying.'

With that despondent look of someone in the dog house, Carrie left them.

'What's the matter with her,' said Hunter.

'It's a long story but the gist of it is this...'

He went on to narrate the known circumstances of Jacquie's misfortune, '...and that's as much as I know but it complicates things somewhat.'

'Did they get the car details?'

'Yes, and they're still looking.'

'They must have followed her to work this morning and waited. Did nobody suspect them hanging around like that?'

'It appears not but uniform are checking the CCTV. According to Long, she last remembers Jacquie checking the mail but she'd had a bad night and fell asleep and when Jacquie did leave the office she left her resting.'

Hunter nodded. 'She would, it's like her and it was mentioned over coffee that Carrie was tired before we left the house that's why she swapped with Simon.'

'There will be an enquiry but she does appear to have mitigating circumstances. I'll leave you now, I'm going back to the crime scene. Keep me posted and by the way your mate's been informed, Mr Hunter. He's on his way. Oh, one more thing. There will be an armed officer here twenty-four-seven.'

As Fearn left them and walked to the lift Hunter said, 'Simon, we're in for a long wait can you grab us a couple of extra chairs?'

Simon disappeared around the corner as Carrie appeared with a tray of steaming coffee and Hunter was the first to take one and speak to her.

'Took your time there, lass. Long way was it?'

She nodded glumly. 'The one in A & E was out of order and I had to go right down to the main cafeteria and it's miles.'

'Never mind, and don't worry about this morning, I'll sort it.'

Simon reappeared with a couple of the ubiquitous plastic seats scattered around hospital corridors and the three of them sat glumly awaiting the consequences.

—

A couple of hours later the lift by them pinged and the doors hissed open and a team of porters and nurses escorted by an armed Policeman carefully manoeuvred a hospital bed draped with tubes and monitors surrounding the inert form of Jacquie across the corridor and into a room in the HDU ward.

Hunter stood up to follow but he was stopped by a Doctor still in scrubs who came out of the lift last.

'Sorry, sir, not yet. Is she a relative?'

Hunter nodded. 'She's my wife.'

The Doctor took Hunter by the elbow and guided him a few

metres away from the others before she spoke. 'I'm Doctor Mrs Isobel Wearne the Emergency Trauma Surgeon, I don't want to raise your hopes as it's early days, Mr Hunter, but although your wife was close to death she's very fit and I think she'll be okay.'

'Her wounds,' said Hunter, 'what were they?'

'She has a through and through gunshot wound to her right thigh which nicked her femoral artery but it was only 40% damaged and we were able to do patch surgery which means she will be scarred on both legs but the prognosis is good if there are no complications.'

'Like what?'

'She lost a lot of blood so there is a chance other organs are affected as well as her lower limb. The next forty-eight hours are crucial. The blow to her head was a concern but she was showing signs of consciousness when they brought her in and the CT scan only showed concussion and no bleeding. She also has a shrapnel wound across her ribcage which is not serious but will give her breathing difficulties for a few weeks.'

Hunter laughed and the Doctor gave him a stern look. Hunter took a deep breath. 'Sorry, Doc, it's an in-joke between us going back to my service days.'

His explanation didn't lighten her mood as she replied, 'That's as maybe, Mr Hunter, but we'll keep her isolated and sedated for thirty-six hours in HDU. She has Police protection, Mr Hunter, why is that?'

'Historical services rendered for the State.'

He took the Doctors hand and shook it. 'A big 'thank you' to you and your team, Doctor.'

'Don't thank us, Mr Hunter, it's the Response Medic you have to thank. It was fortunate he was on hand as I fear another few minutes and she may not have been with us or alternatively the consequences of her injuries could have been more serious.'

—

Tuesday afternoon

Gus Thomas, Simon, DI Fearn and Hunter sat around the coffee table in the Relatives Room and when nobody seemed eager to discuss the morning's events Hunter put his drink down firmly.

'Where's Carrie, Inspector?'

Fearn cleared his throat, 'She's feeling rather distraught about the whole thing and refuses to leave the bedside of Mrs Hunter.'

'She needn't be. It wasn't her fault. If she'd been with Jacquie we would probably be talking of a double shooting.'

'I told her to go home but she insists.'

'I'll have a word before I go. What's the plan now?'

Thomas spoke up for the first time. 'This complicates things, Hunter.'

'I guessed that. Is there any news?'

'We don't know who carried out the attack or why, only that the car was found burning in a field. It was stolen in Liverpool on Sunday morning. SOCO has got it now, but it does suggest that Jacquie is the target.'

Hunter cursed. 'Shit, why her?'

'MI5 are on it as it's internal and they are going over old files. There was some talk of tit for tat for a situation about ten years ago. You were there I believe?'

'That was a coincidence, we just happened on a weapon smuggling thing. They got five years for that. Meanwhile, Gus, we have the Old Bill, MI5 and SIS, all doing their own thing. We know how you love each other. I think these crooks are pretty safe, don't you?'

Fearn coughed. 'Err! If I can just butt in. The shooting is a civil affair, Mr Hunter, and I realise with the extra intervention it makes things a bit more difficult but you have my word that we are doing our utmost to catch whoever is responsible. My major worry is that this is not a local issue.'

Simon banged the table. 'It doesn't matter what branch it is, Mrs Hunter's one of us.'

There was a moment's silence before Thomas spoke. 'You're right, Simon. I'll get onto the 'Firm' tonight and make sure we exchange information. Is there anything else?'

'Yes,' said Hunter, 'what about the Press?'

Fearn put his hand up. 'I've got it covered, at the moment it is just a drive-by and we are looking for two perpetrators. No info regarding MI5 or whatever will be mentioned.'

Hunter stood up. 'Thanks, Inspector. That's it! I've got a Garden Centre business to look after now. You've got my number and I'll check with Carrie.'

While stuffing papers into his briefcase, Thomas said, 'Simon, stick with, Hunter. Inspector Fearn, do you want us to replace Sergeant Long? Someone who's more experienced with firearms maybe?'

Fearn shook his head. 'She's adamant about her role and she's well used to firearms. She was with the Army in Afghanistan.'

'Okay. I'll see you back at the station, Inspector.'

—

Hunter spent ten minutes going through the mail on Jacquie's desk and hadn't got a clue what it was all about except the takeover was in the hands of the solicitors and the new coffee franchise would be in operation in six weeks across the organisation.

'Simon, I've got to take some drastic action here and I'm not sure what.'

Just then there was a knock on the door and Charlotte entered. 'Sorry for the interruption, Mr Hunter, can I get you anything?'

'Charlotte! just the person. Take a seat, you may want it.'

Charlotte looked mystified and slightly alarmed wondering what she had done. She sat on the leather chair opposite Hunter who raised his hand palm outward.

'Don't be alarmed, Charlotte. How long have you been here?'

'Right from the start when Mrs Hunter took over.'

'Good, as of now you have become Mrs Hunter's P.A. You will run the show and your salary will be commensurate. First things first. Come around here and take your seat.'

'But, err... I don't know what to say, Mr Hunter.'

'Say nothing.'

Hunter and Charlotte stood up simultaneously and swapped places before Hunter spoke again. 'Charlotte, I won't interfere but you will liaise with me on any major decisions. I don't know how soon Mrs Hunter will be back but if the takeover crops up we'll cross that bridge when it comes. Meanwhile, the managers will run their own Centres and answer to you. You will need to get a replacement in the outer office.'

'Yes.'

'That's up to you.' He pointed to the paperwork on the desk. 'This mail, I can't make head nor tail of it.'

'It's been covered already, Mr Hunter. Jacquie, I mean Mrs Hunter passed it over to me before she went out this morning.'

'Good, and one more thing. Get a new business smartphone or Ipad or whatever you executives need for the job and get your name on the Insurance for that Range Rover. If you're the boss you must drive like one.'

'I'm already on it, Mr Hunter. I used to run messages and pick people up etc...'

'Charlotte, Jacquie spoke highly of you. Don't let me down.'

'I won't.'

Hunter stood up and offered his hand, 'Welcome to the family, Charlotte. You've got my number, I'm off to the hospital.'

~~~~~
~~~~~

CHAPTER 13

Tuesday evening

'Carrie, go home and I don't want to see you before eight in the morning.'

'Are you sure, Mr Hunter, I feel so bad?'

'Carrie, it's not your fault. Nobody could have foreseen what happened and Jacquie was sympathetic to your condition and let you sleep.'

'But...'

'No buts. See you in the morning.'

With a depressed look in her eyes, Carrie slowly rose from her seat and crossing to the bed sympathetically squeezed the hand of Jacquie before she left the room. Hunter waited and when the coast was clear he leaned over Jacquie and kissed her gently on the forehead while fighting to hold back the sob which seeped through his normally calm exterior.

He whispered, 'Come on, lass, fight,' and as an aside, he added, 'you should see the state of your hair.'

He was sure he saw her eyes move under the closed lids but knew she was sedated to aid her recovery and knowing her hair was her pride and joy he smiled as he dragged the chair closer and took a book from his bag.

It was ten 'o clock when he heard the shift change over in the corridor and Simon poked his head around the door. 'Everything okay, Mr Hunter?'

'Yes, Simon, you shove off. I'm staying overnight.'

'Can I get you anything?'

'No, I've had something to eat and the nurses are keeping me stocked with coffee.'

Simon shut the door quietly and Hunter settled down to a long night and wished he'd asked Simon for his weapon. He shook his head. 'Nah, he'd only get into trouble.'

It was sometime later when a shadowy figure drifted down the car park and as it passed behind Hunter's VW it ducked down and slid something under the rear sill and snapped it onto the exhaust bracket and then hands in pockets walked nonchalantly away.

—

'Wake up, Mr Hunter, would you like some breakfast?'

Hunter jumped and blinked as he woke to the gentle nudge and the soft caring voice.

'Err... Oh... Yes. What time is it? Could I have a cuppa first?'

'It's just after six. I'll get your tea and you could pop down to the Cafe later if you like. The doctor will be doing her last round shortly. Milk and sugar?'

'Just milk, but quite strong.'

She slipped out of the room and returned moments later with a mug of tea. 'Here you are.'

'Thanks, how long have I been asleep?'

'I came around about two-ish and you were dozing so I left you.'

'As long as that?' Looking at Jacquie who was sedated but breathing easily he relaxed but the feeling of guilt remained. 'Sorry, lass.'

He only had time to sip a mouthful when the door opened and a much refreshed Carrie came in. 'Mornin,' Mr Hunter, how is she?'

'Hi, Carrie, you're early and she sounds good.'

'Okay, I'll wait outside. Oh, I nearly forgot. Simon won't be joining us. They said as Mrs Hunter is the target you won't be needing him.'

'Thanks, Carrie.'

With that, she turned and slipped out of the room leaving Hunter to contemplate his cup of tea and how he was going to manage until Jacquie was fit again but within minutes peace was disturbed as the on-duty Doctor entered followed by her entourage.

'Good morning, Mr Hunter, just give me a minute while we do some checks.'

He pushed his chair out of the way while the staff fussed around Jacquie and true to her word the Doctor was with him in a very short time.

'Well, Mr Hunter, your wife is doing better than we expected. Her pulse and BP are good. There doesn't appear to be any problem with her lower limb circulation so our main concern now is what damage the blow to her head caused. The CT scan showed no bleeding but until we wake her we won't know properly.'

'When will you wake her?'

'I'll consult with Mrs Wearne but probably tomorrow. Her stats are fine and her wound is looking good. You carry on with your normal day. De-stress. It won't do your wife any good if you have a heart attack, will it? We'll call you if anything changes.'

'Thanks, Doc. Her minder's here and I can see she's in good hands.'

'Why's she got a minder and an armed Police watch?'

'Historical patriotism.'

The Doctor nodded and left the room while Hunter did a quick tidy around the bed before he called Carrie in. 'You take over, lass. She's in good nick. You've got my number and if you get bored you can chat to the uniform outside. I'll see you around tea time.'

'Okay, Mr Hunter.'

Before he left he leaned across and kissed Jacquie gently on the forehead while choking back a tear. 'Come on, lass, you can do it. Love you!'

~~~~~
~~~~~

CHAPTER 14

Wednesday

'Charlotte, I should have thought about that when we handed over. Set it up and I'll drop by before I go to pick the kids up from school. Meanwhile, I'm under doctors orders to de-stress so I'm going to do a nine-hole bash at the golf club. It's times like this when you need a dog.'

'You've got one, Mr Hunter.'

'I know, but she's two-faced. She's deserted me and won't leave the kids who are staying with my sister.'

Hunter put the phone down, put his jacket on and picked up his golf clubs. As he passed the portrait of Jacquie hanging in the hall he touched it and said quietly, 'Love you, lass.' Hanging alongside it was a photo of Jacquie in her Wren Officers uniform taken at her passing out parade and he resisted the urge to salute as he turned to go out to his car. When he reached for the front door latch he caught a glimpse of himself in the hall mirror. Where there was smoothness there was now lines. His hair was thinner although still clinging to its familiar dark colour which had been the subject of many rumours since he was forty and his eyes showed the stress of his situation.

Slamming the tailgate shut he slid into the driver's seat and revelling in the power gurgling of the exhaust he revved the engine before coasting up the lane. He turned right at the junction with the main road and ignored the innocuous Skoda Yeti which slipped out of the shopping precinct car park opposite and joined the traffic behind him.

He swung into the 19th-century arched gateway which was the combined entrance to the Municipal Golf Course and the side gate of the Church and a hundred metres down the un-metalled track he pulled up outside the Clubhouse.

Twenty minutes later while waiting for the first tee to clear he was joined by Demyan dressed in his finest golfing clobber who nodded a greeting, and said, 'Hi, I'm looking for some practice, shall we make a twosome?'

Hunter after visually checking out Demyan's clubs and the outfit responded, 'If you don't mind knocking around with an amateur.'

'It ain't a problem, pal, it'll be a pleasure to get away from those pro snobs and play proper golf.'

'Right, you're on, Mr... What did you say your name was?'

'Marcus.'

Hunter shoved his hand out. 'Hunter, and whoever is in the lead at the fifth hole buys the bacon butties.'

They shook hands. 'I like it, and I look forward to your English butty.'

'You're not from the UK? On holiday?

'Yes.'

At that point, they got the call to play-on and walked across to the first tee. Hunter took a coin from his pocket and spinning into the air said, 'What do you call, Marcus?'

'The Queen's head.'

'It's a head. Your call.'

'I'll lead off,' said Demyan, 'anything I should look out for?'

'There's a pond on your left and a ditch about halfway.'

Demyan didn't waste any time. He chose his *N°1* wood and after a couple of loosening swings did a good straight drive off the tee.

Hunter admired his technique and muttered quietly to himself, 'Got me hands full here,' and playing safe he chose the more modest *N°3* wood intent merely on staying on the fairway.

With a little social chit-chat, they made steady progress and as Hunter anticipated Demyan was in the lead at the end of the fifth and waving the match behind through they retired to the refreshment van placed tactfully at the side of the green where both dog walkers and players had easy access.

'Introduce me to the bacon butty, Mr Hunter.'

'They do a mean coffee, Marcus, want one?'

'Yes.'

'It's instant Americano.'

Hunter ordered and stood aside to let Demyan pay and they

retreated to some metal garden furniture set out at the side of the trailer.

'You play a mean round of golf, Mr Hunter, I bet you were good when you were younger.'

'I've only been playing ten years.'

'You're kidding?'

'Nope!'

'How so?'

'Money!'

'And you make up for it now?'

'Wednesdays and on Saturday mornings when my wife takes the children out.'

'You have children?'

'Yea, we married late.'

Hunter didn't like the way the conversation was turning and he jumped up. 'Breakfast over, let's move.' He pulled a *4 iron* from his club bag and as he walked over towards the sixth tee he said over his shoulder. 'You to tee off, Marcus?'

Marcus didn't delay. He took a quick look down the *Par 3* fairway before he plucked a club from his bag and after a few loosening swings played a delicate chip onto the green which stopped a metre short of the hole.

Hunter cursed when he realised that he had played his shot with the same iron he had used on the longer *Par 3* fifth and watched as his ball overshot the green and finished in the long grass. 'Shit!,' he muttered, 'why did I do that? How many times have I played that bloody hole?'

He did it in three but par was not what he wanted against a player like Demyan. He made up for it on the short *par 4* seventh which was his favourite. *Woods* and *Drivers* were barred on this hole by club rules so he played it with a traditional *1 iron* and watched Demyan blunder when he played with a *N°1* hybrid iron and with the extra length drop his ball straight into the bunker at the front of the green. Hunter reached the green with a *9 iron* chip shot and was secretly pleased when they reached the bunker and saw that Demyan's ball was plugged into the leading edge. In golf parlance a 'fried egg'.

'I could win one here,' he thought.

Demyan played his first shot sideways but caught the lip and watched it rebound back into the bottom of the bunker. 'Yes!' said Hunter under his breath. The front lip of the bunker was quite high so Demyan opted to play a chip backwards onto the fairway and then play a soft chip onto the green and finished with a five. Hunter could hardly contain himself as he set himself up to play his third. This is where his sniper training came in handy. He took a deep breath, exhaled, held it and putted the final two metres to card a three. He didn't shout but did a small air punch as it dropped.

Demyan didn't like losing any hole to an amateur and walked across to the eighth tee silently but as Hunter took a club from his bag Demyan had time to look around. The eighth hole was a longer *par 4* but was more open. The trees on either side were well spread out and quite low and peaking above the woods behind the clubhouse off to the right of the green he could just see the tip of the church bell tower. He watched quietly while Hunter played a safe *3 Wood* up the centre of the fairway and throwing caution to the wind he plucked his *Driver* from his bag and then watched in dismay as in his eagerness to get revenge for the last hole he carelessly sliced his tee shot over the trees on the right and onto the ninth fairway.

His mood was sour but all was not lost as he could still reach the green over the sparse trees. As he broke through the tree line he breathed a sigh of relief when he noticed a ditch across the fairway with his ball one metre short but the tree directly in line with the hole was the highest in the row and he would have to play a *9 iron* to get the lift. He shrugged and using his upper body strength he dug in and lofted the ball towards the eighth green. His eagerness had got the better of him and with one bounce it rebounded into a small bunker on the left of the green.

Hunter played a *3 iron* onto the green which left him a metre from the hole which that day was set over on the right side. He could hardly retain his glee at his good fortune but he had to make sure of the putt first. He watched tensely as Demyan played a *wedge* onto the green but left himself short and his putt slid agonisingly millimetres past the hole for him to finish with a four.

To calm his nerves Hunter took his time lining up his shot and then had an anxious moment as the ball wavered on the edge but gravity took over and pulled it down. This time he didn't contain himself and shouted, 'YES!' while throwing an air punch.

'Sorry, Marcus, but I haven't played that well for a long time.'

Demyan raised a smile. 'That's okay, George, I've been there many times in my career. One hole to go. Want to bet on it?'

'Nah, don't do gambling.'

'I understand. You to go.'

'Hah, I'm not used to this,' said Hunter with a grin, 'let's hope I can keep it going.'

As they walked off the *eighth green* Demyan had a rueful look at the hole but as he turned he noticed the church bell tower was now visible over the clubhouse and the trees. He kept walking and as they reached the *ninth tee* he had a clear view of the windows in the tower. A plan quickly formed in his mind. He had missed his first opportunity to strike but maybe this was a better one.

'George, you said you play here on Saturdays?'

'Yeah, but not this week. My wife's not well so I've got the kids. I'll be here on Wednesday.'

'Give me your number, George.'

'See me at the clubhouse. When does your holiday finish?'

'I'm on extended furlough and I like your course at Hoylake.'

Demyan was now focussed and *birdied* the narrow *ninth* while Hunter settled for a par. In the clubhouse, Hunter scribbled his phone number on the back of an old card and handed it over. 'You'd better give me yours, Marcus, in case I can't make it or things change with my wife.'

Without thinking, Demyan pulled out his phone and scrolled through the numbers before reading one out to Hunter who wrote it on the back of his scorecard.

'You don't know your number, Marcus?'

'It's a new Brit burner cell.'

Alarm bells clanged. 'What was it that Bill had said in the Swan when discussing the plaque on the bar? Blonde-ish with a funny accent sun tan an' all.'

~~~~~
~~~~~

CHAPTER 15

After storing his clubs Hunter went directly to their bedroom and although he knew he was alone he instinctively closed the curtains before he opened the wardrobe and getting down on his knees keyed in an eight-figure number into the floor safe hidden at the bottom. Lifting open the safe door he withdrew a bundle wrapped in oilcloth and two shoulder holsters before closing the safe again.

In the kitchen, he put the bundle down and unwrapped it to reveal two Glock 17 handguns. He knew Jacquie serviced hers regularly but he gave it a quick check. He filled and emptied the magazine twice to test the spring tension and its movement before loading it once more and clicking it into position on the gun. Satisfied, he flicked on the safety catch and pushed it to one side.

He then stripped the other weapon to its smallest moving part and with careful attention to detail he oiled and tested everything before reassembling it. He did the same exercise on the magazine taking extra care with the spring. Once loaded with one up the spout he fitted the holster under his right arm and after making minor adjustments for his weight gain he popped the gun in and checked that it was ideally positioned to enable an easy draw.

Although it would hinder his draw he settled for a sweater to disguise the weapon. It was a compromise he was prepared to make as it would look a little incongruous to wear a coat all night in the ward. Satisfied he put Jacquie's gun back in the safe and knowingly breaking the law he grabbed his leather jacket and as he went down the hall he touched the portrait and muttered, 'Someone's going to pay for this, lass,' before he drove to the Garden Centre to see Charlotte.

While driving he heard the local radio news announce that the Police were looking for two people in connection to a drive-by shooting of a local Garden Centre proprietor on the Wirral.

—

'Right, Charlotte, have you got those forms for me to sign? I hope it hasn't caused you too much hassle.'

'No, Mr Hunter, the bank was very good. They knew me for all the petty stuff I did for Jacquie... I mean, Mrs Hunter, and they just want your signature to authorise me to sign in her place.'

Hunter scribbled his name across three copies of a form and pushed them over the desk. 'That's it. Anything else?'

'Yes. The coffee franchise is going ahead as planned and the CEO of 'Golden Bloom' has sent his sympathies and said that they are willing to wait until the flak has died down. I shouldn't say this but I think he fancies her.'

'Why?'

'He wanted to know if it was okay to send flowers.'

'Charlotte, I've had to put up with that ever since I've known her and she uses it to her advantage. If there's nothing else I'll go and see my kids before I go to the hospital.'

'There was one more thing, Mr Hunter. The Police came and took our CCTV footage of that date.'

'Are you sure they were the Police?'

'He flashed a badge.'

'Next time insist on a closer look. It's your right.'

'Will do. One moment.' She left the office only to return seconds later with a large bunch of flowers. 'The staff had a whip-round so please give these to Jacquie with our best wishes and we hope she gets better soon.'

'Put them in some water for now and I'll pick them up on my way to the hospital later.'

—

'Daddy, Daddy,' Lesley shouted as she ran towards him and without any thought for her own safety jumped at him. He grabbed her as their bodies came into contact and spun her around giving her a big hug at the same time.

'Hello, baby! Wow, I've missed you. How are you?'

Unconcerned about mothers stood around with alarmed looks on their faces at this man holding a nine-year-old with his hands wrapped under her as she waived some papers in his face, and said, 'Look, look, I've been drawing. We had to draw pictures of our pets today and I've done Tess.' She held a crayon drawing in his face and before he could speak she pulled it away and replaced it with another. 'Do you like them, Dad?'

'That last one's not a pet.'

'No, Dad, silly, it's Henrietta.'

Hunter choked a little to be reminded of the short stories he had written for his children a few years ago when there was a tug on his jacket and he looked down to see Iain. He lowered Lesley to the floor and grabbed the lad. 'Come here, son, give us a hug.'

'Stop it, Dad, they're all looking.'

He tousled Iain's hair and said, 'Get away with you. What would you like to do?'

'Can we come home, Dad?'

He took them both by the hand and walked them to his car. 'Your Mum's very sick so until she comes out of hospital you're staying with your Auntie Kath.'

Lesley shook Hunter's arm. 'Can we go and see Mummy?'

'She's sleeping a lot and I'm going to stay with her again tonight but if everything's okay maybe Saturday.'

'Oh, goody, let's go to MacDonald's.'

'Can't do, Lesley, Auntie Kath has the tea on. We'll go to Costas for a fruit juice and a ginger biscuit. How's that?'

'You only want your coffee, Dad,' said Iain.

Hunter gave him a friendly shove as he held the car door open. 'You know too much, young man. Come on, get in.'

—

He had just finished putting the flowers in a vase when there was a knock on the ward door and he turned to see Gus Thomas poking his head around.

'Hi, Gus, come in.'

Thomas stepped in and spoke immediately. 'Hunter, can we have a little get together down the hall?'

'Is it just you?'

'No, I've got Simon with me.'

'Bring a chair in and we can talk here. Simon can chat with the uniform in the corridor.'

Gus nodded towards Jacquie. 'Is it okay?'

'No problem, Gus. If she butts in I'll have a word.'

Thomas left the room but he was sure he saw Jacquie blink. He returned moments later with a chair and placed it opposite Hunter's armchair.

'Okay, Gus, what is it? Before we start, do you want a coffee or something?'

'Wouldn't mind.'

Hunter stood up. 'Americano?'

Thomas nodded as Hunter went to the door and poked his head outside and acknowledged Simon before he spoke to the policewoman on duty. 'Would you like to exercise your legs? Me and the Inspector would like a coffee.'

She stood up and stretched. 'I'd love to,' she wafted the H & K slung across her body, 'what do I do with this?'

Simon intervened. 'I'll come with you. You can ward off any coffee snatchers.'

'But shouldn't somebody stay here?'

'Mr Thomas is armed so we'll be okay and if anyone says anything tell them he cleared it.'

Simon and the policewoman strolled off towards the lift while Hunter ducked back inside.

'Now, Gus, what is it? I thought the 'Firm' were finished on this case.'

'So did we but something came up. We followed up on Simon's report of a possible tail on you or Jacquie and found this character staying in a hotel nearby. We sent in an Agent to sus him and from her report and DNA sample we found that we have an International gun for hire on our patch.' He took out his smartphone and showed Hunter a photo. 'This is him.'

'Oh, Jeez!'

'What's up?'

Hunter tapped the screen. 'I played golf with him this morning and I think I'm right in saying he was asking questions around the Swan on Monday.'

'He's Demyan Orlov one of the top five known for hire sharpshooters in the world although he's been quiet for some time. He's Russian now domiciled in the U.S. and we've lost him. He sussed our trace and dumped his car and changed hotels. We're tracing the credit card he used to book the hotel but it looks like it was a one-off and he's probably paying cash now.'

There was a knock on the door and Simon came in with two coffees. 'Here you are, Guv, Mr Hunter.'

'Thanks, Simon,' said Thomas, 'I'd let you stay but they only allow two visitors.'

'Okay, Guv, I'm getting on fine with the hit squad out here.'

With that, he closed the door and Thomas continued. 'And now you mentioned he's been around you lately it has changed things. The more I look at this the more I think you're both targets.'

'What about Jacquie's hit?'

'The Fuzz know little more. Two people identified as a man and a woman were caught on CCTV boarding a Liverpool train at Capenhurst Station which is close by where the car was dumped and that's all.'

'Gus, two things.'

'Yes, Hunter?'

'One, I want my carrying permit back.'

'And two?'

'Before I retired I worked with a guy called Duncan Williams. Liverpool is his patch and he would fit in with no problem. I like to team up with him again.'

'This Health and Safety thing, Hunter, makes it a bit awkward. You haven't used for ten years.'

'Elf and Safety, crap! You're with the 'Firm' so don't give me that and if you think I haven't been practising you're in the wrong job.'

'Okay, I give in. I'll see what I can do. This, Williams, is he the guy that looks like Che Guevara?'

'Yep, that's him.'

'Oh! Him? He's a clever dick that one. He's married a Russian woman and speaks Slavic languages fluently now. He was working undercover in Belarus. I'll see what I can do. Why do you need him?'

'This thing with, Jacquie. I think it goes back to her Northern Ireland days. We were doing a job in 2001 looking for Williams when a couple of former IRA activists recognized her. We pulled them in and they did a short term inside but they may still be around and as Williams used to live there he could fit in and do some undercover snooping.'

Jacquie groaned in her enforced sleep and Hunter said, 'Was there something, Madam?'

She sighed and a brief smile crossed her lips.

'Do you think she's waking up?' said Gus.

'Nah, it's wind.'

'Right, Hunter, on that point I'll leave and I'll see what I can do. Aah! one more thing.' He pulled a folded piece of A4 from his inside pocket. 'On here are this months one a day phone numbers. Use them. They'll put you through to me and get a new 'Pay As You Go' SIM card while you're at it.'

They both stood and shook hands and Thomas left the room. Left to his own devices Hunter busied himself tidying things but Carrie had done a good job and there was little he could do. When he had finished, he said, 'What do you reckon, lass, and how do you like the flowers?'

He was sure she smiled as he leaned over and gave her a gentle kiss on the forehead.

—

'What does he mean 'He can't get near him?' The Voice said irritably.

Pat O'Hearne withheld the groan and replied, 'He says the Police are everywhere even when he spends his nights at the hospital.'

'Why's he at the hospital?'

'Cronin doesn't know but there are armed guards outside the room he stays in. Can you help on that one?'

'Are they there because of the first cock-up?'

'He doesn't think so. Since Wednesday morning Hunter is without an escort until he goes home where there is a police presence at the original crime scenes. Talking of which. Do they know where that bomb came from? It wasn't Cronin.'

'I'll look into it but meanwhile tell Cronin to pull his finger out this is costing money.'

'Okay, Boss.'

‘A word, Pat, before you go. Stay in Belfast. You were clocked on your last visits by MI5.’

The Voice rang off and Pat O’Hearne placed the phone gently on its cradle but that was not the way he was feeling. ‘He should try it,’ he muttered.

~~~~~
~~~~~

CHAPTER 16

Thursday

`C′ stood surveying Pall Mall from the top story room of Admiralty Arch. The dull grey sky courtesy of an inconsiderate late spring low-pressure area shedding fine drizzle over London did nothing to lighten his mood as he conjured with the problem that Gus Thomas had put before him. He rubbed his chin thoughtfully and then turned slowly to face Thomas who was waiting patiently on the other side of the extended mahogany table which stretched down the centre of the room.

'This, Hunter. Is he still '*compos mentis*?' By my reckoning he's sixty-eight. Is that correct?'

'Yes, sir, but a more *compos mentis* person you have never met and if there is a conspiracy against his family then I would rather have him on my team.'

'It was his wife who was shot?'

'Yes, she is known to us as Jacquie Riccardi or 'Agent Artemis' and the case so far is a peculiar set of circumstances. We think someone took a pot shot at him on the Saturday night. Overnight on Sunday, someone planted a bomb under her car and then the drive-by on Tuesday. Who was the bomb aimed at? We don't know. Are the incidents related? We don't know. They were both with the `Firm′ so it could be historical revenge targeting both of them or one of them and the Irish connection seems to be the most likely. How their cover was blown is another query? That's why I want him back rather than a loose cannon.'

'And you want, Williams?'

'Yes. They worked together back in 2001 and Williams knows Liverpool. He's also very dextrous if it comes to house-breaking.'

'You know what this means to our budget?'

'Yes.'

'I think this is a police thing or one for MI5 to look after.'

'The police are looking into the drive-by but it is the reason behind these incidents which needs to be sorted by us. 'Artemis' risked her life every day and worked for the 'Firm' out of our Lisburn office. We owe it to her. We can't give out medals but we can look after our own and 'Orion', that's Hunter, likewise.'

'Okay, sign him up expenses only. Williams is on holiday after his tour in Belarus and still lives in that area. Have you any leads?'

'Tentative at best. One of the worlds leading hitmen has been seen in the neighbourhood but he's been off the radar for some time and it may be a coincidence. MI5 tells us that Pat O'Hearne the ageing Belfast IRA Commander has visited Liverpool twice and has been seen in the company of known IRA sympathisers one of whom was Aiden Cronin who did time for a gun crime during the Williams investigation.'

'What was that?'

'Him and another guy recognised 'Artemis' and in their alcoholic stupor took a couple of pot shots at her.'

'Do you think it may be them?'

'There is no evidence yet but 5 are keeping an eye on them and the Police say that two people thought to be the leading suspects in the drive-by boarded a Liverpool train. They are checking CCTV from the intervening stations to see where they got off.'

'Good, keep me up to date.'

'And the leak, sir?'

'We'll call this 'Operation Magpie'. This is purely an internal op to find informants so we tell no one which includes the JIC, the Director General and the Home Secretary. Williams, Hunter and his wife will be known by their codenames. Hunter, that's 'Orion' will take over up there as local commander. You will work from here, Gus, and I'll put it out to the Registry guys that you are to have access to any files you want. You know, routine checking of procedures, that sort of stuff. Be a general pain in the you know where. In particular, you will keep tabs on all the Admin paperwork associated with 'Magpie'. Usual thing, copies given out, copies returned etc...'

'And Agent Bell?'

'Use him as your go-between.'

'One thing, sir. I think Hunter's code name is a bit dated. Let's use his alternative.'

'Which is?'

'Venator.'

'How did you know that?'

'He was my mentor once.'

—

Sean O'Reilly slammed the front door behind him and called down the hall.

'Have you heard anything, Karen?'

The disgruntled reply of a harassed housewife reverberated through the closed kitchen door. 'Stop shouting and come here.'

Sean hung his coat on top of the already overloaded coat hooks and muttering to himself went down the hall and into the kitchen.

'I said, woman, have you heard anything?'

'Oh, I see, I'm your woman now until you want something. Think again.'

Sensing he was on the losing end he changed his approach and said demurely. 'I'm sorry, hen, I've had a hard day at work and didn't mean it like that. Has there been any news?'

Karen stopped what she was doing and wiping her hands on a tea towel she looked at him. 'If you mean has there been any mention of the shooting, the answer's, Yes! But all they said is that they are looking for two people in connection with a drive-by nothing about a murder or death. What have you heard?'

'There's nothing in the daily's.'

'So we don't know if we got the double-crossing bitch.'

'We got her but we don't know how good.'

'Sean, we have to do something. Will Aiden know?'

'We can't tell him.'

'Why not?'

'If he gets picked up, Karen, it may lead them to us. I'll drive over tomorrow and see what's what. Can I have a cuppa?'

'The kettles there. I'm busy, and take your shoes off.'

Sean shrugged and walked back up the hall and kicked his shoes into the cupboard under the stairs before returning to the kitchen and filling the kettle.

'I suppose you want one?' he said.

—

Hunter tapped the red telephone symbol on the Bluetooth receptor and twisted round to face Iain and Lesley. 'I'm sorry, guys; you heard that. I've got to go to that meeting so no playground. I'll take you round to Auntie Kath's.'

'Can we come, Dad?' said Iain, 'it sounds exciting.'

'I would if I had my way but you can't have two adult men watching a kid's playground these days. Sorry, I'll take you another day if the weather stays fine, okay?'

Iain's face dropped. 'Okay, Dad, but it's not fair.'

—

Hunter took his jacket off and slung it over the back of a chair. 'Hi, Simon, why the bloody library?'

'They serve good coffee and when you leave you can carry a book. Have you got a Library Card?'

'Yeah, but I've not used it for years. Why do you need a clandestine meeting anyway?'

'We've upped the game, Mr Hunter or should I call you `Venator′ or Chief?'

'What do you mean, Simon?'

'You're back in the `Firm′. He bent down and pulled some documents from a briefcase under his chair and pushed them over to Hunter. 'Here's your SIS ID and permit to carry and an encrypted phone with a list of one-time burner numbers plus the bumf that goes with it and under the Service cover name of `Venator′ you are the Local Commander of 'Operation Magpie.' Agent `Ernesto′ will be joining you.'

'And who the bloody hell is `Ernesto′?'

'Known to you as, Williams, his contact details are here.' He separated a small sheet of notepaper from the rest and continued, 'Silly question, do you need weapons?'

Hunter leaned forward and raised his hand to the side of his mouth. 'Between you and me, No!'

'After the chat, I had with Mrs Hunter I didn't think so. She will also be referred to internally by her pseudonym 'Artemis'.'

'Simon, am I getting paid for this?'

'Expenses only.'

'That's big of them. Okay, now explain what's changed?'

'You know about Orlov. He came into the country under the name of Dimitrov but after our initial contact he's dropped off the radar...'

'...Except to play golf with me.'

'Yep! We're not sure what he's doing here. He may be just on a golfing holiday but he's still high on the international watch list which may account for Saturday but our main line of enquiry is the historical Irish connection of both you and Mrs Hunter and who tipped them off?'

'Where are the police or 5 in this?'

'The police have their own line of enquiry with the drive-by and 'C' is organising 5 and SIS to work together on this. It's an internal job and we're looking out for our own. There is a downside, however.'

'Oh, aye, and what's that?'

'Everything will be a bit OTT. Like the use of codenames, long phone calls, paperwork, that sort of thing.'

'Why?'

''Operation Magpie' is not only to find who's after you but to try and unearth the mole who is passing on your info.'

'Right, Simon, leave it there. I'm going to grab some dinner before I go to the hospital and now I'm official I can avoid those outrageous parking charges.'

'I'd keep that quiet.'

—

Hunter flashed his ID to the Officer in the corridor who jumped up and held his hand up to stop him. 'I wouldn't go in just yet, sir, the Doctors in there with her entourage.'

'Any idea why?'

'No, but there was no panic so I think it's okay.'

'Thanks, officer, I'll stick my head in anyway and see what's what.'

He eased the door open slightly and peeked in only to push it wider and enter as he saw Jacquie being propped up under the supervision of Doctor Mrs Wearne who looked around to see who was entering her domain. 'Aah, Mr Hunter, just in time. Mrs Hunter is doing so well I've decided to remove her sedation early. She is still drowsy and will fall asleep on and off for quite some time. Are you staying tonight?'

'I certainly am.'

'Good. Just make sure she is well hydrated but the staff will be in regularly to make sure she's okay and she's still hooked up to the monitor. There has been a request to move her to a safer place but I won't allow it at this moment.'

'Who was it?'

'A Senior Agent Thomas. SIS or something.'

'He's good.'

'I'll leave you to it then.'

Carrie was sat quietly in the corner with a look of relief on her face and she smiled at Hunter as the medics left. 'Good news, Mr Hunter?'

He looked at Jacquie who was fast asleep resting on a stack of pillows. 'Hi, Carrie. Yes, it certainly looks that way. I'm sorry I'm late but things have changed and I got called to a meeting. You shoot off home and I'll see you in the morning.'

Carrie scooped her things up and with an affectionate touch of Jacquie's hand she left the room leaving Hunter to drag the chair nearer the bed and prepare himself for a long night but it was not to be as he had no sooner settled when his burner phone vibrated.

'Shit, who is it this time of day?

He dug deep into his jacket pocket and retrieved the phone and groaned inwardly as he saw who it was. 'Williams, your bloody timing is immaculate.'

He glanced at Jacquie and seeing she was still asleep he left the room but stood in the corridor with the door slightly open where he could watch her.

Biting his lip he answered like a man glad to hear from an old pal. 'Hi, Duncan, lad, how are ya! Long time no see.'

Duncan with his usual indifference to seniority replied. 'I'm well, you old git, how are you?'

'Things could be better. What can I do for you?'

'I'm outside your place. Where are you?'

'Countess of Chester Hospital.'

'Are you coming home?'

'No! Make your way here and ask for the High Dependency unit.'

'Why's that?'

'Don't ask, just come.'

'On my way.'

—

Hunter sat opposite Williams who had discarded the 1970's hair style that gave him his codename for a modern shorter fashion.

'Here's the how of it, Dunc, lad. Over the last weekend there were three goes at me...' and pointing '...and Jacquie there, one of which was nearly successful. There are two lines of enquiry. One is the Irish connection involving that Liverpool enclave we bumped into in 2001 and the other is a rogue gun for hire out to get me.'

'First thing, Guv, stop calling me, lad. I'm nearly bloody forty now with a family.'

Hunter raised his hand in acknowledgement. 'I'm sorry, old habits.'

'Okay, now the problem. Do you know why?'

'No; the theory is that its historical tit for tat.'

'And our top gun. What about him. That doesn't fit the bill. Nobody would pay that sort of money just for revenge.'

'That's what I thought. While I follow up on our top gun I want you, Dunc, la... to go back to your old haunts and dig around. Speak to MI5 and see what they've dug up and...' he gave Duncan a piece of paper, 'this is the contact details of DI Fearn the Police Inspector in charge of the drive-by job. Work closely with them.'

'That's handy, my sister lives in Mum's old place.'

'That'll help a lot. How's your wife and you said you had a family.'

'We live up the Wirral and Tanya now speaks better English

than I do and still works as an interpreter. She's taught me Russian and other connected languages and we have two bi-lingual kids, a girl and a boy who both take after their mother...'

Hunter laughed. 'Ha...! At least they've got one thing going for them.'

'Cheeky bastard.' Jacquie let out a quiet groan and Duncan looked across at her. 'Is she checking on me?'

Knowing the past working relationship between Williams and Jacquie he quipped, 'Yep, she's a bit fussy who I mix with.'

'On that note, 'Agent Venator', sir, I'm leaving.' He stood and nodded towards Jacquie, and said, 'Ma'am,' as he went to leave. By the door, he stopped and looked at her again. 'I'm sure she giggled.'

He closed the door behind him while shaking his head.

Checking Jacquie was okay Hunter left her sleeping and spoke to the armed uniform on watch. 'I'm going for some coffee, do you want one?'

'Yes, please.'

'Black or white?'

'Latte, please.'

He continued down to the hospital restaurant and when he returned he gave the uniform his latte. 'Here we are, son, get that down you. What time do you finish?'

'Ten o'clock. How is she?'

'The Doc tells me she's doing better than expected and they've stopped her sedation which means she'll be back to her bossy best in no time at all.'

'That's great, Guv. Can I ask you something?'

'Yep, go ahead.'

'There's some speculation amongst the squad about why we're here. Who is she?'

'I can't reveal who she is but suffice to say that some years ago she did a very dangerous undercover job for her country. We owe her.'

'Is that why she got shot?'

'We think so but it's early days.'

'She's your wife, right?'

'Yep!'

'I'm sorry, Guv, I hope she pulls through okay. I'll tell the gang.'

'Thanks. I've gotta go in now. She'll be giving me earache if I'm not there when she wakes up and I bet you a Mars bar she asks for a coffee.'

He pushed the door open and as he stepped into the room Jacquie opened her eyes. 'Hunter, where the hell have you been, I need caffeine.'

He turned around and poked his head around the door and said, 'You owe me a Mars, pal,' before he nipped over to Jacquie, kissed her and straightened her pillows.

'I don't know if I can give you one,' he said, 'a coffee I mean.'

'Trust you,' she said with a giggle, 'give me some of yours.'

Resigned he handed over his drink. She took a few sips and sat back. 'That's my fix, have you got any chocolate?'

'Charlotte and your gang sent some with those flowers. Do you think you should?'

'Hunter, I've got a hole in my leg, not my stomach.'

He looked anxiously at the drips in her arm and the monitor, shrugged, and taking a bar of her favourite chocolate from the bedside table broke off two squares and gave them to her. When she had devoured them hungrily she stretched, and said, 'Hunter, can you crank up the back of this bed a bit more?'

She leaned forward and he eased the backrest up one notch and straightened her pillows. When he had finished Jacquie pushed herself upright and winced. She ignored the searing pain in her ribs, and said, 'Tell me, Hunter...?'

'...What, lass?'

'Everything.'

He gave her a quick run down of events over the last few days and told her of the arrangements he had made with the business and finished '...and that's that. I'm back on ops and in control.'

'Huh, that's you all over.'

'Hey, watch it. I'll set Duncan on you.'

'Huh,' she chuckled, wincing as she did so, 'a bit of young

blood.'

'It's a good job you're tied up to that thing or I'd show you.'

'Showing is no good, Hunter, I want the real deal.'

'You'll have to wait.'

'I will, and then you'll have to be very inventive.'

'What the hell are they putting in those drips.'

She laughed and clutched her ribcage. 'Enough. What are you going to do about your shooter?'

'There's nothing wrong with it. Oh, you mean the shooter?'

She choked and winced. 'H, you have a one-track mind.'

He knew from experience how much damaged ribs hurt and sympathised as he continued, 'I have a half promise of a return golf match a week on Saturday morning so I'm thinking, 'Why not this week? I'll ask Kath to keep the kids while I try tempting him out and I'll bring Iain and Lesley here on Saturday afternoon.'

'I don't mind a bit, Hunter, but don't put too much on Kath.'

'I don't, I pick the kids up and when I can't I arrange for a taxi so that Kath doesn't have to do the school run. She's down on my expenses as a carer.'

'I feel drowsy, H. Ease me back again and I'll shut my eyes for a few minutes.'

'Okay.'

As he lowered the bed he saw that she was already asleep.

~~~~~
~~~~~

CHAPTER 17

Friday

Hunter turned right out of the lane leading to his house and drove north on the main road. He took little notice of the nondescript silver car that turned into the lane his mind was on formulating a plan to bring the perpetrators out in the open. When he arrived at Hooton train Station on the Mersey Rail Line he thought eighty-pence was a fair price for parking all day and left his car in the only slot available at the top end of the car park and sauntered the length of the car park to the exit where the attendant sat patiently bored in his booth.

Hunter flashed his I.D. and said, 'Are you here all day, mate?'

'I surely am.'

Taking ten pounds from his wallet and pointing to his car, Hunter said, 'See that car? I want you to keep a special eye on it and let me know if anyone goes near it. Have you got a mobile phone?'

'Yep, sure do.'

'With a camera?'

'Better still.' He pointed upwards. 'I've got CCTV on the roof.'

Hunter handed over the money. 'I'm not expecting anyone but you never know.'

'Okay, Guv. Anything to boost my pension.'

'Hunter tapped him on the shoulder. 'Cheers, mate, see you in a few hours.'

—

Andy Roberts was taking a brief look at the weather from his front room window when the silver Ford car coasted past his house and moments later he saw it again as it returned up the hill and slowed noticeably when passing the Hunter bungalow. His instinct told him to take its number but he only managed the first two letters before it disappeared behind the walls and hedges surrounding his neighbour's gardens, nevertheless, he went into the kitchen to scribble them down on a piece of scrap paper when something triggered a memory. What did he do with that number he had noted a week ago?

He looked in the kitchen draws under the work surface and on the magnetic note board, his daughter had installed before thumping the work surface in disgust and knocking his pillbox onto the floor which jogged his memory. His notebook. He picked it up and searched the recent pages and found the number and muttered as he added the first two letters from the silver car, 'I must tell George about that Irishman who came to look at the house.'

At the top of the lane, the car did a left turn out to the main road and drove south until it came to 'Garden Aspects №1' and parked in the lay-by opposite where the drive-by had taken place.

The driver made a call on his mobile before driving across and into the Garden Centre car park. He pulled up alongside the maroon Range Rover Sport and pretended to admire it before walking into the centre and through to the restaurant where he was greeted by Charlotte and a member of staff.

'Good morning, sir,' said Charlotte, 'and congratulations. We are holding a coffee tasting of our new range.' She handed him a form. 'Fill that in and you will go into our prize draw for a holiday in Cuba.'

He took it and answered in his Liverpool Irish brogue, 'Err, thanks, where do I hand it in?'

'Give it to the cashier when you pay. Thank you and enjoy.'

'Err, thank you, miss.'

He studied the form as he walked to the counter and the food array before him made him hungry and ignoring the fact he'd had breakfast earlier he ordered a bacon baguette with his coffee and paid with his debit card before finding a seat where he could watch the office door at the same time fill his form in.

While eating he also read a daily newspaper which was provided free for the clients but after thirty minutes he left and gave his form to the cashier on the way out.

—

The Mersey Rail train to Liverpool was crowded which suited

Hunter as he stood close to one of the doors nonchalantly hanging onto an overhead strap. When the train pulled into the Birkenhead Central interchange he waited until the warning two bell chimes indicated the doors were about to close before darting off as the doors swished shut behind him. Glancing left and right he checked to see if anyone had responded in the same manner and as the train pulled away he double-checked to see if anyone was looking at closed doors in desperation as they swept past.

He only had three minutes to wait for the next train under the River Mersey and when he alighted at Lime Street Station he mingled with other commuters but first, he did the meaningless and now discarded ruse of checking his footwear while sussing those around him and a little later he pretended to check his mobile phone for a signal.

Outside the Station, he called a cab and hoping that a certain pub had not changed its name he directed the driver to take him to the 'Red Lion' on the riverbank on the outskirts of Aigburth. After a quick pint of refreshment, he set off on the mile uphill walk up to the main road and the centre of the suburb.

The area close to Duncan's sister's house hadn't changed much and breathing heavily after the long climb he took his time buying a newspaper while furtively looking about for anyone following. Satisfied it was all clear he wandered off in the direction of Ermine Road.

He stopped on the corner and took a piece of paper from his wallet and studied the place name on the end house before turning up the street and going to N°12. Still holding the piece of paper he knocked on the door which was answered by a neat buxom woman of short stature. After a brief exchange, she stood to one side and invited him in.

As she closed the door behind them Duncan came out of the living room. 'Morning, H, what brings you here and more to the point, 'how's the missies?''

'When I left her this morning, Dunc, she was as bolshie as ever and after you've fixed me up with a cuppa we'll chat about the job.'

He had no sooner lifted his tea to his lips when his internal burner phone buzzed. He put the mug down and took the phone from his inside pocket and without checking who was calling said, 'Hunter!'

A muffled voice spoke for about thirty seconds before he said, 'Okay, got that.'

The voice continued and Hunter interrupted, '...I'm with Williams now,' and then he switched off and threw the phone onto the dining table.

Duncan was surprised by the demonstration of frustration by Hunter. 'What's up, H?'

'This Op, Duncan is doing two things,...' he went on to explain 'Operation Magpie', '...and that last call was part of it. You're lucky, you are only known by your codename and only a couple of people know who you are. By that I mean they don't know what you look like which could be a bonus for them I suppose.'

The dry humour went over Duncan's head and Hunter continued, 'Now tell me how's the lie of the land?'

'I only got here this morning, H. Let's go to the pub for a pint and sus it out.'

'No can do, they know what I look like. Anything else?'

'I've told sis to spread the story I've been away in the Army and I'm looking for work. I shall be integrating myself into the community starting this lunchtime. Are you sure you won't come?'

'Yep! See me out and shake my hand and I'll give you my business card. What number bus to town?'

'I'll check with sis.' He left the room and returned almost immediately. 'It's the 60.'

—

Hunter relived his childhood and headed for the empty front seat on the top deck of the shiny new double-decker bus for the trip to the City Centre and after a short walk from the Bus Station to Lime Street train station, he caught the Mersey Rail connection back to Hooton. The car park was a hundred metres away and he waited until the other commuters had cleared before approaching the kiosk. 'How did it go, mate?' he said to the attendant.

'Oh, Hi, Guv, you were right someone did look over your car

and a right plonker he looked too. He had them camouflage trousers and one of those hunters type gilet things with all the pockets and topped that lot off with one of those American military peak caps. I bet he's never been near the army. I've got it all on video.' He rummaged under the shelf by his window and pulled out a CD. 'Here we are, Guv. Can I have it back soonest?'

Hunter took it off him. 'I'll try and get it back tomorrow. What's your name?'

'Albert, Guv.'

'You mentioned pension, Albert. You're old enough to be retired methinks?'

'Right again, Guv, but I lost my wife four years ago so I thought I may as well sit here all day and get paid as mope at home all lonely like. I've got me little TV and a radio and I get to chat with the likes of you.'

Hunter slipped him another ten pounds. 'Take care, Albert. I'll see you soon.'

—

On the drive leading up to the front door of their bungalow, Hunter stooped and did a check all around the underside of his car until he found what he was looking for attached to the exhaust bracket. A GPS tracking device. 'I thought so,' he muttered, 'we'll leave it there a little longer.'

Indoors he switched on the CD player and after fiddling with the remote he played the video which revealed nothing of value as the man's features were shaded by the cap. He switched it off and reached for the landline phone when he remembered his encrypted burner phone.

He pressed the Contact App and called D.I. Fearn who was reluctant to answer and when he did he was curt and to the point. 'Who is it and what is it?'

'And a nice day to you, Inspector, it's Venator.'

'And who the hell is that?'

'Does the name Hunter ring a bell?'

'Yes, Mr Hunter, what can I do for you?'

'Inspector, I have a CCTV video I want examined. Can your guys do it?'

'Is it to do with the shooting?'

'No, but it is to do with 'Magpie.' As Local Commander, I'm informed we're working together on this.'

Fearn's manner changed abruptly. 'Oh...Oh...! I'm sorry, Mr Hunter, Venator, whatever. I'm up to my neck with these anti-fracking demonstrators and I forgot.'

'Okay, Inspector, can someone check out this video, we may have an I.D.'

'Are you at home, Mr Hunter?'

'Yes.'

'I'll get SOCO to pick it up soonest and by the way, we have withdrawn the police watch on your house as we've done all we can there.'

'I noticed. What about, Carrie?'

'She's staying on attachment with you.'

'Thanks, Inspector. Oh, one more thing. Any news on the drive-by people?'

He could hear papers being shuffled over the phone before Fearn answered. 'Yes, they picked them up on CCTV at Lime Street station and again at the bus station as they walked through but they disappeared into the '*Liverpool One'* Shopping Precinct.'

Hunter rang off and took the piece of his old scorecard out of his wallet and tapped the number Demyan had given him into his phone. 'Let's see if we can get you out in the open, Mr Orlov or whoever you are.'

He let it ring five times before cutting the call and swapping it for his personal un-encrypted phone he tried again. Demyan answered after three rings.

'Hello!'

'George Hunter, here, is that you, Marcus?'

'Err, yes.'

'Good, I'm free in the morning can you make it for our return match say, nine o'clock at the Clubhouse.'

'One moment, I'll check my schedule.' The connection went quiet and Hunter could hear bleeps in the background as Demyan checked his i-pad diary before he answered. 'Yes, I'm free and I will be pleased to give you a round of nine holes or eighteen?'

'Eighteen, Marcus.'

'Good, see you at nine o'clock.'

Hunter put his phone down and began busying himself preparing for the night's vigil at the hospital while Demyan put his phone on the table in his hotel room and studied it thoughtfully mentally planning his course of action for the coming morning.

—

Hunter pushed the door to the ward gently in case Jacquie was asleep and was surprised to hear her laughing and chattering on her smartphone, 'Okay, darling, I'll see you tomorrow put Iain on.'

She looked up at Hunter and waived as she continued, 'Hello, Iain, are you behaving yourself?' She paused for a moment and then laughed. 'I believe you. Your Dad's just come in do you want to speak to him?'

Hunter could hear Iain talking but Jacquie let him speak for a little while before she interrupted him, 'Your Dad is working, Iain, he can't just pop around anytime as he did before...' she paused while Iain said a few words, '...for the Police. You know mummy had an accident, well he's helping to find the people who did it. You're coming tomorrow so I'll try and make sure he's here also.'

As the conversation continued Carrie gathered her things and acknowledging Hunter she left. It was a few more minutes before Jacquie said, 'Okay, darling, see you tomorrow. Love you, and lots of hugs, bye, bye.'

She put the phone down on the movable cross bed table and wiped away a wayward tear with the back of her hand. Hunter pushed the table to one side and leaned over and kissed her. 'Hi, lass, that sounds like I'm in trouble.'

'You're always in trouble, H. Have you been told?'

'I'm the last one to get told. What, exactly?'

Jacquie pushed herself up on the pillows. 'They're moving me.'

'Do you know where?'

'No.'

'I hope it's somewhere the kids can get to see you.'

Jacquie's hand went to her mouth, 'Oh, dear, I hadn't thought of that.'

There was a knock on the door and the Catering Assistant a jolly buxom lady of Afro-Caribbean descent poked her head around the door. 'Sorry, miss, you've got company do you want dinner later?'

'Oh, no, I'm starving. My husbands going to the restaurant.'

'Okay, miss, give me a minute.'

She closed the door behind her and Jacquie spoke to Hunter. 'Bring a bar of dark chocolate back with you, H.'

Hunter saluted and gave her a quick peck and left just as the Catering assistant came in with Jacquie's meal. 'Here're, love.' She put the tray on the movable table and pushed it across the bed. 'You said you were hungry so I've put a little extra on.'

'Thank you,' said, Jacquie, 'it smells delicious. Have you got any red wine?'

'Nah, miss, the meanies left it off the menu.' They laughed together and Jacquie clutched her ribs. 'Ooh, are you okay, miss?'

Jacquie grimaced as she straightened up. 'Yes, it's just my ribs, I shouldn't laugh.'

'You had me worried for a sec. You take care now and I'll see you soon.'

She left the room closing the door quietly behind her.

—

At ten p.m. there was a knock on the door and a porter and a nurse accompanied by two paramedics came in wheeling an ambulance trolley. 'Good evening, Mrs Hunter, your time has come. Are you ready?'

'As I'll ever be. Where are you taking me?'

'Haven't they told you,' said one of the paramedics, 'you're going to the other side of town to the Muirfield Private hospital.'

'Oh, that's okay,' said Jacquie, 'I was worried it would be out in the sticks where my children couldn't make it.'

'I'll call, Kath,' chipped in Hunter.

He left the room to give them space as they gathered Jacquie's things, transferred her drips to the trolley and fitted her up to a portable monitor and ten minutes later lying down with covers up to her neck and wearing a sleeping mask they wheeled her out with the police guard following and took her to the lift.

On the ground floor they pushed her out through the A & E entrance into a waiting ambulance and quietly without ceremony they drove into the night. Hunter walked to his car and after removing the tracking device and placing it in a metal anti-Wi-Fi container he called the Hospital Security on the two-way speaker at the car park exit. 'Agent Hunter leaving car park `A′.'

The barrier raised with a swish and he left the Countess of Chester Hospital mentally thanking them for saving his wife.

Meanwhile, Simon Bell pressed 'send' on his mobile phone and threw it onto the table. Denying himself the pleasure and the stimulation of a stiff whisky he stripped to his birthday suit and proud of his physique and with a hint of despair he strolled uninhibited to the shower room to wash away his inner feelings.

—

Sean O'Reilly plonked his glass down with an angry thump. 'I'm telling you, Karen, I got her, I couldn't miss.'

'But you've seen her car at the Garden Centre so she's back at work.'

'Looks like it.'

'It was her car?'

'Yes, I checked the number.'

'Okay, what are we going to do about it?'

Just then they were joined by Aiden Cronin and Naomi and as they sat down, Aiden said, 'Are we interrupting something?'

Sean shook his head. 'Nah, I thought I'd done a job but I'm not so sure anymore.'

'Sign of old age, mate. What are you having?'

Duncan now with a three days growth of beard played with his smartphone while he watched from across the room and although he had identified Cronin and O'Reilly from the incident ten years previous he had no proof as yet that there was any connection with the current situation. It was time to get to know them better. As Aiden approached the bar Duncan got up from his seat and followed him.

He hung back until Aiden paid and turned from the bar with the drinks in both hands. Duncan stumbled as he stepped forward and knocked Aiden's arm spilling some of the liquid nectar onto the carpet. 'You stupid bastard,' cursed Aiden, 'watch where you're going.'

Duncan answered in his best Scouse accent. 'Whoa, sorry, pal. I stubbed my toe. Here let me get you another.'

Aiden, not one to miss a freebie softened his stance. 'Okay, let me take these over to the table.'

'Right oh! What're ya havin'?'

'Guinness.'

'Okay.'

Duncan turned to the bar and catching the bar girls eye ordered the Guinness and a pint of Beck's beer for himself and as she placed the drinks on the bar Aiden rejoined him. Duncan gave him his Guinness and raised his glass and shoved out his hand. 'I'm Duncan. Cheers, mate, sorry for the boo-boo.'

They shook hands, 'Aye, okay, I'm Aiden, have I seen you before?'

'I used to live around here but I've been away in the Army. I'm staying with my sister while I look for work.'

'What do you do?'

Duncan shrugged. 'Anything and everything. You don't get to learn much as a Para.'

Aiden took more interest at the mention of the Parachute Regiment. 'Did you like it?' he said, 'the Para's I mean.'

Duncan shook his head and mentally apologised to the Regiment. 'Nah, the equipment was crap, the weapons were rubbish and don't mention the food. That's why I left. If they weren't going to look after me I wasn't going to put my life on the line. Two tours in Afghanistan did me.'

'You look a bit old for the Army, Dunc.'

'I joined late. I was a REME Para and joined the Pathfinders as a team mechanic.'

'You know vehicles then?'

'Yeah, a bit.'

'Look, pal, I've gotta join me, missies. I'll ask my mate if he knows anything. See you around.'

Duncan studied his beer as Aiden walked across to join Naomi and the O'Reilly's and as if he'd made a momentous decision he emptied his glass in one swallow and left the pub.

~~~~~
~~~~~

CHAPTER 18

Saturday

Five a.m. and it was still quiet in the village of Sutton and although there were occasional cars up and down the main arterial road nobody paid any attention to Demyan making his way through the churchyard from the side entrance close to the Golf Club car park.

At the Church wall, he stopped and took shelter behind a stone stanchion while he listened and watched for a few minutes before sidling along the wall to a side entrance of the Church. He put his Golf bag down and took a set of large skeleton keys from a pouch on the side and thanked the local clergy for lubricating the two-hundred-year-old mechanism. In a few seconds the lock clicked over and Demyan eased it open. Once again he said a silent thank you for the oiled hinges and he picked up his bag and slid inside closing the door gently behind him. He left it unlocked and waited only for a few moments before he tip-toed along the wall towards an alcove midway down.

He entered and saw the door which led to the steps up to the bell tower. Although nineteenth-century the narrow winding stairs were built in the historical tight clockwise direction and it was difficult to grip his bag and hold onto the fraying rope which had replaced the handrail.

He struggled onto a landing only to be faced with a tall metal stepladder. He climbed up it and pushed open a heavy wooden hatch and with unseemly wriggling dragged himself through with a final flop into a dusty gloom. His eyes became adjusted to the murky light and he saw a low doorway unseen from the outside which led out to a rooftop space about the size of a tabletop. This unexpected bonus provided a panoramic view over the golf course.

He took a swig of water and sat for five minutes regaining his composure and then making sure to keep below the low parapet prepared himself and his weapon for a long vigil.

—

Hunter wandered down to the kitchen and while the kettle boiled he habitually laid out two cereal bowls and two cups and then mentally admonished himself for doing so.

When he had finished his breakfast he went to the bathroom to shower and shave as he did every morning and then through to the bedroom to get dressed. He thought about his shoulder holster and decided against it as it would hinder his swing and putting a gun down the back of his trousers was uncomfortable so he reluctantly left it in the bottom drawer of his bedside locker. He put on a white shirt and a pair of Sandhurst red corduroy trousers and was about to put on a yellow sweater when he had second thoughts and went to his office to dig something out from the top shelf of a cupboard before returning for the sweater.

A few moments later he declared himself ready and as he went down the hall he touched Jacquie's portrait before he went out to his car. He threw the GPS Tracker nonchalantly onto the passenger seat to ping away its message – 'I am here!'

He stopped to pick up a newspaper and at ten minutes to nine a.m. he pulled up outside the Clubhouse. As he took his clubs from the car boot he placed the GPS tracker in a side pocket of the bag, grabbed his shoes and strolled across to the entrance but he could see no sign of Marcus (Demyan). He changed and waited in the Players lounge and watched as other players went ahead of him after his allotted time slot had passed. He was about to give up when his personal mobile rang.

'Hello?'

'Mr Hunter, it's Marcus. I can't make it, something's come up. Can we fix it for mid-week? I'm sure you'll find someone else to knock around with today.'

'I was just about to go home, Marcus, but now you mention it I'll hang around. I'll call you about a re-match.'

'Thanks, Mr Hunter.'

He rang off abruptly.

As Hunter switched off his mobile a tall athletic young couple entered and he wasted no time. 'Good morning. Are you two playing for real or would you mind making a threesome with an old man?'

The young man was the first to speak. 'That's okay, we just come for a knock around and the fresh air. You can join us sure. The names Jeff and my partner is Sherrie.'

Hunter held his hand out. 'Nice to meet you, Jeff and Sherrie. Let's go, I'll buy the drinks at the fifth.'

They waited five minutes swapping small talk before the Club Steward let them out and after winning the toss Hunter teed off.

They played off the Men's 'Yellow' tees and Sherrie with a slight disadvantage on the long holes made up for it on the *Par 3 fourth*, *fifth* and *sixth* holes and she was two up at the end of the *sixth*. The *seventh* they tied on Par and being gentlemen Hunter and Jeff allowed Sherrie to tee off for the *eighth*.

It might be an excuse to get fresh air but she was having none of it. She was out to win and played a slam dunk tee shot right down the middle which left her a chip shot to the flag. Jeff 's ball was a little ahead of her but on the edge of the rough on the left side of the fairway. Not to be outdone, with equal determination Hunter lined himself up and using his sniper technique he took a deep breath, let it out, held it, and played his shot with too much effort. He watched with dismay as the ball drifted off to the right and into the bunker short of the green.

'Shit,' he muttered, 'should have played safe?'

Being farthest from the hole Hunter went first. With his *sand iron,* he played too carefully and dropped the ball on the front edge of the green. He raked over the sand in the bunker and climbed out and took a few steps towards the green. He stopped a couple of metres short and to the right of Sherrie and waited while she played her shot.

She did a few practice swings with her *pitching wedge*, stepped forward and with a glance towards the flag began to play her shot and then gasped as in her peripheral vision she saw Hunter lifted bodily off his feet and thrown backwards and sideways to the ground and milliseconds later she heard the shot.

Sherrie screamed and Jeff shouted, 'Fuckin' Hell! What was that?'

They dropped their clubs and dashed towards Hunter. As they ran Sherrie shouted, 'Jeff, call for the Police and Ambulance!'

He doubled back and cursed as he fumbled trying to get his smartphone from the side pocket of his bag and hit the emergency app.

—

Demyan, having already taken up the first pressure on the trigger watched the action through the telescopic sights on his rifle and cursed in disbelief as Hunter dropped and the sound of the shot reached him. He looked down towards the copse on his left and saw a thin wisp of pale blue smoke coming from the trees and dispersing on the breeze and moments later he detected a figure stooping low moving away from the golf course through the trees. Demyan didn't think twice.

'The bastard's trying to steal my payday.'

Watching his quarry through the sights he tracked the figure as it hurriedly moved through the undergrowth until there was one brief moment when the cover wasn't thick enough. With more hope than certainty Demyan snapped off a quick shot and saw the figure stumble but recover enough to stagger deeper into the woods.

There was no time to think about recrimination. He had to get out of there. He disassembled the rifle and when it was safely stored he made his difficult and treacherous way to ground level.

He negotiated the ladder and trapdoor with little trouble and eased himself into the alcove and silently closed the door behind him and hearing elderly female voices in the church he hugged the wall and listened.

'The weather's nice today, Elsie.'

'Aye, you're right, Betty, and that nice Scottish lady on the tele says it's gonna be good for a couple of days.'

'Oh, do you watch her?'

'Yes, isn't she nice?'

'Yes, but those dresses she wears are too tight.'

'Get on with it,' muttered Demyan.

'Betty, there's a funeral today, can you help me with the flowers before you start cleaning?'

'Of course, I love doing the flowers.'

Demyan breathed a sigh of relief as the dedicated Church volunteers chatting amiably walked down the centre aisle and into the vestry. Keeping close to the wall he slid along to the side exit door and easing it open he slipped out into the graveyard. Once more he paused in the shelter of a stanchion and checked his escape route, before, with measured nonchalance he strolled down the pathway and out of the side gate and across to where his vehicle was parked in the Golf Club car park. He didn't look left or right and with casual deliberation, he threw his bag into the boot before climbing in and driving off.

~~~~~
~~~~~

CHAPTER 19

Aiden got to the edge of the wood and the fence that separated it from the fields and found the gap he had made earlier. Cursing he dragged the gun and the carrying case through and slumped down in the meadow with his back against the hedge. With painful difficulty he wriggled out of his jacket and then pulled a handkerchief from his pocket and rolling it diagonally he pressed it against the bleeding gunshot wound in his arm and holding it in place with his chin he tied it single-handed covering both the entry and the exit wounds.

It was the best he could do and he cursed many times as he struggled to put his jacket on. He heard the alarm sirens of approaching emergency vehicles but still took some time to put the gun in its carrying case before leaning back against a fence post to consider his situation.

'Has that bastard got a bloody guardian angel? The first time I miss him and now this.'

He looked up and down the field and considered his options. Should he go west along the back of the church and try to get to his car parked in a residential cul-de-sac on the other side of the main road or should he keep to the edge of the golf course and go east towards the **M56** Motorway and call Sean, but first he had to ditch his gun. A hundred metres to his right he could see the trees thinned as the wood curved to the north and the wire fencing slung between trees. A safety fence which he guessed must be a pond.

He half crawled and half-ran doubled low down to the pond and searching around found a hollow under a tree root on the edge just above the water line. He shoved the weapon in as far as it would go and then threw some soil and broken twigs over it and satisfied he had done enough to conceal it he doubled back up the field and continued west up to the main road where he halted to assess his position.

After a few minutes, he decided they would never think of

looking for him in plain sight so he crawled along the perimeter hedge to a gate and when the traffic eased he went through the gate and crossed the main road to a bus stop ironically outside 'Garden Aspects №2' Proprietor: J Riccardi.

—

The bus driver looked at Aiden with some concern. 'Are you okay, mate? There's blood all down your arm?'

'Aye, I was fishing for lost golf balls and got caught on some barbed wire.'

'Sit down, mate. There's an NHS drop-in clinic down the road. I'll let you off there.'

'That would be good.'

Forcing himself upright he walked slowly to the first seat available and dropped into it with his injured arm pressing against the side of the bus. Five minutes later the driver called to him and pointed over to the left. 'There you are, matey, just over there.'

Aiden got up from his seat and doing his utmost not to look distressed acknowledged the driver and got off the bus and began walking towards the clinic. When the bus had moved off Aiden returned to the bus stop and plopped down on the narrow plastic bench. He had to reach across his body with his good arm with some difficulty but managed to retrieve his smartphone and call Sean.

—

'Getting shot seems to run in the family, Mr Hunter.'

Dr Isobel Wearne stood patiently by the bed as Hunter squirmed and then winced as he took a breath.

'We don't do it on purpose, Doc.'

She smiled. 'I know, and luckily for you, you were prepared for it. Without that extra body armour, you'd be dead. As it is you have severely bruised ribs and a mild concussion so we'll keep you in overnight. I see you have a few scars in that area already.'

'The story of my life and like I said, the scars are a running joke between us, Doc. Whenever I got injured during my service it always seemed to be my ribcage that got it but that's bye the bye. Can't I leave now? I want to see my kids and Jacquie and I'm supposed to see them at the Muirfield today.'

'Don't worry, Mr Hunter, you will. They'll be along to see you later.'

'Have they released her?'

'You're in the Muirfield and I see you've been here before.'

'A couple of years ago when I had my hip replacement.'

'And how is it?'

'Just fine I don't know I've got it, anyway, how come you're here?'

'I divide my time between the NHS and here, Mr Hunter, and I just happened to be here when they brought you in. Right now the Police want to speak to you, are you feeling up to it?'

'I'd like a bacon butty and a good cuppa.'

'In that order?'

He laughed and then pulled a face as the pain shot around his body. 'Away with you, Doc.'

'Okay, I'll get one of the nurses to fix it.'

She gathered up her notes and left the room and it was only seconds before D.I. Fearn and a fresh-faced Detective Sergeant followed by Simon entered and Fearn came straight to the point.

'Well, Mr Hunter, we've heard the story from your fellow golfers now can we hear it from you?'

Hunter groaned inwardly. 'There's not much to say. I played my shot and waited while Sherrie took hers and the next second I'm lying unconscious. That's it.'

'You had no warning?'

'No, but I went prepared for something and, err...' he nodded towards the Sergeant.

Fearn acknowledged, 'This is Sergeant Jordan, who's only a temp but *au fait* with the case and its security issues.'

Hunter nodded and continued. 'Inspector, you're aware of this international assassin Orlov or Dimitrov who's on the loose?'

'Yes.'

'The plan was to get him out in the open. As of yet, he's done nothing illegal but he's sussed that we're onto to him and gone to ground. I'm in touch with him but he only answers to my personal phone. I arranged a return golf match with him for this morning but he cried off so I latched onto Jeff and Sherrie and you know the rest. And now I think of it, it was him who suggested I stay. What have you got?'

'About the same but we have recovered enough of the bullet to identify it and SOCO are searching the woods to see if they can find more evidence. There was a chap parking his car though who thought he heard a second shot. Not very loud but enough to scare the pigeons and he also heard someone running through the trees towards the fields at the rear of the church.'

'He heard the first shot?'

'Yes, just as he opened the car door, why?'

'A proper shot?'

'Yes.'

'What are you saying, Hunter?' It was the first time Simon had spoken.

'Well if the first shot was loud and the second shot was muffled, Simon, that would suggest two people.'

Fearn glanced between the two of them slightly bewildered and then turned to his Sergeant. 'Jordan, can you recall from your notes the statement from that chap on the car park?'

'Yes, sir.' He flipped open his notepad. 'At approximately...'

'Skip the niceties, Sergeant, get to the second shot.'

Jordan thumbed over the page, 'I climbed from my car wondering who would be shooting in the woods and went to the boot to retrieve my bag and shoes when I heard a crashing noise like someone running through the undergrowth then there was a second muffled shot. It was loud enough to scare the birds and the scuffling continued through the trees.'

'As I said, two people,' said Hunter. It had to be. The first shot without a muffler and the next with.'

'What about one person, two guns?'

'No chance. Your first shot would have been the muffled one in that scenario.'

Simon butted in. 'Mr Hunter's right, Inspector.'

'Are you saying we have a repeat of the first incident?'

Hunter nodded. 'It looks that way.'

Just then there was a polite knock on the door and a pretty nurse poked her head in. 'Your butty and tea, Mr Hunter.'

'I'm sorry, chaps, but that's it for now. Come in lass, ignore this lot they're just leaving.'

Jordan and Fearn filed out but just as Simon was about to leave Hunter stopped him. 'Simon, are you my minder again?'

'I'm sorry, Hunter, you've been downgraded. You only get the uniform out here.'

'Reverse discrimination. She gets two and I get one.'

Simon laughed as he closed the door.

The nurse came in and pushed the overbed sliding table across him and put the refreshments onto it. 'There you are, Mr Hunter, is there anything else?'

'No, lass. I don't get this service at home.'

'We aim to please,' she said with a smile as she left.

—

The ward door burst open and Lesley and Iain entered.

'Daddy! Daddy!, shouted Lesley as she dashed across to Hunter who was sat up on the bed. She threw herself over his legs and hugged him.

Iain, in his inimitable style, walked steadfastly over, and said, 'Hi, Dad, you okay?'

'Whoa! Easy, Lesley. Daddy's got sore ribs. Hi! Iain. Yes, I'm okay, but breathing is hard.'

'What happened, Dad?'

Just then the door swung open and Jacquie entered sat in a wheelchair being pushed by Carrie and his attention immediately was directed towards her. 'Hi, Jay, you're a sight for sore eyes. I thought I was a goner.'

Jacquie pretended to wipe her mouth while holding a discreet finger to her lips, and she said, 'What happened, H?'

Hunter swung round and let his legs dangle over the edge of the bed and put an arm around both children. 'Well, it's like this. I was playing golf and didn't look where I was going and I fell into a deep bunker. I bashed my ribs and banged my head when I hit the bottom. I'll be home tomorrow. Where's, Kath, Jay?'

'She dropped the kids off and has gone into town. She'll be back about four.'

'We must get her something...'

'You're too late as usual, Hunter, I sent some flowers earlier. Can you walk, Hunter?'

'I reckon.'

'Get over here and kiss me or have you changed your affections?'

Hunter took a deep breath in and then blew it out in a huff as he shrugged. 'Watch it, kids, your mother needs attention.'

He slid off the bed and holding his ribs he crossed to Jacquie's side where it was easier to bend without twisting and disregarding the passive audience they kissed. Ignoring the pain Hunter threw his arms around her and hugged her hard as he whispered, 'Love you, Jay.'

She responded, 'Love you too, Hunter.'

He kissed her again before he stepped back. 'Now Carrie, what have you been up to. Is she treating you right?'

'Yes, Mr Hunter, can I have this job permanently?' she said with a giggle.

'Knowing your boss he'll have you off the case at the first opportunity. Have you had a day off since this started?'

'No, I didn't want one but somebody called Jordan has been drafted in and is relieving me just for tomorrow.'

'Right, Carrie, go home now. I'll take it from here and if anyone argues tell them the local SIS Commander gave the okay.'

'Are you sure, Mr Hunter, I mean...'

'Just go, lass.'

Carrie took her bag off the back of the wheelchair and Hunter walked stiffly to the door with her. As she was about to leave Hunter said quietly, 'Give me your gun, Carrie.'

'Are you sure, Mr Hunter?'

'Yes, don't worry, I'll fix it. You'll get it back Monday, okay?'

Carrie dipped her hand into her bag, withdrew the weapon and slid it surreptitiously into Hunter's hand. 'Look after it, Mr Hunter, won't you?'

He patted her on the shoulder. 'I will and we'll give you a job if they sack you.'

She laughed and left the room and as Hunter turned to join his family he dropped the gun into his dressing gown pocket.

'Now then, where were we kids?'

—

Pat O'Hearne spoke with clear desperation in his voice. 'Aiden, how bad is it?'

'The missies has bound it up but we can't stop it bleeding and I'm feeling like shit.'

'Are you bleeding to death?'

'Nah, but the wounds are seeping all the time.'

'Wounds! How many times were you shot?'

'Once, but through and through.'

'Okay, I'll speak to the Boss. You used your landline, you know better than that.'

'It's okay, I blocked caller ID.'

Pat groaned inwardly and hung up while shaking his head in frustration. 'They never learn.'

—

Aiden stiffened visibly when the Voice spoke to him. 'Cronin, listen closely. Have you a pen handy?'

'Yes, but I can't write and use the phone.'

'Get your missies.'

'NAOMI!,' Aiden shouted.

A distant female cry answered, 'WHAT?'

'Come here.'

A few seconds later Naomi entered wiping her hands on a towel. 'Can't a woman have a crap in peace now?'

Aiden held a finger to his lips and offered her his pen. 'Take down what the Boss wants to tell you.'

Naomi took the phone and the pen and said, 'Hello?'

'Mrs Cronin, the '*Cause*' needs your help. Write down this address?'

'That '*Cause*' just got my husband shot. Isn't it time you gave up that nonsense?'

'Mrs Cronin, if you wish to share a future with your husband I suggest you alter your tone. Note this address and get him there a.s.a.p.'

The Voice immediately hung up.

'What did he say, hen?'

'It's a doctors surgery over in Walton. We'd better go.'

—

The Doctor stood back and surveyed his work. 'Well, Mr Cronin, I think that's fine but you've lost a lot of blood and your blood pressure is low. You need a transfusion which I can't do. Go home and take it easy. Come back tomorrow and we'll check it. Stay off the alcohol if you know what's good for you.'

—

Hunter and Jacquie pushed themselves back from the table in Jacquie's room where they had taken dinner when there was a polite knock on the door.

'Come in,' shouted Hunter more vigorously than he intended.

The door opened and Gus Thomas stepped in. 'Evening folks. Hello, Mrs Hunter, you're looking well considering.'

'Thank you. I don't know your name.'

Hunter chipped in. 'It's Gus Thomas, he's with the 'Firm'. He was one of us but he's taken a step up.'

'You've been hospitalised since I joined this case, Mrs Hunter, and Hunter's right, I have moved but I'm still on it.'

'Apology accepted, Gus, I can call you Gus?' she said with a disarming smile.

Thomas blushed and spluttered, ' Err...'

''Scuse me,' interrupted Hunter, 'are you here on business, Gus?'

Thomas, recovered from his reaction to Jacquie's familiarity cleared his throat before continuing, 'Ahem! Yes, but just a catch up really. I've spoken to Fearn and Bell and they've filled me in on the progress so far. Firstly, SOCO found the spot where the first shot was fired and followed the tracks back into the undergrowth before they found blood and a trail which led them to the edge of the wood.'

'And?'

'The trail goes East and West which means he doubled back but which did he do first. One of your Garden Centres is nearby so we would like your car park CCTV to see if there is anything to give us a lead?'

'I'll fix it with, Charlotte.'

Thomas shrugged. 'And as for who shot him, your guess is as good as mine.'

'Gus, in my golf bag there's a tracking device which was attached to my car. Find out who's using it.'

'Give me a moment.' He left the room and was gone five minutes before he returned. 'Fearn has your bag and is sending it to SOCO.'

'And my car?'

'In the Police compound. One more thing. The press has been informed that the incident was a heart attack and that's as much as I can tell you.'

'And you came all the way up here to tell me that?'

'Hunter, you ungrateful... apologies, Mrs Hunter... 'Bastard,' I thought you were dead.'

Jacquie jumped in quickly. 'Gus, you know what he's like and, yes, he is.'

Hunter shuffled uncomfortably. 'I was thinking of what my income tax is being spent on.'

'Hunter, shut up,' Jacquie said sharply. 'Gus, you've been here a while and we haven't offered you refreshment. Would you like a coffee or tea?'

'No thanks, I'll go and set up my digs.' He prepared to leave and as went to the door, he said, 'I'll see you whenever Hunter. Goodnight, Mrs H.'

—

Williams surveyed his pint and thought about his situation. The usual locals were in there, the beer was not the best.

'Doesn't look like there's going to be any action tonight,' he mused, 'I'll call it a day,' and he plonked his glass down on the bar when the doors opened and Cronin assisted by O'Reilly pushed their way in. Sean helped Aiden remove his jacket and settled him into a seat and said, 'What're ya havin'?'

Aiden pushed himself upright with difficulty. 'A double Irish whisky and then a Guinness.'

'Are you sure, bro?'

'Yeah!'

Duncan resumed his seat at the bar and ordered a half and leaning on his elbow to hide his face and using the mirror behind the bar he watched as Sean paid for the drinks and returned to Aiden at the table. Aiden grabbed the whisky and drank it down in one gulp.

He banged the glass down on the table. 'Another!'

'Your missies said you weren't to drink.'

'Fuck her! Get us a whisky.'

Sean got up from his seat and went to the bar and when he returned he plonked the glass down with a solid thump. 'That's it! If you want more you can get it yourself.'

Aiden grumbled and threw his head back and swallowed it again in one gulp and made to get up from the table. He was halfway to his feet when he keeled over and crashed onto the table scattering the glasses before he slid sideways and bounced off a chair before hitting the floor.

Duncan saw his chance. 'Got ya!' he muttered. He slid off his stool and dashed over and tongue in cheek shouted, 'Leave him. I'm a paramedic. I'll see to him.'

Duncan knelt beside the prostrate Aiden and as he reached out to check his pulse he noted the bloodstain spreading on his shirt. He looked up at Sean. 'His pulse is very weak, I'll call an ambulance.'

'You, can't do that.'

'Listen, mate, if you want to see him alive we'd better had.' He raised Aiden's blood-soaked shirt sleeve, and said, 'What's with his arm?'

Sean mumbled something about barbed wire while Duncan dialled 999 and using the 'Firms ' call sign he called for backup before wiping Aiden's blood off his hands with his handkerchief and placing it carefully into his inside jacket pocket.

Minutes later an Emergency Doctor and paramedics arrived and were joined soon after by the Police. While Duncan was being questioned the medics gave Aiden emergency treatment before wheeling him outside and into the waiting ambulance.

When the disturbance had died down Duncan went back to the bar and Sean came over. 'What did the police want?'

'They just asked what had happened and I told them what I saw and that being a trained medic I helped, that's all.'

Sean nodded, 'And where've they took him?'

'The Royal up town.'

'Thanks. Are you from around here? I seem to recognise you.'

'I was brought up around here until I started working away from home. I'm staying at my sisters for a bit, that's all. I told your mate a few days ago.'

'Oh, right. See you, I'd better go and tell his missies.'

Sean wheeled away and headed for the door and after waiting a couple of minutes Duncan did the same and hurried to his sisters to call in. Aware of Hunter's situation he called Gus Thomas and gave him an update and stressed that he had a DNA sample.

Thomas listened intently to Duncan's report before enquiring, 'Agent Williams, why did you take a sample?'

'Because Hunter's attacker was shot and wounded and this guy I've been told to keep an eye on has been injured somehow. I didn't get a look at his wounds but he was bleeding profusely so I put two and two together.'

'Where is he now?'

'Under police wraps in the Royal Hospital, Liverpool.'

'We won't be able to use the sample but we can test it. Can you get it over to DI Fearn?'

'No, I've had a drink. Where's, Hunter?'

'The same place as, Mrs Hunter.'

'Where's that?'

'The Muirfield, Chester.'

'Thanks.'

~~~~~
~~~~~

CHAPTER 20

Monday morning

DI Fearn stood in front of a whiteboard doing the morning briefing. 'Those of you on 'Operation Magpie' stay here the rest of you carry on.'

The majority stood up and scooping up coats, files and computers they filed out leaving behind just four people, Doctor Kerr from SOCO, two female DC's and Sergeant Jordan.

Fearn waved his hand towards one of the DC's. 'Jane, can you nip down to my office, please, and ask Senior Agent Thomas to join us.'

Jane left and returned a few minutes later followed by Thomas and Simon.

'Good morning, chaps, take a seat and I will bring you up to date...' He stopped in mid-sentence as the door swung open and a very sore Hunter carrying a DVD strolled in followed by Williams. 'Good morning, Mr Hunter, are you fit? Who's your companion?'

Hunter plopped down and screwed his face up as he tried to get comfortable. 'Morning, Inspector. I'm held together with miles of crepe bandage but otherwise okay...' pointing to Duncan, '...and this is, Agent Ernesto, otherwise known as Williams.' Can I just say before we start? Gus—I'm sorry about Saturday evening, I wasn't myself. I owe you one.'

'Two, but I can guess how you felt. It's not every day you get shot.'

Fearn cleared his throat. 'Ahem! Gentlemen, let's start. DS Long has requested that she be Mrs Hunter's bodyguard until such times as she's fit. I've acceded to this request and she's now SIS responsibility. I'll send the invoice later. Doctor Kerr, have you anything for us?'

'Yes!' Kerr walked to the front. 'After further investigation at the Golf Club we found a bullet embedded in a tree and because of the blood match we can safely assume it was the one intended for our would-be assassin…' Hunter was about to speak when Kerr held up his hand, '…it was a Dragunov round but not the one used on day one nor the one embedded in your vest, Mr Hunter. They were 7N1rounds from an earlier 320 model. You were lucky in that you doubled up the armour plates in your vest and it hit you at an angle. This new one, however, is a more modern 240 and used the new lethal 7N14 round. If that had hit you, you wouldn't be with us now...'

Hunter guessed who the 240 belonged to but why shoot the guy who had tried to kill him? It didn't make sense.

Dr Kerr continued... 'we also have a blood sample from a suspect who is in police custody in Liverpool. The blood group is a match but we are waiting for the DNA result to confirm. Also, an abandoned car that we think may belong to the suspect was reported this morning in a cul-de-sac opposite the Golf Club entrance. And that gentlemen is all I have.'

Hunter held his hand up to speak when Dr Kerr apologised and said, 'There's one more thing. The shot that injured your would-be assassin, Mr Hunter, came from the church tower.'

'Are you sure,' said Hunter.

Kerr confirmed his surprise disclosure before Hunter added, 'I've got the CCTV from the Garden Centre. I wonder if that will show anything?'

Dr Kerr returned to his seat while Fearn who had been writing the details on the whiteboard turned to face the group when Dr Kerr held his hand up again. 'I'm sorry, Colin, I forgot. Mr Hunter, the tracking device from your car was supplied by the MOD and was being tracked by GCHQ.'

Hunter gasped, 'I'm being tracked by my own people?' He looked directly at Thomas. 'What's all that about?'

Thomas held his hands up as a sign of surrender. 'Why would we do that? Simon, do you know anything?'

Simon shook his head. 'Nope.'

'Dr Kerr—being from the MOD it must have a serial number?'

Dr Kerr nodded. 'Correct.'

'Curious, I'll catch you later. Inspector Fearn! It sounds like we may have solved one incident but what about the shoot and run on Agent `Artemis′?'

'You mean, Mrs Hunter?'

'Yes, Inspector.'

'In a word, No! There doesn't appear to be any connection other than we think whoever did it comes from Liverpool.'

Duncan held his hand up.

'Yes, Mr Williams?'

'Inspector, the guy who was arrested on Saturday night and his mate Sean have a history of IRA allegiance. Do you think they're working together?'

'It's possible but at the moment it looks personal...'

Thomas interrupted...'One moment, Inspector. Duncan—this is SIS speak. Although this is one for the uniform, because of what you have just said, stay on the job and get as much background as you can. Liaise with both sides.'

'Right, Guv, will do.'

'Carry on, Inspector.'

'If there's nothing further to add we'll call it a day. Thank you.'

He placed his marker pen on the bottom of the whiteboard and walked across to speak to Jane and her companion as they left the room.

—

In the Police Station yard, Thomas took Hunter to one side. 'Hunter, this tracker is none of our doing and I will get to the bottom of it. Have you any ideas?'

'No! I thought it was that Russian guy keeping tabs on me but after Saturday I don't know what to believe because I think he shot my attacker. That's weird!'

'So someone else was tipping off your would-be assassin.'

'That's about it but there's something else.'

'What's that?'

'The Dragunov he used is old school which would have been in the Provisional-IRA arsenal.'

'You reckon?'

'Yep.'

'There could be a reprisal thing going on.'

'Yep, and Jacquie is the target and I'm collateral.'

'A bit extreme isn't it, they only know about Jacquie's role in Northern Ireland, not you.

'Gus! When can we interview this guy?'

'You can't, Hunter, you're dead remember'

He gave Thomas a slip of paper 'Gus, check on this phone. It belongs to our Russian and I want to know his whereabouts but I think he's got the GPS App switched off.'

—

Half an hour later, Hunter joined Duncan at a corner table in the 'Garden Aspects №1' cafeteria and plonked the tray down with a sigh of relief and although he tried to disguise his shortness of breath Duncan could see that it had been a struggle.

'Hunter, you daft buggar, you should've let me do it.'

'And I'd never hear the end of it.'

He put the empty tray to one side and sat down opposite. 'Well, Duncan,' he waved a hand towards the interior of the garden centre, 'what do you think?'

'I'm not a garden man myself, Guv, but it looks very orderly.'

'Aye, she's like that and she runs a tight ship but her staff bloody love her.'

'I can imagine.'

'Duncan, I think you may be right with your plot idea. Are these the guys we bumped into ten years ago?'

'The very same.'

'Won't they recognise you?'

'The O'Reilly guy already asked me but I put him off with some bull about the military. They didn't actually see me working with you. It was all that Russian thing, remember?'

'Yep, you're right. It was only me and Jay they saw and it was Jay they were after.'

'You don't think it was that do you?'

'Nah, it's more historical but why me?'

'It could be a sort of blackmail. If we can't get her we'll get you.'

At that moment Charlotte bounced across the cafeteria towards them and said cheerfully, 'Good morning, Mr Hunter, how's Mrs Hunter?'

'Morning, Charlotte. She's almost back to her bossy best.'

'Oh, good. When can I go and see her?'

'Anytime, lass. She's in the Muirfield?'

'Yes, she told us. Was the CCTV from №2 any good, Mr Hunter?'

'They're checking it now.'

'Oh, good. Can I get you or your friend anything?'

'This is Duncan, Charlotte. He works with me. Do you want anything, la... Dunc?'

Duncan shook his head. 'No thanks, miss but the coffee is great.'

'I'm glad. Have you got one of our customer reward cards?'

'No, you're okay, I'm not from around here, besides, I've got the boss or rather her lackey.'

Charlotte laughed. 'On that note, I'm leaving.'

As she left them Hunter said, 'Back to business, Duncan. I want to know everything about this Sean character. What he eats, drinks etc... Oh, and car registration, MOT or insurance. Let's see if we can bring him in for something.'

'Okay, Guv, I'm on it.' He finished his coffee and stood up to leave. 'Keep low, Guv, and don't worry we'll get the bastards. What's with this Russian guy?'

'He's mine.'

~~~~~
~~~~~

CHAPTER 21

Pat O'Hearne slumped moodily in his chair his mind on things other than what he had been called to discuss. He'd sooner be downstairs in the bar of the 'Shady Tree' with his Guinness than stuck up here. 'What now,' he mused.

Pat,' said, The Voice, 'I asked you to do a job and you failed to deliver.'

'What do you mean?'

'Your so-called hitman is in custody.'

'I didn't know. I've had no feedback.'

'That he is in custody is bye the bye but Hunter I'm informed is very much alive. What are you going to do about it?'

'Do you know what happened?'

'Information was given to Cronin of the whereabouts of the target and he went there and took him out or so he thought. The news reported it was a heart attack but I have it on good authority that the target is in good health. Cronin, meanwhile, is injured and in custody trapped by his own blood.'

Pat groaned. 'Cronin's had two goes at this guy and missed both times?'

'Yes.'

'What now?'

'You, Pat, have got to come up with another plan. Have you got anyone else on the books?'

'We have sympathisers but the young blood is too gung ho! and the older ones are just that, like me, they're getting too old for this sort of thing.'

'What about Cronin's buddy?'

'O' Reilly? He's keen but a bit dim. Who else is trying to get this Hunter guy? There's been a couple of attempts that weren't Cronin.'

The Voice leaned back in his chair. 'I don't know, Pat, one of them put Hunter's wife in hospital but I don't think the two are connected. There are further complications. You're being watched and any movement in the UK by any of our sympathisers would be suspicious. We've also lost our GPS tracker and Hunter doesn't use his personal phone.'

'Red says he has, twice, each time to fix up a golf match.'

'Keep tabs on that, Pat, meanwhile I'm due in Stormont but I'll return to London via Liverpool and speak with O'Reilly. Try and think of somebody else but don't take too long, it's costing.'

The door to the upstairs fire escape closed behind The Voice and Pat considered his situation. He didn't ponder long and with a shrug, he went down to the bar convinced the whole thing was a waste of time.

—

The Voice entered the cafeteria of Liverpool Lime Street railway station and spotted Sean O'Reilly waiting in the shadowy far corner of the room sheltered from direct light by heavy curtains hanging across the huge Victorian windows. He delayed long enough to purchase a coffee before crossing the room and ignoring Sean's outstretched hand sat down. Sean remained discreetly quiet while The Voice made himself comfy and had a taste of the mediocre drink before him.

'O'Reilly, are you up to finishing Cronin's work?'

'Err, what was that?'

'You don't know. My, my, he was being discreet.'

'He said he was doing sommat, but he didn't say what.'

The Voice took out a notepad and scribbled something before tearing out the page and pushing it over to Sean. 'On there are the details of what Cronin was doing for the *'Cause'*. We want Hunter removed. Go and see Cronin's wife and see if he's left anything behind. It's likely the authorities have been already but she might know something.' He slid a package out of his jacket pocket and slipped it under the table. 'Here's something towards your expenses. You will get the balance of Cronin's deal if you finish the job which I want done yesterday. Use the phone numbers I've given you and only those. Is that clear?'

Sean took hold of the bulky envelope nudging his knee and

said, 'Err, yes.'

'Good! I have a train to catch. Wait five minutes before you leave.'

Picking up his briefcase The Voice, abruptly stood up, spun on his heel and left. Sean sat there dumfounded but five-thousand pounds richer.

'Five minutes my arse, I'm having a few beers.'

—

'Karen, they want me to bump off that Milligan bitches fella.'

'So! And how much?'

'They're giving me Aiden's pot but how do we do it?'

'The same as we did her?'

'Did we get her?'

'I think so, you've only seen her car.'

'I'll go and sus it out again.'

'We'll make a plan when you get back but I think we need two cars.'

'You said, We!'

'For that money, we're in this together. I want to make sure you're up to it.'

—

Demyan considered his options as he cleaned the residue of the shot from his rifle. Who was trying to kill his target and did they succeed and if they did he had no proof that Hunter was dead so he couldn't claim his payday. Had his employers hired someone else for insurance? 'Unlikely,' he thought but the doubt remained.

Using his thumbnail as a reflector in the bolt access he peered down the barrel. Satisfied, he assembled the gun and put it in his golf bag and after ringing room service for a pot of coffee he replaced the Sim-card in his smartphone before he began scouring the collection of local and National daily newspapers he'd bought earlier that morning.

After a period of frustrating searching to find Hunter dead or alive he decided on drastic action as the solution to his problem. His phone was a no-no because after the shooting Hunter's phone would be checked and double-checked. Lunch in the newly decorated 'Swan Inn' was he concluded the place to start so he put on his flashiest golf outfit to give the impression of a genuine golf tourist.

Before he left to go on his mission he took the time to send a message of love to his wife and children who would, he reckoned, be about to get ready for school anytime soon.

It was five minutes past one p.m. when he arrived at the Swan and he managed to squeeze into the last available parking slot at the rear of the pub. If he was going to play the American tourist he decided he'd best do it right and he put on his golfing cap before he went in.

Bob the landlord acknowledged him as he reached the bar. 'Afternoon, sir, what can I get you?'

'A pint of your best,' replied Demyan, 'and I'd like to see the menu.'

'Yes, sir, coming right up. You might want to look at today's specials on the blackboard over there,' he picked up a menu from the back of the bar and handed it over.

Demyan took the menu and idly scanned through it and when Bob returned with his pint he took his wallet out to pay and Bob said, 'It's okay, sir, put it on the tab and pay for it with your meal. Excuse me asking, sir, weren't you in here when all that hoo-hah was going on?'

'Yes, I met a chap here and we played golf later but I've lost his phone number and I would like a return match.'

'What's his name, sir?'

'George, I think. Getting on a bit with unnatural dark hair.'

'George Hunter?'

'Yep! Where can I find him?'

'His wife's in hospital and he spends a lot of time there.'

'Which hospital?'

Heeding Hunter's earlier warning Bob demurred on the side of caution and answered abruptly, 'It's none of my business. Excuse me, sir, I have work to do.'

Bob immediately turned away and went to his next customer.

Caught in two minds Demyan toyed with the idea of ordering a meal but after a couple of sips of his beer decided against it and choosing his moment he surreptitiously left the bar. In the car park, he asked a passer-by for directions to the nearest hospital and drove off.

The afternoon queue at the Countess hospital was quite long and it took him a considerable time to find a parking place and foregoing his cap he strolled unconcerned into reception and after waiting patiently in line he spoke to the volunteer pensioner receptionist behind the counter.

'Excuse me,' he said, 'but can you tell me where I can find, Mrs Hunter?'

'Have you got an initial?'

'Only her husbands. G.'

She tapped away at the keyboard of her computer for quite a while and then scrutinised a file before she said, 'I'm sorry, sir, we don't have a Mrs Hunter. When did she come in?'

'Oh, sometime last week. Emergency I think. I've just come over from the States and I thought I'd drop in as no one was at home.'

'Oh, I see. Wait one moment and I'll have another check.'

She busied herself once more into the intricacies of the computer and Demyan couldn't help but notice that like most Government agencies they were still using outdated operating systems. Shaking her head the lady picked up the phone and after a few minutes being passed from number to number she put the phone down.

'I'm sorry, sir, we can't help you. It appears we did have a Mrs Hunter but she was only here a couple of nights before she was transferred.'

'Did they say where?'

'No, sir, it's classified.'

He decided not to press it further and thanked her and walked back to the car park where to his frustration he discovered he needed to cancel his parking ticket inside the Hospital and was even more frustrated to find that this last error pushed him over the free half-an-hour limit and distrusting cash machines, in general, he had to ask around for change of a ten-pound note but it did give him a chance to ask if there were other hospitals in the town and was directed to a private hospital called The Muirfield's.

As he pulled into the Muirfield's car park he saw on the back row a white VW Golf. This was going to be a little harder but he brazenly walked into reception where he was accosted by a business-like receptionist straight out of a James Bond movie but Moneypenny she was not.

'Afternoon, sir, what can I do for you?'

'I'm come to see, Mrs Hunter.'

'We don't have a Mrs Hunter, sir.'

'Have you checked?'

'I work here ten hours a day five days a week and I know everyone that passes through these doors, sir. We have no, Mrs Hunter.'

He knew she was lying but realised this was going nowhere and gracefully retired to the car park where he double-checked the VW. 'That's him,' he muttered. When he left the car park and stopped at the main road he took little notice of the commonplace silver Ford that turned in. He did a mental coin toss and turned right and was pleased when he saw next door to the hospital was a Sports Centre and he immediately turned into it and parked close to the entrance where he could also watch the hospital exit.

As he turned the radio on and prepared himself for a long wait he took no notice of the silver car which left the hospital grounds after a quick tour of the carpark but as he flicked through the radio channels for the fourth time there was a knock on his window and he looked up to see a young man in sports gear.

Demyan lowered the window, and said, 'Yes, can I help?'

'Yes, sir,' replied the young man, 'I would like to point out that this is private property and for use by our customers only.'

'Oh, sorry!' said Demyan, 'I was waiting for a friend to join me and we were going to come in. It doesn't look like he's coming so I'll go. Sorry again.'

'That's okay, sir, but the fine for illegal parking by our agent is quite steep so I thought I'd better warn you.'

With that, he turned away and walked back to the Sports centre while Demyan drove to the exit. Fortune favoured him because as he pulled out into the traffic the white VW left the Muirfield and joined the queue behind him. Demyan drove through the town shielded from Hunter's vision by the headrest and when they reached the dual carriageway on the other side of town Demyan slowed and allowed the ever impatient Hunter to overtake and get some way ahead before he increased his speed and followed.

Demyan was curious when Hunter drove past the end of his road and continued through the village and turned right into a residential area and after a few left turns, he turned into a road on a slight hill lined with cars. Hunter managed to squeeze into a space and Demyan drove past him dodging other cars who were also trying to find a decent-sized gap in the mayhem and then Demyan saw the school sign and knew what Hunter was doing.

At the end of the line of cars, Demyan saw the main road and turned into a minor road running parallel to it. He parked and walked back towards the school in time to see the first children leaving the school gates among them Lesley who spotted Hunter and ran towards him with her arms outstretched. Hunter grabbed her and they spun around and she was chatting excitedly when Iain joined them and Hunter put Lesley down and walked to the car with an arm around their shoulders talking as they went.

Demyan watched all this and walked back to his car with mixed feelings as he waited for Hunter to drive past. He followed as Hunter crossed the main road and turned into another residential housing estate and three-quarters of a mile later pull up outside a modest four bed-roomed house. The children ran to the open front door and Hunter joined them at a more leisurely pace. Demyan then parked in what he supposed was a future road junction and hid his car behind an abandoned caravan with just enough vision to watch the front of the house and he settled down for another long wait.

After two hours of wondering if Hunter had a second home, Demyan was about to leave when Hunter came out and gave each of the children a big hug and the lady of the house a kiss on the cheek and went to his car. Demyan started his car and prepared to follow but Hunter surprised him by doing a three-point turn and driving back the way they had come. Demyan quickly dived across the front seats and did not see the curious look that Hunter gave the light brown Skoda Yeti as he drove past.

Demyan waited ten minutes before he followed Hunter and on a whim drove past Hunter's bungalow where he saw the VW parked. Calling it a day, Demyan went back to his hotel and prepared to swap his hire car and hotel yet again.

~~~~~
~~~~~

CHAPTER 22

Tuesday

'It looks like things may be moving, Mr Hunter.' DI Fearn put down his marker pen and turned towards the room. 'There were two enquiries about Agent 'Artemis' by the same person yesterday. One at the Countess and one at the Muirfield and at the Muirfield we were able to get his car details.'

'It wasn't a brown Skoda was it?'

'Yes, Mr Hunter, it was. How did you know?'

'Because the same car was sussing my sister's house last night and I had a phone call this morning telling me that my Russian was making enquiries in the Swan yesterday lunch time.'

'It's a hire car, Mr Hunter, but it was relinquished this morning and your Russian left his hotel so we have lost him again.'

'Well, Inspector, he's done nothing wrong except the illegal use of firearms which actually helped us.'

'You're right. One other thing. Just after our Russian left the Muirfield another car entered the carpark did a tour and then drove off. We have the number and make. Just a minute.' He searched his pockets and moved bits of paper around his desk and triumphantly held up a sticky note. 'Here it is.' He read out the number.

'It's a silver Ford Fusion, Inspector.'

'You appear to be ahead of us, Mr Hunter.'

'It's registered to a Sean O'Reilly. Agent Williams is watching him and he rang me last night to tell me that O'Reilly had visited the hospital which begs the question. Who told him I was there?'

'The Russian found you.'

'Yes, Inspector, he used logic and put two and two together. This other mob was using GPS and we vetoed that so how did he find me? My personal phone is dead and my service phone is only visible to GCHQ.'

Simon who was sat at the back of the room let out a sigh and put his head in his hands.

Hunter turned to look at him. 'What's the matter, Simon?'

'Nothing, Guv, just a bit of a headache. Must be getting a cold or something.'

'Take it easy, Simon. Was there anything else, Inspector?'

'Yes—your Garden Centre CCTV showed Cronin crossing the road and catching a bus and to top that some dog walkers found a gun which SOCO are working on right now It's a Dragunov and it's got blood on it so it's likely to be the weapon used in the shooting.'

'Well, that's Cronin nailed. Where is he?'

'Under police guard in the Liverpool Royal. He'll be moved over to our jurisdiction tomorrow. If there are no more questions we'll call it a day. Mr Hunter, could you stay behind, please?'

During the scraping of chairs and the banging of closed laptops and files, Simon made his way over to Hunter's side. 'Excuse me, Boss,' he said, 'I'll wait outside.'

'Sure, Simon, you go ahead, I'll be with you shortly.'

Hunter joined Fearn by the whiteboard. 'What is it, Inspector?'

'Aah! Hunter, there's been some discussion about the cost of protection for your wife.'

'But I thought you'd put DS Long on our payroll? And I do the nights although I sleep most of the time.'

'Yes, but we need Long back. I have to provide cover for her and SIS are asking for help with the hospital fees. Does she need to be in a private hospital?'

'Oh, that! It's the safest place for her, Inspector. Leave the fees to me but I would like to keep DS Long.'

'I can't promise anything, Mr Hunter, but I can square up this month's accounts if you handle the fees.'

'Done, Inspector, if I have to pay them myself. Would you like to join us for coffee at our №1 Centre?'

'Thanks for the offer but I have a job to do.'

—

Hunter put down his cup and looked at Simon. 'Are you okay?' he said.

'Yes, Guv, I took a pill and it's gone.'

'Good. I'll give Duncan a ring and then we'll see where we go from there.'

He fumbled under his sweater and took his Service smartphone from his shirt pocket. After fiddling with it and finally pressing the contact App, he said, 'I hate these things. The old phones were much simpler.'

He pressed 'Call' and waited and he was about to cancel when a crackly voice said, 'Yes, Guv!'

'Hi, Duncan, any news?'

'Where are you, Guv?'

'In our Cafe.'

'Are you on loudspeaker?'

'Duncan, I don't know how to do that.'

'Okay. Our friend's on the move again. He's going the long way round so I guess he's going to Chester again. Guv, you'll have to give me help here.'

'Why's that?'

'How long is it going to be before he susses my car?'

'I'll send Bell.'

'Is there anyone else?'

'Why?'

'I don't trust southerners.'

'Stick with him, okay!'

'Copy that, Guv.'

Hunter closed the call and put the phone down before he said, 'Simon, I want you to join, Agent Williams. Work together and keep tabs on O'Reilly but don't make contact.'

'What about my current detail?'

'I'll cover that. For now, stay with Williams. He's following our suspect towards Chester at this moment so you head him off and link up.'

He took a card from his inside pocket and scribbled a few numbers on the back of a receipt before sliding it over the table to Simon. 'Here's his contact details.'

'Thanks, boss, and what are you doing?'

'I'll be here for about an hour with Charlotte and then I'm

going to try and tempt our Russian out into the open again.'

Simon stood up. 'I'll be on my way.'

Hunter finished his coffee and watched as Simon made a phone call as he walked through the Garden Centre.

—

It was an hour and a half before he finished his business with Charlotte and as he walked across the car park Hunter glanced at his watch and he muttered to himself, 'Thomas can wait.'

He started the car and slipped it into first gear and drove over to the Exit. He had timed it perfectly. The traffic lights at the junction three-hundred metres down the road were on red and delaying traffic. The road in his direction was clear and the boy racer in him took over and he gunned the throttle just to hear the deep rumble of the exhaust as he accelerated. The smile on his face receded when he slowed for the next traffic control lights and from then on it was a sedate forty miles an hour until he reached Garden Aspects №2 where he dropped off a package. He checked the time and then drove directly across to the Petrol Station on the other side of the main road. As he pulled onto the pumps he took little notice on the tatty blue Peugeot that followed him in and stopped by the end of a line of cars for sale.

The 'Firm' was paying and he filled the tank and squeezed a bit more in before crossing the forecourt to pay. Foregoing the tempting chocolate special offers on sale by the kiosk he paid with the 'Firms' credit card and walked out.

Concentrating on putting the card back into his wallet he was not immediately aware of the roar of a car engine but instinct made him look up and to his right in time to see the Peugeot charging straight at him. In desperation, he threw himself forward but the offside front wing caught him a glancing blow and spun him around and he grunted as his body collided with the concrete island supporting the petrol pumps.

'Shit!' he cursed, 'these bloody ribs will never get better.'

The Peugeot accelerated and smashed into the open door of a young woman alighting from her car before it hurtled out into the main road causing further mayhem and many curses as drivers took avoiding action.

Hunter struggled to his feet screwing up his face with pain as he tried to brush himself down and his bruised ribs complained. Then he saw the young girl jammed behind the car door with blood seeping from a gash in her leg and breathing heavily. The pain from his injuries disappeared as he hurried over to help.

As he reached her the proprietor rushed out and Hunter shouted, 'Get an ambulance quick and the Police!'

'Done it,' the proprietor replied, 'do you need help?'

'No!, but she does. Give me a hand.'

As he reached her he said, 'What's your name, love?'

'Sally.'

'Right, Sally, I'm going to open this door and...' he looked questionably at the proprietor.

'Sam!'

'... Sam here will support you.'

A tall young man in the next bay ran over. 'Can I help!'

'Yes, 'said Hunter, 'go through the car from the passenger side and support Sally's head from behind. Keep her head still!'

With difficulty owing to his size the young man squeezed across the inside of the car and with his knees wedged between the front seats he placed his hands on either side of Sally's head.

'Okay, Sally,' said Hunter, 'I'm going to pull this door off you now. It might hurt as the pressure comes off. Are you ready?'

'Yes,' she panted through clenched teeth, 'but my right leg hurts like shit.'

Hunter bent down and looked under the bottom of the door and he could see her lower leg was badly distorted and the bones out of line but no loss of blood externally other than the surface gash and her foot rapidly turning purple.

'Your leg is broken, Sally, put all your weight on the other one. Keep as still as possible. Are you ready?'

She nodded, 'Yes.'

'You ready, Sam?'

He checked with the lad inside who nodded and with great care Hunter eased the door off the injured Sally.

As the pressure came off her chest she screamed and fainted but Sam and the young man did their job and held her. Hunter grabbed her jacket lapels in one hand and reached around and supported her neck with the other while Sam cradled her legs. Another willing pair of hands rushed over and took over from the young man and between them, they supported her as she was eased from the car and while Hunter maintained the support to her neck she was lowered on her back to the garage forecourt.

In the distance could be heard the wailing of an emergency vehicle. Two minutes later an Ambulance arrived.

The Leading Medic jumped out and Hunter waved him over and he immediately took charge of the situation. He turned to the gathering crowd and shouted, ‘Right, everybody, step back, give us some room.’

He knelt by Hunter, ‘Okay, sir, what have we got?’

‘This is Sally...’ Hunter reiterated the incident and added that Sally had been conscious until the driver's door was moved... ‘and was her passing out my fault?’

The para-medic shook his head. ‘Pain and shock are a good combination, sir, this lady won’t remember much of this, don’t worry.’

He placed an oxygen mask over her face whilst his colleague who had now joined them began observations to ascertain the extent of her injuries and the intervention required. ‘Thanks very much, sir, we’ll take it from here. What about you?’

‘Bashed me ribs when I tumbled over.’

‘Okay, but this may take a while as we’ve got to brace her neck and straighten that leg and as she was crushed it’s quite likely she’s got broken ribs and punctured a lung. We’ll look at you later.’

‘I’ll be around.’

With wailing sirens, two Police cars belatedly screeched to a halt and after they had spoken to the medics the Officers began organising the onlookers and closing off the forecourt.

As Hunter walked back to his car a policewoman called out to him.

‘Excuse me, sir.’ He stopped and waited for her to catch up. ‘I believe you were hurt in the incident, can I ask you a few questions?’

Hunter noted her rank as he went to take his wallet from his inside pocket and a wide-eyed Police Sergeant took a step back. 'Stand still, sir, is that a gun you're carrying?'

Hunter sighed, 'Yes, sergeant, it is, and if you let me get my ID out I'll explain.'

She eased the velcro strap securing her Taser and kept a hand on it. 'Okay, but slowly.'

Hunter took out his wallet and held up his ID. 'SIS.'

She visibly relaxed and took it from him. 'We've been warned you lot were around.' She studied it for a moment. 'That seems in order, Mr Hunter. Is there anything you would like us to do before I take your statement?'

'Can you send a message for D.I Fearn to come here and then confiscate the CCTV from here?'

'Yes, Mr Hunter, will do.'

She went over to her colleague who was talking to Sam and after a few words with him went to her car and called the incident in.

A disgruntled Sam approached Hunter. 'That copper told me you're in charge. Can I open my business now?'

Hunter pointed to where the para-medics were still working on Sally. 'You'll have to wait until they're finished, Sam, and then just the outside row of pumps until SOCO and uniform have done their bit. But stick around I think the medics may need some help.'

'Thanks, I'll do that.'

'When this gets in the papers,' said Hunter, 'you'll be famous and your business will pick up for at least a week.'

Despite the seriousness of the situation Sam laughed and went to see if he could help.

Hunter went back to his car and was mystified when he saw lying on the dash a piece of paper with a phone number and a car registration scribbled on. He slid into his seat and tucked the slip of paper into his shirt pocket and called Duncan.

When he answered Hunter spoke with a hint of aggression in his voice. 'I thought you were following O'Reilly?'

'I am.' Duncan held the phone away and looked at it with raised his eyebrows and pulled a face before saying with a shake of the head, 'He's right here in the drive-through Costa Coffee in

Chester Retail Park. Why? What's up?'

'Some bastards just tried to kill me, that's what's up.'

'It wasn't O'Reilly. Try your Russian?'

'I didn't get a full look but I'm positive it wasn't him. We'll know more when we've checked out the CCTV. Have you linked up with Bell yet?'

'He's inside with O'Reilly enjoying a cappuccino while I'm stuck out here.'

'Did O'Reilly go to the hospital?'

'He drove past it and then made his way here and that's it.'

'Okay, I'll get back to you.'

Hunter climbed from his car and walked over to the Police Sergeant. 'Excuse me, lass, can you do me a favour.'

She pointed to her shoulder tabs. 'Sure, Mr Hunter, what is it?'

He ignored the barbed reference to her rank and gave her the car registration number instead. 'Can you check that out for me I think it may be relevant?'

'Sure, leave it with me.'

—

Hunter settled himself into leather seats of Fearn's Lexus. 'My, my, they're paying you too much, Inspector.'

'It's nice, isn't it, but not taxpayers money. Now tell me, Hunter, what happened?'

Hunter went on to explain the incident up to that moment but conveniently forgot to mention the slip of paper in his car.

'Somebody's got it in for you, Mr Hunter, of that there's no doubt but now we have an extra player.'

'I'm not sure, Inspector, I think we may have a team job.'

'What makes you think that?'

'Someone obliged with the registration number of the car and your Sergeant checked it out. It's a fourteen-year-old banger bought last night from a back street dealer in Liverpool and is not yet registered to the new owner and probably never will be while the number one suspect was leading my team on a wild goose chase.'

'Oh, I see. Any ideas?'

'There's no evidence here except dark blue paint and tyre marks. I've seen the CCTV and couldn't make out the driver although SOCO may do better. The cameras are set to spy on the pumps for non-payers and the car kept close to the building.'

'Ah, I see. The main thing, Hunter, are you okay?'

'Yes, thanks, although I'm black and blue all round now.'

'Well, I can't do any more here, Hunter, so I'll leave you to it. I'll be having the usual debriefing in the morning. Jordan's been sent back to HQ and I'll be introducing my new number two.'

'What's he like?'

'She, my new Sergeant, is straight from University with a Masters Degree in Criminology and Psychology but with the speed, these types get promoted I don't suppose she'll be around long.'

'Best of luck with that one, Inspector, does your wife know?'

—

While Carrie inserted a bookmark and gathered her things together Hunter plonked his overnight bag under the table and winced as the muscles in his shoulders complained.

'Quiet day, Carrie?' he said.

'Yes, Mr Hunter, quite routine.'

'Okay, lass, see you in the morning.'

Carrie gave Jacquie a cheerful wave, 'Goodnight, Mrs Hunter,' and left the room.

Jacquie was the first to speak. 'Right, Hunter, now we're on our own. What have you been up to?'

'Don't I get a kiss first?'

'Hunter! I've been worrying myself sick about you all day now tell me what happened.'

'I went to fill my car and this idiot tried to run me down.'

'That's all? And you're okay?'

'Bruised a bit in the usual places but I'm okay, I promise.'

She got up from the chair and flung her arms around his neck. 'You will be careful, won't you. Nothing silly?'

'Yes, love.'

'Give me a kiss then.' As she leaned forward to clinch she whispered, 'Have you got a wedge to put under that door?'

'No,' he said as he kicked his shoes off so that they rested against the door. It wasn't a lock but it would delay interlopers.

He pushed her gently backwards and when the back of her legs touched the bed he tenderly lowered her down. The temptation was there but they went no further than foreplay and a couple of minutes later they sat together breathlessly on the edge of the bed.

'I'm coming home the day after tomorrow, H.'

'Has Thomas been on at you?'

'No, the physio said I was good and Doctor Wearne agreed but I mustn't do anything physical in case I pull the stitches. You mentioned, Thomas. Has he been making noises?'

'The 'Firm' are complaining about the cost but I didn't tell them that your Insurance would cover it anyway.'

'Were you going too?'

'I was trying to save your no claims bonus.'

She punched him on the shoulder. 'Idiot,' and laughed again when she said, 'have you put the bins out?'

He swung round and grabbed her across her shoulders and pushed her back on the bed and kissed her hard.

'Hunter!' she gasped, 'the physio said nothing physical...' and moments later she whispered, '...be inventive.'

—

'So what do you make of this episode this morning, H?'

'I know who it wasn't, Jay, that's all. We couldn't ID the driver of the vehicle but they're checking the CCTV again from our Garden Centre to see if there's anything.'

'Why are they doing this, H?'

'To get at you, Jay. We thought we'd removed the connection to me but there's obviously a team game going on?'

'And your Russian?'

'He's out to get me but at the moment he's helping me although somewhat belatedly...' He told her about the telephone number and the car registration. '...which is a conundrum I haven't figured. I'm trying to tempt him out again but he's a pro and they plan, whereas these other perps seem to be making it up as they go along.'

~~~~~
~~~~~

CHAPTER 23

Wednesday

'Ladies and gentlemen, and I use the term loosely.' A sprinkle of laughter circulated the room. 'Let me introduce you to my new backup, Detective Sergeant Newlove...' He pointed towards an attractive athletic young woman in her late twenties with short close-cropped blonde hair wearing a tailored pin-striped trouser-suit. There was a spattering of unenthusiastic hand-clapping. '... and I want you to give her your backing and bring her up to speed a.s.a.p. Can you do that, Mr Hunter?'

'Yes, Inspector, if the young lady will stay behind I'll fill her in...' he ignored the titter at the innuendo, '...and I look forward to any insight she may be able to give us.'

Knowing the resentment among some staff about 'fast tracked' university graduates, Fearn spoke in a positive manner. 'Thank you, Mr Hunter. Now team, and I put the emphasis on team, let me bring you up to date with what has happened in the last twenty-four hours...'

He recited the previous days incident right up to the time he left Hunter at the garage, '...and there's been no sighting of the vehicle and I'm afraid that is all we have.' Hunter held his hand up. 'Yes, Hunter?'

'My team followed our prime suspect yesterday and reported he did nothing except drive around in circles for several hours which gives him an alibi and he picked his wife up in Speke on the way home.'

Sergeant Newlove spoke for the first time. 'The Airport is near there. Was he picking her up after a flight?'

'I don't think so, Sergeant, she was home the previous evening and didn't leave with our suspect in the morning.'

'She could have caught a taxi later to the airport and gone on a shopping trip somewhere. Belfast, London maybe. It's only half an hour check-in to local destinations.'

Hunter sensed trouble and adopted a diplomatic approach.

'You could be right, Sergeant, can you to check that out...' he looked at Fearn who confirmed his agreement, '...and you have my contact details?'

'Yes, Mr Hunter.'

'I have a better idea. Meet me at Garden Aspects №1 about one o' clock and I'll go over the background to the whole case. Is that okay?'

Newlove checked with Fearn who approved.

'One o' clock then.'

—

Sean and Karen sat hunched over their breakfast in the local coffee shop discussing the previous day's events but Karen couldn't concentrate and just pushed her scrambled egg around the plate and chewing on a slice of toast in between sips of coffee. She paused with the toast hovering short of her mouth.

'Sean! are you certain you weren't followed?'

'Yeah! I thought I saw that guy from the pub but after Runcorn Bridge, he'd disappeared. I had a good look at all the cars while I was killing time in those damn roadworks on the Expressway at the **M56** junction and after that, I did as you said, I just drove around.'

'Are you sure?'

'Yes!, and I went past that hospital a couple of times. Why?'

'It just seemed too easy. I received that phone call and I got to the Garden Centre just as this Hunter guy was leaving and after that it was simple.'

'Did you get him?'

'I didn't get him cleanly but I left him in a heap wrapped around the bottom of a petrol pump and he wasn't moving.'

'Okay, what are we doing today?'

'I don't know about you, Sean, but I'm going up to *`Liverpool One'* to spend some of that money.'

Sean pushed his plate away looking pleased with himself. He took a sip of his coffee. 'I have a delivery at the lock-up at half-ten.' He looked at his smartphone to check the time, 'and I better get going. See you!'

He stood up grabbed his jacket and left without a glance in

Karen's direction.

Her eyes followed him and the expression on her face spoke unrepeatable volumes.

—

Hunter got to his feet when Newlove approached and he shook her outstretched hand and was quick to observe that they were almost eye to eye. As she sat down he noticed the absence of jewellery. A slim silver watch and a pair of ivy leaf silver earrings were all she wore with no rings on her fingers and her make-up was minimal her lipstick so pale it was hardly noticeable.

'Right, lass, what do I call you, name that is?'

He thought he saw the glimmer of a smile. 'Sergeant would do, Mr Hunter.'

'My, my, we are formal. I'm not the Police, Sergeant Newlove. Give me a proper name or nick name and you can call me, Hunter, everyone else does.'

She sat upright in a stiff uncomfortable position and lowered her voice. 'Promise you won't laugh, Mr Hunter?'

'Promise.'

'It's Ethel...' she held her hand palm outwards, '...my mother was very old fashioned but call me, Effie.'

Hunter smiled and she relaxed when he continued, 'and Miss Effie, what would you like to drink, it's on me?'

'Medium cappuccino, please.'

Aware of her athletic build he knew the answer to his next question before he asked. 'Anything to eat?'

Effie shook her head. 'No, thanks.'

Hunter spun round and caught the eye of a young girl who was cleaning tables and called her over. After a couple of seconds of whispered instructions, the girl smiled, nodded and went towards the coffee counter while he turned his attention back to Effie. 'Right, lass, did you find anything?'

She visibly relaxed at Hunter's easy-going approach. 'You were right...' she paused unsure what to call him but taking a deep breath and taking the bull by the horns she settled on, '...Hunter, but I expect you're used to that?'

'Effie! We all have to start somewhere and this time I guessed right. You made a valid point which had to be checked out after all it was a possible alibi.' At the back of his mind was one city Effie had mentioned with historic connections to the case. 'Is it feasible that she flew to Belfast under an assumed name?'

'I don't think so. I asked them to check passenger CCTV as well as flight manifestos.'

'Good thinking.'

The girl approached with two coffees and hovered prudently but Hunter was quick to see her and waved her forward. She put the coffee on the table and was about to leave when Hunter took her hand, pressed something into it and curled her fingers around it. He smiled, 'Thanks, love, I'll leave you alone now.'

'Thanks, Mr Hunter,' and she turned away while discreetly looking into her hand.

Effie stirred her coffee. 'Hunter, how come you get waiters service?'

He lowered his cup and said simply, 'I own it or rather my wife does and the Staff would give their right arm for her but it all goes on the tab. Nothing is free not even for me. Now then back to business.'

He began to relate the background to `Operation Magpie′ when Charlotte approached. 'Sorry to bother you, Mr Hunter, could you put your signature on these letters, please.'

'Yeah, sure, give them here.'

As he scrawled his illegible signature she stood alongside him and smiled at Effie. The silent signals that flashed between them were electrifying and as Hunter handed her the letters she spoke slightly breathlessly, 'Err..., thank you, Mr Hunter.'

She glanced at Effie and blushed as she turned away.

Hunter was oblivious, and said, 'Right, where were we?'

Despite being briefed on the case by her own department Hunter gave Effie the run down on the lead up to the situation as it stood and the parallel interest by the security services, '...and after toing and froing this latest hit and run incident seems to swing the case back in my direction, Effie.'

'And your wife, Hunter, she's still in hospital?'

'Yes, but not much longer. She's able to get around now and if

I know her she'll be on the exercise bike and down the gym anytime soon. Which reminds me, I'd better tidy the place up or empty the bin at least.'

'You have a good relationship, Hunter?'

'Yep, but we have our moments, and you?'

'I've been too busy.'

'Plenty of time.'

'Okay, Hunter, I've got to go now, Fearn will think I've gone awol.'

Hunter stood up and stuck his hand out. 'Nice meeting you, lass.'

They shook hands and Effie made her way out of the Garden Centre while Hunter went to the front desk and bought a new PAYG Sim before going to his car. After swapping the old Sim in his personal phone for the new one he sat for a few minutes contemplating his next move and then on impulse he sent a message. No words, just a number.

—

The Voice threw his burner phone down on the desk, stood up and strolled over to the window which looked out over the muddy River Thames with the usual ferries and pleasure boats but at least he had a view.

He rubbed his chin thoughtfully. With the loss of the GPS tracker and because his field informant had been allocated to other duties they had no fix on Hunter who was still alive after the latest botched attempt. Using the Belfast connection was stymied since the arrest of Cronin. The job would have to be coordinated from England and his first thought was how to get Hunter isolated. He formulated an idea but first, he needed more heavies and premises.

He went back to his desk and after flicking through his address book and consulting with his diary he dialled the number of a security firm in Lancashire. It was a long drawn out call with many loud words and much haggling and it was obvious from his body language The Voice was not finding it easy to persuade retired activists back into the business and he looked anxiously at his watch a few times before nodding his satisfaction with the deal. He did another quick check of his watch before he dialled his informant and spoke instantly the call was answered.

'Don't speak just listen. I want to know Hunter's routine like when he picks the kids up and how and I want it yesterday.'

There was a polite knock on the office door and he dropped the phone into an open draw and closed it just as his secretary poked her head in. 'Your visitor's here, Mr McGovern.'

'Okay, send him in.'

—

Hunter had just put the bucket and mop into the cupboard when his service phone buzzed. He glanced at the coded name showing on the screen and pressed the key. 'Yes, Gus?'

'Hello, H, just ringing to give you the latest seeing as how you've bumped Bell over to Liverpool.'

'I had to, Gus, we needed extra eyes over there.'

'Okay, about this Russian. We have confirmed that the Skoda was hired out to Dimitrov aka Orlov who has returned it and he's also left the hotel he gave as his residence so he's dropped off the radar so to speak and his home address as you know is mythical.

'How about our leak and the bloody GPS, Gus, who signed that out?'

'The GPS was reported stolen on the day it was signed out before it could be used on the job it was intended for. I'm assuming it was nicked by the same person passing on your details.'

'That means there are two moles.'

'How do you mean?'

'One the guy who nicked it and used it on me and two—the person in GCHG tracking it and passing on the information.'

'Do you want a job here? Unfortunately, H, we don't know who was tracking it. It wasn't the original assignee.'

'What about Cronin? Have you anything there?'

'We have him in a safe house and are questioning him but so far he's saying nothing. We may have to turn him over to the heavies.'

'Why wait, do it!'

'All in good time, Hunter, things have changed since you left.'

'Don't tell me, Human bloody Rights! They try to kill me and shot up my wife. They don't have any rights.'

'Got the message, Hunter, have you anything?'

'Only that Jacquie's coming home tomorrow but you already know that. Can we keep hold of DS Long?'

'Yes, and if that's all we'll call it a day. I'll be in touch.'

Thomas hung up leaving Hunter looking meaningfully at the object in his hand before he set the speed dial to the next scheduled burner number and put it back into his shirt pocket. He glanced at the kitchen clock and grabbed his jacket as he prepared to go and pick up the kids from school.

—

Hunter was late and had to park a long way from the school gates but the walk back gave him time to look around at the other vehicles. He saw nothing untoward and the grannies and mothers gathered around nattering amongst themselves and tripping over each others pushchairs were all familiar.

As usual, Lesley was the first to appear and she ran towards him with her customary enthusiasm waving her latest masterpiece. As he swept her up and swung her around she giggled and shouted, 'Daddy, daddy, look what I drew today. It's you and Mummy.'

She pushed the drawing into his face and he stopped and looked. 'My, my, do I really look like that?'

'Yes you do and the teacher says you need a haircut.'

'Oh, she did, did she?'

Lesley patted his hair, 'Only in the picture, silly.'

Hunter felt a tug on his sleeve and looked down to see Iain. He lowered Lesley to the floor, 'Hi! son, everything okay?'

Iain nodded. 'When can we come home, Dad?'

Hunter took his and Lesley's hand, and said, 'Come on, I'll tell you on the way to the car. I had to park at the end today.' As they started walking he looked down at Iain and continued, 'Your Mum's coming home tomorrow, son, and we'll get her settled in and all sorted and you can come home on Friday after school.'

'Can we see her tomorrow night?'

'I don't see why not. Come home for tea and then sleep over at Auntie Kath's and you know that nice, Carrie? she'll be staying with us for a while.

'I like her,' said Lesley.

Iain as ever was more circumspect. 'Why's she staying, Dad?'

'Your Mum's not fully fit yet, Iain, and Carrie will be keeping an eye on her but when this silly business is over we'll get back to normal. Right now, do you want me to do tea or back to Auntie Kathleen's kitchen?'

'Auntie Kathleen's,' they shouted simultaneously.

'Oh, I see, that's a vote of no confidence on my cooking then.'

'Yes, Dad, I mean, No, Dad, but Auntie Kathleen's doing her homemade beef burgers tonight.'

'In that case, Iain, I'll stay for tea with you.'

He made sure they were secure in the back seat of the car all the time looking around but nothing suspicious caught his eye and grabbing the first opportunity in the school run traffic he managed a three-point turn and drove off towards Kathleen's house.

When he pulled up outside her house he ignored the black taxi that overtook them and didn't see the 4 x 4 pull in between other vehicles parked down the road.

After tea Hunter stood up to ready himself for his stint in the hospital when Kathleen came in from the kitchen. 'Did you see the local news on the television, George?'

He shuddered, she insisted on using his given name. 'No, I didn't, I was busy with the kids. Why? What did I miss?'

'A taxi driver has gone missing from town along with his cab.'

'Locally?'

'Yes—two people were seen getting into his cab last night and since then he's gone missing.'

'He's probably on his way to London or somewhere.'

'But wouldn't he phone home or something?'

'Aye, your right, sis.' He grabbed his jacket off the back of a chair. 'I'd better be going, I have to pop by the house and pick up Jacquie's suitcase. Come here, kids, and give Dad a hug.'

Tess pricked her ears up and stretched while Lesley jumped up from where she had been playing. He picked her up, kissed her and gave her a big hug while Iain looked up from his Pokémon game, 'See you, Dad, give Mum our love.'

'Will do, son, be good.'

With that, he left the room. Kath and Tess followed and when he reached the front door and opened the latch he said to Kath, 'Thanks again, I don't know how we would have managed but it'll be over on Friday.'

'You sure?'

'I think so, we're closing in.' Tess rubbed up to his legs. 'No, you stay here, there's a good girl.'

~~~~~
~~~~~

CHAPTER 24

Thursday

DI Fearn looked up at his assembled team. 'I haven't much for you ladies and gentlemen other than the CCTV from the Garden Centre which gave us no clue as to the driver of the Peugeot but whoever it was driving appeared to have curly hair hanging down below the baseball cap they were wearing.' Looking across to Hunter he added, 'Are you okay, Hunter?'

'Yep, I'm fine, just a few more bruises.'

'Is there any movement over the river?'

'No, Inspector, they seem aware of our surveillance and are leading us around the houses but actually doing nothing. There was one thing. The morning of my car incident our new prime suspect took delivery of something which he stashed in a lock-up.'

'Thanks, Hunter. If that's it team we'll move on. I'm busy with this taxi business. Newlove will be my liaison if anything turns up.'

The assembled company filtered out and as he walked towards the door Hunter had a quick word with Newlove. 'Morning, Effie, you're looking happy this morning.'

'I feel better, I clicked, I mean I met someone last night.'

'Good, see you around, I've got to pick up a certain lady so I must go.'

—

Hunter opened the front door of the bungalow and stood to one side to let Jacquie through. 'Go straight to the lounge, love, and I'll make some tea.'

'Tea is good, H, but if you think I've come home to lie around think again. I've been away two weeks and I want to see what a mess you've made.'

He closed the front door behind them and pulled a face at Jacquie's back as they walked down the hall. She went directly to the kitchen while Hunter put her bags into the bedroom and when he joined her she said, 'Not bad, H, how long did it take you?'

'Welcome home to you too. Now kiss me.'

They met in the middle of the floor and went into a clinch and he murmured into her ear, 'Glad to have you back, lass, I've missed you.'

The doorbell chimed and he looked at the newly installed CCTV monitor and saw Carrie waiting on the doorstep. 'It's Carrie, love, I'll have to let her in.'

She kissed him once more before she let him go. 'Glad to be back, H, I can keep an eye on you now.'

He playfully slapped her buttock and as he left, he quipped, 'Just an eye? Do your job, put the kettle on.'

Moments later he was back with Carrie in tow. 'Dump your bag there, Carrie, and we'll have a cuppa or would you prefer coffee?'

'Tea will be fine, Mr Hunter, thank you.'

Hunter dunked the first of his ginger biscuits into his tea when the front doorbell chimed its reproduction of Big Ben once more.

'It's Andy, H, you'd better see what he wants.'

Hunter slid off his stool and made his way down the hall and opened the door. 'Hi, Andy, everything alright?'

Andy held up a post-it note. 'Yes, George.' Hunter winced at his name again but with Andy, it was protocol with his sister it was something else. Andy continued, 'I saw you come home and I thought I'd show you this while I remembered.'

'Come in, Andy, we've just made a pot of tea would you like a cup?'

'If you don't mind, George, but haven't you brought Jacquie home?'

'That's okay, matey, you're always welcome. Come in.'

Andy heaved himself over the doorstep with the aid of his walking stick. 'George, I swear your drive's getting steeper or I'm getting older.'

'Ha! Ha! I can't imagine which, Andy, go through.'

Andy entered the kitchen and they all shuffled around and made room for him at the front of the table.

'Stool okay, Andy?' said Hunter.

'Better, George, I can just slide off.'

Hunter plonked a mug of tea in front of him. There you are, help yourself to sugar. What was it you wanted to show me?'

Andy pushed the note over the table. 'Those car numbers, George, do they mean anything?'

Hunter looked at them. 'Hang on I'll just check 'em against my notes. They seem familiar especially that first one.'

He left the room and returned a few minutes later and spread his notebook on the table. 'Here we are, Andy. The first one was our prime suspect but he's in custody. The initial letters of the second one belong to our new prime suspect. When did you get these?'

'The first one before all this began, George. It belonged to a guy and his wife who came to look at my house before this shenanigans started.' He turned to Jacquie. 'You may remember this, Jacquie, because he narrowly missed your Jeep on his way up the lane.'

'That Jeep, Andy, is a Range Rover...'

Hunter laughed. 'OOooh! Hark at her, Andy, it's a Range Rover!'

'...before I was rudely interrupted,' Jacquie continued, 'now you mention it, Andy, I do remember. He saw me and was cursing or saying something as he went past as if it was my fault. He fumbled his gears I think. That was the Friday morning before all this got under way, wasn't it?'

'Yes.'

Hunter chipped in. 'Andy, do you think he was sussing the lay of the land or was he really interested in your place?'

'I'd put them down as time-wasters, George, but now you mention it they could have been using the visit to sus you out.' He banged his forehead twice with his hand. 'Oh! my head, I remember now. Just as he was leaving the guy enquired about you. He had an old photo. Looked like a copy from a book or newspaper and he said you were an old Army mate and did I know where you were.'

'And the second one?'

'That was the Friday after Jacquie was shot, George, it went down the road and back like a lot of people do who don't know the meaning of cul-de-sac, but he slowed as he passed your place.'

'Suspect number one checks your house and my car at Hooton Station and suspect number two checks our house and he's been seen at the Garden Centre. He even entered our coffee competition would you believe. They're working together maybe? Then there's our Russian?'

'H,' said Jacquie, 'we know from Andy that number one did a recce on the Friday and took a pot-shot at you on the Saturday night. When he recognised me on the Friday I think he told number two who came after me. He tried the bomb but didn't succeed and then did the drive-by so I don't think they were together but let's say that whoever organised this affair is ignorant about number two operating on his own and has co-opted them to finish the original job.'

'You may have something there, Jay, but that still leaves our Russian. Where the hell does he fit in? I can figure the Irish interest but an International hitman? What's that all about?'

'George!'

'Yes, Andy?'

'I remember you saying years ago you were in Oman once?'

'Yes, Andy, I was.'

'With the BATT?'

'Yes.'

'I have a book on my shelf by a guy called Ranulph Fiennes... err... '*The Feather Men.*' It tells of a group of International killers being paid millions to kill members of the BATT in revenge for the killing of Arabs in that conflict. Do you think this could be a similar thing?'

'There was a period, Andy, when we were told to be on our guard but I thought that ended in the nineties.'

'It might not be associated, George, but is it possible?'

'Murphy's Law says, Yes!

'Is it likely that your Russian is setting you up?'

'Andy, I don't know. You have a point but if that was the case why would he shoot my golf course sniper?'

'To stop him talking?'

'Nah! I think he was going to hit me but the Irish guy got in first and he popped him in a fit of pique but someone else knows besides them.'

Carrie who had sat quietly throughout the conversation piped up, 'How do you mean, Mr Hunter?'

'Because, Carrie, somebody is passing on information that is only available to us.'

'Like?'

'My whereabouts via the GPS. Whoever was using that device passed the info on to our suspects and since.'

'But not, Mrs Hunters?'

'You're right, Carrie. Jacquie is collateral.'

Hunter glanced at his watch. 'Bloody Hell! Is that the time? I'm sorry but I've got to fetch the kids. We'll talk about this later. Thanks for that info, Andy.'

'Glad to help and it gets me out of the house.'

Hunter grabbed his car keys, kissed Jacquie and hurried out to his car.

The still-warm engine rumbled into life and Hunter reversed down the sloping drive and did a handbrake turn at the bottom and while the car was still sliding he pushed it into first and with wheels spinning and gravel flying he shot up the lane towards the main road.

He cursed when a car pulled out in front of him and crawled to the junction and stopped. His angry mutterings aimed at the driver of the car in front diverted his attention until too late he saw another nondescript car coming from the right but instead of turning into the lane, it drove directly towards him aimed at his door. As it smashed into him the driver leapt out and ran to the car in front which was blocking Hunter, jumped in the back seat and it sped away with tyres screaming leaving Hunter trapped, shaken but uninjured.

Hunter shook his head to clear it and counted to ten and his first reaction was to phone his usual Taxi firm.

'Hello! Express cabs.'

'Hi! It's Mr Hunter. I'm sorry I've left it late but can you pick up the kids for me I'm stuck in traffic?'

'Sorry, Mr Hunter, but all our cabs are out. The first one will be in about twenty minutes.'

'Shit! Sorry about that. Thanks, I'll try something else.'

He rang off and called Jacquie. 'Yes, Hunter?'

He quickly told her the situation, '... and can Carrie go to the school for me?'

There was a moment's silence before Jacquie replied. 'Yes, H, she's going now but it will take a few minutes for her to get ready. I'll ring the school but it's late already they'll be out.'

'Okay, I'll leave it with you.'

He rang off and called the Police.

—

Naomi Cronin bent forward and held out the Taxi ID badge with her forefinger obscuring the photo. 'Hello, is your name, Lesley?'

Lesley stopped and looked a little puzzled before answering, 'Yes, where's our usual taxi?'

'The driver's not very well and the firm is busy so they asked me to fetch you. Where's your brother?'

Lesley looked around and pointed. 'There he is. He's always slow.' She waved and shouted, 'Iain! Come on!'

Iain quickened his pace slightly and when he reached them he said, 'Where's Dad?'

Naomi put an arm around his shoulder and guided him towards the taxi as she said, 'He couldn't make it. Said his car was broken or something so they asked me instead. Come on, get in.'

She opened the rear door of the cab and gently nudged Lesley towards it but just as she put her foot on the step she saw the man sat inside and pulled back. Naomi reacted instantly and pushed her in. Iain made to run off but she grabbed him by his collar and as he shouted, 'HELP!' she shoved him on top of Lesley and slammed the door shut. She sprang into the open driver's door, rammed it into gear and ignoring other cars around her pushed her way through and accelerated away.

A young mother waiting for her children shouted, 'Aye! What's going on? You can't do that,' and made a move towards the cab but she was too late. A car was slow to move and the Taxi swerved onto the grass verge and went around it knocking a mirror off another car as it did so before bouncing back onto the road and speeding away.

Other parents alerted by the noise joined the waiting mother as she frantically tried to call the police on her phone at the same time looking out anxiously for her own children.

—

Hunter was stood talking to the policeman who had cordoned off his car when his phone rang. 'Yes, Jacquie?'

'Hunter, did you fix a taxi?'

'No.'

'That's what I thought. Hunter, the kids have been kidnapped.'

'You what!'

'Somebody disguised as a taxi has kidnapped the kids. Get here quickly. Fearn's on his way and the police are already at the school. Carrie's there also.'

'Okay, lass, give me a few minutes.'

Hunter heard her weeping and between sobs utter, 'Hurry, Hunter, I'm frightened.'

He spoke to the policeman alongside him. 'I've got to get home, mate. Can you sort this lot out?'

The policeman hesitated, 'Err, I don't know if I should.'

'That phone call was my wife. My kids have been kidnapped. I'm needed at home.'

'Why didn't you say? Get going, and I'll sort it. Do you need a lift?'

'No, thanks, I only live down the lane and don't worry I'll fix it with the Brass. The brains will be here shortly anyway. Huh! Speak of the devil.'

An unmarked police car pulled up and Newlove approached. 'Hello, Hunter, The DI has sent me round to coordinate.'

'Okay, Effie, take the load of this guy and sort things here and I'll see you later. I'm on the way home. Can't stop! See you!'

He didn't wait for a reply but reached through the passenger door of his car and snatched up his belongings and ran down the lane to his home. He arrived at the bottom of the drive just as Carrie skidded to a halt alongside him and together they hurried through the open front door where a distraught Jacquie met them in the hall and fell into Hunter's arms sobbing.

He hugged her tight and whispered, 'There, there, lass, I've got you, let it all out.'

He could feel himself filling up as her gently heaving body sent the message of her grief to him.

He took a deep breath, and said mentally, 'Someone's going to pay for this.'

He held Jacquie away from him. 'Come on, lass, let's have a cuppa,' and he gently guided her towards the kitchen.

In the kitchen, Jacquie took a deep breath and steadied herself and went immediately to fill the kettle and Hunter went across to help. 'Come here, lass, I'll do that.'

'No, H, you've got enough on your plate and I need to do something. Just find the bastards who did this.'

'There's one up the spout ready,' he said, as he turned to go back up the hall.

~~~~~
~~~~~

CHAPTER 25

Thursday Evening

The Hunter kitchen had been turned into an incident room. Around the large table were several SOCO operators with computers logged into Hunter's Internet system and all landlines and android phones ready to trace any contact while spread around the breakfast bar were the senior officers.

DI Fearn stood by a whiteboard was the first to speak, 'We're all ready, what do we know so far?'

Newlove put her hand up. 'The taxi was using false number plates but we believe it was the one stolen the other day. Witnesses say there was a female driver and two people in the back but that varies as others have said only one person in the back. Also, apart from the GPS tracker on Iain's phone which stopped five minutes after he was taken we have no leads.'

Fearn made a note on the board before speaking again. 'Any news from your watchers in Liverpool, Hunter?'

'No. It looks like they're using our prime as a decoy. He hasn't moved but the wife of Cronin has gone missing.'

Fearn looked across to Gus Thomas who had recently arrived by helicopter from London. 'What about you, Gus, anything?'

'No more than you know already but I suggest we pull in this O'Reilly character. Detain him on some trumped-up charge and I'll get my team to quiz him. What do you think, Hunter?'

'A good idea, and we don't need a trumped-up charge, we can get him for holding illegal firearms. He took delivery of a Kalashnikov and an automatic pistol the other day. What he wants an AK for, God knows?'

'Do we know that?' said Fearn.

Thomas nodded. 'Yes, we broke into his lockup and found them but we didn't remove them.'

'That's it! If you want to question them, Gus, your boys better lift him and his wife.'

Hunter spoke to Thomas. 'I'll organise Williams and Bell but they need back-up.'

'I'll get onto Liverpool now, Hunter,' said Fearn, 'I take it you want the Armed Response Unit and when do you want them?'

'A.S.A.P.! I'm going to call my lads now and you'll have to take out the lock-up at the same time.'

Fearn put his marker down and spoke to Newlove. 'Sergeant, take over here while we organise that.'

Ten minutes later they returned to the table and Jacquie joined them. Hunter slid off his stool and went to her. 'You okay, lass?'

'Yes, I'm good, but getting impatient waiting for something to happen. Surely they should have been in touch by now?'

'You're right, Jay, I spoke to Fearn about this and apart from Iain hitting his panic button which went dead after a few hundred metres we've heard nothing. He also said that it's customary for some notification in the first couple of hours but this is slightly different. We don't think it's for money we think it's to get me and the evenings are getting longer so they may wait.'

'Oh, H, I hope the kids are alright and you know what Iain's like. He's just like you and food and it's way past their teatime.'

'Criminals have to eat, Jay, so they'll be okay.'

'I hope so.'

They shuffled around and made room for Jacquie when the alert for Hunters encrypted service phone jingled and instantly there was activity around the dining table and they gathered around the speakers. He picked his phone up and was just about to slide his finger up to accept the call when there was an urgent shout. 'Don't answer, Hunter, let it ring four times at least.'

He waited and then slid his thumb up the logo to accept the call. 'Hello?'

A refined Irish voice answered him. 'George Hunter?'

'Speaking.'

'Listen carefully. Your children are safe for the moment but if you want to see them again—YOU! will come alone and unarmed to this place...' The Voice read out a location, '...at midnight tonight. I repeat, ALONE!'

Hunter responded quickly, 'How do I know my kids are safe?'

There was silence when a few seconds later Iain spoke, 'Hi, Dad, we're okay.'

'Where are you son?'

'Down the...'

The phone went dead immediately.

'Did anyone get a fix,' he called.

'Yes and no,' said one of the operators, 'it was an encrypted burner phone. The best we can do is that the signal was pinged off the blocks of flats at the bottom end of town.'

Hunter read out the location he had been told to go to. 'Where's that?'

A quick jiggle on a laptop brought up a map and when scrutinised Fearn stood back and said, 'That's a bus stop on Rossdown Road just short of Junction **8** of the **M56**. It's in the open with the nearest building two hundred metres away over a playing field. There's a copse on the other side of the road with a footpath running through it and there are traffic lights two-hundred metres west.'

Gus Thomas stepped in. 'Okay, Hunter, no problem. You will go armed, they'll expect it and you will have a tracking device, in fact, two, and as a backup, we have a trick up our sleeve if, as I expect, you are searched and they find both devices. Overhead we'll have a drone.'

Hunter's screwed up his face and sounded a little incredulous. 'A drone? You employing bees now?'

'It's new tech, Hunter, not widely used yet but one day you'll have your newspapers delivered that way.'

'Let's hope it delivers tonight. Excuse me there's something I have to do.'

He slid off his stool and gave Jacquie a quick squeeze as he left the room. A little way down the hall he stopped and retrieving his personal phone from his pocket he sent a text before returning to the kitchen and taking his place around the breakfast bar.

'Sorry to butt in,' he said, 'but does anyone know how they got my number which is allegedly a ten number encrypted burner?'

The chatter stopped and they all looked at each other before Thomas spoke. 'You know when to drop a depth charge don't you,

Hunter, and you're right. How did they get it? That puts all phones out of operation. Did you give your details to Iain or Lesley?'

'No! They only have my private phone number.'

'Okay, Hunter, I'll get these phones sorted first as they're useless now.'

He picked his phone up and went to dial when Hunter stopped him. 'Not so fast, Gus. Who are you going to contact with a dodgy phone?'

'Head office of course.'

'Who I guess will tell GCHQ?'

'Yes.'

'No! Send one of your team to the corner shop and buy ten PAYG SIM cards and distribute them here and keep two for Williams and Bell. No, better still I'll text Williams and tell him to get their own and then contact us.'

While Thomas organised one of the operations staff to go to the corner shop Hunter sent Williams a text:

SMS: No questions – Service phones are compromised. Buy new PAYG SIM. Venator.

—

'Are you set, Hunter?' said Thomas.

'As I'll ever be.'

'Good. Here take this and put it in the crotch of your 'Y' fronts.' He handed Hunter a small electronic device. 'The chances are they will have a detection apparatus but you never know.'

Hunter took it off him and went into the bathroom and returned moments later. 'All done. Is it pinging?'

One of the team around the table held a thumb up. 'Okay, Mr Hunter, we have a signal.'

'Not too personal I hope?'

'No, but be careful what you think about.'

Hunter gave him two fingers and although he didn't feel it, he said cheerfully, 'Okay, I'm ready to go. Who's driving?'

Jacquie came through from the kitchen dressed in black from head to foot and the slight bulge under her left armpit looked familiar. 'I am, Hunter and we're going in my car.'

'Are you up to it, lass?'

'You'd better believe it, Hunter.'

'But your leg?'

'I've got lycra cycle leggings for support. Come on.'

They walked out to the Range Rover and as Hunter slid into the front passenger seat he spotted Carrie dressed in full Police protective gear sat in the back seat. 'You going as well?' he said.

'Yes, Mr Hunter, this is the 'A' team and we've made our minds up.'

Ten years of marriage had made him wise to the female mindset and he didn't argue but he silently wished that Jacquie wasn't involved.

—

At five minutes to midnight with Carrie lying hidden across the back seat they rolled to a halt at the bus stop as directed. Hunter opened his door and knowing he was visible in the car interior lights he made a show of saying goodbye to Jacquie. With a last peck on the cheek, he got out and slammed the door behind him and watched with a lump in his throat as Jacquie drove off in the direction of the Motorway. She didn't look back.

When she reached the Motorway junction she had to make a decision. Take the old Dock Road into town or go down the Motorway slip road and link up with the old road at the next junction. She chose the Dock Road and after negotiating a series of long bends she pulled into the gateway of the Old Customs House and with lights extinguished but with the engine running she and Carrie, who joined her in the front seat—waited.

—

Hunter watched the tail lights of the Range Rover go over the rise and up to the roundabout of the junction and disappear and resisting the urge to look up he checked the time. Two minutes to midnight and no movement. 'Sticking to the timetable,' he thought when from behind the derelict spice works at the road junction with the nearby trading estate a Peugeot E7 Taxi pulled onto the main road and ignoring the traffic lights drove directly towards Hunter and pulled up with a squeal of brakes.

A masked man jumped out waving a gun while another gun

poked out through the open rear door. 'GET IN, and keep your hands visible,' shouted the Mask.

Hunter stepped forward and as he lowered his head to climb aboard he was shoved from behind and he went sprawling across the floor space reserved for wheelchairs.

'GO! GO! GO!' shouted the hidden figure as he dropped with both knees onto Hunter's back and began patting him down. The masked man jumped in and slammed the door shut and the taxi took off with high engine revs and a clash of gears as the driver tried to emulate a rally car.

The two men searched Hunter and it didn't take long for them to find his gun and the hidden combat knife clipped to his forearm or the GPS stitched onto the back of his collar and before they reached the roundabout at the Motorway junction Hunter was handcuffed.

'A bit amateur, pal,' muttered one of Hunter's captors.

'It was meant to be,' Hunter said mentally.

A dark coloured 4 x 4 without lights crept up the footpath from the thicket opposite and bumping over the kerb joined the road and followed unnoticed at a discreet distance.

—

Jacquie pressed the answer symbol on the Bluetooth relay screen. 'Artemis.'

'Hello, Artemis. Have target on visual and GPS. He has joined the motorway. Signalling off at next junction, Follow the Dock Road and you will come to the same slip road at the next roundabout, Bluebell, over.'

'Got it! Line open, over.'

She quickly engaged gear and without lights took off at speed along the old road towards town.

'Artemis? Target on slip road you should have sight soon. Another vehicle following with no lights, Bluebell, over'

Jacquie accelerated and as she approached the turn-off for the Old Docks she could see the taxi up by the roundabout. She was about to join the slip road when a warning shout filled the cab.

'ARTEMIS! STOP!'

She braked hard and pulled to the side and seconds later the dark 4 x 4 crossed in front of her and followed the target to the roundabout and the next junction. She counted to ten and tagged on behind at a tactful distance. The Taxi didn't go back onto the Motorway instead it went around the roundabout under the Motorway and headed for the town centre. The 4 x 4 hung back a little because of the lighting around the junction and on the main street and, Jacquie, relying on Bluebell to track the Taxi did the same.

'Artemis, target crossing railway bridge, over.'

'Roger, that, Bluebell. What do you know of the second vehicle, over.'

'Zero. Must be a pre-2011. No daylight running lights, over.'

'Bluebell? I haven't. Hunter disabled them, over.'

'Admonished, Artemis! Target slowing and turning left at end of the bridge. Scotts Road, over.'

'Got it, over.'

Jacquie watched the 4 x 4 go over the bridge and out of sight so she accelerated and ignored the traffic lights on the crossroads at the bottom of the bridge which had changed to red. On the top of the bridge, she braked hard and stopped when she saw that the 4 x 4 had pulled up at the bottom of the bridge. It rolled slowly forward the driver leaning forward and peering carefully left watching until he saw the Taxi disappear between two old buildings on Scotts Road.

'Artemis! Target behind the old Social club, Bluebell, over.'

'Bluebell? Second vehicle, over.'

'Artemis? Stopped by old cinema at end of the bridge, over.'

Shielded by the bridge wall Jacquie decided to wait and switched on the parking lights and hazard warning lights to advise any traffic of her presence and she climbed out and went to the wall and looked over. Carrie joined her.

'What do you think, Mrs Hunter?'

'For starters, Carrie, we're in this as a team and you can call me Jay or Jacquie. As for that lot, we'll have to wait until he decides to move. Hunter knows this area better than me but I'm sure we can get around from the other direction.'

'We can, Jay, but it's fiddly as they've changed all the streets and we now have a one-way system.'

'How do you mean?'

'If you went straight ahead at the bottom you could turn left at the next junction and you would be able to get around in a minute as it is now you have to go to the town centre and right around. It could take about five minutes on a good day.'

'It's a good option, Carrie but I'm afraid we are going to break the law if we have to. Look out, he's moving.'

They watched as the 4 x 4 eased into Scotts Road and drove slowly past the Clubhouse.

They got back in the Rover and Jacquie called in. 'Bluebell? Artemis. Where's that 4 x 4 going, over.'

'Artemis? Past the Club and into the next side street. Someone is getting out, over.'

'Bluebell, tell me when he's out of sight and I'll pull around to the front of the old cinema, over.'

'Wilco, Artemis, over.'

'Bluebell? Have you warned the fuzz, over?'

'Roger, Artemis, over.'

The shadowy figure climbed out of the 4 x 4 and pulled a black woollen hat on before he went to the rear of the 4 x 4, opened the tailgate and retrieved a canvas tool bag. He lowered the tailgate but didn't close it and after a quick look around at the surrounding houses unhurriedly walked the ten metres to the end of the road. Lowering himself almost to ground level he cautiously looked around the corner and seeing Scotts Road was all clear he bent double and ran the twenty-five metres to a cobbled back lane at the end of the Social Club and disappeared into it.

'Artemis? Bluebell. All clear, over.'

'Bluebell, Copy, Artemis, over.'

Checking the road was clear of traffic Jacquie extinguished the lights once more and rolled gently down the bridge and did a sharp left u-turn into the slip road outside the old Cinema and parked close to the bridge wall.

'Bluebell? Artemis, in position, over and out.'

Jacquie took a deep breath and looked across at Carrie. 'Right, Carrie, are you okay to go?'

'Jay, I've never been so excited since I left the Army.'

'You got excited in Afghanistan?'

'Yes, it was weird. You knew you could be stepping onto or into danger. It was adrenaline and fear at the same time. I imagine you had similar feelings in Belfast.'

'Hmm! Yes, we'll leave it there. Let's go.'

They clambered out and after checking they had everything, with a firm push they quietly closed the vehicle doors and made their way to the junction with Scotts Road.

With her back to the wall, Jacquie leaned forward far enough to see around the corner of the building. 'All clear, Carrie, straight over to the other side.'

Jacquie went first and on her signal, Carrie followed and bent low keeping close into the buildings they moved quickly to the entrance of what used to be the car park of the Social Club but was now waste ground. They stopped and listened. It was eerily quiet so Jacquie ran across to the end wall of the club and then signalled Carrie to follow.

They waited and listened again and still, there was no sound. Stealthily they moved to the rear corner of the building and took a quick peek. At the back of the waste ground partially hidden by rubbish and undergrowth, they could see the parked Taxi but immediately in front of them there were steps overgrown by shrubs leading up to the old stage entrance and emergency exit. The shrubs were damaged where people had pushed their way through recently but the door was closed. Jacquie gave Carrie the thumbs up and they crept cautiously to the bottom step.

—

The shadowy figure stood with its back to a double gate, which was a disused tradesman's entrance, and surveyed the 19th-century workers houses in front of him and to his right either side of the narrow cobbled backstreet. Except for a few dwellings at the far end, there were no lights visible. He tried the gate but it was locked and after a moment considering his options he decided that going over the wall was the best one. He unwound a long strap from his bag and leaving the bag on the ground he leapt up and got a hold on the sloping coping tiles on the top. With a heave he pulled himself up and sitting on the top of the wall he pulled his bag up and lowered it down on the other side he swung his free leg over and dropped down by the bag.

Quickly rewinding the strap he picked up the bag and ran across the yard and stopped with his back to the wall by a sturdy waste pipe which went up between two old-style sash windows on the first floor both with a wire security screen over them. In the dark, it was hard to see which was the easy one to bust so he tossed a mental coin and chose the right-hand one as it had a sturdier waste pipe running under it which he could stand on. He mentally thanked the Committee of the club for renewing the plumbing before the club had closed.

He tested the pipe and found it was modern stiff plastic and because it was a sewage pipe it was firmly fixed to the wall. Without hesitation, he began to climb reeling out the bag strap behind him. It took him less than a minute to reach the first pipe junction and he was relieved to find that the drain pipe leading off to his right was equally firmly clamped and would take his weight.

He pulled himself up and stood on the branch pipe with a foot resting on separate brackets. He then carefully inched the bag up and clipped it to his belt and retrieved a small crowbar from it. The security screen was held on by masonry nails and popped easily and he swayed to one side to bend it out of the way before he proceeded to work on the window latch.

He had the right tools for the job. Taking a glass cutter from the bag he scribed a square on the glass before applying some Duct tape over it and then he gently thumped it with his elbow. The sound was negligible and he eased the square of glass out and stuck it to the wall with the tape. The window hadn't been opened for years and he had to ease it up with the crowbar a few centimetres at a time. When the gap was large enough he unclipped the bag from his belt and lowered it through the window and then headfirst he wriggled through and was glad to see that whoever had used the toilet last had closed the lid. He athletically lowered himself to the floor and then organised himself.

He removed his jacket to reveal a shoulder holster and automatic pistol. He took off the utility belt which had held his tools. He checked the spare ammunition in his trouser side pockets and then unclipped and reset the magazine on the gun making sure there was one up the spout and retrieving a torch from the bag he was ready to go.

He tiptoed to the door and eased it ajar and found it opened onto a corridor with offices leading off and at the far end another door. He opened this and it led to a flight of stairs. He partially closed the door behind him and started down the stairs with his gun and torch clamped two-handed at the ready. At the bottom, he came to a divided corridor. The passageway straight ahead was closed off by a Fire Door and the other was a corridor at right angles across the width of the building with doors leading off. He chose the corridor. With his back to the wall, he moved swiftly along it and stopped at each door. He gently eased them open and shone his torch inside and was surprised to find they were changing rooms for visiting Stars or celebrities. At the end of the corridor, he turned left and followed what he guessed was the right-hand entrance to a stage. When he came to a heavy curtain he stopped and listened and, 'Yes,' he could hear voices...

—

With her back to the wall and holding her gun upright in front of her, Jacquie cautiously climbed the steps. At the top, she signalled Carrie to follow which she did but not with a gun but with a Taser at the ready. There were ten steps up to a concrete landing and the door and Jacquie crossed to the far side so that Carrie could aim her Taser at the door. Reaching forward Jacquie tried the handle which moved but the door was stiff. She gave a tug and it jerked open suddenly on rusty hinges and she had to take a quick unsteady step back. While she was off balance a deep voice said, 'Holy Shit!' and a large man dressed in black appeared. He made to grab the handle and then he spotted Carrie. 'What the...?

Carrie didn't hesitate. and in the blink of an eye, she pulled the trigger. The probes struck the man in the chest and with a grunt, he doubled up and fell to the floor writhing in agony as the 50,000-volt charge surged through his body before he collapsed unconscious.

Carrie jumped in with Jacquie close behind and following a

practised drill they cuffed him and put tape over his mouth but didn't bother to check his health. Dumping the Taser, Carrie unclipped her gun and they moved him to one side. Holding guns and torches in front of them they followed the corridor they had entered. At the first door they came to they stood on either side and Jacquie gently turned the knob and pushed it open and shone her torch around. She looked in and remained silent as the beam lit up a bulky object in the middle of the room. She stepped back and closed the door, and said, 'It's him, Carrie, the taxi driver. He's dead.'

'Bastards!' said Carrie.'

With Jacquie in the lead, they crept along the corridor until they came to a heavy curtain and Jacquie held her hand up. 'Sshh! I hear voices.'

—

'Alright, you got me. Where's my kids?' said Hunter.

Facing away from the Victorian music hall stage which was across one end of the large ballroom Hunter was tied by his arms and ankles to a wooden office chair that had been left behind when the last man left the Club. There was a bulky armed guard who stood a couple of metres to one side of him and slightly to the front and another near the end of the room by the Ballroom entrance close to a shuttered Bar which stretched across the room.

Pacing backwards and forwards behind Hunter was The Voice. 'Patience, Mr Hunter, it's not that easy.'

'What do you mean, you can let them go now.'

'I can't. They have seen me, they can identify me, so, NO, I can't let them go.'

'Oh, yeh, you Irish bastard, and what do you intend to do? Shoot them as well?'

'That's one possibility but I remind you to watch your tongue or this could take a little longer and definitely not nicer for you.'

At that point, the guard close to Hunter who had been fiddling with an electronic scanning device spoke. 'Hey, Boss, I'm getting more signals.'

'You checked him didn't you?'

'Yes, Boss,'

'Do it again.'

'Yes, Boss.'

The guard came over and ran the device around Hunter's body and stopped with the device in his crotch area. He swung it up and down Hunter's body again and came back to the same spot. 'It's here, Boss.'

Hunter looked at the guard and said socially, 'Does that thing detect titanium?'

The guy looked at Hunter queerly, 'What's that got to do with it?'

Hunter nodded towards his hip. 'Replacement hip, matey.'

'Duh! Yeah, boss, that's it, he's got a hip.'

The Voice looked a bit concerned. 'Are you sure?'

'Yes, Boss.'

Hunter breathed an internal sigh of relief at the guard's lack of knowledge that titanium on its own does not send out electronic signals.

'Ah, so, Mr Hunter, we are getting worn out?'

'Let me go and try me, pillock!

The Voice walked around to the front of Hunter and delivered a sharp right hook to the side of his face.

Hunter grunted and spitting blood from his lip, he said, 'Is that the best you can do.'

The Voice responded with a backhand across the left side of his face.

Hunter spat. 'You're losing it, pal.'

The Voice went to punch him again and stopped frustrated and walked away cursing inwardly that this ancient old soldier could get to him.

Hunter looked at him and grinned through his split lip. 'I know you, so come on, get it over with, you chicken. Lost your bloody nerve or are those dickheads going to do it for you? I should have shot you when I had the chance.'

The Voice spun on his heel. 'What's that??'

'I had you in my sights over thirty years ago when Thatcher stopped me doing my job. You were lucky.'

At this point, The Voice stopped pacing and reached under his jacket and pulled a Glock 17 from the waistband of his trousers. He walked around to confront Hunter and took a silencer from his jacket pocket and with slow deliberate action screwed it to the gun and then cocked the weapon.

'Your time has come, Hunter!

He took a pace back and aimed at Hunter's forehead but instead of fear all he saw was Hunter staring him out before asking, 'Can I see my kids one last time?'

The Voice turned to the guard by the entrance and signalled by waving his gun. 'Fetch them from the office.'

Using his shoulder as a battering ram against the swing doors the guard crashed out of the room and moments later screams and shouting could be heard as Iain and Lesley remonstrated. The entrance door swung open with a bang and the children were shoved through. Both turned to shout and fight with the guard when they stopped and looked across the room.

Lesley was the first to react. 'DADDY!' she screamed and ran towards him. Iain followed instantly shouting, 'Hi, DAD! Help us!'

Lesley threw her arms around Hunter shouting, 'DADDY! DADDY! Help!'

Iain saw Hunter's problem and said more conservatively, 'DAD! What's up? What's happening?'

Hunter could hardly hold himself together and screwed his eyes up to stop a wayward tear. 'Hi, Kids, you okay? They fed you?'

'Yes, Daddy,' said Lesley, 'Chips.'

The Voice called the guards over. 'Move 'em!'

The one from the door seized Iain around the neck and the other made a grab for Lesley but she ran away shouting, 'You can't catch me.'

The guard ran after her while The Voice ignoring the mayhem stepped forward again and aimed his gun at Hunter. 'This is it. You brought this on and now they can see you die.'

As he began to squeeze the trigger a powerful female voice shouted, 'DROP THE GUN!'

Enter stage left, Jacquie closely followed by Carrie. Distracted from his intention The Voice stopped and looked toward the stage and saw Jacquie with her Glock raised and pointing directly at him. The guard holding Iain pushed him away and brought his gun upwards into a firing position when a single shot rang out and he jerked backwards and dropped to the floor as his head exploded. For a moment everybody froze. Enter stage right Demyan with his smoking gun.

The other guard stopped chasing Lesley and swung his gun towards Jacquie when another shot rang out and he spun and tumbled to the floor clutching his chest. Carrie stepped from behind Jacquie moving her Sig-Saur automatic from side to side when she spotted Demyan and swung her gun towards him and Jacquie shouted, 'No, Carrie!'

Mesmerised by the action Iain stood transfixed and in that instant, The Voice grabbed him from behind, put an arm around his neck and pulled him in tight and then pressed his gun hard into Iain's head.

'STOP!' he shouted, 'OR THE BOY GETS IT!'

Demyan, Carrie and Jacquie swung their guns towards The Voice, when Hunter said quietly, 'Give up, mate, you're on a loser.'

'Shut up, Hunter, I hold all the cards here.'

He began to pull Iain backwards towards the Bar when Hunter spoke. 'Remember your boxing training, Iain, when you sway from side to side, what is it you do?'

Iain was alert and remembered the lessons learnt from his father in their back garden and instinctively pretended to faint. He went floppy and dropped to his knees. In the milli-second that The Voice was dragged off-balance, two shots in quick succession echoed around the room. A double-tap straight from the training manual. The Voice was lifted bodily by the force of the hit and spun around before he crashed backwards to the floor.

Jacquie had not forgotten her training with the SAS and Carrie stood open-mouthed as she watched this new Jacquie whose body language was of a person with only one aim in mind. Bent on revenge with her gun held in two hands in front of her Jacquie went steadfastly down the stage steps and walked purposely across the dance floor to where The Voice lay gasping as his life began seeping away. She stopped and stood astride him with her gun aimed at his head. He stared up at her and his eyes widened further as finally recognition seeped into his pain clouded brain. 'Siobhan Milligan?' he gasped.

She nodded, 'Yes, it's been a long time, Martin McGovern, but nobody, and I mean nobody, messes with my children.'

She began to squeeze the trigger when Hunter said, 'NO! Jacquie! Leave it!'

She looked down at McGovern with a degree of pity in her eyes and decided that indeed it would be a waste of ammunition and instead she lowered her gun and walked across to Iain and put her arms around his shaking body. Lesley was quick to join them.

A plaintive cry came from the centre of the room. 'Will somebody cut me out of here?' Hunter looked over his shoulder as he felt the first cut to the rope holding his wrists and his eyes followed Demyan as he came around the front and cut loose his ankles. As Hunter stood up rubbing his wrists the blood bond between two ex-soldiers was instant and they shook hands.

Keeping his voice low, Hunter said, 'Marcus, I thought you wanted to kill me?'

'I did, but that was before I knew about your kids and I don't do kids. I still want you dead but only in a photo and then I get paid. Come on I owe the taxman. Can we do that? And call me Demyan.'

'What do you want me to do?'

Demyan took out his smartphone. 'Lay in that blood and rub some in your hair.'

As he sprawled down, Jacquie said, 'Hunter, what are you doing?'

'I'll explain in a minute. Let's get this done.'

He smeared some blood in his hair and across his forehead and lay with his face half-hidden and his arms spread out. As the camera clicked there were loud crashes as battering rams and sledgehammers were used to break down the solid 19th-century front doors of the Club. This was followed by lots of shouting, 'ARMED POLICE! ARMED POLICE! DROP your weapons. Hands in the air,' and the leading detachment of the Police Armed

Response Team hurled themselves into the ballroom and spread out across the room Heckler & Koch' automatics at the ready swinging from side to side.

Jacquie and Carrie put their guns on the floor and held up their ID while Hunter rolled away and clambered to his feet. From the corner of his eye he saw the stage curtains were still swaying. He felt disappointed but knew that Demyan had to go.

When the Response Team were satisfied the building was secure they stood down and Gus Thomas and Inspector Fearn entered. The two guards were dead and Thomas went to McGovern and checked for a pulse in his neck before he began searching his pockets and removing all identifying assets.

Fearn joined Hunter and the others and when Thomas had finished he waved the waiting para-medics and the SOCO team to come in and see what could be done before the bodies were removed.

Satisfied that everything was secure Thomas joined the group and nodding towards McGovern, he said, 'That was a turn up for the books, Hunter, I wonder why he was involved?'

Hunter looked around for Jacquie for support before he shrugged, 'I don't know, I can't figure it. Did you get anything from Cronin?'

'No. They're holding him on one charge of attempted murder but others will follow. He is trying to claim the status of a prisoner of war saying he was following orders but his bank account tells another story. His wife is a different proposition, however.'

Jacquie who was sat to one side with Carrie comforting the children looked up. 'I heard that. Did you say Cronin's wife?'

'Yes, she was in the front office with the kids and when we moved in she burbled something about being pressurised into the Taxi heist and the kidnapping. We don't know the full story but she says her life was threatened if she didn't play ball. We'll find out more when we get her down to the Station and take a proper statement. She's under caution right now.'

The conversation was interrupted by Dr Kerr. 'Excuse me. Inspector? We've done all we can here will it be alright to move the bodies...'

A paramedic who had been working on the prostrate form of McGovern intervened. 'Sorry to interrupt,' he said, 'the gentleman has died. The shots were only a centimetre apart and the wound too big and too close to his heart.'

Fearn looked around the group but before he could speak he was stopped by Thomas. 'No problems here,' he said and nodding towards McGovern's body, 'so long as you tag him as John Doe. It's nothing personal but it may have repercussions so it is up to someone higher up than me to decide.'

Dr Kerr nodded. 'I understand. So I'm good to go is that what we're saying?'

'Yes, Doctor, you may indulge in your hobby,' said Fearn.

Carrie called across to them, 'The body of the missing taxi driver is up the corridor in a side room and one of the heavies further on.'

Dr Kerr acknowledged and signalled his team to begin bagging up the corpses and Fearn continued, 'Go home and get some sleep. Meet at the Station at ten o'clock for a debrief.'

'One moment,' said, Thomas. 'Hunter! You and Carrie take Jacquie and the kids home.' He put an arm across Fearn's shoulder and led him away. 'Inspector, we have to talk. Now, this was an SIS operation...'

~~~~~
~~~~~

Part 2

Below the Belt

Reprisal is?

Work in progress

CHAPTER 26

Friday morning

Fearn stood in front of the whiteboard with his pen poised when Hunter raised his hand.

'Yes, Mr Hunter, and how are the children?'

'They were still sleeping when I left but I think all this went over their heads. Iain said it was a lot better than his computer games. What I wanted to ask both you and Gus, Inspector, is, how has all this panned out. Who's been charged with what etc...?'

'I was coming to that, Mr Hunter. You know of course that your lot don't do the charging. It's normally Special Branch but we are pursuing a case against O'Reilly and his wife for attempted murder on one count plus the illegal possession of firearms while SB is pushing for two counts of attempted murder and one count of terrorism. Cronin is being held by SB on two charges of attempted murder while we have him on one count of murder.'

'What about their wives?'

'Mrs O'Reilly is being charged with two counts of attempted murder...'

'Two?'

'Yes, Mr Hunter. We found the car that tried to run you down and her DNA etc... was all over it. An attempt had been made to burn it but was unsuccessful and the Fire Brigade notified us of its whereabouts just outside Speke. That plus Mrs Hunter's shooting.'

'And, Mrs Cronin?'

'We are holding her for perverting the cause of justice and we're still looking into her involvement in the kidnapping of the children and your imprisonment but it appears there are mitigating circumstances.'

'Like what, Inspector?'

'The influence of McGovern which needs looking into by both departments but it's early days. If we are finished here I would like to speak to you, Mr Hunter, and Senior Agent Thomas privately in my office. Is there any more questions?'

There was much head shaking and clearing of throats but no one responded and they gathered up their stuff and went about their business. Hunter and Gus joined Fearn and walked with him to his office.

Halfway along the corridor, Hunter stopped. 'Inspector! I'm popping down to the canteen. Can I get you anything?'

Stunned by Hunter's apparent lackadaisical approach to the circumstances Fearn could only nod in amazement. 'No thank you,' he said, 'and please hurry.'

Hunter shrugged. 'What about you, Gus?'

'I'll have a coffee, Hunter.'

Hunter spun on his heel and called over his shoulder as he strode away, 'I won't be long.'

Fearn still looked bemused when they reached his office and he said, 'Tell me, Gus, is Hunter always like that?'

'Hunter doesn't let much get to him, Colin, but he did recently go through a period of PTSD. I put that down to boredom. Since this episode got off the ground he's very much back to his old self.'

'Even when death was staring him in the face?'

'Very much so. I think that's what made him a natural for his career choices.'

There was a click and both of them turned around to see Hunter bent down opening the door with his elbow. The door swung open with a bang and Hunter entered with his hands full.

'Hi, guys,' he said cheerfully, 'some canteen you have there, Inspector. The bacon butty looks good and, Gus, I brought you a choc muffin.'

'Hunter, I said, just coffee.'

'Okay, I'll have it later. Right! Carry on, Inspector. What was it you wanted?'

Fearn pulled out his chair. 'Sit down, chaps.'

When they were both seated Fearn came straight to the point. 'Your wife, Mr Hunter, used a firearm this morning and we are considering charges to that effect.'

'You what!' He sat with his sandwich halfway to his mouth and choked on the remains of the last bite. When he had finished coughing he looked across to Gus for support. 'Gus, what's he on about? Didn't she show her ID this morning?'

Fearn intercepted the reply. 'Yes, Mr Hunter, she did. Her driving licence not an SIS ID or a permit to carry.'

Gus cleared his throat and held a hand up palm out. 'Colin, that's our fault. When we brought Hunter's stuff up from London we overlooked Mrs Hunter's because she was still in hospital. I'll get it sent up *poste haste*.'

'You have twenty-four hours.'

'Colin? It takes two days for the post.'

'Then you'd better get onto it quickly but I must add she is to be commended for her skill. A little too lethal maybe. Does she practice much?'

Hunter chewed slowly while he thought about his answer. 'We both went to the local shooting club to keep our hand in but it's some time since we did.'

'Where did she get the gun?'

Gus interrupted. 'We issued it. She should have received her permit at the same time.'

'Good, but I need to see proof. One more thing before we finish here. DS. Long is coming back to us. She is suspended at the moment while Internal Affairs look into the shootings.'

Again Hunter looked puzzled. 'Why?'

'It's standard procedure.'

'I'm glad to hear it.' He looked across at Thomas. 'Didn't she ask if she could join SIS, Gus?'

He nodded the affirmative. 'Yes.'

'That's all very well, gentlemen,' said Fearn, 'but while she's on our books she has to abide by the rules. Is there anything else?'

Hunter and Gus both shook their heads and stood up ready to leave when Fearn came around his desk holding his hand out. 'I just want to thank you. It's been a pleasure if not frantic working with you although I think your department lacks a little discipline.'

Outside Hunter could hardly hold himself but managed to control the anger seething below the surface.

'Gus, you'd better get onto the 'Firm' pretty damn quick. Do you think you can fiddle it?'

'The permit, yes, but I need both your weapon serial numbers to get them on the books.'

'You don't need the numbers just issue the permit to carry.'

'I don't know. Stop chattering and let's get home quickly.'

—

When they climbed out of the car at the end of the drive the front door opened and Lesley carrying a little blue teddy bear appeared and ran down to greet them. 'Daddy! Daddy!,' she shouted. She grabbed Hunter's hand as they walked towards the door and looked up at him. 'Are you alright, daddy?'

He smiled down at her. 'Yes, darling, I am. Have you slept well?'

'Yes, Daddy and Teddy too.'

'Oh, good.'

Iain waited for him by the door. 'Hi, Dad, you okay?'

Hunter tousled Iain's hair. 'Yes, son, I'm good, and you?'

'Okay.' As he turned to go into the house ahead of Hunter, he said, 'Dad, are all those nasty men gone now?'

Hunter put an arm around his shoulders as they walked down the Hall. 'Yes, son, there's just the clearing up to do.'

Iain stopped and looked at Hunter. 'Dad, why did they try to kill you?'

'Iain, son, it's a long story. I'll have a chat later when I'm finished cleaning up the loose ends, okay?'

'Right, Dad.' He ran off and into his bedroom and called over his shoulder. 'This is a super game Auntie Carrie bought me.'

Hunter let out a sigh of relief. The effects of the previous night had been worrying him but he realised that children could take a lot more than they were given credit for.

He crouched down and kissed Lesley on the forehead. 'Right, lass, you run along and play because daddy has some work to do.'

'Okay, daddy, Auntie Carrie brought me a new colouring book and pencils.'

Before he could answer she darted into her bedroom and in her eagerness she slammed the door behind her. Hunter shrugged and continued to the kitchen where he was met by Jacquie who, relieved of the tension, over the last few days grabbed him without inhibition and gave him a long passionate kiss followed by a hug.

She stood back breathless. 'Are you okay, Hunter?' she said, 'I've been worried sick.'

He held her by both arms and looked her in the eyes. 'I haven't felt better for years, Jay. How about you?'

'I'm alright now the adrenaline has gone but I haven't slept much.'

'Okay, then, are you ready for the bad news?'

'What bad news?'

'Jay, darling, make some coffee and I'll tell you.'

As Jacquie went to make the coffee Hunter acknowledged Carrie who was looking a bit glum. 'Hi, lass, your boss has been telling us about you. You're laid off?'

Carrie nodded. 'Yes, it's protocol but worse still I have to go back. I enjoy the way you guys work.'

Before he spoke Hunter dragged out a stool. 'Gus, what can we do for her?'

'First things first, Hunter, let's sort out Jacquie,' he said, 'and then we'll deal with Carrie.

'I heard that,' said Jacquie, from the other side of the kitchen, 'what have you got to sort out?'

'Gus,' said Hunter, 'hadn't you better start chasing Jacquie's stuff?'

'Yes, take me to your office and turn the computer on and leave me to it.'

'Jay, shan't be a minute. I'll just set Gus up and I'll be right back and tell you all about it.'

Carrie stood up and grabbed her coat from the back of the stool. 'I got to go. I have an interview with Internal Affairs. I'll see you all later.'

—

Jacquie plonked a mug in front of Hunter and sat on a stool beside him. 'So, H, do you think, Gus, can swing it?'

'Yes, lass, he's the Commander of the 'Magpie' team and has a direct line to 'C'. It was only an oversight because you were still in hospital and we didn't consider you'd be part of the team.'

'That changed as soon as they touched the children. Let's hope I don't need it again.'

'You fancy going back in the front line. You and Carrie would make a good team.'

'Now there's a thought.'

There was a knock on the door and Gus joined them. 'Is there any more of that coffee?' he said, as he closed the door.

Hunter slid off his stool and went to the coffee maker and Gus grabbed a stool across from Jacquie. He had hardly settled and she couldn't hold back. 'Okay, Gus, am I going to jail?'

He smiled and teased her. 'I don't know, it depends...'

'...Gus Thomas, if you don't come clean I may have to retrieve the said weapon and persuade you.'

He threw his hands up. 'Whoa! I give in...'

Hunter slid his coffee over to him and butted into the conversation. 'Alright, how'd it go?'

'Hold the tigress back and I'll tell you.'

Hunter wagged his finger at her. 'Jacquie, what have I told you? Right, Mr Thomas, what have you got?'

'You're off the hook, Jacquie. E-mail copies of your Permits and I.D. will be here in about an hour. The real things are coming by messenger and they should be here by morning.'

She breathed a sigh of relief. 'Wow, I'm glad that's sorted. What about Carrie?'

Gus took out his wallet and gave Hunter a card. 'Tell her to fill the forms in and send them to me but advise her not to hand in her notice until she gets the thumbs up, okay?'

Hunter fingered the card. 'Is there a code she can scribble on the top or something?'

Gus held his hand out. 'Give me the card.' He took the card off Hunter and scribbled something on the reverse side and gave it back. 'Tell her to write that on the top left-hand corner and it will get priority.'

'Thanks, Gus.'

He gave the card to Jacquie. 'Can you do that, love?'

She nodded, 'Yes, she's coming back for tea later.'

Gus took a sip of his cold coffee before he spoke again. 'Hunter, have you been in touch with Williams and Bell yet?'

'Williams is with the Merseyside Police. Bell's gone awol.'

'Since when?'

'Immediately after the arrests.'

'Hmm, that's odd. What do you think?'

'Williams said he muttered something about family life and he walked off.'

'Right, Hunter, we'll leave it there. Get your gear you're going to Belfast.'

'Why Belfast?'

'McGovern's place.'

'Silly question—Why?'

'Because when they found his briefcase the stupid bastards sent it by messenger to his Party HQ in Northern Ireland.'

'Didn't they check it first?'

'No.'

'But you got his phones and wallet?'

'There wasn't much in the wallet, H, and his phones were password-protected so we sent them on ahead to the 'Firm'.'

'What am I doing?'

'You are meeting up with Williams at Broughton where a helicopter is waiting. Once there you will do McGovern's Party office. After that, you will move onto his family home. The '*house cleaners*' are already in his Stormont office and his London office.'

'His London office? I thought Northern Ireland MP's didn't take up their seats in Parliament.'

'You're right, but he has a private office over the river from the House. We are yet to find out why.'

'Oh, I see. Jay—you heard all that. Can you manage while I'm away?'

'Yes, Hunter, but just you be careful.'

'Give me a moment to get my stuff ready Gus, it hasn't been used for a while.'

He left the room and was gone for nearly ten minutes before he returned dressed in black from head to toe with a backpack slung over his shoulder.

He dropped the pack to the floor and crossed the kitchen to hug Jacquie. 'Phew,' he said, 'I'd forgotten how heavy they were.'

'You take it easy, Hunter, let Williams do it.' She grabbed him and swallowed him up in a bear hug. ‘Be careful.’

‘Jay, you wear anything but black if anything should happen to me. That’s an order not that it counts for much.’

She tapped him on his right hip. ‘And mind that.’

They kissed again and without another word he left the room followed by Gus.

~~~~~
~~~~~

CHAPTER 27

The Major in command of the Military Intelligence Unit stepped back from the whiteboard. 'That's the layout of the target taken this afternoon, Mr Hunter. What do you think?'

Hunter stepped closer to the board. In the centre was pinned a large aerial view of a Belfast area with street-level photo's pinned around it. His interest was focussed mainly on the rear of the building which was the centre of their attention and after counting off a number to himself he stood back and observed.

'It's lit up like a floodlit football pitch. The houses near it are too close so we need to put them into darkness for at least ten minutes. Can you fix a power cut for three o'clock in the morning with a blip in the middle?'

'I'll get onto the power company.'

'Next! Did we get onto the shutter manufacturer?'

'Yes. We were lucky. They were supplied by an English firm.'

'Good. Is our back-up organised?'

'Yes, two lads from the SAS volunteered and are on standby.'

'And the black ladders?'

'Ready and loaded, Mr Hunter.'

Hunter nodded his satisfaction. 'We know what we're looking for so it should be over in fifteen minutes. If that's it I'm off to the canteen and then I'm getting my head down.' He swivelled around and looked across the room. 'Are you okay with that, Dunc?'

Williams pushed himself upright from the wall. 'Yes, Guv, I'm with you.'

Together they left the operations room with the Northern Ireland Military Intelligence Unit somewhat bemused by their laid-back approach.

—

The long wheel-based Landrover glided to a halt in the gloom. Belfast's long-standing problem with street lights aided them and two black painted multi-purpose aluminium ladders were slid off its roof and four shadowy figures two carrying backpacks and two with H & K close combat weapons climbed over the gates of the local Hospice and into its car park.

They didn't hesitate but ran quickly to the high dividing wall on their right and working in teams climbed and lifted the ladders over the wall into the next business area. Williams watched Hunter's progress and satisfied himself that replacement hip or not Hunter was up for it.

They had entered a narrow alley which opened out into a large car parking area. Down one side was a high wall with buttresses topped with metal spikes separating them from the buildings lining the main road. Dumpsters had been tactfully placed between the buttresses. Keeping low they ignored the first two premises and quickly crossed the yard and sheltered at the bottom of the wall opposite their target. It was a two-storey building illuminated by two powerful halogen lights with three upper storey windows protected by metal roller shutters.

Leaning the ladders against a buttress they each took a corner of the nearest dumpster and gently eased it away from the wall until they had room to both hide and manoeuvre behind it. While they waited they put on surgical rubber gloves and Hunter lifted the cover of his luminous watch. It was close to three o'clock and he hoped the power company clocks were in sync as promised and he began a countdown.

Ten, nine, eight, seven, six, five, four, three, two, one...

Right on cue, all the lights in the locality went out. Working as a team they quickly got one ladder in position and one of them went to the top and pulled the other ladder up and lowered it down the other side. He then climbed over and down and was soon followed by two more of the team. The last man climbed over the wall and balancing on the top rung pulled the first ladder up and over and lowered it down to his team waiting at the bottom.

Dividing into two teams one pair ran across to a position under the light at the left-hand end of the building while the other pair did the same under the right-hand one. Simultaneously they extended the ladders to the height of the lights and two of them raced up the ladders and put a heatproof cover over the lights and tied it in such a way that a long cord hung down to the ground fastened in such a way that one sharp pull on the cord would release the cover.

Sliding down the ladders they quickly moved them to either side of the central shuttered window which was the allocated fire escape and therefore top-hung. Hunter went up one ladder and Williams up the other while the two SAS volunteers steadied the ladders and stood guard. Hunter took what looked like a TV remote from his thigh pocket and held it close to the window.

Williams gave a quick command into his walkie-talkie radio and the power in the area was restored. Hunter pressed the remote and the shutters began to wind open and Williams who had climbed higher pressed a thick piece of sponge against the shutters as they curled over the top to muffle the sound.

When the shutter was fully open Williams spoke into his radio again and the power went off. From his thigh pocket, he pulled out an industrial strength glass cutter and using a metal ruler held by Hunter as a guide Williams made four cuts in a square shape in the outer pane opposite the window catch. Hunter covered it with Duct tape before giving it a sharp tap with a rubber hammer. The glass fell inwards and Hunter eased it out and stuck it to the wall with the tape. They repeated the exercise on the inner pane.

Reaching in they unlocked the catch and eased the top-hung window out to its fullest extent. 'Okay, Dunc, in you go. You've got two minutes to disable the burglar alarm. When the power comes on wipe the CCTV tapes and then switch off the cameras.'

Duncan scrambled in first and went straight for the stairs. Hunter followed and began looking for McGovern's office. He didn't have far to go and using skeleton keys he was in the office as the power came on. The sudden brightness made him jump and he crossed the room swiftly to turn the office lights out which some helpful cleaner had left on and he cursed as he waited for his reduced night vision to return.

Williams joined him a few minutes later and together they searched the room and found the briefcase in a kneehole under the desk in what must have been McGovern's usual spot. They spent a couple of minutes taking photo's of some paperwork and making sure everything was as they found it they left but not before Hunter dropped a business card on the desk.

Locking the door behind them their retreat was the reverse of their entry and when the roller shutter was lowered into place they took the pieces of cut glass with them and slid down the ladders.

Because of the covered lights the rear of the building was in deep shadow and keeping low they could move about freely and they set the ladders up against the spiked rear wall ready. The two SAS volunteers who were each holding a cord gave them a yank and ran for the ladders. They rolled up the covers and were quickly over the wall and the last man dragged the ladder behind him and slid it down and joined the team. They then did a reverse course back to the Hospice car park where Williams uttered the codeword into his radio and five minutes later the Landrover returned and in one minute they were gone.

As they travelled south on the Ulster M1 to Lisburn Hunter became bored and picked up McGovern's expensive leather briefcase which was on the seat between them. He turned it over in his hands a few times and ignored the front which was secured by a combination lock and instead unzipped the laptop section on the back. There was no computer so he searched in the many small pockets and felt an object at the bottom of one of the divisions made for folders. He fished it out and saw it was a black metallic item about the size of a small chocolate bar.

He showed it to Williams. 'What's that, Dunc?'

Under the dull amber glow of the street lights, Williams took a closer look at it. 'That's an SSD external hard drive for a computer. A bit like an oversize memory stick.'

He gave it back to Hunter who zipped up the briefcase and dextrously slipped the SSD into his top pocket before he said, 'Have a go at opening this, Dunc.'

Williams took it from him and holding it close to his ear he played with the numbers. After a few minutes of twiddling, he sat back and smiled. 'I should have tried that first. 1234.'

Both he and Hunter looked inside but didn't touch anything and Williams locked it again. 'We'll leave it for the brains department,' said Hunter.

—

Five Party members stood around McGovern's desk and agreed that apart from the damaged window nothing was missing and appeared all in order. Why? was the mystery, but they were loathe to inform the PSNI of the break-in. One member picked up Hunter's card and looked at it from various angles.

'Does anyone know what this is? It's just a snap of the solar system as far as I can make out.'

He threw it back on the desk and they collectively looked at each other and shook their heads when the youngest member of the group picked it up and took a closer look. 'I recognise that. It's the `Orion′ constellation. See the three stars in the belt and that bright one in the right shoulder that's Betelgeuse.'

No one ventured an opinion other than it was probably something left behind by McGovern.

~~~~~
~~~~~

CHAPTER 28

'Arrangements have been made, Hunter, to pick up Mrs McGovern and fly her over here to identify the body which means you will have the whole night to yourself. Have you sussed the place yet?'

'Yes. The house is up for sale and the estate agents were very helpful. We need an electronics wizard to help. Locks are one thing but this modern stuff they have in some homes today could be tricky.'

'What about, Williams?'

'He's got his doubts.'

'You did okay the other night?'

'That was with the power off but this is something else.'

'It'll take a couple of hours but our experts are on the way as I speak. You'll still have time.'

—

It was a little before noon when the BTIreland van drove into the cul-de-sac and pulled up alongside the green street cable box. The crew were in no hurry. They sat chatting and playing with their smartphones before, with apparent reluctance, getting out and setting up barriers around the rear of the vehicle and a warning sign for pedestrians. The two men retrieved stools and a toolbox from the back of the van and opened the doors of the cable box and sat down and with heads bent low inside pretended to work with the array of wires exposed to them.

A taxi passed them and entered a drive leading to a well-kept property with landscaped gardens and woodland surrounding it and left five minutes later with Mrs Elaine McGovern and her two grown-up children and a minder on board. Immediately one of the men at the box spoke into a concealed radio and two minutes later a van with adverts for double-glazing plastered down the sides drove into the road and reversed into the drive of the same property.

The driver jumped out and opened the rear doors and with a clipboard under his arm set about measuring windows while his co-driver went to the front door and shielded by the van used skeleton keys to open the outer porch door. He did the same with the main door to the house and was inside in less than two minutes.

Inside he hurried to the security alarm box and clamped a small electronic device to the side of it and pressed a button. Digital numbers appeared and began flicking over in quick sequence and with a little ping, it stopped with a four-figure number showing. The operator quickly pressed the appropriate keys on the alarm system keyboard and neutralised it. He wrote the code number on a small post-it note and stuck it on the alarm box.

Job done he went outside and stood blocking the view from the other side of the van and two people dressed in black wearing surgical gloves jumped out and ran into the house. They removed their footwear inside the door and went further into the interior and sat on the floor. The co-driver locked the front doors again and after an unhurried chat with the driver, they added more detail to the clipboard before they drove off.

Mrs McGovern had fortuitously closed the downstairs blinds and in the half-light, Williams mused, 'That wasn't too difficult,' he said, 'we could have done that.'

'Better safe than sorry I guess,' replied Hunter and he lapsed into silence while he pondered his position. Previously when on ops he didn't give it a second thought but now his inner self felt disturbed. He wondered about his feelings if someone broke into his house. This was their home, their refuge, and he felt like he had broken their trust and belief in a safe sanctum. This wasn't an office this was a home.

His thoughts were disturbed by Williams. 'That's ten minutes, Guv, what do you reckon?'

Instantly Hunter's mindset changed and he was back in agent mode. They were squatted in the short hall between the entrance and the kitchen and opposite them was a door.

Familiar with the layout learned from the Estate Agents floor plan Hunter pointed to it. 'Okay, Dunc, that looks like the office, I'll do that, you do the kitchen. Unlock the back patio doors before you start searching and make sure you don't change anything.'

Williams scrambled to his feet and knowing Hunter had a hip

replacement he paused to watch the older mans technique. Hunter slid his right foot under his left and rolled over pushing on the floor with his right fist. When he was on his hands and knees he pulled his right knee forward until he was rested on one knee and then steadying himself on the wall with his left hand he pushed down on his raised knee with his right hand while pushing up with the leg. It looked awkward but with practice, Hunter had it down to a fine art.

Knowing that Hunter wasn't going to be a liability he left him and went into the kitchen. Hunter went to the door opposite and tried the handle. It was locked but he made short work of it with his skeleton keys. He had guessed right it was an office and in typical McGovern style it was spotless and immaculate the same way he had dressed. It was furnished with antique office furniture and there wasn't a paperclip or piece of paper out of place and Hunter knew he would have to be very careful.

He began with the large Chippendale block-front sloping-lid desk. It had nine drawers in the lower section and six smaller ones in the top alcove and everyone was locked but Hunter meticulously opened each one and with the certainty that nobody else would have been allowed access to this very private study and would therefore not have intimate knowledge of what was in there he confiscated items and paperwork he thought were of interest.

He then moved onto the safe which was built into the wall in such a way that it was part of the cupboards in the kitchen/dining room next door. This was William's territory and he went to look for him.

He found him in the utility room at the back of the house.

Williams was bent over delving into an open chest-freezer surrounded by a mountain of files and folders. He stood up when Hunter walked in. 'Hi, looks like we've hit the jackpot, Guv, but there's too much of it. He must have a file on everybody in Sinn Fein's history and guess what else I found?'

Hunter shook his head. 'What?'

'A file on one Siobhan Milligan.'

Hunter smothered a whistle of surprise. 'That was Jacquie's cover. Okay, there's too much here. See if you can find a couple of boxes and fill them with the most interesting files including

Jacquie's and leave them by the back door but before that come and have a go at the safe in the office. Bring your gear.'

They went back to the office and Hunter waved Williams forward. 'There you are what do you think? It fits in with the rest of the furniture in here and is pretty ancient.'

'You're right. Sit quiet and I'll have a go.'

He fumbled around in his pack and took out a stethoscope and squatted down in front of the safe and began twiddling the central dial first one way and then the next. He cursed and bashed the safe with the side of his fist and started again but a little slower this time.

It took him three minutes but he sat back with a grin. 'Got it! I love the old stuff.'

'And the lock, Dunc, can you do that?'

'Give me time, I was just coming to that.'

He fiddled in his bag and brought out what looked like a skeleton adjustable spanner with the jaws facing out. He screwed it down to its minimum width and inserted it into the lock and then twiddled with the adjustments several times trying the mechanism after each one. He withdrew the tool and jerked the safe handle upwards and swung the door open and peered inside.

'Wow! Look at that.'

Hunter crouched beside him. 'What's up?' and then reality struck him. 'Bloody hell! There's got to be half a million quid there if they're all fifties. What do you reckon?'

Williams pointed. 'Probably more as there are some Euros there and there's a folder in here.'

He took it out and gave it to Hunter who opened it on the first page and then let out a small whistle.

'What is it, Guv?'

'I'm quite impressed, Dunc, apparently I'm worth a million smackers.' He gave the file to Williams. 'Keep this and Jay's separate. I think we've found enough but keep looking and don't go upstairs.'

'Why not?'

'Because I said so.'

Williams shrugged and walked back to the utility room with

the file under his arm. Hunter began to renew his search when he sensed the mechanical bleep of a mobile phone. He spun around slowly listening as it rang and he traced it to his backpack. It was one he had confiscated earlier from the desk. The caller I.D. was blank and Hunter let it ring. When it stopped a message came up saying it had transferred to voice mail. A few seconds later it went dead. One for the experts, he muttered and carried on searching.

An hour later they were finished and stretched out on an old crinkled leather sofa which was along one wall of the kitchen/diner. Williams took a water bottle from his backpack and took a swig. 'What do you reckon, Guv?'

'Give it ten minutes and then we'll push those boxes out onto the patio before the security lights are operative. When it's properly dark I'll wait by the doors and you set the alarms. You've got a minute to get out and close the door behind you. After that, we move like hell down the steps into the garden and along the back path towards the woods.'

At nine-thirty Hunter stood waiting by the back door and he gave the thumbs up to Williams who was stood in the grey dimmed light by the hall door. He disappeared and reappeared thirty seconds later. Hunter stepped outside and Williams swiftly crossed the room and stepped out of the rear patio doors and closed them behind him. Because the key had been left in the lock on the inside by Mrs McGovern they couldn't secure the door but hoped that whoever found it open would put it down as a mishap and forget it.

'Did you pick up the sticky note, Dunc?'

'You sound just like my misses. Yep, I did.'

As they scooped up the boxes the motion sensors detected them and the lights came on and they did a speedy retreat across the wooden decking to the steps at the end. Hunter went first and was on the bottom step when he heard Williams attempts to stop a shout and instead give out a muffled scream, 'Aargh!'

He looked around to see Williams tumbling down the steps with loose files flying around him and he landed with a thump moaning at Hunter's feet.

'Shut up!' hissed Hunter, 'you'll wake the neighbourhood?'

Williams groaned. 'Sorry, Guv, I've sprained my ankle.'

'Lie still. We're below the decking and the lights should go out in five minutes.'

They had to wait fifteen minutes for the security lights to go out but when they did Hunter found he could move around easily because as he had previously noted they were below the level of the deck which shielded them from the sensors. He scrabbled about in the dark with a dimmed blue torchlight and gathered in what files he could see and then widened his search to look for others. Satisfied he had retrieved them all he turned his attention to Williams.

'Right, mate, what's your problem?'

'It's my ankle. I missed the top step and it went over on its side and it hurts like shit.'

'Can you get up?'

Hunter pulled Williams to his feet. 'Try and walk.'

Williams attempted a few short steps. 'It's no good, Guv, I'm knackered.'

'You're gonna have to hop. Go down to the perimeter path turn left and follow it into the wooded area. I'll bring the boxes.'

'But, Guv, you can't carry both.'

'I'll have to double back. Get going.'

Hunter picked up one box and left Williams to struggle on his own down to the lower path and along the perimeter which followed the high border hedge. He let out a huge sigh of relief when he got into the trees and saw a small wicket gate that led onto an exit door through the hedge.

It was locked but he left it for Williams to fix and went back for the second box. He passed Williams who was three-quarters of the way tentatively stepping with the toe of his right foot and hopping with the other.

'Unlock the gate, Dunc. Are you up for it?'

Williams gritted his teeth and took a sharp breath. 'No worries. I'll have it done when you get back.'

Back at the steps, Hunter was doing a final search when the kitchen/diner lights came on. 'Shit! Someone's come home.'

He picked up the box and stopped in his tracks as the security lights came on. Stooping low he ducked across the path and slid under a shrub and he had just pushed the box to the back of the bush to shield the lighter colour from prying eyes when a figure came to the handrail around the decking and switched on a torch. Hunter pushed his face into the ground and lay still as the beam swept backwards and forward across the garden but the security lights softened the beam and limited its penetration.

Hunter waited patiently for a couple of minutes before twisting his head enough to see with one eye that the suspicious figure was satisfied that all was safe and had retired when from the corner of his eye he spotted a buff coloured file under a bush the other side of the path. He waited until the lights went out before he crawled on elbows, stomach and knees across the path and retrieved the file. He folded it and stuffed it down the open neck of his combat jacket and slithered back for the box.

He waited a little longer to make sure everything was quiet before he hurried down the path to the shelter of the hedge and the safety of the woods and he just hoped the Williams had the gate open. He did and Williams breathed a sigh of relief when Hunter caught up with him.

'That was close, Guv, did you see who it was?'

'Nope! Let's get moving.'

With Hunter in the lead, they followed a narrow winding path down into a gully before it went diagonally up an embankment and joined a single lane road that disappeared through a tunnel under a railway track. Hunter hurried back for the second box and when he returned they crouched in the undergrowth and Williams called in. Ten minutes later the BTIreland van came through the tunnel and spotted their flashing blue torchlight and in a minute had whisked Hunter and Williams to safety.

—

Such was McGovern's dominance in the household it was a week before anyone ventured into his office. Several people picked up the business card picture of the 'Orion' constellation, looked at it, turned it over, dismissed it and dropped it back on the desk.

~~~~~
~~~~~

CHAPTER 29

Above the barely discernible rumble of traffic going through Admiralty Arch all due to the solid foundations and the stonework of the building which absorbed all but the severest of noise, the china tea and coffee cups clattered onto saucers and were passed down the long table and onto a tray and after a little shuffling and blowing of noses the gathered company which included 'C', Gus Thomas, Hunter and Penny Farthing settled down.

Gus addressed them. 'Good morning chaps and welcome to the latest member of our team Agent Penny Farthing. Penny has been working on 'Operation Magpie' internally more or less since the outset. Hunter! Penny has a similar background to Jacquie and it was she who sussed out our Russian. She will be working with you now we've temporarily lost Williams. Penny—take no nonsense from the grumpy old man.'

Penny practically dressed in a modest trouser suit and cream blouse with polished boots swung her chair so that she faced Hunter who was sat alongside her. She smiled and stuck out a hand. 'How do you do, Mr Hunter.'

Hunter took her hand and liked the firm grip. 'How do you do, but please call me, Hunter.'

'Will do.'

Thomas coughed politely. 'If you two are finished we'll get on. As you know Bell has gone awol.'

'What's happened to him, Gus?'

'We waited a few days after he went missing because he said he was going to see his partner but he never showed and his partner is fictional. We put out an all-points alert for him and the latest is, he left via Gatwick and flew out to Dublin.'

'Gus, is he now a suspect?'

'Yes, and we're pressing our counterparts in Dublin for help.'

'Keep me posted, the two-faced shit!'

Penny had a feeling that Bell might be in serious trouble. With her elbow still resting on the table, she raised a hand.

Gus acknowledged. 'Yes, Penny?'

'Mr Thomas, sir, since we traced Dimitrov or whatever his name is. Did anything come of it after he dropped off the radar?'

'Good question, Penny, and no need for the sir. Hunter was the last person to speak to him. We know he left the country with yet another alias and he's wanted by the boys in blue for firearms offences. Under the circumstances, I don't think we'll be pressing the U.S. for extradition but he's certainly curtailed his travel destination options.

Up until this point, 'C' had remained silent but he now interrupted the proceedings with a polite cough and said, 'Enough! Gus, the stuff that was recovered from McGovern's offices and property, did that help?'

'I was coming to that, sir. He was very efficient and well versed in the security game. The files of IRA sympathisers old and new told us nothing we don't know but he used code names for his connections. Three stand out in this case. Red, Blue and Gold. Blue we think is Bell and Red is buried somewhere in GCHQ and we are still seeking Gold.'

'C' tilted his head and looked up at Thomas. 'And what have we done about it?'

'Well, sir, when we set up 'Operation Magpie' I was going to be the newly promoted kid on the block in Vauxhall Bridge and I buried myself in the basement with the administrators and put it around I was merely bringing myself up to date. Procedures and that sort of thing and to keep me out of the way they were only too glad to help. However, with the shooting of Agent Artemis the exercise widened and I spent most of the time up north so as soon as Penny here was finished with our Russian she took over from me in the basement giving them some excuse I'd been posted elsewhere. Penny! Would you like to continue?'

'Yes, sir...' She stood up and Hunter saw that she had other similarities to Jacquie. She continued, '...with the information Mr Thomas gave me I didn't push it but kept my interest to a month before the date of the first attempt on Agent Hunter and I had easy access to files, withdrawals and more important—returns. Most of it was all to do with International material way beyond my brief and this operation but I did get one break. Someone outside this department took the file relating to 'Magpie.''

'C' immediately looked interested. 'Did you find out who took it?'

'Yes. He returned it later the same day. I made an excuse to go to the restroom but instead went to the print room and while I was flirting with the 'Watcher' I flicked through the register and found he had indeed made a photo-copy of the documents before returning them.'

Hunter interrupted. 'Who was it, Penny?'

'Sir Henry Jackson-Milburn, Deputy Chief of GCHQ.'

'You're sure,' said 'C', 'not one of his personal staff?'

'Yes, sir.'

'Gus?' said 'C', 'are you listing him as a suspect?'

'Yes, sir.'

'And what do you want, Gus?'

'I want covert surveillance, his telephone records and a telephone tap. Oh! and a postal intercept.'

'That could be difficult. He's a senior man, I'll have to speak with the Home Secretary and she's not easily swayed. Meanwhile, I'll get Tech Support on the job. Anything else?'

Hunter intervened. 'Yes! Is he Red?'

There was silence as they looked at each other before Thomas replied, He's too high up the chain to be running agents. I think he's just supplying the info. Why, is another matter.'

'Gus!—a question,' said Hunter, 'have you done a background check?'

'Yes.'

'Did he take any other files?'

'C' spoke up again. 'It's his job Agent Hunter. As second in command at GCHQ he is part of the COBRA and he has access to all files but 'Operation Magpie' is an internal investigation and not a national emergency. He shouldn't have knowledge of it, so it does seem a little odd.'

'What's COBRA, sir?'

'It's the committee which the Prime Minister calls in a National Crisis and it meets in Cabinet Office Briefing Room 'A'. Hence COBRA.'

When he was finished Thomas said, 'Excuse me, sir, but when we set up 'Magpie' did you mention it to the Home Secretary in your weekly meetings?'

'No, Gus, as I said this was meant to be purely internal.'

Hunter thumped his pen down on his pad and sat back. His mind was on other things outside the room. He mentally formed a plan but it could wait until the meeting was over and 'C' continued, 'It's getting late and I have another meeting. If there are no more questions we'll finish and meet again tomorrow when I hope I can give you the okay for Milburn.'

'C' got up from his chair and left the room but before the others could do likewise a young administrator pushed through the door. 'Excuse me,' she said, 'which of you is Agent Thomas?'

Gus stepped forward. 'Me.'

'I've got a message from the Tech guys.' She looked at her pad. 'Agent Bell is in New York and can you give them a call?'

'Thank you, miss, I'll do that.'

She ducked out of the room and Gus walked to the other end of the table and made the call. He was only on the line for a minute when he scribbled something on a sheet of A4 lying on the table before he rejoined Hunter and Penny. 'Good news, Hunter, that phone you confiscated, the one with voice mail...'

'Yes,' said Hunter somewhat impatiently, 'who was it?'

'It was Bell and he left a message saying he was in New York and a contact phone number.'

'Wouldn't he know that McGovern was dead?'

'No, he jumped ship immediately after the incident and as we hadn't broadcast it he wouldn't know but he probably does now.'

'What's that phone number, Gus?' said Hunter.

Thomas shoved the piece of paper over the table. 'Why do you want it?'

'Just for my records. I like to keep things tidy.'

He took an old ATM receipt from his pocket and scribbled the number on the back and then said to Penny, 'Come on, lass, let's grab a coffee and we'll swap info.'

Penny, bag in hand made to follow Hunter when Thomas called out. 'Hunter! One more thing.'

Hunter stopped with one hand resting on the door and turned to face him. 'What's that?'

'There's been a suggestion from above that you should consider changing your name.'

Hunter made to answer but stood briefly open-mouthed unsure what to say and instead uttered, 'Oh!' and a split second later he said, 'I'll think about it. See you!' and he swung away and disappeared down the corridor with Penny close behind.

—

Hunter pushed the cappuccino across to Penny and slid onto the bench alongside her but made sure to keep a respectable distance between them. 'Right, Penny, how do you fancy a trip to New York?'

Her eyes widened and she looked at him. 'Is this a chat-up line?'

Hunter put his cup down. 'Nope! I'm too old for that, lass, I have some unfinished business.'

'And the 'Firm' won't sanction it.'

'You're quick, but it's all in the line of duty. Separate rooms and all that. You can opt-out if you want.'

'Hunter, have you been to New York?'

'No.'

'You need me. When do we go?'

'First, we need more info, Penny. Have you still got your pass into Admin?'

'Yes.'

'I want Bell's file.'

'Leave it with me. Was there anything else?'

'What do we know of this Milburn character?'

'Where are you staying?'

'I'm in the Camden safe house.'

'Okay, see you later.'

She quickly swallowed the rest of her coffee and sweeping up her handbag she left him to his thoughts.

—

The Camden safe house situated in a quiet residential street looked like two semi-detached Victorian properties but inside they had been modified into one. It had three floors and a basement with a walled rear garden that stretched back to the railway tracks. It was conveniently close to Camden Town, the Parks and Primrose Hill with easy access to the Northern Line underground station. Inside there were three apartments. On the top floor was a hi-tech room with recording devices etc... and the housekeepers Mrs Amy Archer and her ex-SAS husband. The two apartments on the first floor were for guests of SIS or Agents like Hunter. The basement was a separate entity comprising two cell-like rooms with toilet facilities and a large open undecorated space with a few chairs and a table which was used for more questionable activities. It had seen little action since the end of the cold war.

Hunter spoke a long loving 'Goodnight' to Jacquie and put down the phone and prepared to watch an evening's appalling entertainment when he heard the doorbell ring. He wondered who was calling at this hour when Mrs Archer's voice crackled on the intercom.

'Mr Hunter, you have a visitor.'

He pushed himself up from the leather sofa and went to the speaker device by the door. 'Who is it, Amy?'

'She says she's Penny Farthing.'

'Send her up, she's one of us.'

'Huh, I bet!'

He opened the door and waited for Penny and when she came in he took her short trench coat and hung it in the small cloakroom space and while he was doing so he had a quick glance at the label.

'Good taste,' he said to himself.

She sat in the middle of the three-seater sofa and kept her large bag close to her.

'Can I get you anything, lass? Coffee or something stronger?'

'Something stronger, Hunter?'

He went to the drinks cabinet and picked up a bottle that was already opened. 'The previous tenant didn't leave anything of note but I have good single malt.'

'Please, with ice.'

He poured some whisky into a glass and went through to the kitchen and returned moments later with ice in a jug. He dropped a couple of cubes into the glass and gave them to her and tactfully sat in an armchair.

'Now then, Penny, what brings you here, it can't be to see me?'

She opened her bag and extracted two files and held them out. He took them from her and nodded appreciatively when he noted the names. 'Are these the originals?'

'No, they're copies for our eyes only.'

Gus had mentioned his new secret weapon and Hunter looked at this *femme-fatale* with wayward dark brown hair, not unlike Jacquie. 'She is something else,' he said mentally.

He flicked open Bell's file, 'Give me a jiffy.'

After a few moments of reading, he lowered it down to his lap and said, 'This tells us nothing. There's no trace of him before his military service. Where did he come from?'

Penny put down her glass. 'I thought that myself. The only reason I can see why there is no background is the fact that he was recommended to us directly from the Military but take a close look at who recommended him.'

Hunter checked and whistled. 'Well, well, that's a turn-up.'

He picked up the Jackson-Millburn file and read for a while and when he stopped for a drink he looked thoughtful and then said to Penny, 'Are you thinking what I'm thinking?'

'If you mean the similarities in the military, yes. A little help do you think?'

'And the Millburn's have a property in Northern Ireland.'

'Hunter, how do we get Bell's background. Who would have it?'

'Our Mr McGovern, Penny. What happened to those files we rescued?'

'They've been passed down to Admin as NFA.'

Hunter smiled at her and said with a grin, 'Penny!'

She laughed, 'I know, can I go to Admin? I'll have to undo another button on my blouse and it will cost you a bottle of single malt.' She held her glass out. 'Right now I'll settle for another.'

'Are you driving?'

'No.'

'Have you far to go?'

'East Finchley.'

'Put it on the 'Magpie' tab or you could stay here in the other apartment. Mrs Archer has emergency supplies.'

'I'll go to my place.'

'Okay, Penny, what are you like with computers?'

'Pretty good, why?'

'I confiscated an external hard drive and it occurred to me it may contain what we are looking for. Hang on, I'll go and get it.'

He got up from his chair and left the room and she could hear stuff being moved around before he eventually emerged holding the SSD up. 'Here it is. As usual, in the last place you look.'

She got up from the sofa and joined him at a computer desk which was wedged alongside a writing desk in the corner of the room. Hunter waved her into the seat and gave her the SSD. 'Do you know how to keep this computer off the firm's network?' he said.

'Yes, a kind man in the training college gave me the info.'

She made herself comfortable and went through the rigmarole of start-up and passwords and when it was up and running she plugged in the SSD into one of three USB sockets handily placed on the front of the computer tower.

She pressed a few buttons and the drive showed up on the screen and a password was required. 'Do you know the password, Hunter?'

'Err, no!' And then he had an idea. 'Try 'Password'.'

'It won't be that simple surely.'

'You'd be surprised how naive people are, Penny.'

She typed it in without success and Hunter said, 'Try 123456.'

Released from its prison the SSD sprang into life showing compressed files of people old and new with connections to the IRA.

'Our Mr McGovern wasn't so smart after all,' mused Hunter.

Using the mouse they scrolled through the files until Hunter, fed up, said, 'Just type Milburn into search, Penny.'

She obliged and so did the SSD. Hunter crouched alongside her and together they studied the life story of Sir Henry Jackson-Milburn. Born in India, brought up in Northern Ireland went to Eton and Cambridge and then joined the Marines and transferred to the SBS and eventually served with SIS under diplomatic cover. Became M.P. from 1983 until 2003. Knighted in 2003 and took up the post at GCHQ. The family still has a residence in Northern Ireland.'

'Busy man,' said Hunter, 'but why the interest by the Pro-IRA. What's that say at the end, Penny?'

She lowered her head slightly and studied the note written in *italics*. 'It says *'Gold'* and then—*see Bell*.'

'Scroll to Bell. Would you like another drink?'

'No, thanks, have you got tea?'

'Yep, carry on and I'll make the tea.'

He got up and stretched and Penny watched as his ageing body gradually unwound as he walked across the room. She had a little smile to herself and got back to the business. When he returned with two mugs he dragged over a dining chair.

'Right, Penny, have you found anything?'

'Yes, and the reason Milburn was giving away intelligence.'

'What's that?'

'He was being blackmailed. Simon Bell, formerly Doyle and his younger brother, Martin, were in a Catholic orphanage and it says here that Jackson-Milburn when he stayed at his country seat was part of a group who regularly took boys from the orphanage and abused them in orgies which included the Bells.'

'Oh, my, my. Why were they in the orphanage?'

'Their father was killed by UK forces in a small action in Belfast and their mother died of cancer and there were no close relatives.'

'The Bells were out for revenge with the help of the Pro-IRA.'

'It looks that way, Hunter.'

'Who's RED?'

'Bells younger brother now known as Martin Parr. He works in GCHQ. He was recommended by you know who.'

'That's why McGovern referred to Milburn as *Gold*, he was a nugget. Okay, Penny, before we call it a day can you print those off for me?'

'Do you know nothing, Hunter?'

She reached under the desk and switched on the small Deskjet printer hidden there and in a few minutes, Hunter had his copies.

'Thanks, Penny, I owe you. Now here's the plan.' He gave her his passport. 'Book two early morning open returns to Paris for tomorrow and a double room in any three-star hotel you fancy so that it looks like a dirty weekend. We check-in and then slip out and fly Premium Cattle Class to New York from Paris using our alias passports. Have you got one?'

'Yes, don't laugh, I'm Penelope Halfpenny.'

He stifled a laugh and said, 'Byewater and Halfpenny, aye. You'll need two bags. One for Paris and one for New York. Make your excuses and another thing, we'll be having dinner with some friends in NY on Friday night. Amy thinks I'm off home to see my wife and kids.' He handed Penny a gold credit card. 'Here's my credit card, use that. Is everything okay?'

He expected a little hesitancy at the thought of going off-piste but she replied without hesitation, 'It's good by me.'

He closed the door behind her and poured another whisky before settling down and planning his next move. A couple of minutes later he leapt up from the sofa and went back to the computer and on a whim, something he had read or heard on the grapevine typed the names of two narcotics into the Google search bar.

He read the spiel about them from several websites and decided that their use was a bit over the top and he would resort to something simpler and for this, he got in touch with the SIS specialist department who after a brief explanation of his needs said they would have the equipment ready and delivered to the safe house early the next morning.

He printed off more copies of the downloaded facts on Bells brother Parr and Jackson-Milburn and then sat at the desk alongside the computer and began writing letters. One he put in an envelope with the downloaded facts about Sir Jackson-Milburn and addressed it to the Guardian Newspaper and the other with Martin Parr's transgressions addressed FAO Gus Thomas.

Checking the time he saw that the U.S. would be up and about and scrolling his personal smartphone contacts he found the New York number he wanted. With a device in each hand, he dialled it on the encrypted 'Firms' burner phone. Five minutes later he did the same again to a number thirteen-hundred miles south in Florida.

Online again but this time on the recommendation of his NY contact he booked rooms in the name of Byewater and Halfpenny in the Cortese Hotel close to Times Square.

Job done, with the last of his whisky he swallowed a couple of painkillers to ease his aching ribs and sat back to video chat with Jacquie on Messenger before he went to bed.

A package containing three blue asthma inhalers arrived early the next morning and he put them into a clear sealable plastic bag ready for airport security.

~~~~~
~~~~~

CHAPTER 30

After safely storing their US bags in the left luggage lockers of Paris CDG airport their journey into Paris itself was a nightmare and try as he might the luxury Uber taxi driver could find no easy way around the mayhem and it took them ninety minutes to reach the Hotel Ascot.

Putting on a brave face they bounced into the hotel reception like star-crossed lovers smiling and laughing through the checking in process and with Penny hanging onto Hunter's arm they followed the porter. He showed them to their room and left with a smile and a wink at Hunter when he saw the tip.

He hadn't been gone two minutes before Hunter put the 'Do Not Disturb' sign on the door and flopped into an armchair exhausted. 'Give it ten minutes, Penny and we'll go down.'

They left the sign hanging on the door and wandered down to the lounge with a good view of the reception desk and they chatted over their coffee watching and waiting. When Hunter thought the receptionist was occupied he gave Penny the signal and they meandered through the lounge arm in arm and out onto the street. Luck was with them and a taxi that had just dropped off more guests was almost too willing to run them to CDG Airport.

Fearing that the earlier delay may have cost them there was a huge sense of relief to find that they were in time for their pre-booked Air France flight to New York but they would have to hurry before check-in closed. They made it and hurried through to Departures and were the last to board.

—

When they walked out of the Arrivals Gate in New York Kennedy Airport a cheroot chewing, grey-haired, medium built man about the same age as Hunter was jumping up and down and waving a card with the name Byewater in large print. 'Hey! Hunter, over here!'

Hunter was looking elsewhere and Penny nudged him. 'I think

someone over there knows you.'

He looked to where she was pointing and said, 'Hank!'

He hurried over and as they came together Hunter dropped his bags and they went into an old comrades man hug. 'Hank, it's good to see you, pal, how are you?'

'I'm great, man...' Penny joined them, '...and who's this, your daughter?'

Hunter introduced them. 'This, Hank, is Penny my number two. Penny, this is Hank, he saved my life way back before you were born.'

Penny held her hand out, 'Pleased to meet you, err, Hank.'

Hank shook her hand enthusiastically, 'Great to see ya, Miss Penny.'

When she managed to free herself they picked up their bags and made their way to the exit. Outside at the cab rank, Hank said, 'I did like you said, Hunter.'

'Thanks, Hank. You pay and I'll settle, okay?'

Next in line they jumped into one of New York's famous 'Yellow Cabs' and Hank gave an address to the driver who mumbled a reply in an unrecognizable Eastern European accent and without looking he swerved out into the traffic. Five minutes later they swung off the main drag between some tall warehouses and pulled up outside a low life Bar.

The driver didn't show any wonderment at their destination and took their money. Hank gave the man a good tip but not so much it would be a significant memory the same reason he didn't give a small tip. They stood on the sidewalk until the taxi disappeared and then they followed Hank to a car parked in the next block. Before they drove off Hank threw a package across to Hunter.

'I got two like you said, unmarked.'

'Let's hope we don't need them. Did you trace that phone number?'

Hank fiddled in his inside jacket pocket and pulled out a slip of paper which he handed to Hunter. 'It's in the South Bronx. I took a look and it's not a bad area for a singly.'

Hunter glanced at it and stuffed it into his jacket. 'Thanks,

Hank, now tell me what you've been up to since we last met.'

'I've retired. The NYPD won't let old bastards like me fly helicopters. Too many lights at night for these old eyes but I got a good pension and a nice place just out of town for me and my wife. The kids drop by to keep an eye on us. My eldest boy wanted to do this job but I chased him.'

'You're staying in the hotel?'

'Yeah, who am I to turn down a trip to Times Square?'

Fifteen minutes later they pulled up outside the Cortese Hotel. The Doorman showed the three of them inside and the car park attendant whisked the car away.

When they had completed check-in they stopped by the elevator and Hunter shook Hanks's hand. 'Thanks for everything, we'll see you at dinner?'

'You bet, I ain't missing a date with a Number Two like that.'

'Is Aaron coming, Hank?'

'He sure is. He's told everyone he's going to a prayer meeting with an old convert.'

They laughed simultaneously and just as the elevator doors swished open Hunter's cell phone buzzed. He ignored it and followed Penny into the elevator and as they zoomed up Hunter checked his messages and smiled when he saw it.

SMS: UOMe $6000. Package in transit. D.

He closed the cell and Penny said, 'I thought you hadn't been to New York. How long have you known Hank and whose Aaron?'

'I've known them about forty-five years. Aaron and I served together in Laos in '66 and Hank was my rescue helicopter pilot. I've been to Washington.'

'You were in the U.S. Army?'

'I was on detachment from the SAS.'

They reached their floor and were reminded by a singularly boring mechanical voice that said 'The doors are opening' to which Hunter replied with a whimsical, 'Thank you.'

They strolled side by side down a never-ending corridor behind the porter and stopped outside the last two rooms. The porter opened the door to Penny's room and took her suitcase inside and then repeated the exercise for Hunter in the room next door.

When the porter had departed, Hunter said, 'This is it, lass, we have to part. See you at seven for dinner. I've got a few calls to make and then I'm taking a nap. This jet-lag thing is doing my head in.'

'You're getting old, Hunter.'

He stuck his tongue out at her as she closed the door and feeling content with his new partner he went to his room pleased with himself.

—

It was midday on Saturday before the small Jiffy envelope arrived and when it did he excused himself and went to the men's washroom.

On his return, he said to Hank. 'We're going upstairs to get our bags and when we come down we'll do the check out thing.'

'Right on, pal,' said Hank, 'you're the Boss.'

When they stepped out of the escalator fifteen minutes later, Hank, who had arranged for his car to be brought around to the front began walking across to the desk when he tripped and as he fell he reached out to steady himself on the desk front and pulled some paperwork down with him. He landed with a thump and began groaning and one of the receptionists dashed around to help as did two porters who were hanging around. In the mayhem, Hunter and Penny carrying their own bags were hurriedly checked out by a receptionist whose attention was diverted elsewhere.

When Hank joined them outside by the car, he said, 'Let's go, they're trying to sign me up for an acting role.'

He engaged 'Drive' and as he pulled out into the early afternoon traffic Hunter said, 'Can we stop at a Diner before we go onto the South Bronx, Hank? While we're eating I want a selfie of us three to add to the others we took at dinner last night.'

Two hours later they swung off the Cross Bronx Expressway and did a series of right turns down to East 175th St into a mixed industrial and residential area when Hank pulled up at a junction and pointed across to a newly renovated seven-storey block of apartments on the opposite corner.

'There it is, Hunter. He's on the third floor to your right. I'll be in the next avenue parked by the garages. When you call I'll be coming down the avenue behind you at the front of the block.'

'Okay, Hank, got it, if this goes well you'll have an extra passenger.'

They clambered out of the car and watched Hank drive off and Hunter went to step into the road. Penny grabbed his arm. 'Whoa, there, Hunter, you're in the US of A. No jaywalking and the traffic comes from the other direction.'

They paused long enough to see the road clear and crossed over one street and did a ninety-degree turn and walked across to the apartment block. Trying not to arouse suspicion and to minimise the view of any CCTV they leaned their heads together and looked at each other like star crossed lovers and breezed into the entrance like it was an everyday occurrence. They stopped outside the elevator and Hunter pressed the button and when he saw it begin its downward journey they pushed through the emergency side door next to it and went up the stairs. On the third floor landing, they followed Hank's instructions and turned right and walked along the corridor to the last apartment.

Hunter drew his gun and said, 'Okay, Penny, leave the talking to me. Are you ready?'

'Yes.'

Following a pre-planned procedure, Penny rang the doorbell and while Hunter stood to one side with his back to the wall she hovered in front of the spy hole. They heard the spyhole cover slide away and then drop back and then the removal of the door bolts and the unclipping of the door latch and as the door began to swing open Hunter flung himself forward and rammed it into Bell who staggered back. Penny and Hunter pushed quickly forward and closed the door behind them. Bell who had recovered his balance made a move to grapple with Hunter when the shiny barrel of a Glock 17 was pushed into his face.

'Back off, Bell, if you know what's good for you.'

Simon knew Hunter's reputation and with hands half-raised went backwards down the hall into the living room and stopped when the back of his legs came into contact with a coffee table. 'Alright, Hunter, what do you want?'

'Sit down and shut up. I'll do the talking,' said Hunter sharply.

After completing her checks of the apartment Penny stood inside the door with her gun held in two hands pointing to the ceiling. 'All clear, Hunter.'

Keeping his gun pointing steadily at Bell's chest he nodded his acknowledgement and gestured for Bell to sit on the sofa. When he had complied, Hunter said, 'Simon, I've come to take you back. Don't piss me about. You're responsible for my wife's gamble with death and also involved my kids so don't think I've come here to be nice.'

Bell raised his hands. 'I'm sorry about the kids and Jacquie. That wasn't supposed to happen.'

'And just what was supposed to happen?'

Bell's accent changed as dropped the pretence of being English. In his native Irish, he said, 'You fucking English killed my father and I wanted revenge and when someone came along and offered to pay to kill you I got the best of both worlds.'

'Has this anything to do with the orphanage?'

'No, I used that as a means and I'm fixing to get those bastards later.'

'That won't happen, Bell, and why me?'

'You killed a guy called McDuggan in '83 and his wife wanted revenge.'

'How do you know it was me?'

'Our help at the top.'

'Why Jacquie?'

'I don't know, she wasn't part of it, that was someone else.'

'You swapped places with Carrie deliberately and put Jacquie in danger and then you set me up and passed the info onto others. You two-faced bastard, if I had my way I'd shoot now but I'll give you a chance to come quietly.'

'You've got no jurisdiction here, Hunter, and I'm not coming.'

Hunter waggled his gun. 'This is my jurisdiction. Your choice. Come with me and you're maybe out in ten years. Stay here and they'll be going for extradition and a longer-term. What is it?'

Bell stood up.

'Sit down, Bell, I haven't finished.

Bell ignored him and Hunter shouted, 'SIT DOWN, or I'll end it now.'

'Bollocks, you're past it you old English twat.'

He arrogantly turned away and started walking towards a chest of draws at the end of the room when Hunter began coughing severely, bent forward and clutched his chest. Bell turned and saw Hunter doubled over and the gun which Hunter had dropped lying on the coffee table. Judging the distance and ignoring Penny he seized his chance and made a dive towards the gun.

Hunter was still bent over coughing in some sort of seizure but when Bell stretched out his arm and reached for the gun Hunter sprang into action. He twisted around and squeezed a spray from an Asthma inhaler directly into Bell's face. The effect of the knock-out gas was instantaneous. When it hit his bronchial tubes Bell faltered and pulled up gasping for breath and when it penetrated his lungs his legs buckled and he dropped to the floor semi-conscious.

Penny momentarily mesmerised by the action lowered her gun and moved forward to help. 'Hunter are you okay?'

'Yes, we've got five minutes, get me a glass of water.'

She hurried into the kitchen area and came back with the water. Hunter knelt beside Bell and in his hand, he had a torpedo-shaped capsule. 'Here, Bell, take this, it's an antidote to the spray. You'll have a headache after but you'll be okay.'

Bell was sleepy but conscious and biddable so he raised his head slightly and opened his mouth and Hunter popped the capsule in. With Hunter's help, Bell sipped some water and washed it down. Hunter put the glass to one side and lowered him to the floor.

'Penny, make sure we've left nothing and then we're going.'

She left the room and Hunter leaned over and spoke into Bell's ear, 'Wrong option, pal, you're dead, you fucking double-crossing bastard!'

He thought about leaving his calling card but decided it was immature and unnecessary and instead he picked up his gun, wiped the glass and took it back into the kitchen area and after another quick look around they left the wheezing figure of Bell on the floor and closed the apartment door behind them. Hunter gave the door a shove to make sure it was locked and hurried after Penny who had started walking towards the stairs.

While they negotiated the stairs he used his cell to call Hank and in the exit hallway, Penny hung onto his arm and with their heads bowed together they pretended to look at something on Hunter's phone. They strolled out into the street and Hank was right on the money. They had no sooner turned the corner into East 175th St when he pulled up beside them and whisked them away towards downtown New York and onward to Kennedy Airport.

As soon as they had turned off the Cross Bronx Highway and were driving alongside the Hudson River unsure and disturbed by what she had witnessed, Penny said, 'Hunter, is Bell okay?'

'He'll recover with a headache and won't remember much.'

'What was that capsule you gave him?'

Hunter smiled but remained silent. She gave him a dubious sideways glance but said nothing.

They drove on in the late afternoon traffic for another twenty minutes and stopped outside the same low life Bar they had used on their arrival. Hank called a taxi and when it pulled up alongside them they said their goodbyes with promises to meet in the future.

Hank watched as they departed and then drove back to the hotel looking forward to a night on the town. He just wished the NYPD had paid him a salary like Hunter did. His work was not over, however. The following morning he had to check out of the hotel and return the 'for hire' handguns.

—

Hunter and Penny caught a Red-Eye flight back to Paris and landed in the early hours of Sunday morning. At the Hotel Ascot, Paris, their dishevelled appearance suggested a hectic night out. For further effect, Hunter had removed his tie and undone a few shirt buttons and Penny had ruffled her hair and undone the top two buttons of her blouse and with rolling jollity, they went up to their room. Hunter flopped into the armchair and Penny jumped on the bed and laughed.

'My, my, Hunter, you know how to give a girl a good time.

I've never been so knackered and it's not for the want of trying.'

'I wish it could have been more entertaining. What time is our flight?'

'We have a couple of hours...' she paused and then continued, '...Hunter!'

'Yes.'

'At dinner the other night Aaron said something about a Congressional Medal of Honour. What did he mean?'

'It's nothing, wake me when it's time.'

She thought he was being modest and set the alarm on her smartphone. In two minutes they were both asleep.

—

He dropped Penny off at her East Finchley lodgings and thanked her profusely before continuing on to the Camden safe house where a stern-faced Mrs Archer was waiting for him and she spoke in a distressed manner.

'Mr Hunter! Where have you been? There's a very irate woman ringing here every few hours wanting to know.'

Hunter knew instinctively who that was. 'It's okay, Amy, if she calls again tell her I'm on my way home.'

An hour later refreshed after a shower and shave he set out for the nightmare drive up to the northwest and a cool reception.

He parked the car at the bottom of the drive behind Jacquie's Range Rover and was retrieving his bag from the car trunk when the front door opened. The look on her face was enough and he remained soberly quiet as he walked towards her.

'Hunter, you'd better explain yourself.'

Her body language as she turned and walked into the house said it all. He dropped his bag in the front hall and followed her to the kitchen where she spun around to face him. Tess sensing the electric atmosphere slunk silently to her bed and rested her head on her paws as Jacquie said bitterly, 'Found a fancy woman have you? Was she good?'

Unsure where to start Hunter took a deep breath and went for it. 'Jacquie, I don't know what you've heard but it's nothing like that, honest.'

'Hunter! I couldn't get you on your phone so I rang the house and I was told you were coming home but it was obvious you weren't so I called HQ and they said there was a rumour you'd gone off for a weekend in Paris with a young woman. Could you keep up?'

'Yes, Jacquie, I mean no, Jacquie. I did go to Paris but it was a decoy for the real mission.'

'Which was?'

'New York.'

'Why?'

'I went to get Bell.'

'Why the cover-up?'

'To extradite him would take years so I went off-piste and I couldn't tell anyone so I dropped hints here and there that we were up to naughties.' He held out his phone. 'Here, look at the photo's.'

She sullenly took the phone and began searching the Photo Gallery. 'That's Hank, and Aaron,' she said, 'Oh!, and that's the young lady—nice! Where's Bell?'

'Did you see the time and date?'

She looked closer at the selfie. 'Ah, yes, but where's Bell?'

'Hank was our chauffeur and he supplied the hardware and as we had the first evening free I arranged dinner for us all. The job was the next day.'

'And Bell?'

'He'll be no more trouble.'

She knew Hunter and didn't query. 'And you did all this in two days?'

'Yes, darling, we did and I'm knackered and by the way, you'll see some unusual activity on our credit card account.'

'Hunter, come here.' He took two paces forward and she threw herself at him and kissed him hard. 'I miss you,' she murmured into his ear and teasingly added, 'was she good?'

He pushed her away and poked her playfully in the ribs. 'Ouch,' she cried, 'be careful, I'm tender there.'

'Oh, love, I'm sorry. Make us a cuppa?'

Jacquie picked the kettle up and as she crossed to the sink she said, 'Gus said you told the housekeepers you were coming home.'

'It was part of the cover-up.'

'Go and put your feet up and I'll bring your tea, and Hunter!'

'What?'

'Slow down you old git.'

He laughed as he went towards the living room and Tess followed him now that the static had subsided. He slumped into his favourite armchair and when she brought his tea he was fast asleep with Tess lying across his feet. She looked down at him and smiled. She knew her man, she knew Hunter. Not faultless but faithful with an underlying ruthlessness.

Lesley and Iain were at a birthday party with friends and that evening when Jacquie picked them she warned them that Daddy was home but they must be quiet as he was asleep but she needn't have worried as he was stood at the front door as she parked the car.

Lesley was the first to respond and she ran up the drive shouting, 'DADDY! Daddy!, I'm coming to get you.'

He stepped outside onto the top of the drive and scooped her up. 'Hello, darling, did you miss me?'

'Yes, yes, yes, and I've done lots of pictures.'

There was a tug on his sleeve and the more pragmatic Iain said, 'Hi, Dad, are you home for good?'

He put his arm around Iain's shoulder and guided him back into the house where he put Lesley down and said, 'There's still some work to do so I'll be going away again tomorrow but only for a short while and then I am definitely finished.'

'Will there be any more shooting, Dad?' said Iain.

'No, son, that's all over.' Iain looked a little disappointed and Hunter added, 'finish your homework before playing games.'

Iain nodded and Lesley dragged Hunter away to show off her pictures.

~~~~~
~~~~~

CHAPTER 31

On Monday morning he waved the children off to school and Jacquie off to work before he prepared for a hectic day driving on the overcrowded Motorways of Britain. The time saved on the Toll Road was no help as twenty minutes later traffic ground to a halt at the road works which had been ongoing for some time.

'I could do this run quicker forty years ago,' he muttered to himself as he fiddled with the channel selector on the radio. He had decided that they were going to be stuck there for some time and settled for *Classic FM* his favoured radio station when suddenly the Bluetooth receptor demanded his attention.

He pressed the green button and sat back glumly when Gus Thomas spoke. 'Hunter, where are you?'

'Hello, Gus,' he said with false cheeriness, 'I'm at the junction of the **M6** and the **M1** and standing still.'

'No time soon then. Give us a call when you get to Camden and we'll have a meet.'

'Okay, tell, Penny.'

'Do we need her?'

'Yes, Gus, she's my Number two.'

'I bet.'

'Less of that, Thomas. It was work only.'

Gus rang off and Hunter switched his phone off. He'd had enough of driving with distractions and he engaged first gear as the queue began to crawl forward. He arrived in London in time for the evening rush hour which added to his frustration and made him feel even less like a meeting that evening.

He dumped his bags in his bedroom and rang Penny.

'Yes, Hunter, what is it. Thomas already told me.'

'Penny, have you eaten?'

'No.'

'Come on over and bring a takeaway. I'll pay.'

'Chinese or Indian?'

'You choose, and bring a bottle or two.'

—

Hunter pushed his plate away, sat back and took a large swig from his glass of red. 'That was lovely, Penny. Did you take a note of the place?'

'I've got their menu. It's about halfway between us. I asked the taxi driver to choose and he was spot on.'

'Did you do anything yesterday?'

'I slept and then lounged around.'

'Well, Penny, rumours are flying around so be prepared. Jacquie's alright but you know what office gossip is.'

'Yes, I get it every time I go on a job. Your Russian is a good example.'

'Why?'

'I did the 'come on' thing and when I got back to HQ you can imagine the backchat. I get fed up with it sometimes. That's why I'm glad they put me with you.'

'Aye, they thought I needed a carer, sorry, minder—Penny! what we did this weekend was outside the box and we may do more. If you would rather not get involved, tell me.'

'I...'

The doorbell chimed and a moment later Mrs Archer called on the intercom. 'It's Mr Thomas, Hunter.'

'Okay, Amy, send him up.'

Thomas came in and threw his coat over the back of a dining chair. 'Either I'm getting as old as you, Hunter, or those stairs are steeper.'

'Keep taking the tablets, Gus. Whisky or wine?'

Thomas looked at his watch. 'Whisky, please.'

Hunter poured a double and took the glass and a small jug of water over to Gus who had bagged one of the easy chairs.

'Thanks, Hunter, now tell me what the weekend was all about.'

'It's simple, Gus. Bell was in the States and as extradition takes bloody years I tried to persuade him to come back voluntary.'

'It was outside our jurisdiction?'

'I paid for it.'

'You didn't succeed?'

'No. We had a heated discussion but he couldn't be persuaded so we left it at that.'

'I see. Tell me, how did you trace him?'

'I have connections.'

Gus shook his head. He knew it, where didn't he have connections? 'We have to go through the rigmarole of extradition then?'

'It looks that way.'

Penny threw a sideways glance at Hunter. Her first thought was it wouldn't be necessary and feeling left out of the discussion she ventured, 'Now that Bell is sidelined what about his brother, Red?'

'I was coming to that,' said Thomas. 'We acted upon your brief, Hunter, but we were too late and Red has done a runner.'

'Surprise, surprise,' said Hunter, 'where?'

'We don't know. He had access to other departments and it looks like he's got himself fake documents so we're checking CCTV at all Ports and Airports.'

'And Jackson-Milburn?'

'He's currently on Police bail. Somebody leaked information about historical sex crimes to the newspapers.'

'Spying and sex, whatever next,' said Hunter, 'that takes it outside 'Magpie' doesn't it?'

'Unfortunately, yes. This could drag on for years.'

'But, Gus, doesn't the countries security come first?'

'He's off COBRA and suspended from GCHQ.'

'Suspended!' said Hunter in disbelief, 'that means he's still on full pay.'

'Yes.'

Hunter sat quietly for a moment with his head resting on his hands in deliberation and when he looked up he was thoughtfully rubbing his chin. 'Gus, are you saying in essence, we're screwed?'

'Yes.'

'So the paedophile who almost got me and Jacquie killed and put my kids in danger is going to get away with a warning.'

'Without witnesses, yes, but he will also be done for leaking information which will probably be a slap on the wrist and he'll lose his knighthood. Not jail time I'm afraid.'

Hunter grimaced and said, 'So, Gus, what do you want us to do?'

'Use your initiative,' said Thomas.

'With the 'Firms' backing?'

Thomas nodded, 'Yes, now give me another whisky.

They sat for another twenty minutes swapping small talk when Thomas stood up. 'I'm going, we'll meet in the morning.'

He picked his coat up off the chair and went towards the door when Penny stood up. 'I'm going too.'

Hunter closed the door behind Thomas and said to Penny. 'Can you hang on half an hour?'

'Yes, sure.'

'Another drink, Pen?'

'Tea, please.'

He made two mugs of tea and joined her in the living room.

'Tomorrow, Pen we need to know where Milburn is staying. You do that and I'll chase up any news on Red. I haven't got a plan as yet and can't formulate one until we have that info.'

'What if this Red or Parr, which is his known GCHQ title, has joined his brother?'

'Then we can go over there legally, Pen, but Milburn is the one I want. He sold his country as well as endangering my family to protect his ancestral title.'

'But won't the Police get priority?'

'That's a good question but as there has been no complaint as yet of any historical sexual depravity we'll have to see. Meet me in Vauxhall Cross in the morning, Pen, I want to get a start before we get together with Gus.'

'Okay, see you tomorrow.'

He held the door for her as she went out and when he closed it he stood for a moment collecting his thoughts before he wandered over to the drinks cabinet and poured another finger of whisky. Half an hour later he still hadn't come up with a plan so he bashed out a quick text to Jacquie and went to bed.

Penny went home glowing. Hunter's use of a nickname meant

she was part of the team.

—

Eschewing the rush hour mayhem into Central London at nine-thirty Hunter caught the N°24 bus which took him to Warren Street. From there he ventured underground on the Victoria Line to Vauxhall Station and he did the last three-hundred metres on foot enjoying the grey but mild summer day and he turned into the entrance of Vauxhall House one of the not so secret offices of the SIS wondering what surprises were in store. The inside of this building was different to other company buildings in that the security was tighter. The Receptionist was fashionably turned out with her Security and Self Defence training well disguised but her male companion was tall and muscular with a demeanour which said, 'Don't mess with me.'

Hunter scanned his ID and pushed through the barrier and walked over to the lift where an equally muscular security guard waited. As he entered the lift Hunter flashed his card which initiated no reaction and he pressed the button for the second floor. He put two fingers up to the monosyllabic warnings from the speakers and stepped from the lift and as he was in no particular hurry he wandered leisurely down the corridor and bumped into Penny coming out of the washroom.

'Mornin', Pen, what have we got?'

She fell in beside him. 'Hello, Hunter. Milburn is in his London apartment. He's ours for the moment as the sex case belongs to the PSNI and Red was seen at Gatwick Airport.'

'They don't know which flight?'

'Not yet.'

'Is Thomas in?'

'Yes.'

'Okay, if that's all we've got let's go and see him.'

They continued to the office at the end of the corridor and knocked. Hunter didn't wait for an answer but bowled straight in.

Thomas was reading from an A4 sheet and he looked up. 'Come in,' he said, 'make yourself at home.'

'Thanks, Gus, have you any coffee?'

'Hunter! You passed a machine in the corridor?'

'Yes.'

Gus remained silent and Hunter, ever the gentleman, said to Penny, 'Would you like a coffee?'

'Yes, Americano if they have it.'

'With milk?'

She nodded and Hunter spun around and disappeared out of the door.

He came back five minutes later with two medium cartons of coffee and sat alongside Penny who had set out two chairs opposite Thomas.

'Where's mine,' said Gus.

'You never asked,' said Hunter.

'Just as well I've had one you tight buggar.' Gus pushed the file he had been perusing to one side. 'Right,' he said, 'what have we got?'

Penny looked at Hunter and with raised eyebrows signalled her approval for him to go ahead. 'Red's done a runner from Gatwick,' he said, 'and they're checking the CCTV to find out where. Sir Jackson-Milburn is under surveillance in his apartment.'

'That's it?' said Gus.

'Yes,' said Hunter, 'and I presume Milburn is firewalled?'

Gus agreed with a nod. 'Yes, and we've spoken to the PSNI and because nobody has made a complaint they can't pursue the historical sex thing yet. It is possible that now it has been brought out into the open other ex-inmates of that orphanage may come forward but our case against him is weak.'

'So,' said Hunter, 'he could get off. What if we had a witness in either case?'

'That would help but...' Thomas's phone buzzed and he picked it up '... Hello?'

The call was short and to the point and he put the phone down with a satisfied look on his face. 'That was Tech support. Red or Parr has gone to Paphos, Cyprus. He used his family name, Doyle.'

Hunter sat up suddenly interested. 'I know Paphos, he said, 'we were there in 2001 and we holiday there regularly.'

'Do you now?' replied Thomas.

'Yes, it was there that Williams first came to our attention.'

'Good, how would you like to go again?'

Hunter tilted his head towards Penny. 'Can I take my number two and I want the whole package. You know, firearms etc...'

'I'll speak to 'C' but as this case is about a breach of national security i.e. GCHQ, I'll set that up and at the same time we'll issue a European arrest warrant.'

Hunter looked thoughtful for a moment before he spoke. 'Gus, that warrant? Only in his GCHQ name of Parr. We'll refer to him as Doyle from now on.'

'Why?'

'Because I don't want the Cypriot police getting involved too early.'

'Is that a problem, Hunter?'

'I have my reasons and there's no need to book hotels as I have a friend with a villa we rent.'

'Okay. I'll get this set up. Go home and get yourself ready. If there's a late flight I want you on it. Leave your sidearm here and you Penny.'

Hunter took his jacket off and unslung the shoulder holster while Penny dug deep into her bag and to Hunter's satisfaction brought out a Glock 17.

'Good choice, Pen.'

'Thanks, Hunter, so glad you approve. What did Jacquie use?'

'The same.'

'When you two have stopped nattering,' said Thomas, 'go and get yourself ready.'

Penny and Hunter stood up together and in unison swung around the chairs crossed the office to the door.

Hunter held it open and stood to one side. 'After you, madam,' he said.

'Oh, thank you, sir,' said Penny with a laugh as she stepped into the corridor.

Hunter joined her and they walked side by side towards the lift.

'Penny?'

'Yes, Hunter.'

'Cyprus is bloody hot this time of year so pack summer gear

and make your work togs light. Come to the Camden house when you're ready.'

'Will do, Boss,' she said with a laugh, 'you got your summer Zimmer frame?'

She took a quick step to the side as Hunter's retaliatory elbow flicked sideways and pressed the button for the lift. As they went down Penny said, 'Are you in your car?'

'No, I slummed it on the underground.'

'I'm going that way, I'll drop you off.'

'Fine by me, Pen.'

As Penny manoeuvred them through the late morning traffic Hunter made a few phone calls and had Penny drop him off at the Camden Town Underground station. He waited while she drove away and disappeared into the traffic before he wandered a hundred metres up the street to a newspaper vendor outside the Market entrance and after a few moments chatter the vendor reached under his small counter and then picked up a daily paper, folded it over his hand and slid it over to Hunter who reciprocated by slipping a folded ten-pound note into his outstretched palm and walking away in the direction of the safe house.

At two-thirty his phone rang. 'Hunter!'

'Hunter, it's Gus. You're booked on the Ryan Air flight from Stansted at ten-past-five. A 'Firms' unmarked car is on its way to pick you up and they're holding the flight for you. An Avis Hire Car will be waiting for you on arrival.'

'Got you, Gus, and Penny?'

'You will pick her up on the way through to the **M11**, and Hunter?'

'Yes.'

'No mishaps.'

'Can't promise.'

He put the phone down and nipped sharply into the bedroom to finish packing and long before the car arrived he heard the klaxons clearing the way.

They didn't waste time as no sooner had he dumped his bag into the trunk and slid into the back seat than the driver engaged gear and they were off. Traffic was slow and the driver once again switched on the hidden blue LED's and the klaxon and they made urgent progress to Penny's place.

Penny was waiting by the gate and before she could catch her breath the driver grabbed her extensive luggage and slung it into the trunk and was back in his seat and once more urgently clearing the road with klaxons and lights.

They skidded to a halt outside the Terminal and while the driver looked after the bags they hurried through to the Check-in desk where a Ryan Air flight Manager was waiting. The driver arrived two minutes later and put their bags on the scales and handed a leather briefcase to the Manager who herded Hunter and Penny hurriedly through Security and down to the departure gate. While the Ticket Attendant checked their boarding passes the Manager went ahead onto the waiting aircraft and gave the briefcase to the pilot. No sooner had they boarded than the doors were shut and the aircraft a Boeing 737-800 was pushed back.

Hunter hated the four and half hour flight grumbling that for a flight of that duration they should give you more legroom. He was only six foot one but his knees were up against the seat in front and it was five minutes to midnight local time when they arrived. He stiffly stepped off the aircraft and manoeuvred his aching legs down the steps and onto the waiting bus. Inside the Terminal building while they were waiting in the long queue for Passport control a policeman approached and spoke to them in English with a strong Greek accent.

'Excuse me, sir, are you Mr Hunter?'

'Yes, how did you know?'

He smiled and pointed over to the waiting Ryan Air pilot. 'He told me. Come with me, sir, and we'll let him go. Have you got your passports ready?'

'Yes,'

He and Penny held their passports out for him to look at and when he handed them back he said, 'Follow me.'

Once through the checkpoint, he took them over to the pilot who stayed airside and handed the briefcase over the barrier to the policeman who gave it to Hunter.

'If you go over there, Mr Hunter, you can collect your bags. Is anyone meeting you? We can lay on a car.'

'Thanks very much but we have a hire car.'

The policeman shook hands with both Hunter and Penny and left them. They followed the crowd over to Belt 4 and waited but not for long as being the last bags on they were the first ones off and easily recognisable. Hunter smiled, the humorous Stansted baggage handlers had wrapped them in blue and white Police tape as they rushed them out to the aircraft. So much for secrecy.

The Avis rep was waiting and took them out to the compound where the hire cars were kept and while they were filling in the paperwork Hunter enquired, 'We're hoping to meet a friend out here but we've lost his address. He only came a couple of days ago and we wondered if he'd hired a car from you. His names Doyle.'

The rep shoved some papers across the desk. 'Sign these where I've put a cross and I'll have a look on the computer.'

He pressed a few keys and scrolled with the mouse before he shook his head. 'Sorry, Mr Hunter. I've checked back a week and we have no Doyle.'

'Thanks all the same, it was just an idea. We have a Cypriot phone so I've no doubt he'll be in touch.'

—

It was the first time Penny had seen Hunter drive and she was impressed by the easy manner he drove the Nissan Qashqai. The four-kilometre drive from the airport to the main road gave Hunter plenty of time to familiarise himself with the vehicle and being after midnight the roads were quiet.

At the main road, he turned left and in his eagerness to get going he pressed down on the fast pedal and two hundred metres later he had to brake hard. It was a few months since he had driven there and in the poor street lighting, he had forgotten the speed bumps at every road junction an EU edict the Cypriot government had taken to heart. Two miles further down the road he turned into what was the UK equivalent of a B road and climbed steadily into the darkness.

'Do you know where you're going, Hunter?' said, Penny.

'Yep, this takes us up to the Motorway and a quick drive to the back of Paphos town. It's my little shortcut.'

Sure enough, as they went over the rise a hundred metres later they turned onto the slip road to the **A6** Motorway. It was like no motorway she had seen before. It was empty, not a vehicle in sight in any direction.

'My, my, is it always like this,' she said.

'Sure is, Pen, it's not much busier during the day.'

'I think I like it here.'

'You would like it here. It's a nice easy-going way of life but the Cypriot drivers are manic. Just give them plenty of room and expect the unexpected. A bit like the UK really, only here you know their bonkers.'

'You sound like you'd like to live here.'

'I would but Jacquie's got a business to run as well as the kids education. It's our second home and we use the same villa.'

'You had your children late, Hunter?'

'Yes, we only met in 2001.'

'You weren't married before?'

'No, I had a couple of near misses.'

Penny didn't press it further. She'd heard about Hunter and Jacquie's relationship on the 'Firms' grapevine.

At the end of the Motorway Hunter took his shortcut as he called it down little side streets avoiding the town centre. They crossed main roads instead of following them until he eventually came to the top road from Paphos Old Town which ran inland until it joined the coast road to Coral Bay ten kilometres north just stopping long enough to buy milk at a 24hr Kiosk.

They came to the Coral Bay turn off which was the head of the Strip as it was called locally but he turned right instead which took them inland and uphill towards the village of Peyia. Five minutes later he took the right fork past the local football stadium and up to a **T** junction where he turned left and fifty metres later bumped up the gradient in the kerb on his right and up a narrow driveway into a small community of villas. Theirs was the second on the right and Hunter swung into the gateway and parked at the side of their villa.

They went around to the front door and Hunter punched a four-figure security code into the key holder security box and extracted a bunch of keys. Inside he switched the lights on and dumped his bag alongside a large round dining table and invited Penny in. 'What do you think, Pen?'

Penny stepped into a large living/dining room. On her right was an open plan staircase and hidden behind that was a small office. To the left was the kitchen and between the two was the downstairs toilet and shower room. Hunter went into the kitchen and put the milk in the fridge and rejoined Penny.

'Hunter, it's lovely what about upstairs?'

'Two double rooms and a single. You take the double directly ahead of you, Pen, and I'll have the one where Jacquie and I usually sleep. Out the back is a pool if we get time.'

'And they're paying?'

'It's cheaper than two in a hotel and more convenient so Gus will be pleased. You don't have to pretend you're a tourist either. Would you like a nightcap?'

'Is there any?'

'Tea or coffee or something stronger?'

'Stronger, please.'

Hunter crossed to a drinks cabinet and opened the doors to a wide collection of spirits. 'Single malt do you?'

'Is it okay, Hunter, won't the vendor mind?'

'What you see is all ours, Pen. Jacquie and I practically own this place. It belongs to an old army pal who's too old to look after it. He's just happy to rent it out to us for the extra tax-free cash and we maintain it. I think we'll be buying it if anything happens to him.'

'A good set-up.'

'Yes, we like it.'

He gave her a glass with a two-finger measure in it and went into the kitchen to get some water. He returned moments later with a small glass jug and gave it to her.

'Hunter, is this local tap water?'

'Yes, but it's the purest water you'll get.'

'How come?'

'We've installed a reverse osmosis filter. Right now I'm for bed.'

'Me too.'

She grabbed her bags and went towards the stairs and Hunter followed with her whisky.

At the top of the stairs he waited and after she had dumped her bags he gave her the glass and said, 'Penny, switch on the anti-mossie thing in the wall plug and you use the upstairs loo and I'll use downstairs.'

'But, Hunter, in the night?'

'No worries, lass. Good night.'

She took the glass off him and he returned downstairs to retrieve his bags and to lock the contents of the briefcase in the wall safe hidden behind a picture.

—

The following morning their body clocks still in the UK they were up late by local time and it was fortuitous that Penny liked muesli as that was all Hunter had in. Over coffee, Hunter put forward his plan.

'Penny, I want to chase up the car hire companies to see if we can trace our friend Doyle so I would suggest that we head back to the airport and start there. If we can't trace him then we'll have to do a bar crawl. What do you think?'

'Do we have a picture of him?' said Penny.

'As it happens we have. Gus sent it overnight to my phone. Have you got Bluetooth switched on?'

She took the latest Apple device from her handbag and after a few minutes twinning with Hunter's modest Nokia he sent the photo to her.

'That's that done. Are you still hungry?'

'I'm good for a bit yet, Hunter, why are you?'

'Always. We'll stop at a kiosk I'll grab a kit-kat or something and then we'll head for the airport. We'll do some supermarket shopping later.'

—

They tried all the major international car hire companies on the airport without success and moved on to the local ones who had depots on the main road in the village of Timi. It was a little confusing as the local businesses shared premises but on their fourth try in a singular run-down little shack attached to the property of a larger outlet they had a success of a kind.

Hunter flashed his SIS I.D. with a hint of a ten euro note sticking up behind and the young Russian who managed the yard on his own was only too eager to help and after offering them a seat he delved into his computer.

'Yes, sir, we have a Mr Doyle.'

'Has he got an address,' said Hunter.'

'Yes, sir,'

He plucked up a pen and scribbled the address onto a scrap piece of paper and gave it to Hunter who looked at it closely.

'He's in Coral Bay, Pen.'

They thanked the lad and Hunter pressed the note into his hand and they left.

'Right, Pen, it's lunchtime.'

Hunter took the same route as they had the previous night but this time in he turned off the Top road and manoeuvring their way down a steep hill between indiscriminately parked cars they crossed over the bottom coast road and stopped at St Georgio's snack bar opposite the church where he was rapturously welcomed in typical Cypriot style as an old patron and shown to a table outside but in the shade.

'Good food here, Pen, and they serve German Lowenbrau bier at two euro's a pint.'

'I thought there was a catch in it somewhere, Hunter. You're loving this aren't you?'

'Good company also, lass.'

An hour later they continued their journey to Coral Bay. They parked halfway down the Strip which is five hundred metres of Bars and Restaurants interspersed with gift shops, travel agents an Opticians a Chemist and the ubiquitous kiosk but all owned by Cypriots.

They sat for a moment pondering what next when Hunter said, 'Come on, lass, I have an idea. Let's go to the opticians.'

'Why, have you got a problem?'

'No, I know the guy there and he can check this address out.'

Penny looked heavenwards and shrugged. 'Is there anywhere this guy doesn't have contacts?'

Again in the opticians, he was warmly welcomed and they were only too keen to help when he showed them the address but the manager and the three assistants said they were sorry they had never heard of it and couldn't help. The next stop was Zentas Bar where he was welcomed with a man hug by the owner Chris, a man of enormous stature.

Looking Penny up and down, he said, 'Mr George, where is your lovely wife?'

'We're here on Police business, Chris, this is, Penny. She's my number two.' He gave Chris the piece of paper. 'Do you know that address?'

Chris looked at it and thought for a while rubbing his hand through his beard before handing it back. 'There is no place with this name, where you get it?'

Hunter took the piece of paperback and was about to leave when he pulled the phone from his shirt pocket and opened the Photo section and showed it to Chris. 'Have you seen this guy, Chris?'

Chris took the phone and turned away from the bright sunlight and looked closer at the picture. 'One moment, I ask my girls.'

Chris checked with the three Russian girls working in his bar and returned. 'Only, Donna over there says she thinks he was here last night.'

'Thanks, Chris, now give me a pint of Keo.' He looked at Penny. 'What will you have, Pen?'

'I'll stick with coffee if they do one.'

Chris bowed. 'Madam! We have best in Cyprus, what you want?'

'Cappuccino?' she asked dubiously.

'Coming up, you like chocolate, miss?' he said with a huge grin.

She couldn't help but like the man and his enthusiasm and she smiled back. 'Yes, please.'

Chris called Donna over and gave her their order and then he took Hunter's hand and nodding his acknowledgement to Penny, he said, 'I have to go now, Mr George, see you again.'

They chose a table under the awning protecting people from

the sun alongside a cage holding two canaries who were engrossed in their own world.

'Hunter, why does he call you, Mr George?'

'I'm not sure. It's something to do with the way they write their names I think.'

Donna brought their drinks over and after he had wet his pallet he said, 'I don't think we'll be here long so we'll just get enough stuff in for breakfast, Penny, and eat out in the evenings, what do you think?'

'You're the boss.'

'Okay, so after dinner tonight we go on a pub crawl.'

Back in the villa after shopping in the local supermarket Penny opted for a swim in the ten-metre pool at the back and took Hunter by surprise when she paraded the skimpiest bikini and he couldn't help but admire her svelte muscular figure. Wiping the sweat off his brow Hunter went into the office and busied himself printing off copies of the picture of Doyle before sending an e-mail to Jacquie and the children.

Penny wrapped tastefully in a sarong joined him later and noticed the photocopies. She picked them up and threw them across the table. 'Hunter! You had me believe you weren't tech-savvy so what's with these?'

'Err...Err...,' he stuttered.

'Stop, Hunter, you'll only make it worse. Go and make some coffee.'

He got up and went to the kitchen and Penny wandered over to the office and stood in the door flabbergasted when she saw the array of computer equipment he had in there and realised he had been testing her.

—

That evening he drove them five kilometres to the Sunset Breeze Restaurant which was his and Jacquie's favourite and he surprised Penny by introducing her to the proprietor as his daughter. To give Doyle time to get out and about they prolonged their meal and refrained from drinking anything but water and it was ten o'clock before they were back on the Strip.

They parked in an area at the rear of the Strip hidden from

holidaymakers and used for deliveries and lingered amongst the throng of international tourists and trawled the Bars and made their drinks last as long as was decently possible before calling it a day just after midnight.

It was three days before they got a hint of Doyle's whereabouts when by accident a tourist picked up one of the photo-fits and said, 'I've just seen this guy.'

Hunter put his beer down and looked up. 'Where was that, mate?'

'In the Irish bar opposite the Coral Beach Hotel. What's he done?'

'Don't worry, mate,' said Hunter, 'it's this young ladies brother and his Mum's been taken ill and wants to see him.'

Penny looked to the heavens and shook her head at the way lies rolled off his tongue and then realised it was something she did like the time she had trapped Demyan.

'Oh, right,' said their informant, 'but it's over an hour since I saw him.'

'Thanks,' said Hunter, 'we'll give it a try anyway and we can always leave a message if it's his favourite pub.'

Trying to appear unhurried he and Penny got up and left the Bar and as soon as they were out in the street they legged it around the back to the 4 x 4.

As they clambered in Penny said, 'Is it far?'

'About a mile.'

Notwithstanding the speed bumps, it took them six minutes to get there and they parked directly opposite the Bar ideally placed to capture thirsty tourists who wanted a cheaper pint than that served in the Hotel. They chose to sit at a table outside and as soon as their drinks were delivered Hunter walked through the Bar supposedly looking for the toilets.

Sat on his own at the bar was Doyle who looked glum and depressed. He was many years younger than his brother Simon also slimmer and had a milder appearance. His brown hair was neat and parted in a 1940's style.

Hunter paid little attention to him and when he returned to Penny he said quietly, 'He's there. I'm going in to join him. Give me ten minutes and then come and distract him...'

She sat back in her seat with a grin, and said, 'Hunter, I'm not a girl like that.'

Picking up his pint he continued, '...and If we speak in there, Pen, call me George.'

He wandered aimlessly inside and stood for a moment in the door undecided and then went to the bar and sat next to Doyle who glanced at him but said nothing and Hunter continued drinking. When his glass was empty he didn't say anything to Doyle but signalled the barman to fill both glasses.

When the drinks were put in front of them Doyle searched in his pockets for money and Hunter stopped him. 'That's okay, mate you look as miserable as I am.' He raised his glass and said, 'Cheers!'

Doyle squared himself with the bar and leaning on his elbows responded with only a slight Northern Irish accent. 'Sláinte, and who might you be?'

Hunter pulled back slightly. 'Oh, Irish, aye? I'm George and I'm pissed off.'

'You are! Join the bloody club.'

Penny sidled into the room and posed in the doorway looking at everybody before she picked on Doyle. She crossed the room and stood by him on the opposite side from Hunter and with her mouth slightly open she ran her tongue over her bottom lip before she said in that voice of caramel and honey she had practised well, 'Mine's whisky.'

For added effect, she wobbled slightly and leaned against him for a brief moment which had the effect she was looking for. Doyle swung around to face her and gave her his full attention as Hunter took something from his shirt pocket and surreptitiously passed his hand over Doyle's glass before he leaned forward and said, 'Hello, Penny, you're out late.'

Doyle signalled the barman and ordered a whisky before he said, 'You two know each other?'

Penny stepped in. 'Take no notice he's not my type.' She eased closer to Doyle and said, 'But you look like you may be.'

Doyle took a huge gulp from his pint and before it had gone

down took another and running his hand over his hair and breathing heavier replied, 'Shall we go somewhere quieter, I'd like to get to know you?'

'Finish your drink and I love that accent,' said, Penny, 'What's your name?'

He took another swallow and said, 'Martin... Martin Doyle.'

It was the proof they needed and Hunter breathed a quiet sigh of relief.

When Doyle put his glass down on the bar he fumbled and nearly knocked it over. 'Whoops!' he said.

Penny was fiddling with her glass and pushed it to one side and took Doyle's glass and went to drink out of it when she saw Hunter frantically shaking his head. He mouthed, 'NO!' and then, 'SLOW DOWN.'

She held the glass up and pulled a face and put the glass down. 'Nah! Beers not my thing, Martin. I'm going to the loo.'

She spun around and walked sensually with a slight wobble across the room towards the washrooms while Doyle obliged and drank the rest of his pint. As he placed the glass on the bar Hunter said, 'She'll be ages, mate. No hard feelings, let's have a whisky while you're hanging around. They've got '*Jamesons'* up there.'

He didn't wait for an answer but Doyle's body language was responsive and he called the barman over and ordered two double shots. They had almost finished before Penny reappeared and when he put his glass down on the bar he lost control of his fingers and knocked it over at the same time his body went limp. Hunter and Penny grabbed him and stopped him sliding to the floor and held him upright mumbling and singing drunkenly under his breath when the barman came over.

'Is he alright?' he asked.

Hunter nodded, 'Yes, he's had a few too many. The cars outside we'll take him home—Come on, Penny, take the other arm.'

Between then they manoeuvred Doyle across the room and down the steps outside and with just a brief stop to let some late-night revellers go by they half carried him and half dragged him over to the 4x4 where they unceremoniously shoved him into the back seat. Hunter felt through Doyle's pockets and fished out his car keys which he handed to Penny.

'Look for his car, Pen, and follow me up to the villa.'

Penny took the keys and together they began walking along the line of cars on both sides of the road. They didn't have far to look as almost immediately the hazard warning lights flashed on a blue Corsa parked nearby.

'Got it, Hunter, see you there.'

'Okay, let's go.'

'Will he be okay, what did you give him?'

'Rohypnol, never to be taken with alcohol.'

'Huh, that's different,' she said as she slid into the driving seat.

—

Twelve hours later Doyle woke up with the headache to beat all headaches and a thirst that would do justice to a Saharan nomad. He tried to move and found himself handcuffed to the metal frame of a folding bed. He had enough free movement to twist his head around and although the blinds were down in the half-light he could see everything in the room. It was some kind of office with a desk and chair complete with computer and printer and in the opposite corner a TV and on the other long wall a bookshelf.

A drink was what he needed.

A hoarse, 'Help...!' was all he had time to say before Hunter walked into the room with his Glock prominently displayed in his waistband.

'Morning,' said Hunter, 'I wondered when you would join us.'

Doyle mumbled, 'I want a drink and a piss.'

'One minute,' said Hunter.'

He went to the door and called Penny and when she came into the room he said, 'Watch him I'm going to release the cuffs,' and to Doyle, he said menacingly, 'One, just one dodgy move, mate and you're dead. Do you understand?'

Doyle mumbled, 'Give us a drink.'

Hunter responded loudly, 'DO YOU UNDERSTAND?'

Doyle nodded, 'Okay,' he said, 'just give us a drink.'

'Penny,' said Hunter, 'can you bring him a glass, please?'

Penny left the room and returned a couple of minutes later with a glass of water which she placed on a low table close to Doyle and when she stepped back and had Doyle covered with her Glock Hunter unfastened one of the cuffs. Doyle who was still drowsy from the effects of the drug managed to swing his legs off the bed and sit facing his captors. With his free hand, he reached for the glass and took a long drink.

He plonked the glass sullenly on the table and looked up at Hunter. 'Can I go for a piss now?'

Hunter nodded. 'Yes, there's a shower room next door with all the stuff in so you can do the works. All outer doors are locked but I warn you one wrong move and your dead and If I don't get you a hungry German Shepherd is waiting outside, okay?'

Penny lifted her eyes heavenward and Hunter released the second cuff and clamped it across both Doyle's wrists. 'Let's go.'

Doyle stood up and Hunter guided him out of the door and showed him the downstairs washroom. 'In there, and don't be too long.'

Just inside the door, Doyle said to Hunter, 'I can't take my shirt off.'

Hunter unlocked one wrist and helped Doyle remove his shirt before cuffing him again. Doyle didn't show any dissent and went quietly into the washroom and closed the door behind him. They heard the lock go on but ignored it. There were bars on the narrow window which were too close for anything but your average butterfly to squeeze through.

Ten minutes later Doyle came out and Hunter signalled with his gun for him to go into the office and cuffed him by one wrist to the bed again. Penny followed them in with a plate of toast and jam and a mug of tea and when she had put it down Hunter said, 'That's the best we can do. Get that down you and we'll start talking.'

Penny and Hunter left him and locked the door behind them and Doyle set about devouring the toast like someone who hadn't had a square meal for some time.

—

They rejoined Doyle half an hour later with two plastic patio chairs and while Penny removed the plate and mug Hunter placed a recording device on the table but before he switched it on, he bent over Doyle and said in a loud whisper, 'Your brother Simon is fucking dead...' Doyle's head jerked back and wide-eyed he stared at Hunter, who continued, '...and if you don't play ball you will be too and I haven't got time to mess around—UNDERSTAND?'

Penny came back and they sat opposite Doyle. Hunter switched on the device and sat back with his Glock dangling from his forefinger and spoke first. 'Martin—we've come to take you back but as you were to blame for my wife's near-death and you involved my kids I haven't come to be nice.'

Doyle shook his head. 'I don't know what you're talking about. Who are you anyway?'

'Hunter, does that ring a bell?'

'No, is it meant to?'

'Don't piss me about, Martin. Did you or did you not pass information from GCHQ to your brother and the IRA about my movements?'

Doyle replied nervously, 'I... I...I don't know. I was given the details of a tracker and some phones and told to report on them in the normal manner which was my job but I did think it was funny that I had to give the information directly to the 2 I/C instead of the usual channels. I didn't know it was you. Besides, it was my job.'

Hunter sat back perturbed and looked at Penny. 'What do you think?'

'It sounds plausible,' she said.

Hunter turned his attention back to Doyle. 'Simon said that he was doing it in revenge for the death of his father and abuse in the orphanage. What about you?'

'Simon had a bad time in the orphanage and they did look at me but left me alone. I'm a lot younger than Simon and I didn't really know my Dad and then Mum died. Simon lead me all the time and I just did as he said.'

Hunter leaned forward with his free hand resting on his knee and looked Doyle straight in the eye. 'Are you telling me you didn't know you were spying for the IRA?'

'No, I mean yes. The section worked that way. We were given the details of the GPS tracker or phone or whatever and reported on it until we were told to stop but we didn't know why or who. Simon cheated sometimes and had me check vehicle registrations for him but that's all. I know nothing about the IRA.'

'So how did you get into GCHQ?'

'Simon was a good brother and he pushed me through school and Uni and then he fixed it for me to get in GCHQ.'

'He used you. You were a bloody sleeper. Why did you do a runner?'

The sudden change of tack caught Doyle by surprise and he stuttered, 'Err... I... Erm... Simon told me to.'

'Why Cyprus? Why didn't you go to the U.S.?'

'Him again. We used to come here on holiday and he said he'd be in touch with new papers.'

'That's not going to happen. Have you got a partner?'

'Yes.'

'Where is she, it is a she, I take it?'

'Yes, and she's in Cheltenham.'

'Any kids?'

'Two.'

'How old?'

'Four and eight.'

Hunter sat back squeezed his chin with his left hand and rubbed his cheeks his mind playing with the dilemma that now faced him. 'Kids.' He looked thoughtfully across at Penny while making up his mind and then promptly put his gun on the table and said, 'Doyle—I'm going to give you a chance—and only one. You cock it up and you follow your brother. You will write a statement. I've recorded it anyway but I want it in writing everything you know and then I'm arresting you on that Euro Warrant. I'll put a good word in. You will get jail time but not much— understand?'

Doyle nodded and Hunter continued, 'Don't mess with me, okay?' He turned to Penny, 'We'll have a spot of lunch while he's writing. I'll pop out and get something from the local bakery and I'll organise the car hire people to come and get his car. Stay there, I'll go and get some paper. Oh! and just another quick word, Doyle,' he said pointing to Penny's Glock, 'she's trained by the SAS and knows how to use that thing.'

Hunter stood up and left the room and Penny spoke to Doyle. 'Martin, don't mess with him and he'll keep his word on both counts. It depends if you want to live or not.'

Doyle raised his head and looked Penny in the eye. 'Is he right about, Simon?'

Still unsure whether Bell was actually dead she continued with Hunter's line, 'Yes, Martin, I was there. It wasn't nice.'

Hunter returned and plonked several sheets of A4 and a pen in front of Doyle and watched to see which hand he used before he said, 'Get started. I'll be back in half an hour with some grub. Are you allergic to anything?'

Doyle shook his head. Penny remained quiet but surprised. That he cared for the welfare of his captive showed another side to the complexity of this man. What next?

—

After lunch, satisfied with Doyle's statement they left him asleep in the office while they lounged around the pool. Hunter nursed a cold beer watching Penny swimming and sunbathing determined to get a proper tan when he suddenly plonked his glass down, and said, 'Penny, I'm going to call Gus and arrange our passage back. Can I get you anything?'

'I'll have some fresh beer when you come back.'

Hunter unwound himself off the sunbed and went indoors and after he had checked on Doyle he called Thomas who answered immediately.

'Thomas here, what is it, Hunter?'

'We've got Doyle and he's coughed. Can you fix transport home on that Warrant?'

'Is it going to help us get Milburn?'

'I don't think so. Doyle was too young when he was in the orphanage.'

'That's a pity. Leave it with me, I'll call you back.'

He rang off without waiting for a response and Hunter rejoined Penny outside but he remained stoically under a sunshade while she, like Jacquie, seemed impervious to ultra-violet and cooked under the Cyprus sun. He didn't mind he readily admitted to himself, he enjoyed the view.

An hour later Thomas called back. 'Hunter, get your bags packed and on your way to Larnaca. Report to the airport police and they will escort you onto the aircraft. You have three seats in business class on the 1930 hrs flight. He will remain cuffed at all times.'

'And the car, Gus?'

'Leave it with the airport police and Avis will collect it.'

'Okay, Gus, we'd better get moving. Cheers!'

He rang off and hurried outside. 'Come on, Pen, we're on the seven-thirty flight from Larnaca and that's a two-hour drive. I'll get Doyle sorted.'

He didn't wait for a reply but spun around and went to the office where he disturbed a sleepy Doyle. 'Come on, wake up, lad.'

Doyle slowly came to life and rubbed his eyes with his free hand. 'What is it?'

'We're going home. Where are you staying, we'll need your passport etc...?'

'Err... Oh! At the Majestic Gardens.'

'That's good, it's on the way.'

He unlocked the cuff from the bed and clamped the cuffs over both wrists. 'Go to the bathroom and get yourself sorted we'll be on our way in fifteen minutes.'

With his gun very much in evidence, he followed Doyle to the bathroom and waited until he came out a few minutes later. 'Sit over there by the dining table and remember—No stupid stuff or you'll travel in a box.'

When Doyle was sat down Hunter clamped him to a chair leg with the cuffs and went to gather his things and passed Penny on the stairs already packed.

His packing technique was quite simple once he was dressed suitably for the journey. Open bag and chuck it in and five minutes later he joined Penny.

'Watch him, Pen, while I put the bags in the car.'

His bag and Penny's cabin bag was no problem but he had to make a second trip for her other more extended luggage and when he was ready he freed Doyle from the chair and cuffed his wrists once more before he marched him out to the 4x4 and when he had him secured in the back seat he left Penny to watch him while he locked the villa and while he was doing that Doyle said to Penny, 'Where's the dog?'

'Don't ask, it's one of those mythical Greek creatures.'

It took five minutes to drive to the Majestic Gardens and Hunter, who had rearranged his holster and gun for a right-handed withdrawal took care to cuff Doyle by his right hand to his left hand and with a jacket tactfully hung between them they marched through to Doyle's Studio apartment.

Packing was a quick affair and Hunter made sure to confiscate all Doyle's papers and they were back in the 4 x 4 in less than ten minutes and on their way.

Hunter's shortcut through the back streets made light work of the traffic and they were on the **A6** Motorway in less than twenty minutes and he ignored the tourist speed limit of 100km's per hour and flogged it all the way to Larnaca and made it with forty-five minutes to spare.

With Doyle cuffed to Hunter's left wrist the forewarned Police checked the Warrant against Doyle's papers and then rushed them through security and onto the aircraft before the regular passengers and they were pushed back only fifteen minutes late.

At Heathrow, they were the last to leave the aircraft and the Airport Police took over the watch duties on Doyle and escorted him away but not before Hunter had reassured him that he would put a good word in.

The ride through London late at night in the 'Firms' car was quite pleasant and Hunter was sorry to say 'Goodnight' to Penny who insisted on going home.

~~~~~
~~~~~

CHAPTER 32

At ten the following morning they were sat around Thomas's desk. Hunter with his obligatory Americano coffee and a stem ginger biscuit while Penny obliged herself with a small bottle of lemon water. Thomas could see Hunter's pale tan caused by the suns rays reflecting off the water in the pool while Penny was a picture of health. 'I wonder?' he thought and immediately dismissed the idea from his mind. He knew Hunter was a window shopper but he wouldn't stray, 'Would he?'

'Right, you two, tell me all about it.'

Between them, Hunter and Penny related the facts as they knew them and gave Thomas the written statement of Doyle and the recording '... and I'm sorry Gus,' said Hunter, 'it doesn't help us to get Millburn, not on anything substantial anyway.'

'No,' said Thomas, 'and to top it all, Doyle's brother, Bell, has committed suicide which means there is no witness in the historical sex case and nothing to prove blackmail if he chooses to deny it. The CPS won't have it.'

'Gus,' said Penny, 'what about the McGovern files and that hard drive? Don't they prove anything and did he leave a note?'

'What hard drive, that's new to me but getting back to Bell.'

'What about him, Gus?'

'The neighbours noticed a nasty smell on Tuesday morning and called the police who broke in and found him dead. The autopsy showed he took cyanide and their estimated time of death is in the early hours of Sunday morning.'

Penny nearly choked, she was both startled and surprised as she looked across at Hunter. Her thoughts were silent but she said mentally, 'This man has a dark side.' Now she knew what was in that capsule but how come the delay. 'Cyanide was instantaneous wasn't it?'

She apologised, 'Sorry, Gus, something stuck in my throat.'

She looked across at Hunter who shrugged while Thomas

continued, 'and the NYPD are looking for a couple seen entering and leaving the apartment Saturday afternoon.' He looked directly at Hunter. 'You wouldn't know anything about that would you, Hunter?'

'Only what I've told you already, that we did visit Bell and I threatened him but I only gave him a warning that the next time would be curtains. I gave him a choice. I really wanted him back here so we could get that bastard Milburn.'

Thomas brushed over Hunter's remark and said, 'And the hard drive, tell me about it.'

Hunter reached down into his jacket which was hanging over the back of his chair and withdrew the SSD and pushed it across the desk to Thomas.

'The stuff I sent to you concerning Milburn and Doyle is all on there.'

Gus picked up the SSD, 'And who leaked Milburn's details to the media?'

'I wouldn't know,' said Hunter, 'maybe the computer in the safe house is hacked. It's not mine so I don't check the anti-virus thingy.'

Thomas pushed the SSD back to Hunter. 'Okay, you pair, take this and go to Admin and check all of it minutely and those files. See if you can find anything.'

With that resigned look that field men have for admin work Hunter stood up and wrenched his jacket from the chair and headed for the door followed by Penny and as they walked towards the lift Hunter apologised to Penny for her involvement.

It was four o'clock when Thomas summoned them back to his office and when they were seated he enquired of their progress. 'Well, have you found anything?'

'No, Gus, we can't add anything of any significance only that this appears to be the only time they used Milburn as a go-between. Other than that Milburn is only guilty of using his influence to get the Doyle's in there in the first place and advancing their careers. Have the 'Watchers' anything to report?'

'Not really, except that he is no longer under surveillance and Milburn's wife has gone to the family home in Northern Ireland.

He's staying in his Eaton Square apartment and he walks to his club every night at about seven and returns about ten-thirty. That's it.'

'What club does he go to?'

'The SFC. He's been a member there since his days as an SBS Officer. Why? Is that important, Hunter?'

Hunter shook his head. 'Nah, just curious.'

'Okay,' said Thomas, 'that'll do for tonight. Come back in the morning and we'll discuss tactics.'

'Would you like a lift, Hunter?' said Penny.

Hunter sat for a moment weighing his options before replying, 'Thanks for the offer, Pen, but I've had an idea.'

He left Penny at the Department Entrance and set off to walk the mile and a half to Belgravia. At a leisurely pace, it took him a little over half an hour and after spending a few minutes wandering the area particularly the distance to the SFC from Milburn's apartment he caught a cab and went back to Camden where he bought a new PAYG Sim and called into the local hostelry.

He picked up his pint from the bar and found himself a quiet retreat in a corner of the lounge. After changing the Sim card he dialled Williams who had been resting his ankle.

Williams answered immediately. 'Williams, who's this?'

Duncan! It's me, Hunter. Make a note of this number and only call it on your private phone, okay?'

'Got you, how can I help?'

'Can you drive yet?'

'Sure can, why?'

'Tomorrow night, drive down to the London Gateway services on the **M1** and meet me on the northbound side at eight-thirty. We will swap cars and you will drive mine back up the **M1** but steadily. That is, not too fast and not too slow. Make two stops. Take the max two hour stop at Newport Pagnell Services and an hour at Norton Services on the **M6 Toll** and if I don't catch you up carry on but take the slow road up the **A41**. Can you do that?'

'Yes.'

'And, Duncan, have you got any false number plates ?'

'Yes, I used them when we were tracking 'O'Reilly.'

'Fit them on your car before you hit the motorway and make this the last phone call.'

'Wilco!'

Hunter finished his pint and on the walk back to the safe house he stopped to pick up a Chinese takeaway and a four-pack of his favourite lager and casually dropped the old Sim card down a road drain on the way.

—

Another boring Friday of file searching but they made no further progress in snaring Milburn for anything more serious that would put him away and at three-thirty Hunter threw in the towel.

'That's it, Penny! I'm going, and after tea, I'm driving north. Tell, Gus, I'll see you all on Tuesday.'

Penny waved from behind her desk. 'Okay, take care and mind how you drive. No pensioners in the fast lane.'

He gave her the Agincourt salute, scooped his jacket up and left. Back at the safe house, he told Amy he would be leaving later that evening and be away for the weekend and then he spent the next couple of hours with his preparations for the evening.

—

Sir Jackson-Milburn was delayed but he left the Special Services Club at twenty-five minutes to eleven and set off for the fifteen-minute stroll to his Eaton Square apartment. It was a pleasant evening still quite light with just a few wispy clouds dawdling across the sky blotting out the few stars visible in the London light cone. He turned into Chesham Place and in the Belgravia peace, his troubles seemed to diminish. He rounded the corner by the Spanish Embassy and walked the last two-hundred metres buoyed by his dinner and a few whisky's and as he turned into Eaton Square he pulled his shoulders back sucked in his paunch and whistling quietly he marched the fifty metres to the front door of the apartments.

He was about to take the first of the steps up to the front door when a man with glasses, blonde hair and wearing an open mackintosh over his black-tie evening outfit approached from under the scaffolding surrounding the premises next door which was undergoing refurbishment.

The man raised his hand palm outwards, and said, 'Excuse me, sir.'

Milburn paused, unsure, but the man appeared well mannered and was sensibly dressed so he was not unduly worried. 'Yes, what is it?'

The man stopped a pace from him, and said, 'I think we know each other.'

Milburn shook his head and said, 'I don't think so, now can I go?'

'We have a mutual friend—Martin McGovern?'

'Oh... Oh, yes, Martin, but he's dead. I have nothing more to do with that.'

'Oh, but you do, Sir. The name's Hunter. George Barrington Hunter to be precise.'

Milburn hesitated and stuttered, 'Oh... Err... err... no, I don't think so.'

Hunter raised his hand to his mouth and leaning forward slightly began coughing and Milburn said, 'Are you alright?'

Hunter's left arm came up and he sprayed an asthma inhaler directly into Milburn's face. Milburn gasped and sucked the gas further into his bronchial tracts and eventually his lungs and his knees buckled. Hunter grabbed him and lowered him to the floor and as he did so a young couple came around the corner and quick thinking Hunter shouted, 'HELP! My friends collapsed, can you lend a hand?'

They hurried over and Hunter said, 'Hold his head up, I'm a Doctor and I have the medication for his angina.'

He took a bottle of water from his coat pocket and showed them a capsule. 'It's glyceryl trinitrate.'

He opened Millburn's mouth and popped the capsule in and gave him a drink of water to wash it down. 'He'll be okay in a couple of minutes. Help me get him up and I'll take him indoors...' pointing to the Apartment Front door, '...he lives here.'

They eased the gasping Milburn to his feet and brushed him down and Hunter thanked the couple for their help. He put Milburn's arm around his neck and half-carrying him guided him up the steps. With little help from Milburn, he found his house keys and opened the entrance door. Once inside Hunter lowered Milburn onto the bottom step of a staircase and while Milburn was still dozy and unaware of his senses he quickly left.

Hunter didn't hurry but when he turned into Belgrave Place he unfolded a pork pie hat from the deep pockets of his coat and put it on for the short walk to Victoria Railway Station.

He retrieved his bag from Left Luggage and in the washrooms he discarded the wig and glasses and changed into his normal day wear and then on the way to retrieve Duncan's car from the nearby Station Car Park he threw a plastic bin bag into a nearby dumpster. He wasted some precious minutes putting information into the TOM TOM GPS before he set out for the **M40** Motorway as quick as the late evening traffic would allow.

With the security of false number plates, he ignored speed limits and on the motorway, where safety would allow, in the thinning night traffic he exceeded one-hundred miles per hour. His progress was slowed in the busy **M42 Smart Motorway** section with its associated speed cameras but once on the **M6 Toll** he made up for it and pulled into the Norton Services with a couple of minutes to spare before Williams was due to leave.

He joined Williams who was working his way through his second cup of coffee and sat down opposite him. He slipped the car keys and an envelope under the table into Williams outstretched hand. 'Here you are, Dunc.'

'No time for coffee, Guv?'

'Not this time but Jacquie and I are planning a get together when this is all over and I'll see you then.'

'I filled up at the last stop, Guv, so you're good to go. What's this all about?'

'The less you know the better, Dunc. Don't remove those false number plates until you've passed through the Toll booths.'

'Got you, Guv. Yours is parked over to the right on the second row as you go out.'

Hunter stood up and reached across the table and shook William's hand taking his car keys as he did so. 'Thanks for that, Dunc, I owe you. Take care and we'll see you soon.'

Happy behind the wheel of his own car he chose the slower

scenic route up the **A41** `A' road away from the prying CCTV on the motorways and made swift progress and was back in his home snuggled up to Jacquie a little over ninety minutes later.

~~~~~
~~~~~

CHAPTER 33

It was after midday when Jacquie and the children arrived back from the Sports Centre and found Hunter pottering around the kitchen making himself a cup of tea having just showered and shaved after a good sleep. Lesley was the first to see him and with her usual enthusiasm dashed down the hall towards him.

'Daddy, Daddy, I see you.'

He scooped her up but in the confines of the kitchen didn't swing her around. 'Hello, my sweet and how are you?'

'I'm okay, Are you staying home now?'

Iain joined them. 'Hi, Dad, how long this time?'

Jacquie remained in the doorway.' Yes, Hunter, how long have we got you for.'

He lowered Lesley to the floor and said rather humbly, 'I'm going back on Tuesday but I think this week will be the last as it's all down to the Establishment and the CPS now and then I can retire again.'

Jacquie came across the kitchen and kissed him. 'Good and then I hope we can get back to normality. Make the tea, Hunter. Come on kids put your stuff away.'

She herded them out of the room while Hunter made tea for all of them and carried the tray with four mugs into the living room. After he had given them out he sat in his favourite chair and said, 'Right, kids, tell me about your swimming.'

'I got my fifty-metre badge this morning, Daddy,' said Lesley, 'and Iain...'

'I'll tell him, Les. She never shuts up that one. I did my two hundred metres mixed medley, Dad, and the lady asked me if I would like to swim for the County.'

Hunter looked at Jacquie. 'Is that right?'

'Sure is, H, they don't take after you in the water department.'

'This calls for a celebration,' said Hunter, 'how about we go out for a meal tonight? Who's for the Stamford?'

'We are,' shouted Iain and Lesley simultaneously.

'Huh, you only want to go there, Hunter, because you like their sticky toffee pudding,' said Jacquie, 'I know you.'

'I fancy a nice steak tonight, Jay. It'll make a pleasant change from takeaways.'

Hunter gathered up the mugs and put them on the tray and as he left the room he said, 'Right, kids, go and find something to do while your Mum brings me up to date with events.'

'Awe, Dad, Mum said she'd take me to Neil's house this avvy,' said Iain,' he's expecting me.'

'Okay, we'll chat later who's for a spot of lunch?'

—

Jacquie returned and poured herself a glass of red wine before she sat down on the long leather sofa and gave Hunter an update on her business and future plans and then out of the blue she said, 'And you, Hunter, what have you and Miss World been up to?'

'I've been to Cyprus in our villa.'

'With her?'

'Err, yes. I slept in our bed and she was next door.'

'What did you go there for?'

'Doyle, as he is now known did a runner and with a little elimination we tracked him down to Coral Bay so we did the obvious and stayed there.'

'How did you get on?'

'Doyle confessed to passing info but was not involved in the child sex problem. He came quietly and is in custody and since then it's been file bashing.'

'And Milburn?'

'He's fireproof and has been suspended pending enquiries.'

'So you have all the suspects?'

'Yes, but the only major witness to get Milburn on something which would have taken years was Simon.

'Hunter, you spoke in the past tense.'

'Leave it there, Jacquie. Let's just say I persuaded him to do the right thing.'

Jacquie looked at Hunter thoughtfully and didn't answer immediately and then she said, 'Hunter! I think it's time for you to stop. Let them worry about the legal side of things.'

'Do you know what, Jay, I think you're right but I'm worried there might be other idiots out there wanting to take a pot shot at us?'

'Talking of which, Hunter, why were they chasing you, and this Russian?'

'The Irish thing was revenge for a job I did in '83. Someone won the lottery and paid the IRA to find out who did it. Milburn supplied the facts but you were shot by a rogue outsider because of your spying and as for the Russian, that's weird. Some Yemeni Arab was on a religious revenge thing for me shooting his son when on an op with the BATT in Oman in '72.'

'Where did this Russian get your info?'

'From what Demyan tells me it was from some historical files left over after a similar multi-hit over a period of years from the same conflict. Different people though.'

'You're on first name terms are you?'

'Yes, and I used him when I was in the States.'

'Hunter, why were you late home last night?'

'I left it late to avoid the traffic and then I stopped a couple of times.'

'Okay, if we're going out tonight I'd better go and get Iain. Pop in on Lesley while I'm away she's got a load of new pictures to show you. We have a budding artist. I wonder who she takes after?'

She didn't give him time to reply as she left the kitchen laughing as she did so.

—

Later that evening when the children were tucked up in bed Hunter poured himself and Jacquie a single malt whisky and he plonked himself down in his armchair and raised the leg rest. 'Jacquie!...' this sounds serious she thought. '...it's been suggested we change our name.

'Is this because they think there may be more reprisals?'

'Yes, for both of us.'

'Oh, I never thought of it. Err...what about Riccardi? That sounds foreign enough.'

‘What about plain old Barrington?’

‘No, H, think of the poor kids having to write that and I think Ricky would sound nicer than Barry on Facebook and Twitter.’

‘Huh! The curse of modern living.’

‘Besides, H, my business name is Riccardi and I wouldn’t have to change anything.’

‘I get your point. Let’s ask the kids in the morning.’ He put his glass down, ‘Is there anything worthwhile on the tele?’

‘Hunter, in your opinion there is nothing worth watching that was made after the seventies and that’s a thought. What would I call you if you changed Hunter?’

‘Come over here and I’ll make a few suggestions.’

She patted the leather sofa she was sat on.’ Try this it’s bigger.’

He pulled himself up from the chair and lunged across to her pushing her sideways as she swung herself lengthways and as they kissed, she murmured, ‘Mind the leg.’

He replied, ‘Let’s go to bed.’

She whispered as she pulled him closer, ‘You do it here or nowhere and be inventive.’

~~~~~
~~~~~

CHAPTER 34

It was a little after ten-thirty on Monday morning when Hunter's phone jangled. He ignored it but when it changed to voicemail whoever it was redialled and it started again.

Hunter picked it up, glanced at the caller ID and let out a low groan before he stroked his finger up the 'accept' app. 'What is it, Gus?'

'Where are you, Hunter?'

'Home, where did you think I was?'

'I don't know but get yourself down here pretty darn quick.'

'Why what's up?'

'The media haven't been told yet but Milburn topped himself over the weekend. Just get down here.'

Hunter sighed with resignation. 'Okay, I'll be as quick as I can.'

He closed the call and sent a message to Jacquie to explain the situation before he finished his packing and called a cab. He'd decided to go by train as the favoured alternative to sitting in a seventy mile an hour traffic jam if you were lucky to be moving at all.

—

He knocked on Thomas's office door a little after a quarter to three and walked in before he was given the all-clear to do so. He threw his bag down behind the door and sat opposite Thomas who ignored him for two minutes as he studied some paperwork and then checked his computer.

When he eventually looked up he said, 'What the hell have you been up to, Hunter?'

Hunters face remained inscrutable as he replied, 'What do you mean?'

'Milburn's suicide, what do you know about it?'

'When did he do it? I went home on Friday night.'

'Early Saturday morning.'

'I was in bed.'

'Hunter! I don't believe you.'

'You believe what you want but you said, and I quote, "Use your initiative" unquote.'

'You turned it into a personal vendetta. You've gone too far this time. Give me your ID and User Permit, you're retired.'

'Do you mean I've come all this way here for that? You could have told me over the bloody phone.'

'While you still have your ID etc... you could be doing anything. Hand them over.'

Hunter removed the required items from his inside pocket and slid them over the desk.

Thomas held his hand out. 'Your gun, Hunter.'

'I'm not carrying and I don't have an issue weapon anyway.'

Thomas sat back and fiddled with the keys of his computer before he said, 'It's being released to the Press now.'

'What's the official verdict?'

'Unexplained death. Suicide by cyanide poisoning most likely. Police are not looking for anyone else. Autopsy pending.'

'Well if anyone had access to it, he did.'

'Hunter, this bears a striking similarity to Bells demise. How did you do it?'

'Off the record?'

'Yes.'

'Switch off that computer and your phone.'

Thomas complied and when Hunter was satisfied he said, 'It's cold war technology, Gus. A delayed action capsule. One end is ceramic and immune to the effects of the digestive juices and the other is like your average pain-killer. The two halves are separated by a copper membrane It can take as much as ten hours before the cyanide is released!'

'Where do you get all this stuff, Hunter?'

'I read the right books.'

Hunter stood up, crossed the room and picked his bag up and as he went to open the door, Thomas said, 'Give my regards to Jacquie. She remains on the payroll until we think all danger is passed.'

Hunter said nothing but swung the door open and left the room unperturbed. It was bound to happen but he didn't know when and his conscience was clear. Justice had been done in his eyes and his family safe.

Were there other people out there with a grievance? Would there be repercussions? Who knows but one thing was clear he would have to move from his family home and the thought of the name, Riccardi! Ugh! 'Oh, well, goes with the territory I suppose,' he said to no one in particular as he strolled down the corridor. 'Job done! Time for a pint of *Stella* methinks.'

—

He arrived home that evening very subdued and he apologised to Jacquie and the children for his behaviour after dinner as he chose to shut himself in his office and quietly drunk himself to sleep with his favourite malt whisky.

The following morning nursing a hangover and getting little sympathy from Jacquie and foregoing his atheist doctrine he walked the mile to the local Parish Church. He paused at the antique gateway pondering his thoughts when his inner feelings carried him forward down the crumbling path through the well-kept churchyard. His spirits were lifted by the fresh flowers laid on the graves old and new and he was surprised to find the church door open. He found out later that the church was open on Tuesday and Thursday mornings for visitors.

The interior was bright and airy and the stained glass windows depicting scenes from the diocese in 2004 turned the sunlight into a myriad of multi-coloured spotlights. There were vases of fresh flowers dotted around and the variety of colours contrasted perfectly with the light. Their perfume gave the place that feeling of tranquillity and he sat in a pew in the middle of this pastoral atmosphere. For no other reason than he felt the need he leaned forward and resting his head on his hands he said a silent prayer.

He had been sitting contemplating his life for few minutes when the comforting voice of the Rev John Fraser disturbed his composure. 'Good morning, can I be of any help?'

Hunter jerked upright and turned to face the intruder in his thoughts.

'I'm sorry,' said the Reverend, 'I startled you.'

Hunter made to stand up and the Reverend with a movement of his hand begged him not to. 'Please stay seated. Don't I know you?' he said.

'Not because of my presence in church but over the last few years I did help my wife deliver trees and plants etc... mainly at Easter and Christmas.'

'Ah, that's it. You must be Mr Riccardi?'

Hunter smiled. 'No, not yet anyway. I'm George Hunter her husband.'

'Oh, I see. What brings you here, Mr Hunter?'

'Because of my early career choices my family were put into grave danger and when asked to don my official guise to help solve the problem I cried, 'FOUL' and lost my conscience.'

'Did anyone die?'

Hunter paused and spent a few seconds pondering his answer before he spoke. 'Yes!'

'And you feel guilty?'

'Yes, but under the circumstances, if I had not acted they would have escaped justice and it seemed the right thing to do. I was doing my job.'

'What did the authorities think of this?'

'I can't say anymore, sir, but I will point out that the culprits shot my wife and kidnapped my children to get at me and were about to kill me when the tables were turned.'

'In those circumstances, Mr Hunter, I may have forgotten my principles. Join me in a short prayer and seek forgiveness and repentance for those unfortunate people who chose to go down the path of evil.'

The Reverend knelt in the pew across the aisle from Hunter and recited a short prayer. When they had finished they shook hands and said nothing but when Hunter reached the main door he turned to face the Reverend who was stood watching him, and said, 'The next time we meet I'll probably be Mr Riccardi.'

THE END

ADDENDUM

Agincourt salute
J.I.C. : Joint Intelligence Committee
PSNI: Police Service Northern Ireland
SIS: Secret Intelligence Service
DCI: Detective Chief Inspector
DI: Detective Inspector
DS: Detective Sergeant
DC: Detective Constable
SOCO: Scenes of Crime Officers
CPS: Crown Prosecution Service
BATT's: British Army Training Teams

About the author.

My name is **JB. Woods** a retired soldier and fibre optics industrial operative. I turned my hand to writing after researching my wife's family history which inspired my first novel—**'Stolen Birthright'**

I then joined the *'Paphos Writers Group.'* As a result of lessons learnt with them I had many short stories published in local magazines and I continued writing and edit other peoples work in a small way.

Next came:
Book 1 of the Hunter series: **REBOUND**
Book 2 of the Hunter series**: 'Below the Belt'**
Book 3 of the Hunter series: **Upstart**

'Henrietta – Tales from the Farmyard' Twelve short stories for grown ups and children alike about the adventures of Henrietta the matriarch of Village Farm.
'A Cry of the Heart' (Amber Zacharia) — an edited biography. An account of the traumatic life story of a young woman from Zimbabwe.
and **'Gems from my Pen'** which is a selection of my short stories in one volume.

I am currently working on my next book, a historical novel set in Cumbria, Lancashire and Australia.

Printed in Great Britain
by Amazon